# THE
# LAST CARD

A NOVEL BY **KOLTON LEE**

# THE
# LAST
# CARD

**LEE**

Published in 2007 by
The Maia Press Limited
82 Forest Road
London E8 3BH
www.maiapress.com

Song lyrics pp. 58–59 by Notorious B.I.G., 'Dead
Wrong' from *Born Again*, 2000; p. 123 by Mad Lion,
'Play De Selection' from *Real Thing*, 1995; p. 174 by
Buena Vista Social Club, 'Candela', from *Buena Vista
Social Club*, 1999; p. 192 by Tim Dogg, 'Low Down
Nigga' from *Penicillin*, 1991

ISBN 978 1 904559 25 2

A CIP catalogue record for this book is available
from the British Library

Printed and bound in Great Britain

The Maia Press and Kolton Lee are indebted
to Arts Council England for financial support

'WHAT BOXING DEMANDS, PRIMARILY, IS THE HUNGER TO MAKE THE GRADE AND THE COURAGE TO ENDURE SETBACKS AND DISAPPOINTMENTS.

'SELF-BELIEF IS A PREREQUISITE: IF A MAN DOES NOT BELIEVE ABSOLUTELY IN HIS OWN ABILITY, HOW CAN HE PERSUADE OTHERS TO DO SO FOR HIM?'

**Harry Mullan**
**Writer and journalist**

**15 JUNE 1998**

H was floating, moving in a different time. His control over his body was perfect. His years of training, dedication, conditioning had all led to these nine minutes; three three-minute rounds of flowing, balletic motion.

It was the second round and the action was following the course of the first. H was fighting in the finals of the English Amateur Boxing Association. As South of England champion he was fighting his northern counterpart, Henry 'Bugle Boy' Mancini. They called him Bugle Boy because he played the bugle when he wasn't boxing. He didn't play it well, in fact he could barely toot out 'Three Blind Mice', but he played it, and the press latched on to it, an angle for their human interest stories. H scowled every time he thought of it. Fuck Mancini and fuck his bugle. They say you need good lips to play brass. By the time H was through pounding Mancini's face, the man would have to take up the guitar.

The arena, a sports centre in Birmingham, was packed. Three thousand people: punters, minor celebrities, the country's amateur boxing cognoscenti. And they were all cheering for H. Because H was putting on a show and making the artistry of boxing look like the easiest thing in the world.

Despite media spin, Mancini was a tough, stocky, big-boned kid from Hulme, Manchester's equivalent of the south Bronx. He was also a bully. With a jaw carved from the concrete of the council flats he grew up in, Mancini could take a punch. He thought nothing of wading through two, three or four of his opponent's punches to land one of his. And Mancini could punch. He was a banger. He'd bulldoze his opponents, not only taking their blows but flaunting the fact that he could do so and still keep coming. The public liked watching

**9**

Mancini not because he was good but because he was exciting. A bit like Nigel Benn in the early years.

But the public also liked watching H. H wasn't a banger, he was a dancer. Slim, lean and whippet-fast. He didn't just dance, he could punch as well, but he didn't have Mancini's weight of punch. On the way to this final bout, H's knockouts were fewer; his journey was less spectacular, but no less decisive. Where Mancini would land the dazzling blow that could separate his opponent from his senses, H would land three that would put his man down, unable to beat the count. Stunned but not out. So the hype leading up to this fight was all about how the Bugle Boy with the knock-out blow would handle the cold-eyed Shuffler.

H was called 'Shuffler' because his patented move was the Ali shuffle. Having seen the great man do it countless times on video, H had imitated and then practised the move to perfection. To the point where he had made it his own. It was now somewhere between the Ali shuffle and a Michael Jackson moonwalk. Whenever H had an opponent on the run, or if it was a closely fought bout and H wanted to momentarily bamboozle an opponent, he would begin shuffling his feet and gliding smoothly round the ring. There were those who thought he was showboating but most people loved the entertainment. Either way, H's smooth, fluid movements would invariably bring the watching crowd, hungry for violence and action, to its feet, roaring approval. For H, the shuffle wasn't so much arrogance as an expression of fun, the almost childlike joy he took in his sport and his ability to do it well. He revelled in his ability to make what he did look easy and the crowd responded, loved him for it.

And so it was that halfway through the second round of the finals of the English Amateur Boxing Association H began to shuffle. But only after peppering Mancini with any amount of stiff lefts that caused the Bugle Boy's lips to bulge; only after a sweet one-two-three combination, the three being an uppercut that jolted Mancini's head back, the sweat flying from his close-cropped head; only after a body shot that doubled the bullying Bugle Boy from Hulme. Only after all these things did H finally allow Mancini to close in. And when Mancini did, H promptly dropped his hands to his sides and shuffled his feet in a blur of motion that carried him out of harm's way. The crowd began to rise, the front sections at first, and then further back throughout the arena, as a roar of applause, approval and love built to a crescendo, crashing around H with the force of a waterfall.

For the first time in his life, H knew what it meant to feel drunk, intoxicated, inebriated on sheer ability.

Mancini stood, floundering, in the centre of the ring. H could see that he was bemused, befuddled and embarrassed. Through swollen eyes he glared at H. And the crowd roared. Like a mammal reared in water and finding himself on land for the first time, Mancini was confused; life wasn't supposed to be like this. Movement was supposed to be fluid, taking in oxygen was not supposed to be something you thought about, and bashing opponents was supposed to come easy. Now none of this was true. H watched as, with resolve, Mancini again went for him. Bravely, he stepped forward, glaring, murder in his eyes. Rat-a-tat-tat! H peppered him with light, fast punches. Mancini brushed them aside and swung. Air. He missed, H was gone. Kept moving forward. H stopped shuffling, he was dancing, up on his toes, bang! a right to the side of Mancini's head, Mancini swung, H bobbed, under the blow – bang! another left to Mancini's face, the Bugle Boy's lips this time and Mancini's mouth sagged. He was trying to breathe, his mouth hung open, gasping for air, H in again, combination, one-two-three, bang-bang-bang! Mancini lunged, grabbed on to the Shuffler, clinging, holding.

Break! The referee stepped in and separated the combatants. His left eye closing now, Mancini again came in, like a bull, all upper-body beef, looking for the blow that would put an end to this. And again H shuffled, just out of reach. He was playing to the crowd, returning the love that they sent towards him in waves.

Ding, ding! The bell rang to end the round. With all the noise in the arena only the referee heard it and had to step between the fighters, sending them back to their respective corners. On their way, they passed each other.

'Are you gonna dance all night, bitch?'

'Maybe.'

'I thought blacks were supposed to be tough?'

H let this lie as he floated to his corner. Nick and Matt, his corner men, slid through the ropes and into the ring. With the precision of Swiss watch manufacturers, they set to work. A stool was planted in the corner, H was pulled on to it. A bucket of cold water with a sponge in it was slapped to one side. Matt, the sixteen-year-old sponge boy, put his hand in H's mouth, pulled out his gum-shield, dropped it into the bucket. He dipped the sponge into the water and mopped H's face, squeezing the cooling water over the crisp, clean cut of his features. Matt's father Nick, a grizzled Irishman from the slums of Belfast, had already dropped to one knee. He looked piercingly into H's eyes and spoke with calm but urgent authority.

'What did he say?'

'Stand and fight.'

'What?'

'Stand and fight. He wants me to stand and fight him.'

'Forget him! He's an animal! Dis is it son, all we've been working for. Look at me! It's in de fuckin' bag, just keep movin', movin', workin' de jab, stickin' it in 'is face, and shufflin'. Look at me!'

H's eyes wandered over to look at Mancini in the far corner. Nick yanked his face back.

'Keep keepin' outta trouble, stay loose, stay focused, remember everythin' we've worked for, back in de gym. Dis is yours! Dis is your day! Fuck dis Mancunian arsehole, you're goin' ta make him pay de proice for turning up in de same ring as you. What's de proice? What's de proice?!'

H was no longer listening. His breathing was easy, his head felt light. He deliberately slowed his breathing further. His gaze was clear. While Nick talked H stared, clear-eyed, across the ring. In contrast to the calm efficiency of his own corner, Mancini's was a mess. Blood oozed from the cut above Mancini's eye, his mouth was swollen and cut, two cotton buds were jammed up his nostrils. One of his corner men feverishly slapped grease over his red-raw eyebrows and fore-head, another slopped water down his chest, into his trunks.

'Look at me, H! What's de proice?'

'Defeat.'

'Not defeat! Not defeat! Annoihilation! Crush dis guy! Like a bug! Leave no doubt in de judges' moinds! Dere is no doubt already, but I want even less! Just keep doin' what you're doin', no change of game plan, DMS – dancin', movin', shufflin'. Dis is de last round you'll ever foight as an amateur. Make it one to remember. You're next fight is as a professional and we go and make some real fuckin' money with de big dogs. Now go out and jab his fuckin' head off, H. What are you?'

Matt took the gum-shield and slipped it back into H's mouth.

'I'm a champ.'

'I can't hear you!'

'I'm a champ!'

'I can't fuckin' hear you!'

'I'm a champ!'

'You're a fuckin' god! Now go out dere and prove it!'

Ding! Last round. Nick struggled up from arthritic knees back to his feet. He and Matt both kissed H before climbing out of the ring. H rose. He looked across at Mancini. The adrenaline spurted, still coursing through his veins. He shook his arms out, rocked his head from side to side, working out the kinks, he eased his gum-shield into a more comfortable place in his mouth.

The referee now waved him and Mancini to the centre of the ring, looked them both in the eye, paying special attention to the bloody Mancini. He was happy. As far as he was concerned, they were both able to box. He waved them together, stepped back. H looked at Mancini, Mancini glared back. H banged his boxing gloves together, ready to get it on . . .

\*\*\*

Years later, when H looked back on his performance against the short, stocky fighter from Manchester, he would always find goose-pimples rising on his arms. Pure adrenaline, not blood, flowed through your veins. Moving so fucking fast you think you're about to defy gravity and lift off the face of the planet. But now, with the benefit of those added years, H realised what he had been experiencing was the celebration of unbridled, unfettered, pure and un-adulterated, one hundred per cent concentrated youth.

# 1.

The room was cold and dark, the cloakroom of an old, Victorian dance hall. The fact that it had once possessed a quiet grandeur did nothing to improve H's mood. He sat on a low bench, a grille with hooks for coats over his head, staring at nothing. Steam rose from his overheated body as he allowed the cool of the room to evaporate his sweat. His hands, still encased in bulbous boxing gloves, hung by his sides and his back sagged as he slouched against the grille. H was tired.

The door was suddenly thrust open and Matt strode in. Now a sturdy young man of twenty-three, he wore a chunky gold chain around his neck and an equally chunky ID bracelet on his wrist. He flicked on the light. He was surprised to see H sitting in the dark.

'What's up with you? You've got a face like a well-slapped arse!'

H looked at him out of a partially closed eye. He said nothing.

Setting down his trusty bucket and sponge, Matt pulled up a wooden stool and dropped it in front of H. Without a word H rose and sat on the stool. Matt removed the towel from round his neck and slowly began to rub H's head, shoulders and back.

'Don't worry about it, H, you were fucking robbed. You know it, I know it and the punters know it. The only one who doesn't know it is the one-eyed, bald-headed cunt who calls himself a referee. That cunt is a fucking disgrace. He should be struck off.'

H continued to stare at nothing, the throbbing from the black eye becoming more pronounced.

Matt's practised fingers kneaded the baby dreads that sprouted from H's scalp. The relationship between them went back almost fifteen years. H felt his head bob rhythmically back and forth as his friend worked his fingers in the towel, going from the base of the skull, down the neck to the shoulders and then the back. H raised his arms, one of them more gingerly than the other, so that Matt could gain a greater purchase on his back.

'What's the matter, H? Why so quiet?'

H turned to look back at him but still said nothing. Matt finished rubbing down his spine. He then pulled up another stool and sat himself in front of H. He took a pocket-knife from his tracksuit and opened it up. H extended his gloved hands out in front of him and Matt moved on to the second part of the ritual. He unlaced H's boxing gloves, first one, then the other. H's fists were tightly packed in thick white masking-tape. Matt took his knife and carefully cut through the taping of H's right hand. Every so often he looked up. H was staring at him out of his one good eye.

'Come on, mate, snap out of it.' It seemed Matt couldn't take the silence any longer. 'It wasn't that fucking bad, I've seen worse. You didn't see Taps fight last week. Taps had this black geezer from Brixton – big fucker he was! – Taps had him down twice in the second round; it was a six-round fight, knocked him spark off his feet in the fifth, and the ref gave it to your man from Brixton! Couldn't fucking believe it! It was a joke!'

'How come they gave it to the guy from Brixton?'

'Fucked if I know. Could've had something to do with the cut Taps had on his bonce. It was pretty deep, but Christ Almighty, Taps had this bloke looking like a fucking amateur. He is a fucking amateur! He works down at the Fridge as a fucking bouncer, d'you know what I mean? There should have been a fucking riot. Taps is a class above.'

'What class is that, then?'

'What?'

'You said Taps was a class above: what class is that, then?'

H wasn't really trying to be difficult. It was just that, today, he'd had one low-rent fight too many, in front of a clearly unqualified adjudicator, before a small but ignorant audience who had no real idea of what they were watching. H was not the fighter he once was. While he used to be ridged with hard, distinct muscle, those very same muscles were now soft; while his waist always used to be eleven and a half inches smaller than his chest, it was now only six inches smaller; and while his feet used to dance and shuffle with the precision of a Gene Kelly . . . H's feet now slipped and shuffled with the dexterity of an old man tottering carefully on an icy pathway.

This last point had been rammed home with callous cruelty when, earlier that evening, H had again tried to evoke the memory of the fighter he had once been. In the third round the forty-one-year-old brickie that H was fighting had caught him with one too many body shots. H could see them coming. The problem was that when his brain, crisp and clear as ever, told his stubborn and perverse body to move, it refused to obey. Consequently his ribs took a pounding that they should not have taken. H had tried to shuffle out of harm's way. The move that used to bring crowds of two, three, four thousand people to their feet in admiration now brought twenty-five drunken louts to a state of heightened derision. They were laughing at him! For as H had tried to shuffle, his thirty-two-year-old feet had somehow become entangled with each other and H had crashed, without grace or style, on to his elbow.

'Taps is a boxer!' Matt snapped. 'He's not a fucking brawler! He understands what the game is all about.'

This answer afforded H no satisfaction whatsoever.

'I woke up this morning and pulled a pubic hair from my groin.'

Matt gave H a cheeky grin. 'Ey, ey! You dirty bastard! One of Bev's I hope.'

'No, Matt, it wasn't one of Bev's, it was one of mine. And it was grey.'

This was not the male patter that Matt was expecting and he remained silent while he finished cutting through the tape on H's right hand. Moments later, flexing his freed fingers, H dunked the hand into the bucket in front of him. It was two-thirds full of iced water. Matt began to cut his way through the tape on the left hand.

'It gets us all in the end, mate. When the grey ones outnumber the black ones,' Matt continued, 'that's when you have to worry. You've got a few years yet, sunshine.'

H cast him a withering look. 'I need a holiday.' He said the words as though the idea had just occurred to him. It had. 'I need a holiday,' he said again, more conviction this time.

Matt looked at him with surprise. 'I'm not trying to be funny, H, but . . . you don't even have a job!'

H rose abruptly, wincing from the pounding his ribs had taken,

# THE LAST CARD

and walked over to his nearby kit-bag. The battered old leather holdall was chained to the coat rack with a huge bicycle lock. H pulled out his mobile. He had a text message from Beverley. Later for that. Ignoring the text, H found the number and dialled.

'You're right, I don't have a job,' H said to Matt, listening to the telephone ringing at the other end. 'But, man . . . I'm really tired.'

\*\*\*

The Mercedes was gunmetal grey. It was a 1973 model, a classic, the bodywork in mint condition. H parked it and then eased his bruised body out, pausing before deciding whether he should lock it after him. One of the few things that actually worked properly in the car was a cheap cassette deck. If anyone wanted to steal it, it was better to leave the car unlocked rather than risk a window being smashed. But something about leaving his Mercedes unlocked offended H's sense of ownership. He did what he usually did; he left the car unlocked, turned and walked down towards Oxford Street.

It was a cool, clear, spring night, just after half-past ten and the centre of the city was teeming. Clubbers, tourists, the gay crowd, trendies, workers, drinkers, diners, streetwalkers, theatre-goers, cab drivers . . . the list was endless and it was one of the things H loved about the city. Whatever the nature of London's unpredictable weather, the city teemed with life. As he strode purposefully towards Blackie's shebeen, wearing his lucky suit, H momentarily felt a part of all that was good about London.

Truth to tell, H did indeed look good. He had on his one good suit, a two-piece, charcoal-grey, one-hundred-per-cent wool affair, made by the black designer, Derek Lilliard. It was his lucky suit, the suit that he wore on his special gambling holidays. For that's where H was going, into the throbbing, underground heart of the gambling shebeens of Soho.

H turned off noisy Wardour Street, into the quieter Broadwick Street. He paused outside Agent Provocateur before crossing the road and heading into Duck Lane. Duck Lane finished in a dead end, but a little way before that H came to a plain, metal door. He rapped on it twice. Almost immediately, with the slow grinding squeal of metal on concrete, the door opened.

H entered a dimly lit hallway. In front of him, leading the way, was a short, dumpy, doughy-faced Chinese woman. She led him up two flights of stairs, both barely lit, and then into the room where the gambling went on. It was spartan and dark. In the centre of the room stood a large green baize gambling table, and eight wooden chairs. On either side of this were two smaller tables. The far end of the room was a small kitchen area and on the kitchen counter were sandwiches and drinks.

High on one of the walls, a silent TV was showing a fight. H's eyes immediately turned to it: there was Mancini, in the middle of an elimination bout H knew would earn him a crack at the world title. In a packed-out Albert Hall, Mancini was putting the final touches to the destruction of Colin 'Sweetwater' Joseph. Joseph may have been sweet before this meeting, but he wasn't sweet tonight. In the seven years since H had fought Mancini, the Bugle Boy from the bad side of Manchester had gone from strength to strength. His upper body had bulked, he'd learned one or two classy combinations and someone, somewhere, had taught him how to bob and move. Mancini could now box. The Trinidadian was finding it out the tough way.

H looked away. He could no longer stand watching boxing on television.

Various unsavoury characters milled about the room, drinking and chatting. Some H recognised, some he didn't. In the middle of one group sat Ghadaffi, the smartly suited, Oxbridge-educated, Libyan nightclub owner; beside him was Boo, Nigerian hard man and petty thief. Sharon, a thin, pale junkie from east London, was helping himself to a sandwich and ignoring Stammer, a big dumb-looking Jamaican in a white shell-suit and heavy gold chains, who played alone, as usual, on a one-armed bandit. There was Sammy, south London's hardest-working mini-cab driver; and finally Dipak, a Ugandan Asian, who had seen good days, bad days, and was old enough to know that gambling was an addiction. Dipak owned the all-night grocer's on Shepherd's Bush Green and was one of Blackie's best punters.

Sitting at the large table stacking chips sat a soberly dressed, dark-skinned Jamaican. Blackie. Blackie's skin was so black it almost looked blue. He was the houseman; this was his shebeen, newly moved from a spot in Ladbroke Grove.

Blackie wasn't big but nobody ever crossed him. Not twice anyway. The last person to do that, as far as H could remember, was

# THE LAST CARD

Cookie, a young, smooth-talking Tunisian. Cookie loved the sound of his own voice and could talk his way out of any kind of problem. Cookie especially loved to talk on telephones, loudly and without inhibition. Women loved to hear him because he could string together wonderfully fragrant phrases; sentences that could charm a nun. H winced as he remembered the story. Blackie had been playing a big game in a shebeen in north London: five-card poker, or stud poker as some people call it. It was a big hand, there was a lot of money on the table, and the man playing opposite Blackie was a fish. He had his own carpentry business and was loaded. Blackie had, apparently, been stringing him along all evening, allowing the fish to win just enough of the small hands to sucker him into a big hand where Blackie would move in for the kill. As the hand approached its climax, a hush had descended over the game. Blackie was slowly reeling the fish in when Cookie entered the room, talking on his mobile. Checking out the clientele, Cookie had doubtless seen a number of attractive women in the house. And so, instead of lowering his voice as protocol dictated – given the stage of the hand Blackie was playing – Cookie raised it. Braying loudly into his phone, he looked around to see who was listening in to his conversation.

Blackie, apparently, didn't react immediately. According to the story he kept his focus, his eyes trained on the businessman. The man's forehead glowed as he chomped with apparent nonchalance on a fat cigar. It was his move. For Blackie, this moment was the difference between collecting the pot as it stood, or at least doubling it. The moment was tense. But for Cookie's braying. Anyone who looked closely would have seen the vein in Blackie's left temple begin to throb: the first indication that all was not well. When his right hand began to paw distractedly at the baize of the table, it should have been a clear warning for anyone who knew Blackie. But Cookie wasn't looking at Blackie. He was looking at the full, frank bosom of an attractive Ghanaian woman.

Finally, Blackie turned to Cookie. 'Stop oonu blood clat chat, no man! You cian' see we playin?!'

Cookie looked round, startled. But at that moment Blackie was undone. Once he had taken his eyes away from the businessman, the man felt the pressure ease. He folded his hand. Blackie was going to walk away with over two thousand pounds, but with the losses he had taken he would clear maybe eight hundred. He had been looking at a score of just under five grand.

Without a word and without even pausing to collect his winnings, Blackie rose from the table and barged his way out of the room. A few moments passed, during which, hindsight established, he had flown down to the kitchens at the back of the shebeen. Blackie returned wielding a meat cleaver. The panic that ensued did not prevent Blackie catching Cookie, slamming his right hand to the flat of the gambling table and chopping it off. It may or may not have been a coincidence that this was the hand in which Cookie had been holding his mobile.

Cookie survived the maiming but his smooth patter was never quite as smooth again. Soon after this incident Cookie disappeared. The word on the street was that he had returned to Tunisia.

H crossed the room and slapped Blackie on the back.

'Blackie, man, wassup!' Blackie turned to H, a smile of recognition creasing his scarred, battered, fifty-three-year-old face.

'Ey! Watcha now, my yout'! Wha' gwan?!' Blackie jumped up and the two friends embraced.

'Good to see you, man, how've you been?'

'Me a cool, you know. Me jussa try to keep a level vibe.'

'So this is your new place?'

'Yeah, man, me a hit de big time now, you know. I tired a run race in de Grove so me say, me a move wid man an' man in de West End.'

'Looking good, my brother!' H stood back and looked Blackie over. In reality Blackie was not looking good at all. Since H had last seen him Blackie had become thinner, almost gaunt. One of his front teeth was missing. He was also sporting a long, thick scar on his forehead. H had heard this was left behind by an irate out-of-town fish who had entered Blackie's shebeen in the Grove with over two thousand pounds. A straight thirty-six hours later, the fish had left, laughter ringing in his ears, with all his money gone, bar a crisp twenty-pound note for his cab home. The fish did not leave quietly.

'So you come to give me a spin tonight?'

'What, you think I'm here to watch?'

Blackie laughed and the two again embraced. The Chinese woman who had opened the door approached.

'Drink? Something to eat?' Blackie threw an arm around her

# THE LAST CARD

waist, drawing her into his body. 'H, dis 'ere is Shampa. A good woman. Shampa, dis is H.'

Despite H's smile of greeting, nothing about him seemed to please Shampa. The sullen look on her fleshy face remained as tight as ever.

'Hi, pleased to meet you.'

Shampa ignored him and there was a moment's pause.

'What you want to drink? Every t'ing on de house tonight.' Blackie's joie de vivre interceded.

'In that case I'll have a Jack. Jack Daniels.'

Blackie turned Shampa's shoulders and playfully slapped her arse, sending her off in the direction of the kitchen.

'Who's the new girl? She looks like fun.' The ambiguity of H's comment was deliberate. It didn't do to be too playful with Blackie.

'Das my sweetheart, man. I love 'er! Love 'er to deat'!' H and Blackie watched her take short, quick steps on her way to the kitchen. Boo, the good-natured Nigerian, piped up. Despite being in his late thirties Boo liked to speak with the florid cadences of a teenage, African-American, Harlem homeboy.

'Yo, nigger, wazzzzzup?' With a bear-like hug he wrapped his big arms around H, squeezing him until he squirmed.

'Man! You need to back up!' said H, gasping for air.

'And look at you, man!' Boo continued. 'Wearing your lucky suit 'n' shit! Yeah, boeeeey!' He slapped H's hand, hard.

'I'm not like you bums,' countered H. 'I've got things to do outside of gambling.' He turned to Blackie. 'So these are your new premises.' H looked around. 'This place has . . . life.' Blackie's new shebeen could probably have jostled with The London Dungeon for gruesomeness and lack of life. Despite there being something of a crowd tonight, the collection of dead-beats, hustlers and petty criminals, combined with the general pall of poverty that hung over the room, reminded H of the funeral of a boxing buddy he'd once attended in Birmingham.

Stammer, the big Jamaican, ambled over and broke into the conversation. 'B . . . B . . . Blackie, b . . . b . . . business good, boy!'

H gave him a quizzical half-smile. A thought, once again and not for the last time, flashed through his mind: he really ought to give up gambling. Why did he need it? Blackie was okay, but there were few people in this room that H really liked. Something inside him would just not let him walk away. Always, always, either when he was down, or when Bev was giving him earache, or when he just felt like he had to get away, he was drawn back to this nocturnal world.

Shampa returned with H's drink. The small shot glass was barely wet with the tiny measure of Jack Daniels in it. To show his contempt for her portion H reached out a hand and, with barely a pause in motion, downed the drink in one, handing back the empty glass. The Chinese woman with the Indian name surprised H with her harsh east London accent.

'Are you firsty or wot?'

'What's it to you?'

'This stuff's expensive, d'you know what I mean.'

'So? Are you buying it?'

'No, but . . .'

'Well keep it coming and stop squawking!'

'Oooo-oooh!' Both Stammer and Boo liked that one. H glanced over at Blackie but Blackie just shrugged and turned back to sorting the chips on the table.

'You better check the next one carefully . . . you might find some gob in it!' She turned and walked away. Blackie looked up, his face creased into a broad smile.

'I don' know wha' 'appen to she, but she 'ave fire in she body. You ready to play?'

The group wandered over to the main table and took their seats. Including H, there were eight players. All put money on the table, varying from £100 to £500. The serious money wouldn't come out until later in the evening.

As the players settled themselves down at the the table, Ghadaffi pulled Blackie aside, steering him away from the table and its prying ears.

'What are you doing next Thursday?' Ghadaffi wanted to know.

'Why?

'You know my place up in Chelsea? Well, I've started a quiet game with some businessmen on a Thursday night. It's nothing fancy but it's regular. Very respectable. My usual houseman can't make it this week. You want to take his place, as a one-off? You and Shampa? I'll pay you three hundred each.'

# THE LAST CARD

Blackie looked at Ghadaffi, watching him blink rapidly. 'You tarking five hundred each?'

Ghadaffi continued to blink, a scowl forming on his face.

'You don't play around, do you Blackie?'

'Me is a businessman, you know. I don' 'ave time to play aroun'.'

'Okay. Five hundred.' They shook on it. 'Call me on my mobile tomorrow and I'll tell you what time I need you to show up. But do me one favour: don't tell anyone else here about the game. I don't want these hard-faced professionals scaring away the fish.'

Shampa returned with H's drink and slammed it on the table next to him. H checked it carefully as the others sniggered. Shampa then sat, picked up two new packs of playing cards and handed each to a player on either side of her. Stammer and H broke the seals on the cards and handed them back. For one with such short and stubby hands, Shampa shuffled the two packs together with extravagant skill.

As the players round the table sat quietly watching her, H dipped his hand into his pocket and pulled out his Zippo lighter. H rarely smoked these days. A few years back he was on a seriously destructive jag and smoking was part of his attempt to give himself an excuse for losing in the ring. He was through that now but he still liked the smooth, weighty feel of the Zippo in his hands.

H twisted the lighter – his talisman – round in his hands before placing it gently on the table next to his money.

Shampa finished shuffling the cards. She dealt, gracefully and accurately, flicking the cards across the table to the eight players: one card each, face down, in the hole. As Shampa dealt, each player tossed their opening stake, ten pounds, into the middle of the table.

'Anyone blind?' Shampa droned mechanically as she looked round the group. The players all shook their heads. Shampa then dealt each player a second card, face up this time. As the cards slid smoothly across the table, Shampa called out the name of each one.

'Nine of spades, queen of clubs, jack of hearts, eight of diamonds . . .'

H watched her deal. No wonder Blackie had latched on to this woman. She may not be the life and soul of the party, but bring her into a sleazy, all-night, illegal shebeen and boy, did she know her way around.

23

'. . . Ten of clubs, ace of diamonds, queen of hearts, king of spades. Ace of diamonds starts the bidding.' Shampa finished dealing the hand and scanned the players at the table.

Sammy had the ace and considered his cards. The game was on. H's heart began to beat just a little bit faster, the adrenaline kicking in. He picked up his talisman and fingered it. This was why he gambled! It wasn't for the camaraderie; it wasn't for the patter; and it certainly wasn't for the women. It was for the buzz. Something that had been lacking from his boxing for some time.

'Twenty.' Sammy, a conservative player at the best of times, tossed a twenty-pound note into the middle of the table. Shampa deftly changed it for the round plastic house chips. H studied Sammy's face; Sammy's eyes flicked up, made contact with H's, and then dropped back to his cards. Too quickly for H. Wanker! The wanker was bluffing. Still; this was the first hand. And the first game of five-card stud that H had played for nearly six months. No need to go on the offensive first game back. H was going to ease himself in. Savour the moments. Enjoy them. Luxuriate in the feeling of being back, being on holiday, indulging himself in a favoured pastime.

\*\*\*

Hours had passed; the room was heavy with smoke. It hung in the air, glowing red from the light in the window, white from the light above the table, blue from the glow of the silent television. The thickness of the air seemed to muffle sound as the players concentrated on their game. Movement in the room, be it the collecting of money, the passing of cards, the scratching of a forehead, was made efficiently, economically. The only gamblers left were those around the central table, hunched together like conspirators. As H looked around he was acutely aware of something: these people weren't here to play, they were here to work. For the patrons of Blackie's shebeen gambling was a way of life. H knew he couldn't stay in the gambling world for too much longer. Maybe until he'd had one more big win. Just one. Really.

The money and chips which lay on the table had now shifted around according to each player's respective fortune. H and Dipak were having a good night and large stacks of notes and chips sat in front of them. H's talisman was nowhere to be seen, buried deep in his pocket.

Shampa dealt the next round of cards.

'Eight of clubs, nine of diamonds, king of spades, jack of spades, jack of hearts. King of spades starts the bidding.' She looked blankly over at H. H sat staring at a pair of kings with a nine card. Not bad. Not bad at all. He flicked a glance over at Sammy and the loot sitting before him on the table. Six hundred quid. H casually tossed six hundred pounds of his own into the pot. Bosh! If the wad of notes could have landed with a crash it would have. The pot in the middle of the table was already piled high with big notes and fat chips. H even noticed some funny money, some Euro notes, in with the real stuff. A big hand.

'Maximum bet, all in. Stammer?'

Stammer had a pair of queens and an ace showing. H thought about the cards that were already on the table, the cards that had passed through the pack, and the various permutations which Stammer might try. It was a tough decision, he could swing a number of ways with this. Stammer might not be the smartest guy on the planet but he knew how to play the cards. He was the kind of dingbat who would happily lose two hundred pounds in a one-armed bandit in the course of an hour, but would play poker for five hours to win twenty pounds. He looked over at H, a thoughtful look on his face. H stared back at him, blank, non-committal.

Stammer, reluctantly, covered the bet. Next to go was Sammy. Sammy had a pair of tens showing with a king. Sammy let a minute go by. Sammy carefully peeked at his card in the hole. Sammy let another minute go by.

'What are you doing? Are you playing de game or are you not playing de game?' Boo had a lot of money riding on this hand and the pressure was telling. The Harlem homeboy accent was gone and what H heard now was hard-core downtown Lagos. 'Shit, man, I've seen cream curdle faster dan de way you seem to play de game!'

'Yeah, mate, must be the cream between your toes.' Sammy spoke but it was Dipak that laughed.

'What did you say?'

H looked at his watch. The game had been going for just under five hours and he could see that Boo had already lost most of his money. Not that he needed to see it. The note of challenge in Boo's voice would have told him. It was time for H to think about moving on.

'I said shutcha yap, I'm trying to think here.' This would normally pass for everyday conversation, but the note of edge in Boo's voice should have warned Sammy to be more diplomatic. But then Sammy, a man passing through his sixty-eighth year and still driving an illegal cab for a living while gambling away anything of any value that his family had ever managed to acquire, was not the most sensitive punter around. Again Dipak laughed.

'And wha' de hell you laughing at?' Boo demanded of Dipak. Dipak, having a good night, chose to reply in Urdu. Neither H nor anyone else spoke Urdu but the words 'drug dealer' and 'motherfucker' needed no translation. One of the few shebeen rules however, over which there was no flexibility, was the foreign language rule. Blackie quickly enforced it now.

'No foreign, my friend, no foreign.'

H thought that despite Britain's all-pervasive class system – with the queen sitting at the top – gambling was perhaps the country's greatest social and racial leveller. In Blackie's shebeen, and most shebeens throughout London, you could speak the Queen's English, Jeremy Paxman's English, Chris Eubanks' English, even Jonathan Ross's English, but it had to be English.

'Yeah, man, speakie English! Where the fuck you think you at?' Boo was back to Harlem homie speak. H shifted in his seat, recognising that the flash point had passed. Boo had regained control of his frayed nerves.

Sammy tossed the last of his money into the pot. Boo cursed and threw his cards in, as did the casual Dipak. Shampa dealt the remaining players their last cards, face down. H, Stammer and Sammy looked at their cards and, one by one, they turned them up.

H now had two pairs, kings and nines; Stammer also had two pairs, aces and queens; Sammy had a pair of tens, plus a king and an eight.

'Stammer to bid, ace of hearts.'

H looked at Shampa and had to admire her technique. Whatever shit went down at this table, she was sure as hell going to maintain her cool.

# THE LAST CARD

'Check.' Stammer knocked once on the table. Sammy did the same. H considered his hand. He lifted up his hidden card and took a peek. He thought carefully about his next move, dipping his hand into his pocket, pulling out his lighter and fingering it. And then he made his decision. He shoved the lighter back into his pocket and looked over at Stammer. He casually tossed three grand into the middle of the table. The noise of air being expelled through gritted teeth and pursed lips was heard throughout the room.

'Godt . . . dammn, nigger! You cooking with gas!' Boo's eyes bugged from his head.

'Three thousand pounds is the bet. Stammer?'

Stammer looked away but he knew H was still looking at him. He stood abruptly and walked aggressively towards H. As he reached him he leant behind H and picked up a heavy black leather coat. He put it on, zipped it up to his throat and threw up the hood. He returned to his place glaring round at the others. They were all staring at him.

'My lucky c . . . c . . . coat.' He bent down and, lifting one of the legs of his satiny white Nike track bottoms, he dug into a fluffy white Nike sock. He pulled out a bundle of high-denomination notes and tossed them into the middle of the table. Boo let out another low whistle, whiplashing his big, rusty index finger on to the finger next to it. A loud whhap! cracked around the room.

'Get-the-fuck-outta-here-nigger!'

'You'd better check those notes for cobwebs,' Dipak laughed. Yes, big fun for everyone who wasn't still in the hand.

Stammer fixed Dipak with a glare that silenced his laughter. He turned to Sammy. 'M . . . m . . . make your m . . . m . . . move!'

H looked at Sammy and could tell that yet another shot of adrenaline had just kicked in. His nicotine-stained fingers were trembling.

'Please, Stammer! Please! Please! I'm thinking!' No amount of politeness could hide the effects of what was suddenly coursing through Sammy's body. H could see it and so could the smiling Stammer. Jokingly, Stammer pretended to lean over and look at Sammy's cards. Sammy snatched them away.

'Fuck off!'

Stammer fucked off with a laugh. And now that he was no longer in the hand, Boo was also up for some fun.

'Take him, Sammy, this is your house, man, this is your pot . . .'

While all eyes turned back to Sammy, Blackie cracked the knuckles of hands that had surprisingly well-manicured nails. H remained impassive. By his calculations he had a good, a reasonable, chance of winning this hand and if he did it would be his biggest win in a while. No point in blowing it now with a 'tell': a sign that his heart-rate had suddenly picked up and that the room was beginning to feel oppressively hot . . .

Sammy suddenly stacked, flinging his cards to the middle of the table. H allowed himself to breathe an inward sigh of relief and suddenly everyone wanted to talk.

''E's got a full 'ouse! I know it!' Sammy was shouting now. ''E's got a full fucking 'ouse! I'm telling ya!'

H continued his blank look. It would take more than Sammy's hysterical bleating to cause the merest flicker of emotion to register on his face.

'So why did you put in your twelve hundred?' An urbane Ghadaffi.

'B . . . b . . . because the man is a f . . . f . . . f . . .'

'F . . . f . . . f . . . fuck you, Stammer!' Sammy.

'F . . . f . . . f . . .'

Boo slapped Stammer on the back.

'Fool!' Stammer was practically snorting with the effort of making the one-word observation.

'Turn over, gentlemen, please.' Now that there were only two left in the game Shampa wanted to move things on. H flipped over his blind card. Bodies craned forward to see what he was showing. Sammy was right. A full house: two kings, three nines. The rubber necks now turned to Stammer.

'Stammer? Your card?'

Stammer did not do as he was bid. Instead, he flipped his cards face down across the table. The move was quickly followed by loud 'oohs' and 'aahs'.

'Full house takes it.'

The laughter from Sammy was now unnecessarily loud and obviously false.

'Ha! I told you! I told you he had a full . . !' But Stammer was in no mood to hear that H had a full whatever.

H shrugged, almost apologetically. Almost.

# THE LAST CARD

'Easy, man, relax you'self, Stammer.' Blackie had no reason yet to be concerned. H reached forward to sweep up the cash and chips from the centre of the table. This was his biggest win in some time but even though he'd won the hand he still couldn't relax. No, that didn't happen until he left the premises, the money safely tucked in a wallet nestling against hip or chest. Accordingly, the expression H showed the room as his hand dropped on the money and chips was blank. It remained so even after Stammer's big hand slapped down on top of his. Only then did Blackie ease forward, ready to intervene.

And that's when the evening took a surprisingly violent twist. It was the moment that was to shape the rest of H's life.

# 2.

**G**avin sat in the front seat of the champagne-pink BMW with the cream leather seats and stewed. He was annoyed. He had a thumping headache, it was 3.30 in the morning and he was tired. He had just spent an unforgiving three hours at home in Purley, Surrey, enjoying the pleasures of his latest conquest, green-eyed Brenda. Now finding himself in the middle of the West End at this time of the morning was not his idea of fun. And so he sat in silence next to his Spanish driver, Emanuel, and stewed. He could feel the two monkeys behind him staring at his back, impatiently waiting for the action to start.

'Er . . . what's the hold-up, Gav?' That was Eric, possibly the dimmest man Gavin had ever had the misfortune to meet. Eric was so dim that when Gavin first met him he was sure he had premature Alzheimer's disease. But twenty-six-year-old Eric, who still lived within one square mile of where he was born, in Brentford, west London, was just dim.

Next to Eric sat Hodges. Hodges was all right. If you didn't spend too much time in a confined space with him. Hodges turned the body's natural cooling system into an art form, sweating with reckless abandon.

These were the thoughts that ran through Gavin's throbbing head as he cursed his ill luck while sitting in his champagne-pink BMW in the middle of the West End at 3.30 in the morning.

'Gavin? What's the . . .?'

'Yes, I heard you! I'm thinking!' He paused. 'Okay. This is what we do: we go in, you leave the talking to me.' Gavin stopped to twist round in his seat. He was trying to keep his sentences short, his instructions clear, with enough pauses between each sentence to give the meaning time to sink in. 'I tell the Negro that's moved in about the new realities of his lease; then I collect the rent.' He again paused. 'If there's a problem at this point that's when I would like you to make your presence felt.' He looked Hodges, and then Eric, in the eye. 'But only if there's a problem. I'm not expecting one.' Hodges nodded, Eric looked blank.

'What kind of problem?'

Gavin's head began to throb a little harder.

'Well, for example . . . if the Negro decides he doesn't want to pay?'

'Oh. That kind of problem.' Eric smiled through broken and battered teeth.

'Any more questions?' Both Hodges and Eric were now clear on the modus operandi. 'So let's go.' Gavin turned to Emanuel. 'I'll see you back at the club.' Emanuel shrugged. The three exited the car into Broadwick Street. Emanuel started the engine and pulled away.

The street was quietening down now. The prancing homosexual frenzy that Gavin thought Soho had become was just a memory. The coming day would start the merry-go-round all over again but for now the area was quiet. Gavin hated homosexuals. He couldn't understand how they had been allowed to colonise Soho the way they had. He glanced into the store for women's underwear, Agent Provocateur. His eyes caressed the frilly see-through knickers that barely covered the mannequin's bottom.

Gavin now turned into Duck Lane. He eased his head from side to side, hearing his thick neck give a pleasing crack as he approached the nondescript door. He'd left green-eyed Brenda in such a hurry he'd had no time for his morning stretches. First glancing behind him to check that Eric and Hodges were there, Gavin knocked on the door.

Moments later a thin, sleepy, anaemic-looking man in his early twenties opened up. Without a word he stood to one side, allowing Gavin, Eric and Hodges to enter.

They swept past him and along the dimly lit hallway. In a trundle of steps on naked floorboards, the three mounted two flights of stairs. As they approached the closed wooden door at the top, they could hear muffled voices. A red light leaked out from under the door. Gavin paused, Eric and Hodges readied themselves behind him. The pale young man who had let them in was on the landing below. Through hooded eyes he observed them as they paused outside the door. Without a word, he turned on his heel and went back down the stairs.

Gavin suddenly and violently kicked the door open and he, Eric and Hodges strode into the room. As they entered the room, all action froze. Now what? thought Gavin as he surveyed the room. He had two large Negroes, each with a hand on a large pile of money. Although it was hot, one of them was still wearing his fancy leather coat. The only man standing was smaller, with a scar on his head. He had to be Blackie.

The only woman in the room was a dumpy-looking Chinese, staring at Gavin with dark eyes. In fact all nine people round the table were staring at him.

The one with the scar now spoke.

'Wha' de blood clat you a deal wid! A come in my yard and kick off de door!'

Gavin ignored the outburst, walking slowly round the table. Eric and Hodges stayed by the door, feet spread, hands hanging loosely by their sides. They bristled with aggression. All eyes followed Gavin as he made his way round the table.

'My name is Gavin.' Passing the only window in the room he caught a glimpse of his reflection. He paused and rocked back on his heels to take another look. He looked good. His strawberry blonde hair was beginning to thin, but it didn't show. Gavin walked on.

'I'm here on behalf of my business associate, who I'm sure you've all heard of. White Alan.'

'But wait! You a step in my yard ana chat 'bout . . !'

'Quiet!' The authority in Gavin's voice forced Blackie to silence. 'White Alan would like you to know that since you've moved into the area – without a word of permission from him – you're likely to need his protection. There are some big, nasty people out there, with big, nasty guns.' Gavin looked meaningfully at Eric and Hodges. Eric caught the look and unzipped the bomber jacket he wore. Tucked into the waistband of his jeans was a German-built, heavy-looking Mauser Parabellum with a three-inch barrel. The move naturally attracted the eyes of those around the table. Gavin knew he had the attention of the room now. The two men with their hands on the money in the middle of the table slowly leaned back in their seats.

# THE LAST CARD

'We don't want no trouble in here, my friend.' Blackie's tone was suddenly much less belligerent.

'Exactly. Neither does White Alan.' Gavin looked down at the money lying on the table. 'To make sure that this . . . establishment has a long and prosperous history, all he wants is three thousand pounds. Every week.'

'You fuckin' jokin', man!' Blackie's eyes narrowed, his lips poked out, he looked like an angry gargoyle.

Eric and Hodges stepped forward but Gavin raised a hand to stop them. He knew his tailored blazer emphasised his strong, well-built shoulders, hiding the spreading girth that he spent hours trying to keep in check on the Stairmaster. He not only towered over Blackie, he was probably twice as heavy.

'What did you say?' Gavin stared coldly down at the black man. Blackie didn't flinch but he didn't say anything either. Gavin and Blackie eyeballed each other for a good thirty seconds. When it was clear to Gavin that Blackie was neither going to say or do anything he turned to Hodges.

'Count up this money. Take out three thousand pounds and let's go.' He pointed to the cash on the table.

Hodges, a sheen of sweat now clearly visible on his forehead, nose and upper lip, stepped forward and began to pick out the cash amongst the chips. Gavin, meanwhile, continued on his way, walking slowly round the room.

'This money doesn't belong to the house.'

Gavin glanced around at the gambler who spoke.

'It's okay, don't worry.' Gavin dismissed the intervention and turned back to examine his reflection in the window. The thought struck him that he looked damned good for forty-nine. Not that anyone knew that was his age. As far as White Alan and green-eyed Brenda were concerned he was thirty-nine.

'This money belongs to me. I just won it.'

'Tough luck!'

Gavin didn't even bother to turn round this time. Thus it was that, behind his back, one of the black men took Hodges completely by surprise when he swept his hand off the money and punched him smack in the middle of the face. Gavin whipped round to the commotion behind him and saw Hodges stagger backwards across the room. The loud crack that had accompanied the blow suggested that Hodges's nose was probably broken. Eric yanked his gun out from his waistband, flicked the security catch and aimed it. Everybody immediately scattered, ducking down or hitting the floor. As Eric fired, the black gambler dived behind an elderly Asian man who caught the bullet in his stomach. At the sudden deafening blast of the Mauser everyone froze. The Asian man dropped, screaming, blood ballooning beneath the ratty yellow cardigan he was wearing.

Gavin couldn't quite believe what he was seeing. The Asian man continued to scream and the room suddenly came alive. A number of the gamblers scrambled to their feet and headed for the door; Eric, apparently in a state of shock, made no move to stop them. He just stood there, looking at the writhing man on the floor, the gun hanging limply in his hand.

Hodges, who had been leaning up against the wall holding his face in his hands as they pooled with blood, gave an enraged yell. He charged at the man who had punched him. Gavin continued to stare. This wasn't supposed to be happening! The man was big, but surprising nimble on his feet. As Hodges charged at him, the big man stepped back to give himself room and then used Hodges' forward momentum to headbutt him in the face. Gavin winced sharply as Hodges staggered back, tripped and banged his head on the wall as he hit the floor. He rolled on to his side and stayed there, dazed. Eric came alive and again raised his arm to aim the gun. But this time Blackie was too quick. He slapped Eric's arm away, knocking the gun sliding across the floor. He grabbed him round the neck, yanking him forwards. Eric struggled in the headlock but, red in the face and with saliva drooling, he soon gave up. It was all over in a flash.

Gavin looked at Blackie, then looked at the man who had done for Hodges. Apart from those two, only the Chinese woman, the wounded man whimpering and gurgling on the floor, and an old white guy remained in the room. Gavin turned back to Blackie.

'This doesn't change anything, you know. You're still going to have to pay.' Slowly, carefully, he approached Blackie and gently eased aside the arm locked around Eric's head. Eric choked and spluttered as air was suddenly allowed back into his windpipe.

## THE LAST CARD

Meanwhile, the man who had dealt with Hodges went over to the discarded Mauser and picked it up. He didn't aim it at anyone, holding it in his hand openly for Gavin to see. Moving with as much authority as he could muster in a situation that had clearly veered wildly out of his control, Gavin went to the fallen Hodges and helped him to his feet. The three of them headed for the door. First Eric, then Hodges went out. Just before Gavin left he turned back to the black with the gun, staring at him.

'And you,' despite the throbbing in his head, Gavin tried to grin. 'We'll meet again. You can count on that.'

They kept eye contact for a moment, and then Gavin left, closing the door quietly behind him.

# 3.

**H** looked around the room. What the hell just happened? Blackie and Shampa stood side by side, Blackie with his arm around her; Sammy picked himself up from the floor and dusted himself down; Dipak lay on the floor where he had dropped after the skinny guy had shot him. His eyes were open, but he wasn't moving. He was lying in a spreading pool of blood. That's when H realised he still had the big gun in his hand.

Blackie looked at it and then went quickly to the window. He looked out for a moment watching as the three gangsters walked quickly away, and then turned back to H.

'Kiss me back-foot!' He whispered the words. H looked on while Sammy knelt down by Dipak's body, careful not to step in the blood, and picked up his wrist, feeling for his pulse.

'Is he dead?' H wanted to know. The way Sammy looked back at him gave him his answer.

'I'm out of here, Blackie, mate. I can't fucking deal with this.' Sammy gently laid Dipak's arm to the floor, picked up his remaining possessions from the table and headed for the door. Before he left he turned back to Blackie. 'Sorry to leave you like this, but . . . are you gonna call the old bill?'

'Wha' you want me tell dem?' Again Blackie spoke in a voice just above a whisper. Sammy shrugged. This was clearly a new one for him too. He left.

'What're you gonna do with him?' H asked the question that was on all their minds. Although he'd aimed it at Blackie, it was Shampa who answered.

'I don't know what we're gonna do with him, but we ain't doing a stretch for being accessories to murder.' She spoke with the efficiency with which she handled the playing cards. She looked at Blackie. 'We're gonna have to get rid of him.'

H and Blackie both knew she was right. H used the corner of his jacket to wipe clean of all possible prints the gun that was still in his hands. Then he went to the gambling table and swept up all the money from the last hand. That was his. The chips he collected into a pile and counted.

'There's twelve hundred and twenty-five pounds here.'

Shampa went to the cash box that sat on the table and opened it up. It was stuffed with money that the table had taken over the course of the night's gambling. She counted out H's cash and handed it to him.

'A pleasure doing business.' He looked over at Blackie. Blackie had now gone back to the window and was again looking out, his back to the room.

'Hey, Blackie, man, did you know those guys were coming?' Blackie didn't answer. Dipak had been a punter at Blackie's various clubs for at least twelve years. That didn't necessarily mean that Blackie knew anything about him outside of his life as a gambler, but twelve years is twelve years. As H well knew, the gambler's life could be all-consuming. Character is always revealed during times of stress and the ebb and flow of life that surrounded the gambling table could be considered a seductive form of stress. Over the twelve years of support that Dipak had given Blackie's games, H would guess that Blackie probably knew Dipak as well as anyone. He searched for something to say.

'Still tired of running race in the Grove?' It wasn't the most appropriate comment but H was shocked by what had just happened. When Blackie didn't answer he knew it was time to chip.

'Adios amigos. Welcome to the West End.' With that, he picked up his shot glass, downed the remaining Jack Daniels, and walked quickly from the room.

\*\*\*

As H hit the cool night air and made his way back up Wardour Street, he suddenly realised how tired he was. Dipak's death had briefly shocked the tiredness out of him. He'd pulled his first late-night gambling session for some time. His body wasn't yet used to the shift in time. Something like jet lag.

H crossed quickly into Oxford Street and could see his Mercedes up ahead. Leaning against it was a figure wearing white shell pants and a hooded leather coat. H approached, eyeing Stammer warily.

'Where's mmmmmy m . . . m . . . money?'

H couldn't believe it. The fatigue seeped out of his body as he could feel himself becoming more and more angry.

'Leave it, Stammer, just leave it. And why are you leaning on my car?' He kept the edge out of his voice, but it was hard.

'You m . . . m . . . mmmust . . .' H didn't know what Stammer was trying to say but the effort of waiting had used up his remaining patience.

'Didn't you see what just happened to Dipak? I'm not in the mood for any bullshit, you're going to have to deal with it.' He stood opposite Stammer now, feet spread, hands hanging loosely at his side. As he'd shown when facing up to the thug at Blackie's, H might have been on a downward trajectory as a boxer, but for the average man on the street, he was still in good shape.

The two men stared at each other for a long moment. Stammer kissed his teeth, loud and long. Casually, without a word, he hoisted himself off the car. With an exaggerated rolling gait, Stammer headed past H, walking back to Oxford Street. H turned to watch him go.

\*\*\*

H's Mercedes glided smoothly through Knightsbridge, along Sloane Street, round Sloane Square and along the King's Road. Yeah, man. This was H's London. He loved driving through the streets at night when there was almost zero traffic and the Merc could cruise thirty without the constant shifting of gears. Tonight was almost one of those nights. In all the excitement around the sudden end to the session at Blackie's, H had forgotten that he had walked out with nearly £5,000 in his pocket. Five grand! A massive result! What was more, normal gambling etiquette dictated that he couldn't just leave after a big win like that. Under usual circumstances he would have had to give the other players at least some chance to win their money back. As it was, the way the game had broken up meant that he could legitimately walk out with his winnings intact and his head held high. That was why Stammer had taken the unusual step of waiting for him. Tough shit for Stammer! H had worked hard for that money. And as every gambler was secretly aware, over the long haul, they were all ultimately losers. So what the hell was he hassling H for?

No, it wasn't the temerity of Stammer's actions that ruined H's post-session high. He was driving through the quiet streets of Knightsbridge, he had the Merc's window wide open, he had Linton Kwesi Johnson – dub poet supreme and chronicler of life for Britain's black community – blaring unconvincingly through bad, tinny speakers. At any other time H would've felt good. But Dipak's death and the things that had caused it were playing on his mind. In all the time Blackie had run his shebeen in Ladbroke Grove, the heart of one of London's toughest black communities, no one had ever died. Sure, there'd been trouble; illegal gambling was a rough business that attracted rough people. But no one had ever been killed. Now, after twelve years, when Blackie moved into the white people's area, suddenly there was death and mayhem. Not for the first time H wondered why it was that white people loved to cramp a black man whenever he tried to improve himself.

It wasn't enough that with gentrification happening all over Ladbroke Grove and Notting Hill black people were already under siege and being forced out of an area that they had lived in and made home for over fifty years. The 'grey' film *Notting Hill* said it all. Black people had made the area fashionable with their Caribbean culture and lifestyle, the street life and music, the carnival and colour they added to what was a run-down, squalid, depressed corner of London. Yet if you saw the *Notting Hill* film you would have been hard-pressed to spot a black face anywhere. Airbrushed out! And that's what you supposedly call progress. So Blackie is forced to move out of the area, and now he and Dipak are victims of that same progress. H liked to think of himself as well-read. Even smart. Smart? White people living in Hampstead were smart. No one was moving into their area, cramping their style and slowly easing them out. They were smart. He thought about Blackie and Dipak and slowly shook his head. My people, my people.

Beverley would be asleep when H finally made it home but in the morning when she readied herself for work he would tell her about his win – carefully avoiding any mention of how the session ended. Maybe they could go shopping this weekend for some things they needed for the kitchen. Beverley liked to shop and, damn, they could buy a new toaster! How long was it since the old one burst into flames, pouring out thick black smoke? And they definitely needed a bread bin of some kind. Bread was always left in its bag on the worktop next to the cooker and it looked a mess. No, shopping would be good and it might put the two of them in a better place. Things had been getting on top of them recently and the strain was showing. H put it down to the pressure Beverley was under as a teacher but a niggling thought told him that it might be more than that. H also thought about taking Cyrus with them and buying him the *Shark's Tale* DVD he had been going on about. H didn't get it but for some reason Cyrus – H's five-year-old boy – had become obsessed with Will Smith.

H turned left off the King's Road into Beaufort Street, heading towards Battersea Bridge. With the traffic lights running in his favour, he drove straight over the bridge and into Battersea. In less than five minutes, H drove the Merc into the council-owned Surrey Lane housing estate, one of the few remaining enclaves for working-class people in the area. Over the last ten years the area had become surrounded by walled-off and gated luxury accommodation – much of it riverside. Such was the price of progress.

H parked up next to his block of flats, Cranmer House, left the car unlocked, and headed for the block entrance.

\*\*\*

The lift doors opened and H stepped out on the eighth floor. The light in the hallway had been smashed yet again. He pulled out his front door keys in the dim light and fumbled one of them into the lock.

He entered the short hallway and saw a flickering light coming from the living room. That was funny. Both Beverley and Cyrus should have been in bed asleep a long time ago. He walked through the hallway, rounded the corner and entered the small living room. Curled up asleep, in front of the silently flickering television, was Beverley.

A trim five feet four with boyishly slim hips and a smooth, clear complexion the colour of an After Eight chocolate, Beverley woke as

# THE LAST CARD

H stepped into the room. Her eyes opened and looked at him but took a moment to focus. When they did, they became cold and hard. Beverley had clearly just remembered why she was curled up on the sofa at nearly 4.30 in the morning. She uncurled and sat up. Without a word she folded her arms in front of her and stretched out her legs, wriggling her toes. She had good legs, Beverley. Slim and shapely, without a hint of cellulite.

The look on her face told H what he needed to know about why she was up at this hour of the morning. Her processed hair, normally cut into a fashionable bob, was now crushed on the side she had been sleeping on. Although she was sitting up, the hair remained sticking up at the angle at which it had been pressed by her sleeping head. At another time H might have laughed, but he could forget about laughing now.

'You're up?' This comment, H felt, was suitably innocuous.

'What the hell do you think you're doing coming in at this time? Where have you been?' Pause. 'Didn't you get my text?! Not that I need to ask!'

H just stood and looked at her, resignation on his face.

She carried on. 'You've been gambling again, haven't you?'

Caught! Bang to rights. H braced himself for the coming onslaught.

'When are you going to learn that you can't win at gambling! Get it? Arsehole! You-can't-win! And you aren't the only loser here, H! I am! And your son is!' Beverley rose and approached, jabbing him in the chest with her finger. 'He's your son! How much more of this shit . . .' she waved a hand around their sparse excuse for a home, 'How much more of this shit are you going to put us through, H? When are you going to grow up and be a man!' She stood in front of him, hands on hips. 'Do I have to assume all the responsibilities in this relationship for ever? Am I going to be the only one earning money for ever? Or are you going to do something? Anything?!' Her last word was shrieked. She looked at H, waiting for his response to this outburst.

H turned and walked out of the living room and into the kitchen. All thoughts of toasters, bread bins and Will Smith DVDs had long gone.

# 4.

**G**avin, Eric and Hodges made their way into Walker's Court. It was quiet, but as the three of them approached Roxy's, White Alan's nightclub, Gavin could see people leaving. He guessed the action in the club would be almost over. That was bad news – he wanted a lot of people to be around when he told White Alan what had happened.

Roxy's was a throwback to the '70s: glittery, camp and trashy. The club catered for two types of people: one type was . . . how could he put it? Ambiguous about their sexuality? The type who liked to see men dressing as women? The type who liked to flirt with members of the same sex? All of these things were true at Roxy's and Gavin had no idea what to make of it. Where he came from this type of thing was sneered at. There was nothing queer about Gavin!

The other type of person that Roxy's catered for were groups of women looking to behave in a raucous, undignified and generally sluttish manner. To Gavin's way of thinking, drinking heavily, lip-synching to trashy '70s disco numbers and generally waving arms in the air as if you just didn't care . . . that was the kind of behaviour he would expect from men. Which was perfectly fine. But women had no good reason to be behaving like this. All in all, over the last five weeks, Gavin had found himself thinking more and more about his whole involvement with White Alan . . .

Gavin had met White Alan some three years earlier when he had been working at a health club based in one of west London's smarter hotels. Gavin was a fitness guru. One of his clients was an up-and-coming young boxer, by the name of 'Beanpole' Barnes. Barnes, managed by White Alan, was an excellent amateur prospect. His problem was that he was having trouble maintaining himself in the super-bantamweight category. At the age of twenty-one it was clear that he would soon have to step up a division, into the feather-weights. More importantly, he wanted to turn to professional boxing. And that, potentially, was his problem. Beanpole Barnes could certainly box. But he had a punch that was only slightly heavier than that of an angry six-year-old. The Beanpole needed bulking up to prepare for his step into the professional ranks and Gavin was the man charged with doing it.

Gavin – who had briefly been a member of England's four-man bobsleigh team, competing in the 1980 Winter Olympics at Lake Placid – knew nothing about boxing but he knew about body conditioning. White Alan had been introduced to Gavin as a local businessman and philanthropist, given to taking an interest in up-and-coming boxing prospects. It transpired that he and his brother Paul ran a boxing stable in east London and Alan would often take on the expense of training and preparing particularly talented young fighters. Thus it was that Gavin, after driving up from his modest home in Purley, was confronted in the hotel health club with the Beanpole and a man introducing himself as Mr Alan Akers.

Alan Akers was in most respects an unexceptional man. He was of average height, slim build, in his early forties. What made him striking, however, was the fact that although this first meeting happened in early February, Akers was dressed from head to toe in white. He wore a white three-piece suit, he had on white Italian slip-on shoes and wore a crisp, open-necked white shirt. His skin tone, which should have been white, was in fact a deeply burnished sunbed orange. The look was topped with collar-length peroxide-white hair.

At this first meeting Gavin was almost compelled to laugh. Looking at Alan Akers, it was as though someone had turned up the brightness of Gavin's vision. He wanted to whip out a pair of sunglasses. But despite the sartorial idiosyncrasy, as far as Gavin was concerned, Alan Akers' saving grace was that he was rich. He was not only rich, he was grand and he was flamboyant. Speaking in the contorted vowels of the northern nouveau riche, he was given to grand statements; he wanted you to know he was a man of vision, a man used to giving orders and having them obeyed. For this, he paid the people that worked for him generously, if not always promptly.

Having seen all of this in that first meeting three years ago, Gavin had eagerly taken on the task of beefing up the Beanpole. He had done such a good job with his young charge that Gavin was offered the responsibility of looking after the fitness and dietary regimes of more of Alan Akers' fighters. The modest home in Purley could certainly do with the extra income and, before long, the majority of Gavin's income was being provided by Akers. Slowly but surely, Gavin's managerial skills and leadership abilities were being recognised, and before Gavin knew what had happened he was taken into the inner sanctum of Akers' world.

This new world of boxers, nightclubs, gambling and protection racketeering was certainly not what Gavin had come to expect from his life. But then again Gavin was in his late forties, pretending to be in his late thirties; he was single; and he had no discernible talents other than working in an hotel health club aiding those waging a losing battle with middle-age spread. The offer Akers had made to Gavin, to be his second lieutenant, his man in the field, was certainly a lucrative one. If it meant Gavin living in denial about the social acceptability of his work, well, Gavin was prepared to accept that. Certainly he was for a while. But Gavin could see there would come a day when Akers and his particular brand of haute couture would no longer be a feature of his life.

That day, however, was not today. Today, Gavin had the unenviable task of informing White Alan that the protection money from a new and upstart shebeen had not been collected. Gavin had failed to perform what should have been a simple task, and this pained him because he took a professional pride in his work. More importantly, White Alan was not a man to take bad news well. In fact, of late, White Alan was becoming more and more fractious and his reaction to news such as this less and less predictable.

With Eric and Hodges still behind him, Gavin stepped up to the entrance to the club. They passed through a short passageway that opened out into the body of the club. There was a stage at one end, a bar that ran the length of one wall, and a dance floor which took up half of the area in front of the stage. The other half was filled with tables and chairs for those who opted to chance the over-priced pleasures of 'Roxy's' kitchen.

The club was winding down and a number of the well-muscled, handsome men behind the bar lounged, counting the minutes until the end of the night; similarly, the 'waitresses' – tall, outrageously dressed transvestites – were also waiting for the night to end.

While Eric and Hodges sat at the bar and ordered drinks, Gavin made his way round the side. He was about to go through a door leading upstairs but he paused. Nina, the house singer with the unnaturally clear porcelain skin, mounted the stage to sing her last song for the night. Nina was the only thing that gave Roxy's a semblance of class. Statuesque in build and poise, she looked good. She was wearing a long, tight evening dress that glistened under the small spotlight. Without any introduction she unhooked the microphone from its stand, sat on the stool that was placed before it and began a melancholy, sentimental torch song. The few clubbers who were still around knew enough to pay attention because, although Nina wasn't a great singer, she wasn't bad. She exuded sex appeal and she knew how to invest a song with emotion.

But Gavin had pressing business. He moved on, disappearing through the door next to the bar, passing through a narrow hallway, and climbed the stairs at the end. He walked with a heavy tread. As he neared the top he met four bovine-looking toughs sitting and standing, looking awkward. It was one thing about working for White Alan that he'd never entirely accustomed himself to: the number of moronic-looking toughs – 'knuckle boys' he called them – who were constantly hanging around waiting to be told what to do. As Gavin approached these particular four, their awkwardness and unease became more apparent. Nina's torrid song of love could still be heard, just, floating up from the stage. Over this however, Gavin became aware of muffled, rhythmic grunts.

At the top of the stairs Gavin could hear more distinctly. The noise was coming from White Alan's office, a short landing away. Gavin looked round at the four men with raised eyebrows. What was going on? The grunts were louder now, bestial. The four men looked nervously back at him. Whatever shabby existence had spat out these four specimens of manhood, it had not prepared them for the uninhibited noises emanating from behind White Alan's door. Gavin, however, was of a different ilk. He stepped forward boldly and knocked. There was no answer.

Gavin cautiously opened the door. The grunts were now loud and clear. The room was dark. As Gavin's eyes adjusted to the lack of light, odd things caught his attention: the light from the door falling on the black-and-white photograph on the wall of White Alan and his slightly younger brother, Paul. They stood on either side of a punch bag in a gymnasium. On a shelf beneath that was a small lead statue of a laughing circus clown, arms spread, riding a one-wheeled cycle. Gavin had never noticed that before.

The grunting continued. It came from the end of the office, deep in shadow. As Gavin's eyes adjusted he soon had a pretty good view of what was going on. White Alan was standing behind a shadowy figure lying face down, bent over the desk. Alan was thrusting his groin in and out of this person's arse. The guttural, animalistic sounds came from the throat of White Alan. It was now clear to Gavin that they were expressions of pleasure.

Gavin stood for a moment, transfixed. What to do? Did Alan know he was there? Should he interrupt? While Gavin pondered his next move, the decision was taken away from him. One of the knuckle boys, displaying a discretion and sensitivity that Gavin would never have given them credit for, gently closed the door behind him. Gavin was shut in! And almost as if to emphasise his predicament, White Alan suddenly began grunting and thrusting more feverishly now, grunting and thrusting, grunting and thrusting, pounding away into the unseen figure's arse. With one last thrust and a last extended growl, it was over. White Alan stepped back. Breathing heavily, he zipped up his fly.

Without turning he said, 'Don't you ever knock?' He said it breathlessly but without embarrassment. He turned, flicking on a desk light. The figure who had just been rhythmically violated groaned quietly but made no move to rise, remaining bent over the desk. White Alan sat on the desk. He was wearing his customary white suit, and he had on a white shirt with ruffles down the front and at the cuffs. His face glowed from his recent efforts.

'I did,' said Gavin. He stepped closer to the table. Gavin was seeing something new about White Alan and he could feel horror, revulsion and fear welling up inside his stomach. The figure moved now, rising, turning over. It was a man. His face bashed and bloodied. He was dazed, disoriented. He staggered as he tried to prop himself up on one arm.

# THE LAST CARD

'Don't answer back, Gavin, I don't like it. And get him out of here.'

Gavin stepped quickly back to the door and opened it a fraction. The four men outside had edged closer to the door. As Gavin opened it they jumped back. Gavin beckoned two of them in.

'He's ready to go.'

Two of the four men silently entered and, instinctively averting their eyes from both Gavin and Alan, each took an arm of the man on the desk, hoisted him up and dragged him out. It was only now, as he was being dragged out, that Gavin recognised him: a troublesome nightclub owner who, only two days earlier, had crossed Alan for the third time in the last two months. He'd been late with a payment.

Once the man was outside Gavin closed the door behind him. He could feel his head beginning to pound again. Alan walked briskly around the desk and sat in his executive chair. Before he spoke he opened one of the desk drawers, pulled out a small canister and sprayed a little breath-freshener into his mouth. He then tossed the canister back into the drawer, slammed it shut, ran a hand through his hair, rubbed his nose loudly. Only then did he look up at Gavin.

'What's so urgent?' He drummed his hands on the desk. Like a man who had just had a refreshing shower.

'We had trouble from the new shebeen tonight, Alan.' Gavin worked hard at keeping his voice steady. The drumming stopped. 'I need to go back with some more of the boys.'

'What kind of trouble?' Alan looked back at Gavin, surprise replacing contentment.

'They wouldn't pay.'

'They wouldn't pay? They wouldn't fucking pay?' Gavin looked at his boss. This he could understand. Alan was angry. Soon he would be fuming, given the mood he seemed to be in these days. That other thing, the thing he'd witnessed earlier when he came in, that, he didn't like. In fact, for the first time in the three years that he'd had worked with White Alan, Gavin was frightened.

# 5.

**N**ina finished her last song for the night, an old one from the mid-90s – Des'ree's 'You Gotta Be'. Nina wasn't a great fan of all the gospel stuff that came with Des'ree, but you couldn't argue with her voice: the woman could sing. And Nina had always found the lyrics uplifting. That's why she always chose to make this the song that she performed at the end of the night – for all the women out there.

Nina took her bow and the applause from the sparse crowd was enthusiastic. With a gracious smile she left the stage and trod delicately over to the bar. She lifted the bottom of her dress so she could sit on one of the bar stools. As she sat down, loud, pumping disco music started up. Nina turned to survey the room. The gracious smile she had beamed down to her audience at the end of her song was now replaced with a surly look. She glanced quickly at her reflection in the mirror behind the bar. Two small, vertical lines appeared in her otherwise smooth forehead, just above her eyebrows. They always appeared when Nina had this particular expression on her face and she always had this particular expression on her face when she was unhappy. Those two lines had become almost constant companions over the last month or so. When she first noticed them she tried to smooth them out by using one hand to pull the skin between her eyebrows to the left and the other hand pulling the skin to the right. It didn't work. As soon as she stopped pulling, the two small, vertical lines reappeared. This made her feel surlier. The lines became deeper. She had decided the only way to stop these two small, vertical lines appearing in her forehead was to stop wearing a surly expression. She had to smile more. But now, as she forgot this resolution and wore the surly expression, she turned back to look round the room.

'Every time, Nina. You bring tears to my eyes.' Tony, the barman, was a nice guy. He was from Nigeria, very dark-skinned, good body, and camp as a Spanish bullfighter.

'Bring tears to my eyes, Tony, and fix me the usual. A double, please.' As she ordered her drink, White Alan, with Gavin following behind, made his way over.

'It's off tonight, Nina. I've got business, I've got to go home.' White Alan often dispensed with the formalities of greetings these days. And if Nina had thought carefully about how this made her feel, she would have realised that this was one of the main reasons why she had two small, vertical lines furrowing the smooth, clear skin of her forehead.

'But what about the party at Janine's?'

'I've got to work, I've . . .'

'But I want to go to the party! It was her first night on stage tonight and, and . . .' Nina lapsed into silence. The look Alan now gave her was encouragement to nothing less.

'I'll take you home.' Now that he had silence from Nina and had told her of her new arrangements, he turned to Gavin.

'What did Dunstan say when he rang?'

'He said he had a problem with Paul; he wants to deliver directly to you this month.'

'Coont!' Alan's expletive made Nina flinch. She knew tonight was not going to be a good one.

'And what does Paul say?' Alan continued.

'He says it's a local problem. He can handle it.'

Alan looked at Gavin as though he was the cunt and it was him who was saying he could handle it.

'He can handle "it"? But he didn't say what "it" was?'

'No.'

'Right! Ring him back and tell him his big brother wants to know what the fook is going on! I'm sick of this shite!' Tony returned with Nina's double Tanqueray and tonic. Alan swept it from the bar and took a big gulp. He spluttered into his hand and glared at Tony.

'What the hell is this?' Alan slammed the glass on to the bar. Tony stepped forward and took it from Alan's hand. He bent down smelling the remaining contents of the glass as though he, Tony, had not just poured the drink himself. Sixty seconds later, having smelt and examined the glass and its contents in minute detail, he looked nervously over at Alan.

'Smells like, like, gin and tonic to me.'

'So why are you giving me a gin and tonic when you know I only drink dry Martinis?'

'Er . . . I wasn't, I wasn't giving it to . . .'

'Forget it! You're fired! I can't stand this fooking incompetence all around me! Fook off!'

'What? Alan, I wasn't, I didn't . . .'

'You're fired! Go! Gone! You're history!'

Without another word Tony turned and left the bar area. Nina stole a glance at Gavin. He caught the look but made a point of not holding it for more than one, maybe two nano-seconds.

Alan suddenly remembered something. 'Give me two minutes, Nina.' And he left, round the side of the bar and back up the stairs. Nina watched him go.

'What's his problem now?' She spat the words out as she looked up at Gavin. She didn't like Gavin – he walked around as though he had a poker up his arse. The kind of pompous idiot who thought he was better than everybody else. She certainly couldn't trust him, but the way she was feeling right this minute she had to let her feelings out to someone. Gavin paused before he spoke, weighing his words carefully.

'You know what I think? I think he's going through a mid-life crisis.'

'So see a therapist!'

'That's not exactly his style.'

'Can't you make it his style? You're his batman!' As soon as she'd said it Nina knew she'd said too much, but Alan was making her feel increasingly uneasy these days. She had no time for Gavin's delicate sensibilities. Gavin looked at her coldly.

'He has his own style.'

Nina waved to another barman, gesturing for him to fix her another drink. Gavin paused again before he continued. 'Alan carried out his threat.'

'Oh, God, no!' Nina's hand flew to her mouth, horrified.

'The nightclub owner? He . . .?' Gavin nodded. 'Sweet Jesus!'

# THE LAST CARD

Nina leant over the bar to where one of the barmen had left a packet of cigarettes. Fingers outstretched, she lifted one out. She put it in her mouth and tried to light it with a book of matches from the ashtray in front of her. Her hand shook so badly she couldn't do it. Gavin carefully took the matches from her and lit the cigarette.

'I thought you stopped smoking?'

'I did.'

Gavin watched her inhale hungrily and then he continued. 'It gets worse. Paul went cocaine crazy, then went AWOL. Or some other madness. Now there's mutiny amongst the ranks; some kind of trouble happening back in Hackney.'

Nina looked at him without comprehension.

'So?'

'So I think it's all getting too much for Alan. I think he might be looking for a way out.'

'He could just leave, couldn't he? He's got enough money!'

'Has he? How much is enough?' Before Nina could even begin to answer that one Gavin spoke up again. 'I think Alan's looking for a big pay-day. I would be if I were him. And there's too much stuff going on right now to walk away. Like the fact that the man that runs the new shebeen on Duck Lane, he wouldn't pay up.'

Nina pulled hard on her cigarette. 'Does he know who he's up against?'

Gavin gave a mirthless chuckle. 'I suspect not.'

Nina's drink arrived, she took a big swallow. 'I've got a horrible feeling something very bad is going to happen.' She said the words softly, without inflection, not expecting an answer from Gavin.

'That's what I'm thinking.'

Her surprise at his response prompted her to go further than she probably should have.'I've got to get out of this scene, Gavin. I can feel it, something is very wrong here.'

* * *

Nina and White Alan made their exit from the club. They left Walker's Court and turned right on to Brewer Street. Alan's white Rolls Royce was parked nearby. The casually dressed Jimmy, White

Alan's driver, spotted them, stepped out of the car and nipped round to the rear passenger door to let them in to the veritable landscape of white of the Rolls Royce interior.

Nina ensconced herself on the back seat, as far away from White Alan as she could possibly squeeze.

'Where to, Mr Akers?' Jimmy was one of a dying breed: a chirpy cockney, satisfied with his lot in life, with no desire to become a TV presenter or a singer or even an actor. As he looked in the rear view mirror, his eyes met Nina's.

Nina turned away, peering out of the window, not looking at anything in particular. Alan had raped a man that evening – raped! It sent waves of horror and revulsion through her that she did not know how to begin to deal with. Why had he chosen this particularly violent way to teach the man a lesson?

As the Rolls Royce eased its way through the West End, all kinds of questions were circling in Nina's mind. And as they circled ever more furiously, her body language became more and more distant. She squeezed herself further into the corner of the car. Alan looked across the snowy expanse of the back seat, eyeing Nina's back.

'Better make it Holland Park first, Jimmy, then up to Hampstead.' Holland Park was where Nina lived. In a mews house rented by Alan. Alan lived in a sumptuous house in Hampstead village.

Nina stared fixedly out of her window. Every so often Alan turned to her, about to speak, but then thought better of it and turned away. To distract himself he removed a small canister of breath freshener, sprayed it twice into his mouth and then slipped it back in his pocket. While Nina maintained her frigid silence, Alan's hand took on a life of its own. It made its way across the back seat of the car and an errant finger tickled the edges of Nina's coat. No response. The hand took this as encouragement and made its way round the coat and on to a thigh. The thigh flinched at the touch and the hand scurried hurriedly back from whence it came.

White Alan looked casually ahead of him. Nina caught Jimmy watching them via the rear-view mirror. Jimmy quickly flicked his eyes back to the road ahead. White Alan touched Nina's arm.

'Why don't you stay with me tonight?'

'I'm tired, Alan. I think . . . I'd rather go home.'

# THE LAST CARD

Nina had been hoping that tonight of all nights, Alan would not ask her back to his place. They had been together for four and a half years. Early in their relationship Alan had a live-in girlfriend, Zoe, and Nina had insisted that he had paid for Nina to have her own place in Holland Park. Now that Zoe was history, Nina had continually resisted Alan's attempts to have her move in with him. She did not intend to give up her independence lightly, small though it was. Tonight, however, she knew that if she turned Alan down in a way that offended his masculinity, as a matter of principle he would insist that she return with him to Hampstead. Consequently, she had tried to add a note of disappointment to her refusal. Apparently, she hadn't tried hard enough.

'I thought you wanted to go to Janine's party?'

'That was earlier.'

'So? What's changed?'

Nina racked her brains to think of something that had changed. She could think of nothing. About to say anything and stall for time, Alan pre-empted her.

'I tell you what Jimmy, why don't you drive directly to my place.'

'Right you are, Mr Akers.'

And that was that. The Rolls pulled to the side of the road, did a three-point turn and headed back the way it came.

# 6.

**W**ha Gwan watched as the slightly built Indian girl entered the twenty-four-hour grocery store on the corner of the Uxbridge Road. The chill in the air reflected his mood. He hunched his powerful shoulders against the cold and sniffed loudly. His nose had been running since he had been sitting on the exposed bench in the middle of west London's Shepherds Bush Green for some time. A line of snot trickled, untroubled, down on to his upper lip.

The bench was an oasis favoured by the neighbourhood drunks; three of them loitered nearby. If any of them felt brave enough to question the heavy-set Wha Gwan about the temerity he had shown in usurping their position on the bench, they let it slide. The hurt on Wha Gwan's face, the tension in those powerful shoulders, the very set of his body as he eyed the three Indian people entering the grocery shop on the other side of the Green, told them that now was not the time to question his presence on the bench. Whatever was bothering the young man in the full-length padded parka that loudly proclaimed its origins as 'New Jersey', it was a problem that he was best left alone to deal with. Full-time drunks tend to be better acquainted than most with the harsh realities of life, and the glistening, brimming eyes with which the young man stared out at the world were no more than was to be expected.

# 7.

With sweat running into his eyes and his arms beginning to feel like lead, H took big, slow, methodical swings at the heavy bag. This wasn't the way he usually worked. He usually used his time training with the heavy bag to work on his body movement, bobbing and weaving from the waist, aware of his footwork as he manoeuvred himself around the swinging bag. He usually gave it a jab, stepped to the left, the bag swung back, thwack! another jab, bend from the waist, to the left, to the right, thwack! two steps to the right, never crossing the legs, keeping his imaginary opponent off-balance, never letting them predict your next move, thwack! thwack! a one-two combination, big step to the left, move your head, always presenting a moving target, thwack! big right hand. That was his usual routine. But not today. Today H pounded the bag with all his strength, on every swing. Without his usual energy, without his usual bounce . . .

H had started the day with a row with Beverley. Days had been starting like this more and more often recently, but today's row was different. Beverley had finally had enough of H's gambling – that H had heard before – but this time she was saying she wanted out of their relationship. Beverley had threatened to move out and take Cyrus with her. H told her she was out of her mind. Despite the fact that they'd been together five and a half years, three years living together, she seemed not to be listening, she still didn't seem to understand when he was serious and when he was jesting. He was certainly not jesting about Cyrus. If she wanted to move her black arse out of his council flat that was her choice. But take his son with her? She was out of her fucking mind!

The argument had escalated almost to the point of violence. Not quite, because although H was a cruiser weight and came in at a chunky 188 pounds, Beverley was a woman you didn't want to go down that road with. They both understood that. If violence were ever to flare between them someone was sure to be very seriously hurt and neither knew which of them it would be. Beverley had nails like a big cat, she was as stubborn as a mule and she had a memory like an elephant; she could probably remember every day of her twenty-eight years. H had once seen her leave a scratch on the face of a woman who had wronged her and the scratch looked as though it had been made by a mountain cougar. No, fighting was not for them. But certainly the argument this morning had been heated.

As usual, while H slept, it was Beverley who had risen and pre-pared Cyrus for school. As usual. She took him into school. As usual. What wasn't usual was that instead of going straight to work she had returned home. Just as H was rising from his bed, scratching his balls and ambling casually into the kitchen to see what was in the fridge. He was surprised to see her back at home and said as much. That's when things became heated and nasty. It turned out that Beverley had come specifically to see him and talk.

At first H tried to laugh off the serious expression that Beverley wore, but once he could see that she meant business he felt his anger begin to rise. What really stirred him was that she didn't imme-diately complain about his gambling, which is what he'd expected. They'd been over that course a thousand times before. At least this time H had five Gs, five big ones burning a hole in his pocket. No, this time Beverley came at him from a completely different angle. She attacked his boxing. She wanted to know how long he was going to put off doing real, honest work, to continue pursuing a dream that was long past its sell-by date.

Oh, shit!

His boxing was a taboo subject. It was accepted that this was his world, he knew what he was doing and Beverley should keep her opin-ions to herself. This morning that had all changed. Beverley attacked him about how his dream was ruining her dream, which was for the three of them to be happy; H's dream was ruining their lives. She seemed to think that H's gambling was somehow linked to his boxing and that if he gave up the fight game then his desire to gamble would fall away. H was stunned. As far as he was aware he had never, ever expressed anything about a 'dream' to her! So why did she assume that he had a 'dream' that needed fulfilling as a boxer? But that wasn't even the worst. Her next blow was her rabbit punch. It blindsided H completely. Beverley didn't go to yoga on Thursday nights. She went secretly to a Gamblers Anonymous meeting.

What?

H considered himself a conscious man and a cool customer but at that moment he could happily have torn out a clump of the hair Beverley was so proud of. Instead he offered to box her face. Beverley stood up and said if he was a man let him try. After the silence that followed she told him that he was an ignorant ox, he didn't know what he had with her and Cyrus, and he was killing her love for him.

Beverley claimed to know him better than he knew himself. She said that she could see he was trying somehow to redeem himself through boxing, but if he didn't hurry up and do it he was going to throw his life away trying. But she, Beverley Angela Hyacinth Fredricks, was not going to let him throw her life away. And hell would freeze over before she let him deprive their son of the rights and opportunities he deserved. It was tough enough out there already. Cyrus should not have to grow up with a punch-drunk gambling addict for a father who was never there and never had nothing to offer nohow!

H stepped back, reeling, when he heard all of this. His heart raced as he sat himself down at the cheap kitchen table. Was she asking him to choose between his family and his boxing? She told him to read her lips. That was precisely what she was asking.

\*\*\*

And so H was in the run-down gymnasium in south London where he had trained for over ten years, pounding hell out of a heavy leather bag that looked older than he did, thinking about life. Around him, the gym with its peeling paintwork, its dust and its grime, was abuzz with activity. Ten other boxers trained hard at various stations, on speed bags, shadow boxing, skipping, floor work. At one end of the gym there was an elevated boxing ring. Two boxers sparred with each other while Nick, the man from Belfast who set up the gym some twenty-four years earlier and who was now its gnarled trainer, watched from one corner. Six other boxers stood around the ropes.

The staccato, syncopated orchestration of the gym's movement was held in place by the booming sound system that pumped out the music and words of the American rapper, the late Notorious B.I.G.

**. . . SMELL THE INDONESIA, BEATS YOU TO A SEIZURE,**
**THEN FUCK YOUR MOMS, HIT THE SKINS TO AMNESIA . . .**

The pounding, slapping, scuffling of leather throughout the gym mysteriously kept time to the music that dripped with the depraved violence of the deceased New York gangsta rapper.

**. . . SUCKING ON THE TITS,**
**HAD THE HOOKER BEGGING FOR THE DICK . . .**

H didn't particularly like rap music, but the brutality of the lyrics and the beat somehow complemented his colleagues' and his own pursuit of violence.

Matt walked past H with a bundle of skipping ropes. Matt was now training and managing fighters in his own right. He joined his father, standing outside the corner of the ring watching the two talented boxers, one in his early twenties, the other in his late teens. Both boxers were black – Sam and Blood – and both sparred stylishly with each other in their head guards. Blood, nineteen years old, was clearly the more talented; if he kept his rate of progress up, he would be destined for good things.

Nick watched the action with intense concentration, screaming his commands. He was old and grizzled now, wearing grey stubble and a sweat-stained tee-shirt.

'No punches to de head . . . I said no fuckin' punches to de head! . . . Dat's good, dat's good . . . keep movin', keep movin' . . . slip dat jab, Sam, slip de fuckin' jab! . . . for Chroist's sake willya move your fuckin' feet!'

Nick looked over at the big clock on the wall with the red minute hand.

'Roight, toime! Good work, Blood, you're lookin' good, son.'

Sam and Blood touched gloves. Sam climbed through the ropes and out of the ring, joining the others outside. Blood, meanwhile, prowled inside, staying loose. Nick looked around the gym.

'So who's next?' Although he shouted this into the body of the gym his voice was drowned out by the gems delivered by the Notorious one.

# THE LAST CARD

**. . . AFTER SHE SUCKED THE DICK I STABBED HER BROTHER WITH THE ICE PICK . . .**

'Oi!' Nick gave a shrill, piercing whistle. 'Which one of you useless fuckin' toime-wasters is next?'

You can take the man out Belfast's south side but can you ever take Belfast out of the man? H didn't think so.

**. . . BECAUSE HE WANTED ME TO FUCK HIM FROM THE BACK . . .**

'Turn dat fuckin' rap music shite off!' Nick's face went beetroot red and flecks of spittle flew from his mouth.

Benjamin, a lanky white fighter from New Cross, stepped quickly over to the battered old stereo sitting on a shelf on the wall and pressed 'stop'. There was a sudden quiet in the gym.

'T'ank fuckin' Chroist for de sound a soilence! Now which one a you brain-dead, prickless excuses for proize foighters hasn't yet been up here?' Nick looked around at the open faces of the boxers below. 'Have you all been in?' Silence. People now began to go back to their workout, most of them already having been in the ring with Blood.

'What about H?' It was Matt. Nick looked over at H standing by the heavy bag, hands on hips, blowing hard.

'D'you fancy a turn in the ring, H?' Nick said it scornfully. H ambled slowly over and climbed up to the outside of the apron.

'I thought you'd forgotten I was alive.'

'I had!'

'Come on, H, I need a good punch bag. You know't I mean?' That was Blood. He smiled as he slammed his boxing gloves together and chewed on his gum-shield like a skittish horse. In the boxing fraternity Blood had just thrown out a challenge that couldn't be ignored. Although H had at least fourteen pounds on Blood, he was also thirteen years older.

H nodded and climbed into the ring. He beckoned Matt to take the gum-shield from the back pocket of his shorts and slip it into his mouth. Nick looked at the big wall clock and watched the minute hand approaching the sixty-second mark.

'Your t'ree minutes are starting now.' Nick looked over to Blood. 'And dis is your last round, Blood, so go to work.'

'Head shots?'

'Yep. Unload de lot.'

Matt climbed quickly back through the ropes to grab a headguard for H. Nick stayed his hand.

'Leave it.'

Matt gave his father a surprised look but Nick shrugged it off.

'He's a big man, he can take it.'

H and Blood began to box, H circling, testing, exploratory jabs, moving, looking for an opening. Blood flew at him, two-handed, throwing ones, twos, snorting loudly with each thrown punch. Fitter and faster than H, at the peak of condition in readiness for an upcoming fight, Blood pushed forward, peppering H from every angle as he bobbed and moved, jabbed and drove. At first H was able to contain him; holding his own, moving, staying out of trouble. But as he tired, ninety seconds into the round, one hundred seconds, H's arms drooped. More and more of Blood's shots connected.

H took a big one flush on the chin – bang! He staggered; his technique crumbled. He tried desperately to fend off Blood's blows. Matt looked at the wall clock and winced. One hundred and twenty seconds had passed, sixty to go.

'Take it easy, Blood!' muttered Matt.

'Don't you fuckin' dare!' Nick screamed at his protégé. 'You've got another minute.'

Other boxers were paying attention now, wincing with concern as H took another heavy blow to the head. He dropped to one knee. Blood stopped, looking to Nick.

'What are you lookin' at me for! You've got another t'irty seconds!'

Humiliated, H stayed down. He took two deep breaths. He passed a glove over his forehead to wipe the sweat from his eyes then rose. Straight into another cluster of blows. Blood was making it look good now, better than it was, dancing and posing. Blood was beating on H from all angles and, like a man wading through mud, H vainly tried to defend himself. He was again knocked to the canvas.

With a satisfied look on his face Nick turned to the clock.

'T'ree . . . two . . . one . . . toime. Good job, Blood, good workout, son, you're looking grand in dere.'

Blood helped a groggy H to his feet and then trotted over to Nick.

Nick unstrapped his headguard. 'You look as dough you're about ready to me.'

# THE LAST CARD

\*\*\*

In the changing room H slumped down on a bench, his back against the wall. Using his teeth, he took his time unlacing the gloves. Beverley. Blood. Jesus Christ, what a day.

H could hear his phone ringing from inside his locker. He didn't care. As he sat, without making a move, the changing room door clattered open and Blood strode in carrying his tee-shirt and gloves. H looked at his young body. It was ripped.

'Hey, man, sorry about that out there. You know what Nick's like, he gets carried away. He doesn't mean anything.'

'No problem.' He said it but he didn't mean it. It was a problem. Blood turned to one of the lockers and fiddled with the combination lock. H rose and slipped a small key from inside his sock and fitted it into the padlock on his own locker. His mobile was still ringing.

'Who're you fighting?' asked H.

Blood pulled out his wash-bag. As he stripped off his shorts and trunks he turned to H with a grin.

'Glen Patterson. Up in Sheffield, next Monday.' He dropped to the bench to unlace his boots. Brand new Nikes. Glen Patterson was a seasoned pro fighting out of a gym in Wincobank, Sheffield, a place run by another displaced Irishman. His fighters were known for their defensive style and were notoriously difficult to beat.

'Yeah, Patterson is ranked three in the division and he's looking to get an easy win so he can make a charge for the top.'

As a young fighter, Blood had already made a name for himself as a useful contender. Unnecessarily flashy, but useful. The flashiness meant the fight would draw a crowd and the crowd would make some noise. Patterson was probably banking on his experience and durability to wear his younger, less experienced opponent down. He'd earn a useful pay-day and grab some headlines that would add leverage to his request for a crack at the title.

'What he doesn't know is I've got something for his lilywhite arse.' Blood stripped off his boots, rose and stalked naked as a jay-bird for the showers. 'Dynamite in both hands. I'm the real deal, baby. Bam!' Blood threw a punch to emphasise his point. His laughter echoed round the showers.

H shook his head. He couldn't complain. Blood was H ten years ago. He opened up his locker. His mobile was still ringing. As he answered it he looked down at his own boots. They were Nikes, but his were scuffed, the laces were frayed and the soles were worn as smooth as glass.

'Hello?'

'H?'

'Blackie. What's up?'

'Me cool, man, me cool. Listen, dread, I wanted to t'ank you for de lickle trouble we 'ad de udder night, seen.'

'No diggidy, no doubt. I just hope you managed to sort things out.'

'Everyt'ing cool, man, me a sort it all out. I t'ink I gwan 'affu pay dem man de, still; but evert'ing else, me a work it out.'

\*\*\*

Wearing trainers, jeans and a leather biking jacket, H left the gym. He carried his gear in his old leather holdall. As he hit the street he saw a champagne-pink BMW, a convertible with tinted windows parked opposite. He eyed it as he walked by. You didn't see many of those on the Old Kent Road, and H wondered who it belonged to. The next moment his idle curiosity was resolved.

'We meet again.'

H turned. Facing him was the big blond guy who'd burst into Blackie's the other night. Oh, shit.

'In the car. I've got someone who wants to meet you.'

As H assessed his aggressor, deciding what to say, the back doors of the car opened and two large men stepped out. They didn't look as though they meant to take no for an answer.

# 8.

**N**ina sat in a corner of White Alan's office. Since the other night when she'd heard about Alan raping – raping! – the nightclub owner things between the two of them had been . . . difficult. He'd told her he was feeling the pressure to maintain his business and for the first time since they had been a couple, she didn't care. She had admitted to herself, finally, that this relationship was one she wanted out of. Worryingly, she had admitted this to Gavin and she didn't know if Gavin was someone she could trust. But this didn't worry her half as much as Alan's apparently deteriorating mental state. He'd raped a man! He'd then insisted she go back to his place and share his bed with him.

Nina was aware that she wasn't a great singer but for a young girl who had grown up in the council estates of Stoke Newington she had paid her dues. She deserved a chance. It was Alan that had given her a chance and for that she would always be grateful. On the other hand they were both aware of what Alan gained from his 'philanthropy': Nina McGuire. And for Nina, that was a problem.

As Nina sat absentmindedly staring out of a window, her troubles ran back and forth through her mind. She unwrapped a stick of nicotine chewing gum and popped it in her mouth. The thing about Alan was that, despite the money and the power, it was never enough. What he couldn't understand, and people like him never seemed to understand this, was that you can't own people forever. Alan wanted her around so she had to sit here. That was the power he had over her. For now.

Alan sat behind his desk, an elegantly manicured fingernail digging inelegantly at a piece of spinach stuck between his teeth. Nina turned to look at him and stared as he absentmindedly switched between thumb and forefinger, twisting, straining and grimacing to remove the little strip of green. It was disgusting. She felt the two small, vertical lines appear in her forehead, just above her eyebrows.

With his other hand Alan wrote in a ledger that sat in front of him. Alan worked hard, of that there was no doubt. He was ambitious and he was ruthless. Despite an unhealthy preoccupation with dental hygiene, in the early days Nina had liked him for all these reasons; she liked him because he had helped this struggling woman who was desperate to make a name for herself; she liked him because he adored her. But she only fell in love with him because, unlike the kind of men she grew up with, he could bend the world into the shape he wanted it to be. Things were so because he said they were so . . .

Nina's Irish immigrant father left the flat that she and her two younger sisters grew up in when she was seven. She was the oldest daughter and close to her father. But even at that age Nina could tell that her parents were not suited to each other. They fought, they argued; they argued, they fought. Nina never knew what the problem was because once her father left, that was it, none of the family ever saw him again. And her mother, Jean, never spoke about him.

When Nina turned thirteen and tentatively asked her mother about the big man that she remembered as her father, Jean had slapped her hard across the face and then promptly burst into tears. Dry-eyed but shocked, Nina had never mentioned her father again. The one thing she could remember about him, however, and desperately held on to, happened one night after a particularly nasty row between her parents.

Nina and Dymphna had climbed out of bed and sat on the top of the stairs, listening to the drama that was taking place below them. Maureen was just a baby at the time and was asleep in her cot. At some point Nina and Dymphna crept along the landing and climbed back into bed. Nina didn't know if her parents had heard them or not but a short time later her father had opened their bedroom door and stood in the doorway. Nina and Dymphna were pretending to be asleep. After what seemed like an age Nina finally turned over to see if he was still there. He was. Seeing her move he came into the room and sat down on the edge of the bed. He stroked Nina's long, shiny hair. Nina had asked what the matter was and her father had just looked at her. It was only then that she could see that her father was crying.

# THE LAST CARD

Across the room Dymphna stopped pretending to sleep and slipped into bed beside Nina. At the sight of his tears the two young girls hugged each other and their father and all three of them cried. Then her father said something that Nina had always remembered. His words had come back to her many times over the years and were one reason why she was attracted to Alan.

Her father had said that some men are constantly at odds with the world and this was not a happy position to be in. When a man is faced with this situation he can only really do one of three things. He can either change what he believes and what he does so that he can fit in with the world; or he can drive himself so hard that he changes the world to believe what he believes. Or he can go mad trying to do either one of these things. Nina never knew what path her father chose, all she knew was that some time after this night her father left home and never returned.

Nina's father was a distant man and this memory was his only legacy. It was a legacy that left her with a taste for troubled men, men who could clearly be identified as people who had chosen one of these paths. Alan was such a man.

Alan had told Nina how he and his brother Paul started their business as petty drug dealers, but had gone on to buy into nightclubs and provide 'insurance' for them; Alan told her about his love for the noble art of boxing and what it meant to him. Nina could see the passion in his eyes as he talked, about his businesses and the boxing, and she had fallen for his drive and energy. Here was a man out of step with the world, who had the drive and the willpower to change the world to his way of being. Here was a man who had turned a tragic past in a poor, wretched mining town into the triumph of owning a home in Hampstead village, a nightclub in one of the most exclusive areas of central London and a custom-built Rolls Royce. This was the man Nina had fallen for. But as she stared at him now, grimacing like a gargoyle, mindlessly pawing at the detritus between his teeth, all she could think about was him raping – raping! – a man who had crossed him.

Nina unwrapped another stick of nicotine gum and turned away. She thought about how she could slip away and call her girlfriend, Maxine. Maxine was a receptionist for a law firm over on Baker Street and was one of her best friends. They often had lunch together.

'Do you have to make that noise?' Alan was scowling at her. 'I'm trying to concentrate.'

'What noise?'

'With your mouth! I've seen camels chew with more finesse than you!'

'Then go out with a camel!' Nina stomped her way to the office door. She stopped as a large stapler crashed against it.

'Sit your arse down! You're just like a bloody camel! How come you've always got the hump these days?'

Nina glared at him. She could feel the two small, vertical lines deepening in her forehead and the fact that she sensed their presence made them deepen even more.

'I'm trying to run a business here! And it's bloody hard work! Can you not see?'

Nina stomped back to her seat in the corner. As she sat someone knocked at the door.

'Come in!' Alan roared. The door opened a fraction and Gavin's balding head poked in. 'Well come in then, for fook's sake, man!' The door swung back and in stumbled a tallish black man with baby dreadlocks. Nina sat up. This looked interesting.

The man was about six feet tall and built with the loose-limbed precision of an athlete, slim with long limbs. The short dreadlocks that sprouted from the top of his head crowned what would have been a smooth-skinned, open, almost handsome face, but for a heaviness that settled over his eyebrows. The man looked startled as he stumbled, held from behind. Watching him closely, Nina saw he had the posture and body language of a man not used to being pushed. Pinning his arms was one of what Nina called Alan's 'beefeaters' – his heavies.

'Who the hell are you?! And what the fuck do you want with me?' The man's tone was insolent. Nina guessed it had been a long time since anyone had spoken to Alan like that.

Casually, Alan opened a drawer, pulled out a little tub of toothpicks, extracted one and began to pick at his teeth. He looked the black man up and down. The man stared back, waiting for an answer. Alan sprayed two squirts of breath freshener into his mouth and replaced the canister in the drawer. He continued to delve into the recesses of his mouth for the remains of the day's detritus. Finally he spoke.

'So you're the man with his hand in my pocket. Me sky rocket.' Alan leaned back in his chair, eyeing the man in front of him.

'Listen up, bad man, I was just hanging on to what was mine.'

Alan paused for a moment, taking this in. He pulled out the tooth-pick, examined a minute fragment of bacon skewered on the end of it, and sucked it off. He then nodded to one of the beefeaters. The beefeater stepped forward and slapped the black guy hard in the face. Nina winced and looked away. When she looked back she was surprised to see the man looking down at Alan, almost with pity. Gavin stood quietly by the door. There was a long silence.

'I don't know what you thought was yours but you were wrong. It was mine. Now you owe me five grand. It was three but for your fooking cheek I'm making it five. Have you got it?'

'You're out of your mind.' Calm, untroubled.

More silence.

Alan again nodded to the beefeater and he again slapped the black man in the face, harder this time.

'Have you got my five grand? It's a simple question.'

The man locked eyes with the man who had slapped him twice. He slowly turned his head back to Alan.

'No.'

'Surprise, surprise. Where the fook would you get five grand?' Alan looked around at Gavin and his beefeaters. This was their cue to smile. Gavin gave a polite grimace, the beefeaters smiled broadly. Nina didn't smile at all.

'Seven days. I want you back here with my money, understood?'

The man remained silent, staring down at Alan. From where Nina sat the man's defiance, insolence, seemed obvious but Alan stared back at him thinking . . . what?

After a moment Alan nodded again to the frisky beefeater. Again, he used his open palm to slap the black man in the face, putting even more enthusiasm into it this time. Blood trickled from the black man's mouth. It glowed hot from the three blows it had taken. Nina again winced, allowing herself a soft 'no!' this time. Alan looked at her but said nothing.

'It's just gone up to ten grand. Do you understand me now?'

Nina spun round to look at Alan. He looked back at her, allowing himself a little smile. She realised he was playing with this man for her benefit.

'Have you been eating onions?' This was the black guy. The question hung in the air. The little smile that gambled playfully on Alan's lips had gone. In the silence the door knocked. Gavin poked his head outside for a moment.

'It's Dunstan.'

Alan nodded and turned his attention back to the black guy.

'You obviously don't know who I am, do you?'

Alan was all business now. While the beefeaters seemed to find the meeting was going exactly to their liking, Nina was sitting very still and very quiet. The explosion was coming. She looked over at Gavin. He too looked serious.

'You now owe me fifteen grand.' Alan paused. 'I'm giving you seven days to get me my money and if you don't I will have no hesitation in having you killed. Do you believe me?'

Whether the man believed Alan or not, Nina could see that he had his attention. It was in his eyes, the way he was staring at Alan, the way he licked his lips. His gaze drifted round the room and for a moment, he was looking directly at Nina. The two of them boring into each other. Suddenly Alan seemed to arrive at a decision.

'Hold him tight.'

The beefeater holding the man's arms behind his back now gripped them more securely. The man struggled but there was nothing he could do. Alan rose from his seat and walked slowly round his desk, dropping his toothpick into the wastepaper basket. Sitting on the edge of his desk, he looked directly into the black man's face. With his eyes locked to the man's he held out his hand to the other beefeater. Nina realised she was holding her breath.

'Knife.' The beefeater looked around, puzzled. Alan slowly turned his gaze on to him. 'Do you have a knife?' Dry.

'Er, no, boss, not with me.'

Alan gave him a withering look and turned to the letter-opener on his desk. It had a long, thin, blunt blade. He picked it up.

The man's eyes were following Alan's every movement. As Alan picked up the letter-opener the man struggled, but the beefeater's grip was too strong. Alan stroked the flat of the blade along the man's neck, then down his chest to the top of his jeans. He casually undid the belt and gently pulled the man's trousers down to his knees. The man struggled more urgently, but the movement of his legs was restricted by his trousers. Alan pulled down his underpants.

'What the fuck are you doing?' the man hissed. Nina stared, eyes on stalks, still holding her breath. Alan used the blade of the letter opener to ease the man's penis to one side and stroked it along his scrotum. The man strained to twist his hips away but he was being held too tightly. Suddenly Alan sat back on the edge of his desk.

'I could cut your fooking balls off, do you know that?'

The man just stared at him, sweat on his brow, his breath coming in short bursts now.

'Seven days. Okay?'

The black guy gave a dry, cracked swallow but made no other movement. Alan smiled. He turned away, then turned back, fast, grabbed the man's ear, dug the letter-opener into the lobe and yanked it down. The man let out a scream of pain.

'Get him out. Bring Dunstan in.'

Nina drew breath. She watched as the man's screams were quickly choked back, held in through clenched teeth. Alan walked quickly back round his desk and sat down. Gavin, also looking visibly shaken, opened the door while the beefeaters shuffled the man out. Alan was finished with him, his point was made. He pulled a tissue from a box on his desk and wiped the tip of the letter-opener. Alan looked at Nina as he tossed the blood-spotted tissue into the wastepaper basket. It nestled alongside a tangle of discarded toothpicks.

'You see? Now you see what I have to deal with?' He spoke as if Nina had no idea why he was so busy and what he was preoccupied with. In a way he was right. She was no longer absentmindedly chewing her gum.

She sat very quiet and still as Dunstan entered. Dunstan was a black teenager from Hackney. He was dressed in the ubiquitous urban uniform: the latest Michael Jordan Air basketball shoes, jeans so baggy the crotch hung just above his knees, and an oversized white sweatshirt with the hood poking out of a black, shiny blouson jacket. Emblazoned on the back of the jacket were the letters NYU. His hair stood upright like an Angela Davis afro and, in a parody of a wedding hat, a dark, wooden afro comb poked out of the back.

Nina had seen Dunstan twice before, once when he came to the office to meet Alan and once in passing in Hackney's Mare Street. On both occasions Dunstan walked as though he had the world at his feet. He didn't walk, he strolled with a loping gait, high-stepping as though one foot was about an inch shorter than the other. It wasn't a limp, it was a kind of ambling cool; swinging the shorter leg round as he took each step. Although Nina had seen this before, Dunstan's street walk was so pronounced she felt sure he must have practised it at home.

Dunstan must have heard black guy's scream of pain because as the two passed in the doorway he seemed without his usual swagger. He carried a briefcase, and if Nina hadn't know better she would have thought it held his homework. He looked around warily, looked at Nina, looked at Gavin. Then he pulled up a chair and with the brief-case at his feet, he looked up at Alan. There was a moment's pause, and he began.

'It's about Paul, Alan, you know't I mean? 'E hasn't got your management skills, guy.' Dunstan's voice was high and whiny.

'Yes? And?' Alan stared back at the boy in front of him.

'I don't know what it is! De man's just gone power-mad.'

Nina could see that Dunstan was beginning to relax as he realised that Alan was at least hearing him out.

''E's orderin' guys about, 'e's movin' people around that I've placed, 'e's even dissing some of de boys down on de street! In front of deir own soldiers!

'I know you left 'im in charge when you moved,' Dunstan continued, 'but dat was to oversee. I'm de one running t'ings out dere, you get me? I know how to handle de boys. 'E's making me look bad, Alan, you know't I mean?'

'But the goods are still selling?'

'Yeah, everyt'ing's cris', cook and curry, but I can't talk to Paul, you get me? 'E's crazy! De man can't leave de product alone, de geezer's always high. You gotta talk to 'im or somefen, you know't I mean!'

'Something? And what would you suggest?'

Nina knew from the tone in Alan's voice that Dunstan would be wise to tread carefully here. Unfortunately, Dunstan did not.

'Well, 'e's your brovver, you know't I mean? Is you left 'im in charge. But I'd slap 'im into shape if it were down to me, you get me!'

At this point Nina sensed that the youth had already said too much, but the loquacious Dunstan blundered on.

'And dere's anovver fing. I didn't wanna bring dis up but cozza de way Paul's been acting, some of de boys have been thinking; dey t'ink you're taking liberties, you're taking too much out of de . . .'

'Fook all of you wogs and niggers!'

It was here. The storm that Nina had anticipated had arrived.

'Me and Paul are running things, who the fook do you think you're dealing with?'

Dunstan sat quiet. He knew that much at least. Alan stood up, clasping his letter-opener dagger, and walked to the back of the office, pacing behind Dunstan. Dunstan didn't move a muscle.

'When you jungle bunnies were slicing each other up over your fooking chump change, me an' Paul came in and taught you lot how to organise things properly. The white man's discipline! Bring some fooking order to that madness out on the street! We made some real fooking money! For everyone! So don't fooking come in here talking about 'diss'-respect! You fooking monkey! You respect me!'

Dunstan turned in his seat. 'No, Alan, I didn't mean . . .'

'Shut it!' Alan sat on the edge of his desk again. Opposite another black man. He fiddled with the letter-opener while Dunstan looked at him. And then Alan suddenly smiled.

'Sorry for that outburst. That was a joke. Have you got the money?'

Looking as though he didn't get the joke, Dunstan slid his brief-case on to the desk and clicked it open. It contained stacks of cash, neatly fastened with elastic bands. Alan smiled more broadly.

'I like you, Dunstan. But you're still a boy. Don't, don't get above yourself, man. Do you know what I mean?' Alan was attempting a parody of Dunstan's street vernacular. 'Me and Paul, we started this business, Dunstan, we do what we want.' Alan turned to Nina looking smug.

Nina thought that if the point of this meeting was for Alan to demonstrate that he was a man still in charge of his own destiny, it had only partially succeeded. Noting the look on Dunstan's face, the set of his jaw, Nina couldn't help feeling that somehow matters would not be allowed to rest here.

# 9.

**D**unstan bounced out of Poxy's, as he and his crew referred to Alan's nightclub. He stepped high with the confidence to which he was accustomed. If Dunstan was honest he'd been shaken by the strangled scream and the sight of the tall brother who'd clearly taken some licks. But his own meeting with Alan had forced that from his mind. 'Fuck all of you wogs and niggers!' Dunstan looked up and down Brewer Street trying to remember where he'd parked the Jeep. He was so angry he'd forgotten.

'What a fucking raaaas! White Alan! 'Bout 'im a play meee! Dunstan Cuthbert Winston Churchill!' In his rage, Dunstan was actually talking to himself. His lips moved as he peered short-sightedly back and forth. His mother had told him time and time again to have his eyes tested. But Dunstan had thought, with good reason, that the crew he hung with would not appreciate with the same fear and respect Dunstan Cuthbert Winston Churchill in glasses.

He spotted his rag-top black Wrangler Sahara Jeep and high-stepped towards it. As he neared the car that he had paid a little under twenty thousand pounds cash for, his pace slowed and his afro reasserted its former glory. He aimed his security fob at the Jeep and lights flashed, accompanied by three shrill blasts. He pressed another button on the fob to open the doors. Normally the locks would release with a seductive 'thunk'. Not this time. Dunstan pressed the fob a number of times. Fuck it. He high-stepped around the car and jammed the key into the lock. Only he missed the lock and scraped the key along the pristine paintwork. Underneath the black was silver.

Dunstan was now apoplectic with fury.

'I'm gonna fucking kill somebody, guy! I am! I'm gonna fucking kill somebody!'

# THE LAST CARD

At his second, more careful attempt, Dunstan opened the door and climbed into the driver's seat. Climbed, because after buying the Jeep from a dealer in Camden he had immediately discarded the prosaic sixteen-inch Icon Alloys it came with and installed a much larger, chunkier and altogether more masculine set of wheels. The Jeep was now jacked so high off the ground a small child would have needed a grappling iron to climb in.

Dunstan slipped the key in the lock and turned on the ignition. The area around the car, within a radius of fifty metres, was immediately blasted with the music and lyrics of the New York rapper, Sho Nuff Money.

**OH BABY! OH BABY, I'LL EAT THE GOODS FROM RIGHT OUT OF YOUR ASS . . !**

Dunstan reached into the inside of his jacket and pulled out his mobile. It was a gold-plated, diamond-encrusted Nokia, the 8850. He had had it imported especially, from Saudi Arabia. Dunstan liked to bling. The mobile retailed at a cool ten thousand pounds and for the kudos it gave Dunstan it was worth every penny. He flipped it open and pressed a button to speed-dial. After four rings the telephone at the other end was answered.

'Ade?' Dunstan had to raise his voice because the music in his Jeep was so loud.

'Who dis?'

'Ade?'

'Hello?'

'Ade!' Dunstan was now shouting into the mobile.

**I DON'T HAVE NO TROUBLE WITH YOU SUCKING MY DICK**
**BUT I HAVE A LITTLE PROBLEM WITH YOU NOT SUCKING MY DICK . . .**

'I can't hear you!' It didn't occur to Dunstan to turn the music down. He pressed an index finger into his free ear. Ol' Dirty Bastard was cut out, at least for Dunstan.

'Ade, you fuck, is that you?' Dunstan was now screaming into the telephone.

'It's Jan. Who's this?'

'Where's Ade?'

'Who is this?'

'Don't fuck with me, Jan, where's Ade?'

'What? I can't hear you? Where are you?'

Dunstan glared at the mobile telephone and nearly hurled it through the windscreen. He pressed it to his ear and screamed into it again.

'Where. The fuck. Is Ade?'

Knock, knock. A man was knocking the front window on the passenger side, trying to attract his attention. Dunstan ignored him.

'Yeah?' Ade's voice was deep and rich.

'It's me. I'll be back at my yard in half an 'our. Fuckin' be there.' Dunstan flipped shut the mobile. He lowered the window the man was knocking at.

'What the fuck do you . . ?' Recognising the man looking into the Jeep, Dunstan cut short his question and turned the music down.

'Wha Gwan, D?' The voice was hoarse.

'Wha Gwan. Wassup?' Dunstan put an arm out of the window and the two touched fists.

'I'm looking for a shebeen. Run by a Grove man, called Blackie. You know him?'

Dunstan pretended to think for a nano-second then shook his head. 'Nah, never heard of him. Gotta go man, gotta go.' Squinting into the rear-view mirror, Dunstan dropped the clutch and grabbed the gear stick, slipping it into first. Wha Gwan's hand slapped the bonnet of the car with a resounding thunk.

'I said I'm looking for a brer called Blackie! Do you know him, blood?'

Dunstan scowled at Wha Gwan through the open window but this time he paused before he spoke.

'No. I told you, I don't know him. Sorry, mate, I'm in a real hurry.' Dunstan made sure to keep his voice even and respectful. After a moment Wha Gwan withdrew his hand. Dunstan nodded, lifted the clutch and the Jeep pulled out into the middle of the street.

**. . . BABY YOU KNOW I'M IN LOVE WITH YOU**
**COZ YOUR TITS ARE BIG AND YOUR ASS IS TOO . . .**

The lyrics of Ol' Dirty Bastard filled the car again. What nobody realised at that point was that, although they were indeed profane and violent, they were nothing to the mayhem that was gradually being unleashed.

# THE LAST CARD

***

Wha Gwan stared at the disappearing Jeep with its blaring music. He waited until it had turned out of sight before he shifted his gaze. He shifted it to the doorway Dunstan had emerged from. A nightclub called Roxy's. He looked at it for a moment and then turned away, walking on down the street.

# 10.

**G**avin stood on the landing outside Alan's office. He took a couple of deep breaths and a moment to collect his thoughts. Alan had ordered him to go down into the bar, fix him a large dry Martini and bring it back. As though he were a manservant. But this wasn't why Gavin was hesitating.

There were things about this business, Alan's business, that Gavin knew, but chose not to concern himself with. Like the small fact that they were involved with major crime. And in the business of major crime there is often violence. To be fair to Gavin, he had been unaware of this in the early days. By the time he had any real sense of what he was involved with, it was too late. Gavin had become used to the large cheques. They paid for the new marble bathroom suite that his home had cried out for; the rather fine kitchen recommended by a chap at the Conran store in Marylebone High street. Unfortunately, however, Gavin found violence, real street violence, ugly and brutal. Uncivilised. He himself had had some training in the ancient martial art of ju-jitsu but that, thought Gavin, was a different kind of violence. That was civilised. Given the full extent of Alan's business interests, he knew discipline had to be maintained. But Gavin preferred to believe that it wasn't the violence itself that maintained discipline, but the threat of it. So Gavin told himself the lie that Alan was a businessman and he was merely Alan's business manager.

In any event, the fact that Alan now displayed his ugly form of discipline openly and without shame appalled Gavin. Although Dunstan was young, Gavin did not believe he should have been treated in quite such a dismissive fashion. First, Dunstan was right about Paul. Paul had been snorting cocaine for years and was now a stumbling, shambling degenerate. Secondly, Dunstan had a personal kudos and clout on the street that was valuable. And since Paul garnered zero respect amongst the 'staff' who ran Alan's various businesses for him, Dunstan's services were varied and necessary. Certainly he could be replaced, but the smart way to do that was in a manner and at a time of their – Gavin's and Alan's – choosing. Calling the young Negro a 'nigger' to his face was not helpful. From Gavin's knowledge of Dunstan, this could well lead to trouble.

Then there was Hilary James. He had certainly needed to be taught a lesson, but Gavin was certain that the threat of a simple beating in a back alley would have sufficed.

No. These latest outbursts of Alan's were uncharacteristic and Gavin wasn't sure what was causing them. Whatever it was, Gavin was worried. He knew he needed to act. An idea had occurred to him, but it had only just occurred and he was still thinking it through. It involved Nina.

Gavin stepped away from the office door and skipped quickly down the stairs. He often skipped up and down stairs because he had less and less time to go to the gym these days. The exercise was good for him.

Gavin entered the club and there, sitting in front of the bar, was the very person he needed to see. She was sipping a coffee and smoking. She looked up quickly, startled as he entered, and her momentary look of fright told Gavin all he needed to know.

'Smoking. Again.' He said it with a smile, to put her at her ease. She didn't smile back.

'My timing's way off. This is no time to go through withdrawal.' Nina sipped her coffee.

'I thought you were having lunch with your friend Maxine?' Gavin spoke with care. The germ of the idea that was growing in Gavin's mind. It needed careful nurturing.

'Alan's flipped, Gavin!' She looked at him with worried eyes.

'He's certainly not behaving with his usual . . . discretion . . .'

'Discretion! Did you see what he did to that man's ear?!' Nina ran a manicured hand through her long, dark hair. 'Why? I don't understand.'

'Are the two of you . . . getting on okay?'

'What's that supposed to mean?' Nina snapped.

'I'm not saying you're anything to do with this,' Gavin said hurriedly. 'I'm just trying to work out where Alan's head might be.'

'It's disappearing up his arse!'

'So what do you think we should do about it?'

'What can we do? All I know is I've got to get out of this situation. Soon!' She gulped down the rest of her coffee.

'Either that . . . or we take over. Me and you.'

Nina stared at him. 'Are you crazy?' She now spoke in a low hiss. 'Did you miss what just happened?'

Gavin looked around the club. They were definitely alone. He leant down on the bar, his face close to Nina's.

'Remove Alan and this operation could be so . . . good. You know the Negro that Alan cut? The one upstairs?'

'We're not in the nineteenth century, Gavin, he's a black man.'

'Whatever. I'm thinking there's a way to get him into this that can solve all our problems.'

In the silence that followed, both tried to work out if the person opposite was to be trusted.

# 11.

**H** pulled the Merc into the car park bordering his block of flats. As he turned the engine off he sighed with relief. He had been driving with one hand while the other pressed a pair of sweaty shorts to his throbbing, mutilated ear. Fuck, it hurt! But H put the pain to one side as he sat and thought. From the car he idly watched a group of removal men loading a nearby van with furniture.

Now what? H took a deep breath. He needed to find £15,000 in seven days! Impossible. But the meeting with Akers convinced him that he had to do the impossible because the alternative was unimaginable. H was not a man to allow himself to be pushed around but, Jesus Christ, Akers was a fucking psycho! There was a time to fight back and there was a time to know better. He racked his brains. He still had nearly five grand from his win at Blackie's last night. Beverley probably had about two thousand saved in her account. That was seven. He only needed to find eight fucking grand in seven days! Neither of H's parents were alive and, for a second, he thought about asking Beverley's mother. The idea swiftly left his head.

Who the hell did he know who had eight grand, five grand or even two grand? The sad fact was H didn't know those kinds of people. In fact Beverley was probably the only person H knew with a bank account . . .

H remembered when he and Beverley had met at Compendium, a nightclub in Islington. H and his man Blue had been chilling at one side of the club, near the bar, checking out the talent. It was a Friday night, they both had money in their pockets, were looking a bit tasty and were seeking fun for the weekend. They were footloose and fancy-free and the club was bubbling with women; they were feeling good. Blue, a tall and bony mixed-race brother with a mountain of dreadlocks piled high on his head, nudged him in the ribs and said 'Oiya!' Three attractive women had entered their field of vision. The women, one of whom was white, had come from one of the other two dance floors in the club to jiggy to some R'n'B.

The three women all looked to be in their early twenties, dressed in their finest, and equally keen to have some fun. As they approached, H could see Blue coming alive. His sleepy eyes belied a keen sense of timing where women were concerned. Tracking the movement of the women across the dance floor, he spoke out of the side of his mouth.

'Punany approaching; one o'clock . . . two o'clock . . . three o'clock.'

Picking up and then following Blue's coordinates H was able to track their progress. The women found a spot they were happy with amongst the other moving bodies and began to dance.

'What d'you reckon?'

'Yeah, man, let's cherps it.' Blue was like a wolf, licking his lips with anticipation.

'Which one d'you fancy?'

'Which one don't I fancy! Come on, man, you're wasting time!' Blue stepped forward, easing his way unhurriedly through the dancing bodies, homing in on the prey.

As Blue reached the women he began bobbing his shoulders and nodding his head in perfect time with the music. H came up quickly behind him, also falling effortlessly in with the beat.

Blue began casually chatting to the women. H joined in. They soon discovered that the three women were teachers at a secondary school in west London. They were at the club celebrating a birthday. As the night progressed it soon became clear that Blue was going to end the evening with the white woman. That left the birthday girl and Beverley for H. He had his eye on Beverley but it wasn't clear until the very last slowie whom H would choose. He was sitting between the two women when 'Alright' came on. D'Angelo. Perfect. There was a pause in the conversation; both H and the women knew this was crunch time, a decision had to be made. H looked at Beverley, she looked at him. And with Saffron, the birthday girl, watching, the two of them, without a word, stepped out on to the dance floor. They had been together ever since.

# THE LAST CARD

As H sat in his Mercedes holding his damaged ear, he smiled despite the pain, remembering some of the fun he and Beverley had had together. Especially in the early years. Things weren't too clever at the moment, that was for damn sure, but it had to improve in the future. Didn't it?

He finally climbed out of his car. Approaching his building he could see the activity with the removal men was still going on. Three of them were now manoeuvring an old brown sofa through the doors. Hang on a minute! H squinted as he looked at the threadbare two-seater. That was his fucking sofa! He quickened his step, breaking into a jog. Jesus Christ, what was going on here? Still keeping one hand pressed to his ear and holding his kit bag with the other, H fairly ran towards the workmen now humping his sofa – his sofa! – into the back of the removal van.

By the time he arrived the sofa was almost in. H looked into the back of the van. Alongside his sofa was the wardrobe from his bedroom, the big chest of drawers, the bed, the television, two armchairs and the kitchen table.

'Oi, mate, what are you doing? What's going on?'

The workmen finished struggling with the sofa. One of them, standing up inside the van, looked down at H with irritation.

'What's it look like we're doing?'

H felt panic rising in his stomach as he rushed into the tower block.

Out of the lift, into the corridor, round the corner and there was his front door, wide open. H paused. He could hear someone pulling something heavy across the floor. H strode inside.

Beverley was busy dragging the washing machine out of the kitchen and into the living room. Cyrus was sitting on the floor happily playing with his Gameboy. They both looked up as H entered. Beverley wore a frantic, guilty look.

'Daddy, Daddy, Mummy and I are going to live with Grandma!' Cyrus innocently announced what Beverley had presumably been planning for some time. H felt a sickening jolt to his system.

'You're back.' Beverley straightened up, facing him, stretching her back.

'What's going on?'

'We've had enough, H, we can't take it any more.'

'"We"? What do you mean "we"?' H bent down, gently took the Gameboy out of Cyrus's hands and picked him up. Beverley stepped forward and roughly pulled the child to her. H didn't want to fight over their son. He let the boy go.

'Beverley!'

'Don't start, Hilary . . .'

'What? When were you going to tell me?'

'I've tried to tell you but you won't listen! I'm tired of your childish, stupid . . .'

'Listen,' H interrupted her quickly, looking at Cyrus. 'Can we do this somewhere . . .' But Beverley went on.

'. . . stupid arrogance. Your gambling, your staying out all night! Your wasting our money! Just throwing it away when we're trying to move forward!'

H stood there and took it. She was glaring at him, challenging him to come back at her. She wanted this fight, probably to make what she was doing that much easier. But H could see the fear and upset welling in Cyrus's eyes. A noise in the silence made him look round. The three removal men were standing behind him. One of them delicately cleared his throat.

'Look, put Cyrus down and let's go outside to talk this through.' He reached over to take Cyrus from her arms but she jerked back as though he had something contagious.

'No, Hilary! No, no, no, no, no!' She was shouting at him.

'You can't just walk out!'

'Oh, yes I can! You just watch me!' She tried to push past him, heading for the front door. H blocked her path.

'Beverley . . .' She tried to step round him but he again stepped in her path.

'Don't do it, Hilary.'

'But, Bev . . .' She set Cyrus down on the floor, aimed him at the door and patted his behind.

'We're going! Go on Cyrus, you go down with the nice man and Mummy will be down in a minute.' Her eyes told one of the workmen to go down in the lift with Cyrus, but Cyrus wanted none of this. He turned back to his father.

'But, Daddy, I want . . .'

Beverley interrupted sharply. 'Go on! I'll be down in a minute.'

# THE LAST CARD

H moved towards her. 'Please, Bev.'

'It's too late.'

'Let's just talk it . . .'

'I tried that this morning.'

'Let's try again . . .'

'No! You've got to grow up sometime, H. Be a man. That's all we want. Just face up to your responsibilities.'

She pushed past H, grabbed Cyrus's arm, swept past the removal men and was gone. The front door slammed behind them.

H stood, leaning, his back to the door. It was done. They'd gone. H walked in a daze to the living room. It was a sad, grey, dusty mess: a stack of Jamaican reggae albums were pushed against a wall, a few old boxing magazines and newspapers lay scattered about the floor, some clothes – including H's lucky suit – were piled in a corner. In the middle of the room, sitting on a high stool, was a glass bowl with a small goldfish in it. At that moment, this small fish felt like H's only friend. H looked around, slowly surveying the wreckage of his life.

*\*\*\**

Later H stood in the shower, jets of hot water shooting down at him, bursting over his body, running down the contours of his skin. Over his deep chest, down what remained of his abdominal muscles, through the stiff wire of his pubic hair, down the big, strong, rounded quadriceps and on to his feet. He watched as the water ran from his body and drained away. It was scalding hot. H wanted to cleanse himself of the day.

Beverley was right. She had tried to talk to him. Time and time and time again. But he had put her off. He'd silenced her. He'd ignored her. He'd argued with her and shut her down. He'd accused her of nagging him. Nag, nag, nag, that's all she ever did these days. At least that's what he'd told her. He had not wanted to face what he knew to be true. That he had become addicted to gambling, to a scene that he knew was destroying him, that was eating his time, his energy, his money. Why couldn't he stop? Because he fucking liked it, stupid! It was a buzz! A crack! It was exciting! He was good at this! And he made money! Sometimes. Hadn't he just had a huge win?

He turned off the water but continued to stand there, dripping in the bath. He had just had a huge win, but so what? Now what? What did the money mean to him? So, he had a bit of extra scratch in his pocket, so what? He'd only lose it again the next time he played. Did that matter? Isn't that what life was about? The ebb and flow of money? Here today, gone tomorrow? What he was doing was buying some fun. He knew that, he wasn't stupid. So what was the problem? He stepped out of the bath and looked for a towel to dry himself. Beverley had taken all the towels. Dripping, he stepped out of the bathroom and looked in the closet in the hallway. She'd left him one. He dried himself with that and went into the living room.

What was the problem? The problem was that the money that came and went left nothing, or not very much for Beverley and Cyrus. He supposed. Much of the money he gambled was the money that Beverley spent her days earning. He supposed. Maybe that was it. He looked around the flat. He had cleaned up and put things away but it still wasn't much. All that was left in the way of furniture was his stereo, a stool and his goldfish. Not much to show for thirty-two years of life on the planet. It suddenly hit H that everything Beverley had taken had been hers. Beverley had paid for it. What had he paid for? The stereo. A Nakamichi. And the goldfish.

With his towel wrapped around his waist he padded over the thin, cheap carpet and put on his favourite CD – Junior Murvin's 'Police and Thieves'. An old skool classic. The world might be a cruel and harsh place but some things make it more bearable and this was one of them. He put the track on repeat and cranked up the volume. Once was never enough for Junior Murvin.

He walked into the kitchen, found a little pot of fish food and returned to the living room. He tipped some of the food into the bowl and watched the fish rise up and nibble the flakes floating on the water's surface.

The flat was on the eighth floor and from the window he could see much of south London spread out before him. Darkness had crept over the capital while he had been in the shower and as he looked out, lights were winking on and off. The city looked unbelievably beautiful; romantic, alive, pregnant with possibility.

Sitting on the stool, leant against the goldfish bowl, was a postcard. It was from H's older brother, Sean, who was now living in the

# THE LAST CARD

Caribbean, in Montserrat. He lived in a big house which had belonged to their mother, in Virgin Isles, an area on the north-western part of the island. According to Sean money was hard to find but life was good. He'd moved there with his wife and two children, Jamie and Isaac, ten and eight years old, and was always writing to H asking him to come out. H knew that a part of Sean missed south London, where the two of them had grown up, but H could also tell that Sean was happy: it was as if he'd found himself. Montserrat gave Sean something that London couldn't.

He looked at the card. It was the classic image of the Caribbean; a sunset, a beautiful woman in silhouette. She was leaning against a tree and behind her lay a golden beach and the sparkling ocean, stretching out to the horizon. Written across the card was the motto 'Grab the opportunity – Montserrat is for you.' H thought about that. Why didn't he just clear out and forget about that psycho Akers? No, he couldn't leave Cyrus and Beverley like that.

H sat cross-legged in the middle of the empty room looking at the wall. His babymother had just dumped him, taken his son with her and stripped the flat bare. He owed Alan Akers £15,000 and he had seven days to pay him. Apart from that, everything was fine. H gave an involuntary shudder.

He looked around for something to distract himself, saw the stack of newspapers that he had tidied up earlier and dragged them over. The first thing he saw on turning a tabloid over to look at the sports page was the headline 'Mancini Jumps For Joy'. Underneath was a picture of Mancini in the ring with his arms held up in victory.

H tossed the papers aside, re-crossed his legs, straightened his back and closed his eyes. He stayed like this for a while, breathing deeply as Junior Murvin's 'Police and Thieves' played on.

Still wearing just his towel, H entered what used to be his and Beverley's bedroom. The furnishing now consisted of a futon mattress on the floor, a blanket box against the wall and a clothes-line strung across the room. On the blanket box H had set up his silver boxing trophies. A number of them were statuettes of boxers on top of tall, Grecian columns; three more were large medals, set in crushed velvet, in wooden boxes. He had five cut-glass statuettes of boxers and nine smaller medals with the image of a boxer on each. H had set up the blanket box as a kind of shrine to his prowess as a warrior.

These were the trophies of his youth, the last tangible reminders of what he had been. He would have defended them to the death. In H's imagination this shrine was set up in the living room, in a cabinet with swirling, flashing lights, designed and built specifically to show off these prizes. Soft music would have played and sticks of sweet-smelling incense would have been constantly burning. But Beverley had put her foot down and insisted that the decor of the whole living room could not possibly be organised around H's boxing trophies. She was not going to stand for it. She admired what they stood for, apparently, but would much rather they were kept in the bedroom. Out of sight. She had made such a fuss when H had tried to explain what they meant to him that he had been forced to back down.

Aside from the trophies, hanging on the line that was strung across the room was H's lucky suit. He took it down, laid it out on the mattress and dropped his towel. Fuck it. If Beverley was going to just move out like that – and take Cyrus with her! – he might as well do what he always did when the going became too tough.

\*\*\*

The G-spot was an intimate jazz hang out. At the front there was a tiny bar and a small performance area. Although it was cramped for the punters, it made for a good atmosphere for the musicians.

Currently in residence was Tessa Souter, a British jazz chanteuse who lived in New York but was in the middle of a five-week tour of the UK. Just past the performance area was a short hallway and then the club opened out into a large and cavernous dinning area. H assumed this was where the G-spot made its money, subsidising Ghadaffi's love of jazz.

By the time H walked into the entrance, wearing a sticking plaster over his damaged ear, the front of the club was packed. Good. He wanted to forget about Beverley, forget about Alan Akers and just enjoy himself. It was only 9.30 p.m. and already there was a buzz in the air. Tessa was in the middle of her version of John Coltrane's 'Wise One' and the crystal-clear tones of her voice awed the crowd.

H stood by the doorway watching Tessa do her thing. He looked around at the audience. And then, just beyond the drummer in

# THE LAST CARD

Tessa's quartet, H saw what he was looking for. Smart dark suit, crisp open-necked shirt. Ghadaffi was talking to a waiter at the mouth of the dining area.

H eased himself through the scrum around the bar and moments later he was standing next to Ghadaffi. He glanced over with a scowl. Ghadaffi finished his conversation with the waiter and then turned to H.

'Hi, Ghadaffi. Where's the action?'

Ghadaffi was clearly not impressed. Not least because his name wasn't Ghadaffi. That was just his nickname amongst the gamblers; in that circuit, people very rarely knew anyone's real name. Ghadaffi took his time looking H up and down.

'I see you have your lucky suit on.'

H smoothed it down. It had spent most of the afternoon crumpled on the living room floor.

'It's Thursday night, I'm feeling lucky.'

Ghadaffi continued to eye him.

'What action are you talking about? There's no action here.'

It was H's turn to give Ghadaffi the look.

'Forget it, Ghadaffi. It's too late, man, your cover's been blown.'

'Who told you?'

'Does it matter?'

'My father always told me I should never mix with gamblers.'

'Bloody good advice, I'd say.' H left it there and waited to see when – and not if – Ghadaffi would spring with the information. The pause grew longer and neither of them moved a muscle. Finally a customer attempted to walk from the performance area through to the dining area. Someone had to move. It was Ghadaffi, he took a step back to let the man through. Once the man had passed Ghadaffi just looked at H and gestured with his head for H to follow him.

Ghadaffi walked to the far end of the dining area, between the tables, to a door marked 'For Employees Only'. He took a bunch of keys from his pocket and opened the door. They walked along a short, unfinished hallway and up some stairs, both lit with naked bulbs.

At the top of the stairs Ghadaffi opened another door and suddenly H was in a dark, smallish room where a naked black woman and a naked white man, lit from below, were dancing erotically on a small stage. A group of ten men, city types, sat at a low counter in front of the stage, silently drinking and watching the action. H took in an eyeful as he followed Ghadaffi through the room, heading towards another door at the far end.

Ghadaffi stopped and turned so suddenly outside the door that H, still looking at the naked floor show behind him, ran into Ghadaffi's back. The look Ghadaffi gave H suggested he thought H was some kind of country bumpkin.

'You're a dark horse. I didn't know you had all this going on up here.'

'How do you think I pay for the jazz?' Ghadaffi was all business.

'I thought the dining area . . .'

'No. Not nearly.'

'Shows you how much I know about business.'

'You said it.' He jerked his thumb at the door. 'They're in there. And you're the last.' Without a second look, Ghadaffi walked back past the stage and down the stairs.

H stepped through the door. On the other side there were ten people playing stud poker. H made his way quietly into the room and headed for a side cabinet laden with bottles. He searched among the spirits and mixers for his usual, Jack Daniels. H poured himself a large one, took a hit and refilled the glass. As long as the juice was flowing free, no need to be stingy. With the jolt of alcohol seeping into his bloodstream H turned to check out who was in the house tonight.

As H looked around the plush gambling room he realised that he had learnt more about Ghadaffi in the last five minutes than he had in the previous three years that he had known him. Ghadaffi's set-up was sweet! He not only had jazz, the bar, the dining area and the erotic floor show, he also had this upmarket gambling room, with the air of a West End gentlemen's club. The room was plushly set up with two old leather Chesterfield sofas, a thick red carpet, lush red-and-cream wallpaper, a chandelier and soft, subtle wall lights at various points around the room. Jesus Christ! As he looked around H realised that he had badly misjudged Ghadaffi. H had always looked down on him, in a way that he himself was unaware of until now, because Ghadaffi wasn't a particularly good gambler, though he was always at Blackie's throwing his money around. Or perhaps, H thought to himself, it was just that H had a superiority complex; he wasn't addicted to gambling like the others, he had a life.

# THE LAST CARD

In the centre of the room was a large, eight-seat gambling table. At one end of it was Shampa, handling the cards like the professional that she was. Behind her stood Blackie, one hand resting gently on her shoulder. Not for the first time H marvelled at the blackness of Blackie's skin. It was so dark it seemed to be sucking light from the room. Sitting at the table on one side were a collection of professional, low-life gamblers that H was mostly familiar with: Boo, Sharon, Sammy and another guy he only vaguely knew. On the other side of the table were four wealthy-looking businessmen.

As H took in the number of professionals who had descended on the game he now knew why Ghadaffi was unimpressed with his arrival: word had spread through the West End about the session here. While there were large piles of money and chips in front of the businessmen, in front of the West End professionals the piles of cash and chips were significantly smaller. And knowing West End professionals, this was not the pleasant evening of social gambling the businessmen expected. The West End boys had come here to work – to earn money from four unsuspecting fish. They had not come to have fun, they had not come to make friends and they had certainly not come here to lose money. That didn't mean they were going to cheat, they were just going to play such a tight, joyless game, leaving nothing to chance, that over the course of the session they couldn't lose.

H stood there in his crumpled shiny suit, taking this all in, the truth of his situation hitting him with force. Everything he thought about the West End gamblers and hustlers was equally true for him.

H dipped his hand in his pocket and pulled out his talisman. His fingers caressed its smooth edges. Blackie quietly left Shampa's side and approached him.

'Wha' 'appen, man? You look sick.'

# 12.

**W**ha Gwan watched Meena stare blankly at the steaming rice, gunga beans and chicken stew in front of her. Not even a cup of the peanut punch that she loved so much could brighten her mood.

'Come on, Meena, you have to talk to me.'

As Dipak Chadda's only daughter raised her head, a tear cusped her left eye and slowly tracked its way down her cheek. Sighing, Meena stared at Wha Gwan. Wha Gwan watched the tear as it hung ponderously from the end of her chin. He waited for it to fall. When it didn't, he reached out, gently lifted it with his finger and wiped it on the sleeve of his coat.

Meena wore her hair short like a boy. Despite being large-hipped, she was not really overweight, she was just short – five feet three inches – and pear-shaped. She was by no means a classic beauty. But as Wha Gwan stared at her dark eyes and sunken cheeks he had to swallow deeply to stop the love he felt for her welling up from his stomach and pouring out of him in a howl of – what? – rage? fear? vulnerability? Wha Gwan felt all of those things. Everything he'd ever felt for Meena in those two years that he had been seeing her poured up from his stomach and jammed his throat.

'Let it . . .' He coughed to cover the emotion that caused his eyes to water. 'Let it out, Meena, you'll feel better.'

But Meena wouldn't let it out. She merely lowered her head as the tears flowed freely, miserably, down her cheeks. Wha Gwan rose and scooted round the table. He slid a comforting arm around her shoulders.

Joseph, the Roti Shack's Trinidadian chef, glanced over at the two of them from behind the counter and shook his head.

# THE LAST CARD

'If dere's anyt'ing I can do you know de two a you only have to ask. You know dat, don't you?'

Wha Gwan acknowledged the kindness with a wave. He then leant into Meena and spoke softly.

'Your father's gone but your mother's still here. And your brothers. They need you to be strong. Especially your mum, Meena, you know she's going to struggle.'

Meena responded to Wha Gwan's words by leaning into his chest and burrowing her face into his padded coat. When she finally spoke, she aimed the words at the J in 'Jersey' on Wha Gwan's coat.

'He was always a fucking bastard; a selfish, mean, irritable bastard.' Meena stopped and gasped as though the effort of finally formulating words had tired her out. 'But he was our bastard; my bastard. And now he's gone.'

Meena burrowed her face deeper into the J of 'Jersey' and clung to Wha Gwan as though he was everything she had in the whole world. Wha Gwan looked down at the top of her head, smelt the slightly garlicky funk coming from her hair, then looked up and out on to Shepherds Bush. Life ebbed and flowed in front of the Roti Shack, but Wha Gwan saw none of it. No. His thoughts were filled with revenge. Whoever had killed Meena's father was going to pay. If it was the last thing Wha Gwan ever did, Dipak's killer was going to pay.

# 13.

Ade stared out, concerned, as the black Wrangler Jeep turned off Brentford High Street and into North Road. Dunstan drove slowly down the quiet road and turned the Jeep left into a small car park, pulling up at the edge of the estate. Through the darkness Ade could see four tower blocks, but only one of them was of interest. Its name was on its side in big letters: Maudsley House. Perfect.

Ade and Dunstan were still in west London but as far as Ade was concerned they might as well have been in the Cotswolds. This was about as far west as you could go and still call it London. Ade didn't like it at all and it showed on his face, but this was something that had to be done if honour was to be restored. If it meant coming out to the 'country' then so be it. Ade was nothing if not professional. Dunstan abruptly turned off the in-car entertainment and the sounds of the ludicrously named P. Diddy died with the engine. Ade looked over at his friend but Dunstan kept his eyes fixed on the road ahead.

'Back in five.'

Dunstan nodded but said nothing. Ade opened up the hidden compartment in the passenger-side door by pressing the pressure-release point. The compartment clicked and sagged open. Nestling inside was a small bag of salted cashew nuts, underneath which was an Israeli-built, black, shiny, semi-automatic Desert Eagle. Although the weapon was Ade's, it was kept in Dunstan's car because Ade refused to keep it in his. He pulled it out and tucked it under his jacket, folding his long body out of the Jeep with difficulty. This is a nice ride, he thought, but too small for a man, you know? A Wrangler Jeep was a car for a boy. That's why he drove a Range Rover. Top of the range, racing green. And whenever Babylon came with their foolishness, pulling him over for no reason, he always had his papers ready in the glove compartment.

As Ade climbed out of the jacked-up Jeep he stepped straight into a puddle, splat! You see, Ade thought, that's what happens when you drive a car like this. He slammed the door shut behind him and, stepping on to the kerb, he shook the rainwater off his buckskin, tan-coloured Timberland boot. The leg of the olive-green Armani suit that he wore was also wet. He looked back at Dunstan with a scowl, but Dunstan just silently shooed him on his way.

With one wet trouser-leg Ade set off, heading towards the tower block on the Green Dragon Lane Estate. The Desert Eagle was a big weapon made bigger by the silencer screwed tight to the gun's muzzle. Ade liked it because it was big and flashy and when people saw it pointing at them it frightened them. He liked that. He had it nestled under his jacket, tucked into the top of his trousers. He kept it in place with one arm held close to his side. It was a good job he had on his good suit, the new one. Coming all this way out to country where you didn't see too many black people, he didn't want to look too conspicuous. Ade was barely twenty-one and the suit had cost him over £3,000. The trousers were so baggy the bottom of the legs trailed over and under his sixteen-hole Timberlands. The jacket was so roomy a family of badgers could have moved in. The look was topped with a black, high-neck John Smedley and a close cropped haircut, a number one. No fade, no markings, no bullshit.

Ade didn't roll with the high step that Dunstan employed but he was equally bad. Nobody messed with Ade. Ade had always been big for his age and from as early as he could remember he had been aware that he was a Nigerian, from the Yoruba tribe. Yoruba were warriors according to his father and that's what he had told the boys he had grown up with in east London.

But it was only when he'd begun hanging out with Dunstan, two years ago, that his reputation really began to pay dividends. Dunstan was in the recreation business, dealing recreational drugs. Dunstan needed a man to roll with when he went about controlling his growing empire. He and Ade had first become partners and then become friends. The two were now almost inseparable. Ade and Dunstan moved together and people didn't mess with either of them.

By now Ade was at the foot of Maudsley House. He and Dunstan had done their homework. Eric Griffin lived on the fifteenth floor, flat 15G. Ade approached the entrance of the block and indiscriminately slapped about six or seven buzzers. Amongst a flurry of 'Hello,' 'Who is it?' and 'Oi! Stop,' one of the tenants kindly buzzed back, releasing the lock. Ade quickly pulled the security door open and slipped inside.

The ground-floor hallway gave off a stench that Ade was used to from a life lived in public housing. This may have been 'country' but it smelt just like the inner city: piss, alcohol and stale cigarette smoke. Ade slapped at the button next to the lift. Only then did he notice the sign that read 'Out of Order'. Shit! Ade silently cursed. His experience told him to call the job off. If he were to walk all the way to the fifteenth floor there would be much more of a chance that he would be spotted. The whole job would take that much longer. On the other hand, Akers needed to know that he couldn't take the piss. Not with his boy Dunstan. Ade looked at the foot of the stairs. Also, if he did the job now, then he and Dunstan wouldn't have to come back. And that was the clincher. He started walking.

Ade walked with a slow tread, a methodical pace. He didn't want to attract any more attention to himself than he had to. He had no idea how many black people lived in this building. So his approach to Griffin's flat was unhurried, quiet and relentless.

Ade arrived on the landing of the fifteenth floor. He peeked through the glass of the fire door that led into the hallway of flats. All was quiet. He opened the door, walked through. The first door he looked at was 15A. He kept on walking. B, C, D, E, F . . . G. Stuck to the solid wooden door was a picture of an aggressive, barking British bulldog with the line 'Say Hello To My Little Friend . . .' below. In another context Ade might have smiled at this, but not now. He was here to work. Inside the flat he could hear the television blaring and laughter. Griffin. Ade knew it was Griffin because the man lived alone. Ade and Dunstan had done their homework. Ade stood squarely in front of the door, undid the top button on his jacket so that it now hung open, and pressed the door bell.

Moments later he could hear Griffin's tread as he came to answer. When it stopped Ade knew that Griffin was looking at him through the spy hole. This was nothing to worry about because anybody who lived in a council flat automatically looked through the spy hole before they opened the door. Ade smiled, showing his gold tooth, and waved.

Ade heard a chain being taken off and a bolt being withdrawn. The door was pulled open, a smiling Griffin standing on his welcome mat in a white vest and underpants. The vest was stained yellow round the arm holes, and had drops of what was probably curry on the front. Griffin's underpants were bunched up round his genitals. His legs were whiter than his underwear, stork-thin and covered in thick, black hair. Lovely. Griffin was holding a foil dish of what smelt like chicken biryani.

Griffin was an unpleasant-looking man, no doubt about it, and that made what Ade had to do next that much easier.

'Ade, mate! What you doing round here?' The question was not aggressive, Griffin seemingly pleased to see the man who was going to kill him. The question was asked in a spirit of friendship, camaraderie. Although Ade was lower down the pecking order than Griffin, Griffin was pleased to see another of Alan Akers' employees.

'I wanted to have a chat with you, Eric.' Ade did not want to have a chat, he wanted to be on the inside as quickly as possible. He stepped into the hallway of Griffin's flat, whipped out the Desert Eagle with one hand, grabbed Eric Griffin's throat with the other. He used his boot to close the door behind him. With one arm now locked stiff in front of him, ending in Griffin's throat, the other with the Desert Eagle pointing at Griffin's forehead, Ade frogmarched him backwards, through the hallway into the living room. Eric, of course, had no more interest in his food and promptly dropped it. His face wore an expression of shock, fear and hurt, all at the same time.

As they entered the living room Ade glanced at the television. Playing on the screen was *The Little Mermaid.* Ade turned back to Griffin.

'You sick bastard!'

Griffin's eyes bugged as he struggled for air. He waved thin arms about, reaching, clawing for Ade. Ade squeezed his neck that much tighter, looking at Griffin as though he were some kind of insect. Ade looked around the flat. It was a mess. The television – a huge one – was in one corner with an old sofa slumped opposite. That was it. Spread all over the floor, however, were old newspapers, beer cans, take-away food boxes, piles of clothes and other rubbish. Ade forced

Griffin through the debris towards the french doors on the far wall. As his eyes bulged, Griffin's mouth worked, opening and shutting, gasping for air. One of the doors was ajar and Ade used Griffin's shoulder to nudge it open.

The wall around the balcony was waist-high. They were at the back of the block, away from the road. Beneath them was the car park. Griffin was struggling furiously now, desperate to extract himself from what he had finally realised was more serious than he could imagine. But it was far too late. Ade had been prepared to use the Desert Eagle if necessary but Eric Griffin had made that null and void. With the gun pointing in Griffin's terrified face Ade pushed him over the balcony. Over the side of the building. From the fifteenth floor.

Ade could still hear the scream as he walked quickly back through the french doors. The move against Akers had begun.

# 14.

It was late as H, Boo, Sharon, Sammy, Shampa and Blackie spilled out of the G-spot and into the cool of the night. The Kings Road was quiet, hardly any traffic. Despite the nightmare of H's day, his night had been a good one. In fact, the night had been good for all the West End gamblers. For once they were all winners and the competitive element that usually that existed between them was absent. Goodbyes and general sentiments of goodwill were sincerely meant. Sammy headed for his mini-cab and the drive back to east London while Sharon and Boo walked off towards the West End. H, Blackie and Shampa headed towards H's Mercedes, parked on the corner of Flood Street.

In the afterglow of success H's mood was surprisingly sombre. In truth, he'd had a very good night, far better than he could have expected given the events of the day. Perhaps he'd had a good night because of his day. H had arrived in the session late and immediately begun taking chances that he wouldn't normally take. Some of the gambles he'd taken had verged on the reckless. Had he been playing strictly professional gamblers no doubt he would have been made to pay. However, playing with three fish at the table meant that there was a constant flow of money. The fish had entered inro the spirit of H's game, allowing their egos to rule their heads, but they couldn't hope to compete with his level of play. The overall effect of H's presence at the table was to make money for all the West End professionals.

Had the mood been less euphoric, H probably would have registered the significance of the metallic blue BMW Z3 Roadster sitting opposite Flood Street, or recognised the beautiful woman inside. But he didn't. It was H's first big mistake of the night.

'How much?' Blackie asked with a grin. Not only had there been no trouble in the game, making Blackie's night an easy one, but Ghadaffi was so pleased at the level of tax the table had taken that he'd said he would use Blackie and Shampa again while his usual houseman was away.

'About eighteen hundred,' H replied.

Blackie slapped him on the back. 'Seen, man, seen! Is a good night! Why you face favour a donkey, it look so long?'

H gave a grim smile. 'Blackie, let me ask you something: tonight was a good night . . . but what about tomorrow? I mean, don't you ever think you're getting too old for this?'

Blackie could see where this was going and gestured to Shampa.

'Wait in de car fo' me no', baby.' He kissed her, and watched her walk back past the club to Blackie's huge old Volvo.

'Of course we too old, man! But das not de point!' They walked on, arriving at H's car and leaning up against it. 'You know me, H, we know each udder a long time. Me is a man dat like to work; I been a driver, I work construction, I do lickle factory work; an' I serve my time as a guest of 'er Majesty.' Blackie paused, looking closely at H. 'But 'ear now: dis las' time inside people is tarkin' 'bout 'ow England change up now under dis New Labour. De people fling out de set a Tory dawgs and t'ieves and dey tarkin' 'bout how England is a meritocracy. Well kiss me foot, dey may be right! I'm not a clever man so I don' know. But what I know is dat for you and me, as black people in dis country, maybe we is part of a, of a los' generation.' Blackie looked away as though he felt guilty about what he was saying or he wasn't sure if he was talking out of turn. He corrected himself. 'Whedder is Tony Blair or Gordon Brown . . . de Labour Party cian't do nutten for me, at least. I too old, I too black an' I too nasty! But gamblin' is somet'in' I love. I might still get to be rich one day, you knowa mean?'

H just listened. He didn't agree with everything the older man was saying but he recognised that Blackie was speaking from the heart and paying the man respect meant listening and thinking about what he had to say.

Looking back, H would wonder how he had failed to notice the shadowy figures hiding by the side of his car. 'Everyone wants to be rich,' H said, 'but there has to be more to life than that.'

# THE LAST CARD

Blackie just laughed. 'I live de life an' I 'ave my dreams; what more you want outta life?'

H thought about that for a moment. 'Beverley's moved out. She's taken Cyrus with her.'

'Lawd, God, me sorry to 'ear dat, sah! Me really sorry.' Blackie patted H on the back with concern.

'I guess it was bound to happen sooner or later, the way we were going.' H paused as he thought about what he was saying. 'What I need is a regular life, Blackie. A regular job, regular hours.'

''Ear what; I spen' a large parta my life looking for a regular life, you know! You t'ink I come from Jamaica lookin' dis kinda work? No, sah! When I come to dis country life was hhharsh and hhhhard! Dey didn't want us when we come 'ere fe look work. Calling you a "black bastard" an' all dis shit. "Go 'ome you black bastard!" You know 'ow many times I did hear dat? Under de circumstances one 'as to mek choices and mek you own way in life. In de bes' way you cian. When water run down a hill an' you block it off, de water still haffu run. I don' know how I start in dis business, I cian' remember, but for me now, gambling . . . allows de juices to flow, seen? It brings . . . light. And what is a life widout light?'

H kept his silence. He looked at Blackie's battered teeth, the scar on his forehead and his generally battered, gnarled appearance. Blackie's words were simple, unembellished and to the point. But H knew there was a wealth of experience beneath them that he wasn't talking about and he didn't need to. Blackie continued. 'Relax you'-self, man. Y'ave a good win. Enjoy it becau' dis is as good as it gets. Go 'ome, sah. Ketch some sleep.'

H pulled him into a tight embrace. He suddenly felt emotional but he didn't know why.

'G'night, man, sleep well, yeah? And thanks.' H watched Blackie walk quickly away, back on to the King's Road and his own car. Suddenly somebody shortish and heavy-set stepped towards him. It was a man wearing a long, padded coat, with half his hair in a cane row style, the other half loose. H glanced at him and then looked away, thinking he'd seen him somewhere before. When no one came to mind he turned away and bent to open the front door of his own car. At that moment the Z3 Roadster from across the street suddenly roared to life.

Its engine kicked in and its headlights sprang on, full beam. As H looked over, the roadster swung round in an arc and pulled up alongside him. The driver, a beautiful woman, lowered the window. It took H about a second to recognise her. It was the woman that he'd seen in Alan Akers' office. She was alone.

'Remember me?' She said it with a smile as though the one time they had met wasn't when his life was threatened and his ear mutilated.

He looked down at her coldly. 'How could I forget?'

'Where are you going?'

'What's it to you?'

'Just interested.'

'Home.'

'A man like you shouldn't have to go home alone.'

H bent down and looked in the car. This was weird. Why was this woman who he'd met once, under less than perfect circumstances, coming on to him?

'Why not? I like the company.'

'So would two be a crowd?'

Jesus Christ! This woman was pushy. She was fit though.

'Depends on the context.'

'Me. You. My car. My place.' There it was. On a plate. A punany platter.

'How do you know I don't have someone waiting for me at home?' H was smiling now, despite himself.

'Do you?'

'No.'

'So what are we talking about?' She looked up at him and she too was smiling, her eyes large and open.

'What are you doing out here, anyway?'

'I'm feeling lonely.' She said it in a sad and campy voice, adding to the effect by leaning over and opening the passenger door. H thought about it, he did. But no, she was working too hard, there had to be a catch somewhere. H had done his gambling for the night.

'Maybe another time.'

He turned back to his Mercedes. And it was then that H paid the price for the second of the mistakes he'd made that night. Two men

# THE LAST CARD

rushed him from behind his car. One of them grabbed H from behind, pinning his arms behind his back. The other stood in front of him and proceeded to drop a lick on H that he hadn't taken in a long, long time. He lost consciousness.

# 15.

It had been a long, long time since Nina had played the role of nurse. Being the eldest of three children with a mother who was always working meant that she had often had to babysit her younger sisters. And when she and Alan had first started going together he had often seemed happiest when she had taken him in her arms, held him tight and gently rubbed his back. Maternal instincts that she had always been aware of came out at odd moments.

Tonight provided one of those moments. The man Gavin had called Hilary was slumped in the passenger seat of her car. Nina had reclined the seat and his head lolled on the head rest. She dabbed at the egg-sized lump on his forehead with a small sponge that was really for washing dishes but which Nina kept in the car to wipe the windscreen. She'd dampened it with a bottle of Evian and used this to stem the blood. Hilary seemed to be regaining consciousness and was making low moaning noises. Nina continued to squat outside the car, working on him gently, with care.

For some reason, as she wiped away the blood that had run down his cheek and under his chin, Nina noticed Hilary's lips. They were full, thick lips; the upper one a dark brown while the lower one was a more reddish colour. Funny that, she had a lot of black friends but it had never occurred to her to look closely, really closely at their lips. They were so unlike her own. Hers were longer, thinner. There seemed to be a pale line, a pale shade of brown around Hilary's mouth that highlighted it, made it seem like a caricature, a stylised version of what a pair of lips should look like. She'd never noticed that about anyone before. They seemed pillowy and soft, like a comfortable bed . . .

# THE LAST CARD

H suddenly came round, opening his eyes and trying to sit up. Nina backed away, still squatting outside the car. She could see his eyes focusing on where he was, trying to remember how he had arrived in the passenger seat of her car. He looked at her, blankly at first and then recognition seemed to dawn. He raised a hand to his head, touching the lump where he'd been struck. He immediately yanked his hand away, wincing with pain.

'What happened?'

'Some old friends of yours, apparently. One of them was a Mr . . . Stammer?'

This seemed to be especially bad news and Hilary groaned, loudly this time.

'They left you this.' Nina picked a black leather wallet up from the pavement by her feet. She handed it to Hilary. He again looked blank.

'A wallet?'

'It's yours.'

'Shit!' H's memory seemed to be clearing now. 'You let them take my money?'

'What could I do?'

'All of it? Over six grand?'

'There were two of them! What was I supposed to do?!' Nina stared back as H glowered at her, trying to intimidate and make her feel guilty.

'Where are we?'

'You don't know where you are?'

H looked around him, still dazed.

'I've got no idea. Is this your car?'

'This is my car and I don't think you should go home alone tonight. You're not well.'

'I am well. What makes you think I'm not well?' He looked at her with the same look of confusion that people have when they've suddenly been roused from a deep sleep. Nina had to smile.

'Because you're outside a club called the G-spot. You were in there for at least six hours.'

H looked blankly out at the front of the club.

'Come on, I'm taking you home.'

'What about my car? If I leave it here it'll get towed.'

'Good. They can tow it straight to the scrap yard. Save you some money.' With that she made sure Hilary was secure in the car, strapping his seat belt on. She slammed the door, walked round to the driver's side and climbed in. She started the engine.

'Don't you need to know where I live?'

'Why?'

'You're taking me home!'

'Not your home; mine.'

Nina was a good driver. Given the little traffic at this time, it took her barely ten minutes to race down the New King's Road, make a right on Beaufort Street, cross the Fulham Road, Old Brompton Road, through Earl's Court, on to Holland Road, hit the roundabout, make a right, then a left down Portland Road until she hit Pottery Lane. Way down near the bottom was Nina's small mews house. Home.

Nina climbed out, went round the car, opened the door for her passenger and helped him out. H was still groggy and as he climbed out he suddenly pitched forwards.

'Here, lean on me.'

'Lean on you? Can you handle it?'

'I can handle you.'

'Oh yeah? What makes you so sure?'

'Confidence. I was born with it.'

'That kind of confidence can get you in trouble.'

'Are you going to keep talking or do you want to come in?' She took one of his arms and, with H offering no resistance, draped it heavily round her shoulders. Struggling to prop the big man up, Nina staggered with him straight into a large, modern kitchen. Nina flicked on the lights as she slumped H down at a wooden kitchen table. Next to the refrigerator was a side cupboard where Nina kept her overflow of spirits. She pulled out a bottle of brandy. She lifted two glass tumblers from a cupboard above the sink and poured two generous helpings. She carried them both over to H who by now, was looking around him.

'Nice place you've got here.' He took a sip of his brandy, and his eyes rested on the huge silver Alessi toaster that sat on the counter by the cooker.

'I was just about to buy one of those.'

# THE LAST CARD

'If you hurry there's a sale on at Harrods.' She watched while he turned to look at her, not sure how to respond.

'Are you taking the piss?'

'Me?' Nina widened her eyes and added a splash of innocence to her tone. 'Why would I do that?' H continued to stare and she held his look. Finally he turned away. This was going to be easier than she had thought.

H continued sipping his brandy, taking it in slowly, letting it do its work. Nina cradled her glass in both hands, not drinking, just watching this large well-built man sitting at her kitchen table. Even in the way he sat, he had a grace, an ease about him. Here was a man who seemed comfortable with his body. Not just because it looked good but he seemed comfortable with the way it worked. She stared at his face. Baby face. He looked as though he had only recently started to shave. But she could tell by his eyes that H had lived. His eyes were constantly moving, they were a deep . . . H glanced over at her.

'What?'

'Better?'

H gingerly felt the bump on his head.

'A bit.'

'You've got some rough friends.'

'So have you!' He pointed to the plaster that covered his mutilated ear. 'Remember?'

'I'll drink to that.' She took her first sip of the brandy. There was another pause. H was looking at her, his eyes taking their time, taking her in, as they lingered on her face. Nina held his look but for the first time she became aware that she was nervous. There was suddenly a tension between them. It was H that broke it.

'To what . . . do I owe the rescue?'

'You're too good-looking to leave lying in the gutter.' She said it straight, keeping her eyes on his. She wanted to see how he would react.

'You think you're hot stuff, don't you?'

'I know I'm hot stuff.'

'A regular angel of mercy.'

'Only when I want to be.'

There was another silence.

'What now?' Nina could hear the edge to his voice.

'My name's Nina. And you are?'

'I thought you and the albino knew all about me?'

'Maybe I just want to hear it from you.'

'H.'

'Is that H with an 'A' or does H stand for something less fashionable?'

'Hilary Chester Zechariah James.'

'Impressive. I like a name that trips easily off the tongue.' She said it with a smile.

'Have you got a boyfriend?'

'Why?'

'Because I can tell that you're a woman that needs some discipline.'

Nina dropped the smile her face 'And if I didn't have a boyfriend would you be the man to discipline me?'

'Only if you ask me nicely.' Now it was H's turn to smile. He finished his brandy with a gulp and looked down at his watch. Nina glanced at the clock on the wall above the door. 4.27 a.m.

'It's late . . . are you going to give me a ride back to my car?'

'You're not going anywhere in your condition . . .'

'What?'

'I insist. Have another drink.' Without giving him time to continue his protest she left the room. She took a duvet, a sheet and two pillows from a closet and carried them upstairs to the spare bedroom. H called to her from the kitchen below.

'Okay. But the sofa'll be fine!'

Nina didn't even bother to glance back. Yeah, right. How was she going to make him feel beholden to her if she allowed him to sleep on the sofa? She began making up the double bed. The room was sparsely furnished with Habitat chic. She stripped the existing sheet off the bed and threw it into a corner. She then spread the clean sheet in its place and was busily smoothing it out when H appeared standing in the doorway. He was sipping his brandy, watching her lean over the bed, no doubt admiring the view. She could tell he was feeling better.

'So are you going to ask me?'

'Ask you what?'

# THE LAST CARD

'If I'm going to discipline you?'

Nina glanced round at him 'You better make that brandy your last. You're getting far too frisky.'

The way he was watching her was beginning to make her feel uneasy again.

'I said the sofa'll be fine.'

'Nonsense . . .' Before Nina could finish making her point H had stepped over to her and grabbed her arm. He jerked her up and spun her round to face him.

'Hey! Careful, hard man!' They stood there, face to face, neither saying anything. Then H slowly let go of her arm. She turned away and continued smoothing out the bottom sheet. With his eyes following her every move she picked up the pillows, plumped them and dropped them at the head of the bed. From having been in some kind of control earlier, Nina suddenly felt vulnerable, clumsily aware of every move she made. She finished off by sweeping the duvet into place. She turned to him.

'There you go. All done.'

He didn't answer. A hint of a smile played on his lips. Nina was suddenly feeling a little breathless. She headed for the door. He may well be drinking his last brandy but she wasn't. She was going to fix herself another one right now.

Standing in the doorway, he made no move to let her through. As she squeezed past her breasts brushed against his chest. He was looking down at her. She stopped, the two of them chest-to-chest in the narrow doorway. Nina looked up at his lips. H bent down to kiss her. He put his hand on the back of her head, grabbing a bunch of her long, brown hair and roughly pulled her head towards his. Their mouths met in an awkward clash, their teeth bumping. But their lips fought for purchase and sorted themselves into a position that fitted. H's tongue darted into her mouth, probing, exploring. Nina's was more reserved, only coming out in small flicks, testing, tasting . . .

As suddenly as H had kissed her, he suddenly pulled her head away. She really was breathless now. She glowered up at him while he smiled down. And then she slapped him across the face, hard.

'Do you know who you're dealing with?'

'Do you care who you're dealing with?'

Nina went to slap him again but H caught her wrist this time and held it tight.

'I think you're just about ready for bed.' She slowly eased his hand off her wrist, turned and stalked away, downstairs. She could feel his eyes boring into her back. Damn! That hadn't gone to plan!

\*\*\*

Morning. Early. Nine. Virgin Radio blared and H ground his teeth as he slowly munched through a bowl of cornflakes. The noise was infuriating. Nina wasn't quite sure why, but it was. The man looked to be in a world of his own, like a cow chewing grass. When you watched a cow chewing grass could you possibly know what it was thinking? And that's what this man looked like sitting at her kitchen table spooning huge mounds of cornflakes, dripping the milk, slowly chewing. Big, dumb and slow.

Nina watched him surreptitiously from the sink. After last night she had to regain the upper hand. Games of sexual chemistry were games that she was used to playing and used to winning. Then once she had him . . . on to phase two.

She was making herself a latte but as she waited for the milk to heat up she slyly watched H out of the corner of her eye. She had brushed her hair and was wearing a skimpy, sheer negligee – mauve – that was just long enough to cover her arse. Over this she wore a light cotton dressing-gown that she had artfully left open from the waist down, deliberately exposing mucho thigh. Her legs were her best feature. They were long, slender and smooth and H, if he bothered to look, would be able to see them from the top of one creamy thigh all the way down to her bare feet.

But all this big, dumb ox could do was chew cornflakes and look dazed.

'Are you sure you don't want eggs or bacon?' She worked hard at keeping the irritation from her voice. Here she was asking if she could feed his fat mouth more food, and he could barely bring himself to look at her. This was too much.

'I said do you want . . .'

'Shhhhh!' He pointed to the radio. He was listening to it! Could you believe this ox? Not enough that she had to listen to his bovine munchings but now she wasn't allowed to speak in her own kitchen. She whipped her dressing-gown round her and turned back to her latte. She poured the milk into the coffee and padded with as much aggression as she could muster to the kitchen table. She sat opposite him. She was aware that those two, small, vertical lines had reappeared in her forehead. Just to further annoy her. She looked over at H. He was looking at her, but he wasn't looking at her. His eyes were far away. He was listening to the radio. Nina tuned herself in.

'. . . number one contender for the WBC's World super-middle-weight title, has finally been given his chance. After months of negotiations, a date is to be announced when he'll take on the American champion, Robert Howard.'

'I'm having one warm-up fight and then bring on this "great" American champion. I'll beat him like his daddy used to beat him.'

'What do you think, Chris? Do you think Rob Howard will be shaking at the prospect of facing our Henry Mancini?'

'I couldn't give a monkey's, John, go on, get out, I hate boxing.'

The DJ cut off the sports chatter with 'Wake Me Up Before You Go-Go'.

Nina glanced at H. He was still somewhere else. Where? She put out a hand and laid it with care on his; the one without the spoon that was feeding ever larger mounds of cornflakes into his big trap.

'Are you all right, Hilary?'

He shook himself as though waking from a dream. 'Yeah, yeah, I'm fine. Sorry about that, something on the radio . . . You got any coffee?'

She looked at him. This guy – like most men! – is a Neanderthal. What can you do with them? She rose and began making him a latte.

'Did you sleep all right?' she ventured.

'Great. Slept like a top. It must have been that brandy.'

'Good.' He carried on eating while she made his latte. She brought it back to the table. While he spooned in sugar she sat and watched him. Typical man. The dumber they were, the sounder they slept. She could see she was going to have her work cut out to move things on to stage two. H looked as though he was going to be a tougher nut to crack than she had anticipated. She tried another tack.

'You didn't tell me why you have a girl's name?'

'My mother wanted girls but she ended up having two boys. We've both got names that could be boys' or girls' names. I'm Hilary and my brother's called Sean.' H carried on eating, every so often taking a slurp of coffee. He sounded like a plumber wrestling with a blocked drain. Nina fought hard to keep the disgust out of her voice.

'You know, you were kind of rude last night, Hilary.'

'Call me 'H'. I don't like Hilary.'

'I don't like 'H'. I'll call you Hilary.' That drew his attention. He stopped the crackling and crunching of his jaws to look at Nina in surprise.

'You're feisty, you know that, woman?'

She let that go. To deal with it now would have meant a long digression and she had more important seeds to sow.

'Yeah, whatever. So tell me, what was last night all about?'

'The kiss? Put it down to your charm and good looks.'

'So are you involved with anyone at the moment?'

'I asked you the same thing last night.'

'Yes, but the question takes on a whole new level of meaning when it's the woman who asks the man.'

# 16.

**A**de sat in an old Ford Granada. Stolen. It was parked up in front of what looked like a peeling, run-down old shed. Ade had his eyes pinned on the shed. He was waiting. And while he was waiting he was thinking. Thinking about what Dunstan had said that morning . . .

'It's globalisation, ennit, you know't I mean.'

'No.' Ade didn't have a clue what Dunstan was talking about.

'You don't know what globalisation is?' Dunstan's voice became shrill. 'Globalisation is when big companies swallow little companies and the big companies get bigger and bigger.' He paused, to think through what he'd just said and check that it made sense. 'It's like McDonalds, right, dey make deir burgers and den when a nex' man wants to make his burgers dey run 'im outta town because 'im would take up some a deir burger market, you get me? So das 'ow dey expand 'till dey're controllin' de fast food market all over de world, you get me?'

'Yeah . . .' Ade wasn't sure that he did. 'So globalisation is really when dem big-up people afight each udder to keep hold of their market?' Ade left the questioning tone in his voice just to cover himself.

'Yes, man! Is so me a tell you! I was reading about dis de udder day. Dey call it globalisation because de bigger companies are now operating worldwide; globally. So when a yout' in India is dreaming about biggin' up himself and operating his own chain of burger shops, 'e better t'ink again! McDonalds is coming for his rarse!'

'Dey got McDonalds in India?'

Dunstan almost whiplashed round to squint at Ade. 'Dey got McDonalds everywhere, dread! Dat company is cookin' wid gas, guy! Osama Book Binder is fronting it out wid Bush now, cos America are kicking a McDonalds into Baghdad, Kandahar and all dem Arab places, dread, I'm telling ya!'

'But I thought dem Muslims don't eat meat?' Ade was aware that Dunstan liked to bullshit sometimes, play like he knew more than he really did.

'Ade, man, you better start read newspaper. Dis is a dangerous world we're living in, you know't I mean! Wid all dis globalisation business. It's not Muslims dat don't eat meat it's de Indians. An' I t'ink it's just beef dey don't eat, anyways.'

'So what dey doing wid a McDonalds den?' Ade said triumphantly.

'Ade, Ade, you're missing de point; de point is globalisation. Dat man Akers vex me up, guy, you know't I mean! So I'm t'inkin' how can we deal wid dis man? 'Bout 'im stan' up in my face and chattin' about "fuck all you wogs and niggers"!'

Ade sighed grimly. This wasn't the first time he'd had to listen to Dunstan fulminating against Akers.

''E musta thought he was talkin' to dem Paki boys up in Leeds or somefen! 'Bout "fuck all you wogs and niggers"! Den dis man chat up in my face, pushing out 'is chest, talkin' "We do what we want"! I shouldda slap 'im two times in 'is face!'

Ade again inwardly sighed. He knew enough about Dunstan to know he was not about to slap Alan Akers.

'Anyway. I'm t'inkin' Akers made 'is money by startin' a ganja delivery service. Den he expanded; brought in people like me an you. Now we're running t'ings but insteada workin' for ourselves, we're workin' for 'im! That cunt! Why is it de black man always ends up workin' for de white man?'

Ade had a theory about that but he could tell that Dunstan wasn't looking for an answer.

'I tell you why, Ade, cos we ain't got no fuckin' balls! Me nah like dat man Akers, but fair play to 'im! He took 'is chances and made 'is money. Now it's our turn. Globalisation. We're doing all de fuckin' work anyway, we're going to take 'im down. And expand. Wha' d'you think?'

Ade thought for a moment. 'Where we gonna expand to, Dunstan?'

'First, London. We eivver join up wiv some uvver crews in de recreational management business or we take dem over. People like Wha Gwan. I hear say he's running a crew over in north London now. We "globalise". And den when we're controlling t'ings in London we take on other cities, Birmingham, Manchester, Liverpool. We go fuckin' large man! Me and you!'

Ade couldn't see it. For two reasons. One, Wha Gwan was a tough customer who ran a crew in north London with an iron discipline. He would not easily bend to the idea of being 'taken over'. And secondly, Dunstan did have some good ideas, it was true, but he was the kind of brother who, when push comes to shove, didn't always follow through. Still, Ade thought, no point in stifling a man in the middle of his creative flow.

'Yeah, yeah, I can see it, why not?'

'Exactly! Why fuckin' not! Why not me an' you?! Dream big, Ade, always dream big!' Dunstan was so pumped he slapped Ade a high five and then took the afro comb from the tropical growth of his hair and picked at it excitedly. It stood tall and proud. 'That's why we take out more of Aker's people and den, when de time is right, we drop a lash on Akers himself! But only when de time is right. Too early and we won't have enough people behind us to continue business as usual, you get me?'

'You think it's our time, Dunstan? You think it's really our time?'

'It is our time, dread; London is changing, you get me? Dem old style gangsta ways is finished. It's like Akers is always goin' on about de Krays. De Krays and the Richardsons. Fuck de Krays and fuck de Richardsons! An' 'e's talking 'bout "fuck all you wogs and niggers"!'

This time Ade had to laugh. Dunstan demanded to know what the hell was so funny. But Ade was laughing too hard to answer. Eventually, the two of them were rolling around Dunstan's bedroom laughing their faces off. '"Fuck all you wogs and niggers."' Ho, ho, ho, ha, ha, ha! '"We do what we want."' Hee, hee, hee, huh, huh, huh!

It was only later, sitting in this Ford Granada, while Ade was thinking it all through, that he realised what they were actually laughing at. It was that history was on Ade's and Dunstan's side. Of course Akers would say 'fuck all you wogs and niggers'. What else could he say? He was trying to hold back the march of time, the march of progress. And as Ade's Yoruba father had told him, on more than one occasion, it was exactly what the white man had tried to do in Africa. Slavery, imperialism, colonialism. But then independence. The white man had tried to hang on to Africa and he'd failed. So why shouldn't Akers fail now, Ade reasoned to himself? And even if it wasn't Ade and Dunstan who brought about change, well, Akers was fucked anyway because globalisation was all about change. Akers was all about maintaining the status quo. Sooner or later someone, from somewhere, was going to take him down. If that was the case, Ade reasoned, it might as well be them. And if not them, him. Ade. Because, apart from the joy of taking out White Alan, there was also a lot of money at stake here. Cash. Ade liked cash.

He sat back in the front seat with a smile on his face. He could see it now: him and Dunstan, big office, big cigar, running an empire that stretched from London to Edinburgh. Anything you want: smoke, smack, crack, ecstasy, charlie, anything you wanted, they would supply it. It would be like a factory. Like Marks & Spencer. *Dunstan & Ade.* No, no, *Ade & Dunstan.*

His pleasant daydream was interrupted as two boxers, one white, one black, exited the old shed. Ade sat up. Moments later, another man came out and followed them. Mark Hodges.

As Hodges picked his way over the wasteland Ade dropped a hand under his seat. He pulled out the black and shiny semi-automatic Desert Eagle, tucked it under his jacket and climbed out of the car. He nipped quickly towards Hodges, coming at him from the right and slightly behind his line of vision. The first two boxers were now a little further on but it didn't matter to Ade. The hood of his sweatshirt covered his head and most of his face. He called out Hodges' name.

'Hey! Mark Hodges!' Hodges turned. Ade got a good look at him. It wouldn't do to take out the wrong man. He had a huge bandage over his nose. Apparently some bruiser in a West End shebeen had given him a Glaswegian love bite when he'd tried to collect White Alan's rent. Yep, it was Hodges all right. Ade opened his jacket and pulled out the Desert Eagle. The fitted silencer made it seem huge. At the sight of it Hodges froze, then backed away. But too late. Ade opened fire, pumping him with a short burst. As the bullets ripped through his chest, Hodges didn't have time to make a sound. He leapt in the air and then staggered back, finally dropping to the ground, dead.

Without waiting to see who had or hadn't seen, Ade walked quickly back to the Granada, started the engine and pulled smoothly away.

# 17.

Alice sat opposite her daughter, Beverley, on the plastic sheeting which covered her favourite sofa. She was knitting and her needles clacked and clicked at a furious pace. Her daughter's boyfriend and the father of her grandson, Cyrus, was coming over and she was not looking forward to the visit. Alice sat with a set to her jaw and a scowl on her face that could have been carved with an axe.

The problem for Alice was that once you had a child with somebody you were stuck with that person. That child is a tangible reminder of what once was. And so it was that Beverley was stuck with Hilary. As Alice thought about Hilary she loudly kissed her teeth, schtupsing over the sound of her knitting needles. If it was at all possible to remove a person from the face of the planet with the strength of a schtups, Hilary would have disappeared at that moment.

Beverley sat on an armchair that matched the sofa, the plastic sticking uncomfortably to her bare legs. She was reading, keeping her eyes on the page, out of harm's way. She had already been told, at some length, about the waste she was making of her life and the danger she was putting Alice's grandson into.

Alice was nearing sixty. She'd led a hard life but a full and active one. She had few regrets about the shape her life had taken since she'd arrived in England almost forty years before, but the few regrets she had were all to do with men. She'd married twice and both men had no principles, no ambition, and were no damn good. Consequently, Alice had had to make her own way in the world and everything that she had she'd worked hard for. The three-bedroomed house she and her daughter now sat in, in Hanwell, west London – she paid for it; the little plot of land with the house in Cork Hill in Montserrat, even if it was now in a volcano exclusion zone – she paid for it. These

**115**

were, she reflected, notable achievements for a black woman coming to England alone at the tender age of twenty. However, to Alice's mind, one sucess stood head and shoulders above all others. Beverley. Beverley was Alice's crowning achievement.

Alice had grown up in a poor, rural area of Montserrat, born out of wedlock to a mother who was too young to be a mother. Alice had been raised by her grandmother. Alice loved her grandmother but the woman had been a tough disciplinarian. A single woman herself, she supported her family by running a small grocery store – a low, two-roomed, wooden structure with the store in the front room and Alice and her grandmother living in the back.

It was the toughness of this upbringing that Alice brought with her when she came to England. Life had been difficult for her in the early years but she had vowed that if she were ever to have children, life for them would be easier.

Alice's first husband, Sam, was tall, good-looking, dressed sharp – but was as pig-headed and violent as a man could be. Seven married years and four single years later, Alice's second husband was as unlike her first as it was possible to be. Charles was caring, he was easy, he was quiet, he was polite. At last, thought Alice, here is a man who I can share my life with. Unfortunately, Charles was as dull as a donkey.

And then Alice, who by that time had given up on the idea of ever having children, became pregnant. Beverley, Alice's miracle child, was born. She was seven pounds three ounces of joy! Soon after Beverley's birth Alice finally gave Charles his marching orders.

Alice's parenting skills, such as they were, were learned at the knee of her grandmother. She was disciplined, hard, sometimes lacking in affection. But her drive for Beverley's success paid off. Beverley was a good student, she was sociable and had many friends. Alice knew that when her daughter had been at university she'd met one or two boys but none had seemed special to her. When Beverley graduated with a 2:1 and became a Bachelor of Arts in History, Alice was very, very proud.

When Beverley found her first job as a teacher in a comprehensive school, Alice could see her highest hopes for her daughter gradually coming to fruition. She felt that her major mission in life was almost complete.

# THE LAST CARD

And then Beverley – Alice's joy, Alice's pride, Alice's masterwork! – met Hilary, a thick-eared, hard-headed boxer.

When Cyrus was born Alice had been forced to admit that Hilary was a devoted father. But then things began to go downhill.

One day Alice had a quiet sit-down with her daughter and it all came tumbling out. Amidst the tears came the stories of Hilary's gambling, his staying out all night, his running around with strange characters, his constantly borrowing money from Beverley. It came out higgledy-piggledy but by the end of their talk Alice had a very clear idea of what was happening over in Battersea.

Alice had learnt a lot and changed a lot since she first arrived in England as a shy, diffident slip of a thing. She had filled out somewhat and the long limbs and hour-glass figure had been replaced with – what? The thing her body most closely resembled was the side of an upright piano, straight up and down with a bulge in her middle. It may not have been flattering but it made her path through life a little easier. It gave her a certain . . . authority. In addition to this she had acquired a sharp, cutting edge to her tongue. More than one English workman who had asked for a 'cuppa tea, darling' while he fixed the plumbing had felt the lash of it. Yes, Alice had changed since the '60s and could be fierce if she felt the situation warranted it.

And so it was about four months before, when Alice had taken it upon herself to pay Hilary a 'friendly' visit. It was not long after her heart-to-heart with Beverley. She tramped into the doorway of the gym on the Old Kent Road and paused, looking around for Hilary. Some haaaaard-core west-coast gangsta rap blared from the gym's sound system.

**ROLLING ON MY HOMIE WITH MY GUN IN HIS FACE,**
**GOT HIS BITCH DOWN LOW WITH MY DICK IN HER ASS . . .**

The lyrics were harsh and Alice's expression hardened. Her bottom jaw pushed forward. She finally caught sight of Hilary and tramped forward, attracting startled looks in her wake. By the time she reached Hilary almost all activity in the gym had ceased.

Alice stood right in front of him and Hilary was forced to stop skipping. He eyed her warily. He knew why she was there. Someone, no doubt afraid of missing something, turned the music off. Someone else, the gym's resident wag, helpfully called out to Hilary: 'Hey, Hilary, your girlfriend's come to see you!' Alice spun round with the speed of a twitching nerve. A young man tempted to laugh quickly stifled the impulse, the guffaw strangling in his throat. Alice cast her eyes over the crowd of gawking boxers.

'I don' want any trouble from any of you all . . . but if I have to put me han' on you, I put such a slap on all you faces you wouldn't be cheeky again!' The loud schtups she gave as she kissed her teeth seemed to make the ropes of the boxing ring vibrate. There was total silence. She turned to Hilary, raising an index finger and jabbing it harshly and repetitively, inches from his face. 'And you, you ought to be ashame' of you'self! Is wha' kin' a man you call you'self? I have to come all de way to dis place dat ssssstinking of sweat because I want to waaaaarn you! Don't. Mess. Wid my. Daughter! I warning you! If you want to mess wid someone . . . try me! You t'ink you is de firs' man I would have to put me han on?' At this she looked around the gym at the gawking boxers. Nobody said a word. She turned back to Hilary. 'And don' budder start trouble wid Beverley, becau' she never tell me anyt'ing dat I didn't work out meself.' She paused for breath. 'De bot' of us know what we talking about! An' if I hear any more, any more about you foolish attitude and you foolish behaviour . . . I coming fa you! Das all I want to say: I coming fa you!'

And with that, Alice spun round and tramped back out of the gym. The gawking boxers stepped back as she made her way to the door, parting like the Red Sea before Moses.

In the four months since that visit Alice hadn't told Beverley about her trip to the gym, but she had gently let it be known that there was always space for her and Cyrus in Hanwell. They could stay as long as they needed to get themselves back on their feet.

Two mornings ago Alice had picked up her telephone to hear her daughter weeping at the other end of the line. Between sobs and chokes she said she'd had enough. She couldn't take it any more, she wanted out. And now Hilary had telephoned and said he wanted to see Beverley and Cyrus. Alice's knitting needles clacked manically in anticipation of Hilary's arrival. She glanced up at the fake wood panelling of the grandmother clock on the wall. Ten minutes past two. Hilary was late. She looked back down at her knitting needles as they flashed through the wool they were working into a small jumper for Cyrus. Just as she was about to say something derisory about Hilary, the doorbell rang. Both she and Beverley looked up. Beverley looked nervous as she rose to open the door.

When she returned with a sheepish Hilary behind her, Alice had a sudden flash of her daughter as a young, carefree girl of thirteen. Alice remembered her confidently dancing and laughing in front of the mirror in this very living room. And here she was now, walking on eggshells, because of this man Hilary! With his hair 'locksed up' in one foolish hair style! As she looked at Hilary Alice felt her bottom jaw jut out a little further.

Beverley returned to her armchair, while Hilary approached Alice.

'Hi, Mrs Fredricks.' The boy held out his hand for her to shake. Alice didn't even look up. After a moment Alice heard him back away and sit on the other good armchair. For a moment there was a pregnant silence in the room, the sound of Alice's knitting needles loud over the distant traffic noise from the street.

'Is Cyrus still at school?'

Hmmph! That was the boy's opening gambit.

'Of course.' Beverley now had her stockinged feet curled up on the chair and was looking at Hilary, her arms folded defensively in front of her.

'How is he?' the boy asked.

Alice couldn't contain herself. 'If you weren't such a damn fool you would know for yourself!'

'Mum!'

Alice glanced at her scowling daughter. Click, clack, click, clack. The needles flashed ever more quickly as Alice's thick fingers worked them. She had promised that she wouldn't interfere but she had insisted on being present during this first meeting with Hilary. Beverley was her only child and she was definitely going to give her some support.

'He's all right. He misses you.'

Alice let out a schtups that was so loud and so strong it seemed to echo round the room. She didn't look up as she felt her daughter's hot gaze on her.

'He knows his dad loves him, that's why.'

Alice couldn't see but she could hear the defiance in the boy's voice. She had to admit, he was probably right.

'You've still got some of your things at the house,' he said.

'I know. I'll come and pick them up one day when you're out.'

'Eh-heh!' Again! It just popped out. Alice felt a little ashamed of herself. Beverley was glaring at her.

'Please, Mum!'

Alice had gone too far with her last interruption and Beverley wanted her out of the room. Well. It was up to her. Alice rose unsteadily to her feet and threw down her knitting.

'I hope you know what you doing, Beverley! This fool certainly doesn't!' Alice tramped into the kitchen before creeping softly, silently back down the hallway, back to the slightly open door of the living room. She stopped, held her breath and turned her ear to the crack. She had no qualms about eavesdropping on a private conversation. Where her daughter was concerned, all was fair.

'Come back, Bev!'

'Nothing's changed though, has it?'

'Please! Please, come back!'

'Why? It'll just be more of the same. It doesn't work between us.'

'It can do. I've been thinking about what you said . . .'

'And?'

'You're right.' As Alice listened there was a pause. She couldn't see but she imagined her daughter, who had played it well so far, beginning to melt. Alice thought this was bad, definitely bad; too early to show signs of forgiveness. Hilary continued.

'But I just need a bit of time, Bev. I promise you, I'm trying to sort myself out. Bev . . . I need some money . . .'

'Oh, God, Hilary, not again . . !'

'No, you don't understand, it's not my fault this time . . .'

This was too much for Alice, never mind Beverley. She charged into the room like a buffalo stampeding across the plains of North America. Hilary was one foolish man and if this was the best he could do to win back Beverley – her Beverley! – then he had to go.

'Out! Get out! And don't come back, I don't want you in here!'

And that was that.

# 18.

**H** had his fight at the Grundy Park Leisure Centre in Cheshunt, Hertfordshire. It was scheduled as a six-round contest against 'Spider' McKenzie, a bald-headed bruiser from Aberdeen. He had a tough chin, he had long arms and he fought dirty. At this level of the professional fight game there are no television cameras, there are no celebrities in the audience, there are no glamorous women around. For H, each bout was becoming more and more like a Victorian freak show; about entertaining a screaming mob eager to see violence. Once H had taken the elbow to his face, just above the eye, the spring drained from his legs. Judging from their cheers the illegal blow was seen by the entire audience, but not, apparently, by the referee. H no longer heard the crowd's desperate baying for blood.

The stripped fluorescent lighting was harsh. H sat on the stool under it in the changing room, his back against the wall. The cut above his right eye was plastered, but the sweat from the fight still came out of his skin as little, tiny pinpricks. He held his arms out in front of him and Matt unlaced his boxing gloves and cut the white sticky-tape that bound H's hands.

Matt discarded the tape in a nearby bin and picked up the bucket of iced water. Next to it was a brown envelope.

'Where'd you want your money?'

'Just leave it here.' H gestured to the floor next to him. Matt dropped the envelope and H plunged both hands into the bucket. He waited until Matt was stood behind him rubbing his shoulders down with a towel.

'Can I ask you something, Matt?'

''Course you can, mate.'

'You know I wouldn't ask if it wasn't serious . . .'

'How much?'

'Fifteen thousand pounds.'

'*How* much?' Although Matt had been here before he was stumped by this figure.

'I know, I know, I know, I know . . .'

'I can't put my hands on that kind of money, H! And to be honest . . .'

'Don't! Don't be honest.' Coming on top of the honesty aimed at him by Beverley's mother, H had had more than enough honesty for one day. He took one of his hands out of the water. With dripping fingers he picked up the envelope and opened it. Inside was the princely sum, the magnificent total, the gargantuan amount . . . of £300: a cockney carpet.

H looked at the crumpled, used notes. It was all the money he had in the world but it was still nowhere near enough for Alan Akers. On the other hand . . . it was just enough to secure a place at VJ's poker table in Whitechapel.

# 19.

Dunstan was vex. He tried to centre himself as he sat in the front seat of his Jeep, building up a nine-Rizla super-spliff. A Japanese origami master would have been proud of it. To construct a spliff of such architectural complexity, such splendour, gave Dunstan a sense of peace and wellbeing at least equal to the lick the mighty herb would give him once he'd torched it.

Dunstan's head bobbed to Mad Lion's wicked, old skool lyrics on 'Play De Selection'. The music was waging a war with his eardrums. The terrifyingly loud one-drop bass-line beat was so intense the reverberations rattled his ribs and his heart seemed to pump and bounce to the music of its own accord. To Dunstan, the music was sweet and calming.

**GET 'PON DE FLOOR AND DANCE YOUR ARSE OFF.**
**SMOKE UP YOUR WEED AND DRINK UP YOUR BOOZE . . .**

Dunstan's head rocked to the reggae, his afro bobbing just behind the beat. It waved like the leaves of a palm tree in a gentle Hawaiian breeze. As Dunstan worked on his spliff and listened to Mad Lion's ruff and gruff dance-hall chanting, he could feel the vexation gradually lifting out of him.

Dunstan glanced over at Ade sitting next to him. Ade neither seemed to be listening to the music, nor was he building a spliff. He stared ahead with a fixed and rigid expression. Dunstan could feel the hostility emanating from Ade like heat from an oven.

'Wha' 'appen to you?'

'Nutten.'

'How you mean "nutten"?'

'I said nutten, didn't I?' Ade spoke without turning to look at Dunstan. It took some of the heat out of his snapped response and

Dunstan was glad of that. He liked Ade but – cha! – he didn't want to have to get nasty and tell him about himself.

'Man, you should take up some yoga or somefen; cool you nerves.'

Ade turned to look at him. Having finished building his spliff Dunstan enthusiastically licked it together.

'What did you say?'

'Said you should take up some yoga or somefen. Chill you out a bit.' Now that the spliff was finished and with the music pumping, Dunstan was relaxed enough to smile.

'Wha' are you talkin' about? Wha' de fuck you know abou' yoga?' Ade was badly irritated and Dunstan took his time before answering. He took out his lighter and lit the end of his spliff, sucking on it greedily.

'Come on, Ade, I'm jus' winding you up, man. You cian' take a joke?' Dunstan held up the spliff for him. Ade made no move so Dunstan manoeuvred it towards the ashtray. He missed, and an ashy slagheap fell on the car's pristine upholstery.

'Fuck sake, man! I jus' clean up de car yesterday, you know't I mean!'

Ade eyed his misfortune with a broad grin. 'Dat'll fucking teach you!' he snapped. He leant over and snatched the spliff from Dunstan's hand. ''Bout youa chat 'bout yoga!' He took a short pull on the spliff and let it out quickly. He handed the spliff back to Dunstan. Dunstan knew that Ade was not a man to smoke too much ganja and rarely in public. Ade's theory was that it dulled the mind and slowed reactions. But once in a while he liked to indulge himself. They had time to kill while they waited for Paul Akers to show.

Paul Akers, the fool, the man they had come to kill, was the cause of the present vexation between the two friends.

Earlier that day Ade had been chilling in his council crib with Janet. Ade had his own place because his uncle worked for the local authority in Hackney and was a senior member of the housing department. It was widely known amongst certain circles that for a not-so-small fee Mr Isiakpere would make it his business to put any name he chose at the top of the list for available council flats. Since Dunstan was far too busy running his recreational activities on the streets of east and north London to learn how to pronounce 'Isiakpere', he often referred to Ade's uncle as 'Boo-Boo'. Being something of a diplomat however, Dunstan refrained from using this name when Ade was within earshot.

# THE LAST CARD

Unfortunately, earlier that day, Dunstan, annoyed with Ade, had forgotten his manners.

Dunstan had driven over to Ade's in his Jeep, expecting to pick him up so that the two of them could drive over to Streatham, meet up with Paul and do what they had to do. Dunstan was keen to take this business with White Alan to the next level. Tonight.

He'd expected Ade to be ready and waiting. What he'd found was Ade, still in his underwear, sprawled on his sofa with a nearly naked Janet, watching *Scary Movie 2*.

'What kin'a fuckrise is dis! We're suppose to be down outside Caesar's in half an 'our!'

'Er . . . yeah, yeah, I overslept.' Ade looked at his watch. It was just after ten. Still half-asleep he rose and stumbled from the room.

'You 'ave to come into de place screamin' and shoutin'?' This was Janet. In just her bra and knickers she sat up and glared at Dunstan, completely unembarrassed by her state of undress. As Dunstan looked down at her it occurred to him that he loved to put a woman in a headlock and drag her down as much as the next man. And he had to admit Janet was fit like a butcher's dog: she had long slim legs, a tight arse and ebony skin; she had her hair fixed with long, braided extensions. Yes, Dunstan thought, she was well fit but he still didn't care for her too tough. In his opinion the woman was so hasty she was feisty and no matter how fit she was, man is man and man has his business to do.

'Yeah, well das wha' being in business is all about, you get me!' Dunstan fixed her with an evil eye. 'Too many black people come like dis is joke business; dis is not joke business, you know!'

'Yeah, well dis is our home, you know't I mean, I don't like you jus' walkin' in here giving orders! Wha' about some privacy?'

'Listen Janet, don' let me 'ave to get ignoran' on you, you get me? You t'ink say you fit so dat give you licence to run race wid man!' Janet continued to glare at him. A few seconds later she shook her head, a gesture which seemed to indicate nothing but pity and contempt for Dunstan. She rose, picked up two half-finished bowls of peanut soup from the floor and sauntered from the room. Dunstan's eyes, squinting, followed her every step of the way.

'Don' even bodder to try flex wid me, Janet! Dis crib ain't even yours anyway!'

Janet stopped and turned. 'Wha' you talkin' abaht? Ade's uncle gave dis to us, dis is our home!'

Dunstan showed her an evil smile. 'You mean Boo-Boo? You should shu' you mout', bitch, cos Boo-Boo soon gone get ketchup! You t'ink say dem council man dere can go on wid dem teefing ways for too long? Nah, man, I don't t'ink so! Dey soon come and take back dis flat!'

Ade had been coming down the hallway, tucking his shirt into his trousers and had heard this exchange

'And anyway, dis is Ade's place, not yours!'

Janet decided to take another tack, one she'd tried before and knew to be effective.

'You're not jealous, are you Dunstan?' Her voice was now soft and seductive. 'I know you'd like to sleep wiv Ade but . . .?' Janet didn't have time to finish her thoughts on Dunstan's sleeping arrangements. He stepped towards her looking to give her one slap in her neck bone. Janet saw it coming and scooted towards the door, colliding with Ade as he came in from the hall. The bowls of soup she was carrying bounced off his chest; the soup poured down his front and the bowls crashed to the floor.

It was only when Dunstan and Ade were on the way to Streatham that Ade complained that his Salvatore Ferragamo trousers were ruined. Still vex himself, Dunstan asked if Salvatore Ferragamo was the crusty Italian man who ran the chip shop by the traffic lights on Mare Street.

Ade exploded. He did not appreciate Dunstan's brand of humour and he did not appreciate Dunstan referring to his uncle as Boo-Boo. And if there was any more of this kind of fuckrise he would have to reconsider his friendship with Dunstan. Dunstan could deal with Paul Akers on his own. And there you had it. They both understood the root of the argument and it had nothing to do with being late or peanut soup.

Since the argument about Ferragamo, neither had spoken a word. But Dunstan built up his super-spliff and calmed down. He looked at his friend.

'You all right now? You cool?' He smiled. Ade smiled back.

'Don't smoke too much of that shit, man, we got work to do, you know.'

# THE LAST CARD

'Don' worry about it, every t'ing cook and curry.' Dunstan's demeanour became serious as he paused, thinking about what to say next. The powerful sensi worked through him and he felt easier. 'As soon as we tek dis man out . . . I wanna bust a move on Alan.'

'So we're gonna do it?' Ade's smile broadened.

'Yeah, we're gonna do it.'

'Okay. I didn't hear you mention anything about globalisation for a while so I thought maybe you gone cold on the idea.'

'Nah, man, I'm down. But it's all abaht timing, innit? You can't fuck up a move like dis, because you only get one shot, you know't I mean?'

'For real . . .'

'I'm jus' t'inking abaht dat man, Gavin. White Alan's slave. You t'ink you could take him?'

'You even need to ask?'

'You de man, Ade. Dat's why we make such a good team.'

\* \* \*

It was 1.43 a.m. and the Jeep was still parked opposite Caesar's on the corner of Streatham High Street and Amesbury Avenue. Dunstan and Ade had long finished the spliff and the two of them sat smoking cigarettes as they kept their eyes peeled on the front of the club. People had been leaving in ones and twos since about one, so Dunstan and Ade paid rapt attention.

Their diligence paid off. Paul left the club with another man, about the same age. Dunstan and Ade looked at each other. Dunstan could tell from the shrug of Ade's shoulders that he didn't know the second man. As far as they knew he wasn't part of Akers' gang. As far as they knew.

Both men were in high spirits, laughing together as they left the club and turned on to the high street. Shit! The Jeep was across the road, facing right: the opposite direction! Dunstan gunned the engine and swung out to the traffic lights at the end of the block. They were red. While Dunstan kept his eyes on the lights, Ade peered behind him, watching Paul and the man with him. They turned down a side street.

'Fuck sake, man, they've just turned a corner!'

'Just keep your eye on that corner!' The lights changed to amber. Dunstan performed a dramatic U-turn that had his wheels screaming.

They raced back past Caesar's, one eye on the lookout for Babylon. They passed the end of the block and Dunstan dropped the Jeep into second, slowly approaching the turning Paul had taken. Barrhill Road – short, quiet and residential. The Jeep eased around the corner, picking up speed as it made its way down to the T-junction at its end. Another quiet residential street. Which way? They looked to the left. Nothing. They looked to the right. A little way down the road a long, low XJS was parked up. Standing next to it, no more than ten metres away, was Paul Akers.

Paul was at the open door of the Jaguar, bending as he spoke to the driver. The man with him leant with his back against the rear door. Dunstan slowly drove round the corner; there was nothing else he could do. Staying where they were would immediately have attracted attention. Despite their youth, he thought to himself, despite their bickering, despite the sudden and unexpected emergence of their quarry round the corner, Dunstan and Ade were good at what they did.

As they drove past, Ade leant down to the concealed compartment in his passenger door. He pressed the pressure point to release the cover. He pulled out the Desert Eagle. He lifted it up to the level of the window and, as the Jeep cruised past the Jaguar, Ade let fly. The man with his back to them danced as his body was riddled with bullets. Paul had a split-second warning. As the bullet flew towards him Paul dropped to the ground and rolled away from the car.

Having supplied the XJS with a new ventilation system, taking down one man and possibly taking out the driver, Dunstan stopped the Jeep, engine running.

Inside, he and Ade craned their necks, their eyes wide, searching for Paul. No sign. Where was he? After the explosion of gunfire there was now silence. The engine idled, dogs barked, lights were going on in the houses in the road.

'Did you get him?'

'Reverse! Go back!'

'Did you fuckin' get him?'

'I don't know!' Silence, heavy breathing. Nobody moved by the smoking, ruined Jaguar. In another nearby flat the light snapped on. Curtains were twitching. Dunstan slammed the car into reverse, raced it back, screeched to a stop. Ade peered out of his window. Silence. Nothing. His eyes searched the Jaguar, straining to see under it, behind it. Still nothing. He opened his door. About to step out. Wa-wa, wa-wa, wa-wa, wa-wa! It was faint but they could hear it. Babylon coming! Dunstan rammcd the Jeep into first, slammed his foot down, popped the clutch. The back of the Jeep smoked as the huge wheels screamed for purchase. Purchase found, engine roaring, still in first, Dunstan and Ade tore into the night.

\* \* \*

Blairderry Road was once again quiet. More lights came on now, more curtains twitched, bodies were silhouetted in the bright glass. A window opened and an elderly man looked out, squinting into the night. His eyesight wasn't what it used to be and he leant forward, peering into a dark and blurry world. Had he taken the trouble to find his glasses, he would have seen a nearly new XJS with its front door open, a number of its windows shattered, and the windows that remained splashed with blood. The old man would have seen the body of a black man, balding, probably in his mid-thirties, lying face-up, half in and half out of the driver's seat. If the elderly man had been able to stand it and continue looking, he would have seen another man, a white man this time, about the same age, lying outside the car. This man too had been hit with bullets, in his back, on his arms, through the centre of his right temple. His broken body lay awkwardly across the pavement leaking the evidence of its abuse.

As the street slowly came alive to take note of the aftermath of the American-style drive-by, a figure, not seen by the old man in the window, lay huddled in his neighbour's front garden. The fact that the figure had his elbow embedded in a relatively fresh dog turd in no way altered the gratitude with which he cleaved to the shadows of the hedge. The figure was Paul Akers and he was shaking, shaken and had his eyes wide open. Unlike his two colleagues, Paul Akers was very much alive.

# 20.

In an alleyway off Vallance Road in Whitechapel, the back door of a shebeen burst open with the force of a kick. Three burly Bengali men piled out, dragging a struggling and dishevelled H. In the cool of the night, H was tossed like a sack of potatoes on to a smelly, sweating pile of rubbish. Looking down at H without pity, Shohidur, one of the Bengali men, dug his hand into the pocket of his cargo trousers and pulled out a thick coil of notes.

'Take a taxi, H. Get some sleep.' Shohidur peeled off a twenty-pound note and tossed it at him. The night was airless and the note fluttered back and forth, falling gently to the greasy ground. H, bleary-eyed and reeking of smoke and alcohol, sat up on the rubbish to face his persecutors. He ignored the note lying next to him, examining instead the tear that had appeared along the seam of his lucky suit, under his right arm. He looked up at Shohidur. One of the other Bengali men smiled down at H and said something in Sylheti. All three of the Bengalis laughed and H's face darkened.

'Ask me, Shohidur.' H was aware of a thick burr to his voice, put there by the six shots of Jack Daniels he'd had in quick succession.

'Ask you what?'

'Ask me why the three of you look so fucking ugly when you laugh!' The three stopped laughing. 'You're like the three fucking gargoyles on the corners of the Chrysler building in New York. You know the one I mean? Yeah, yeah, the three of you are like, like, like masterpieces of gothic masonry. It's the extended foreheads and the big mouths full of brown stained . . .'

That was as far as H could get before the side of Shohidur's shoe caught him a glancing blow on his cheek. Luckily he'd seen it coming and had just managed to move his head. Had he caught its full weight it could have been all she wrote. Shohidur leant down and picked up the twenty-pound note he'd so casually dropped for H's taxi-ride home.

And with that the three Bengalis were gone. H heard the door being heavily bolted and barred from inside.

He sat on the pile of rubbish for several minutes, his chin resting on his hands. As he stared blankly into the blackness of the night he gradually became aware of the poster on the wall opposite. It was a billboard poster of a boxer. The poster was old, advertising an up-and-coming fight that had, in fact, long gone. The boxer whose picture hung smiling in the blackness of that grubby, Whitechapel alleyway was Henry 'Bugle Boy' Mancini.

H had come straight down from the Grundy Park Leisure Centre to this Bengali-run shebeen in Whitechapel. Operated by the diminutive VJ, Whitechapel's longest-running illegal gambling den was a haven for less-than-devout Muslims from all over London. As well as the Muslims, the usual West End habitués often stopped in to give VJ's a run and the games were accompanied by entertainingly raucous and sometimes violent discussion about world affairs. The mood H had been in that night meant it was exactly the atmosphere he needed: a reminder that the world had problems bigger than his.

H didn't necessarily have to participate in these discussions; just listening was entertainment enough. He could remember one particularly entertaining night when the topic of discussion had been Bill Clinton and his ill-fated affair with Monica Lewinski. A number of the clientele in the shebeen that night were big fans of Clinton. They couldn't understand what all the fuss was about.

The topic in the house on this particular evening was the continuing presence of George W. Bush's American troops in Iraq. As H sat himself down at the table with worries of his own swirling around in his head, the discussion was already in free flow. Since the ramifications of Bush's decision were of particular significance to the largely Muslim gamblers, the mood round the table was as raucous as usual but less humorous.

'That fucking Bush! He needs to be dealt with,' scowled a young Pakistani mechanic called Harwant who had arrived in London from Birmingham two or three years ago. He threw his beaten hand into the middle of the table in disgust. 'They should deal with him like the IRA used to; shoot off his kneecaps.' The violence of his comment was no doubt prompted by the failure of his pair of aces to result in a win.

Whatever the reason, it was received with general nods of approval – despite Harwant's failure to outline who 'they' should be. H, meanwhile had also lost the last hand and as his worries mounted he listened to the conversation flowing around him with only half an ear.

'Wha' you tarkin' about? You cian' do dat to the President!' This was the elderly and feisty Sanjay, the Trinidadian Indian who had lived in London for the last twenty-five years and who smoked incessantly.

'Why not? They shot the Kennedys, they shot Martin Luther King, they can shoot Bush!' Harwant drained his rum and coke and held up his empty glass. A plump woman in a sari silently took it from him and went away to refill it.

'You don' see de man 'ave body guard aroun' him 24-7?' Sanjay was so incensed by Harwant's naivety that he coughed and hawked loudly into a handkerchief. He carefully examined the result of his loud lung evacuation, wrapped it up and slipped it into his trouser pocket.

'I don't care about that; he's a dangerous man.'

'And you don't think Bin Laden is equally dangerous?' Devinder was a Bengali man in his late sixties and was generally accepted as being the most widely read of the shebeen's habitués as well as being a fair poker player. In keeping with the esteem with which he was held by the other Muslim players, he spoke in a soft voice.

'Bush is a colonialist and the world has seen enough of colonialists!'

'Dis is not a colonial war. Were you not dere to see the pictures of the two towers in New York burning?'

H was only vaguely aware of who Devinder was but by this point in the evening he didn't care. Things were not going well for him and an element of desperation had entered his play. His customary coolness under pressure had deserted him and he was still waiting for his first win of the night.

VJ always allowed the alcohol to flow freely, and despite the number of Muslims in the house the drinks were always consumed with enthusiasm. H was no slouch in the drinking stakes and was well into his third Jack Daniels.

'Terrorism is an evil! It's an evil! It has been taken to a new low. And it has made the world a much more dangerous place.'

# THE LAST CARD

'And who are you to define who is a terrorist and who is not a terrorist?' This was Manmohan, the manager of the petrol station on Cambridge Heath Road.

'More dangerous than terrorism is that black woman who hangs on Bush's shoulder like a vulture. What's her name? Something Rice?'

'She's a hawk, not a vulture.'

'She looks like a love machine. I quite like her.'

'That's because you haven't had sex in a long time, sir.'

'Fucking hell! That woman should be forcibly strapped in a burqa.'

'And that is precisely my point,' said Devinder in a silky voice. 'The burqa is an instrument of repression that is holding much of the population in the Middle East in bondage.'

Devinder's observation made the others stop and think. But not so deeply that they would look at the plump woman in the sari in a new light as she returned with Harwant's rum and coke. Devinder now waved her over. He handed her his full glass of whisky and water.

'This tastes like mosquito piss, take it back. Bring it back with a decent amount of whisky in it.' He imperiously waved her away and turned back to more important things. 'You see the problem with the worst excesses of Islam, fundamentalists like those bastards the Taliban, is that the oppression of women is a wastage of human resources. The state of much of the Middle East today suggests to me that they cannot afford to waste fifty per cent of their intellectual resources.'

'You tarkin' like you smart, Devinder, but you tarkin' shit! You see my wife?' Sanjay squinted at the hand that had just been dealt to him. 'I would love to hol' 'er in a burqa.' He suddenly whiplashed his index finger and the finger next to it together with loud crack. Evidently Sanjay was pleased with the cards he had been dealt. 'I tell she me is a man an' I want to come out and pass some time wid de boys,' he smiled broadly at his cards as he sorted them out in his hand, 'an' she want to start!' He looked up and around the table. 'Who going firs'?'

For H, who went first no longer mattered. He would usually have interjected with his own thoughts on the banter that flowed all around him. Tonight, however, was not one of those nights. He lost his hand and over the next two hours he lost many more. It was at the loss of his last £20 – from the £300 that had been his purse from the evening's boxing – that he finally lost his temper too. H rose unsteadily to his feet, grabbed the edge of the gambling table and tipped the whole thing – cards, money, drinks – over on its side. The shouting, cursing and threats that followed were ended when the houseman, Shohidur, and his henchmen grabbed H. They frog-marched him to the exit at the rear of the shebeen and threw him into the rubbish.

\*\*\*

As H sat and contemplated his fate, he looked away from the image of the smiling Mancini, apparently sent to taunt him, and dipped his hand into the pocket of his jacket. He pulled out his talisman. He looked at it for a long time, waiting for it to explain why his life was going so badly wrong. He had four days left with which to find £15,000. Four days! Having stared drunkenly at the lighter for a while and found no answers, H slipped it back into his pocket, eased him-self off the rubbish heap and headed for the end of the alley.

Back on Vallance and rubbing the cheek where he'd been kicked, H turned right and walked with difficulty to Hanbury Street, where his car was parked in the shadow of a tower block. The first thing he saw was the broken glass on the passenger's seat. Suddenly he knew this night could still get worse. He walked round the car and saw that the front window had been smashed. The stereo had been ripped out. Adding insult to injury was the front door on the driver's side, unlocked. The smashed windows were a wanton act of vandalism. H walked around the car to see if any other damage had been done. The front two tyres had been slashed. Why?

'Fucking . . . Jesus Christ!' H swore under his breath. The insult to his gunmetal-grey vintage Mercedes, circa 1973, sobered him. He stood up straight, hoping to see the vandal. The streets were empty. He turned, pulled up the collars on his lucky suit and wandered off, back past the shebeen to the Whitechapel Road. He didn't know where he was going but did know that he couldn't face his empty flat in Battersea.

Tired and footsore, H walked down Wardour street. He hadn't been heading anywhere in particular, but as he neared the centre of town it seemed natural to aim for Blackie's shebeen. The night was warm and H had walked all the way from Whitechapel. And while he walked, H thought. About Beverley, about Akers, about his boxing, about his life.

Did he really love Beverley? Or was she just a convenience? Certainly he loved Cyrus but the fact that he was less certain about Beverley worried him. He was deeply hurt by her abandonment of their relationship. Why had she done that? Of course, he knew why she'd done it, but still . . . why had she done it? Then he thought about his boxing. Why did he continue? Was he trying to prove something? Did he even enjoy boxing any more? And what about the connection Beverley saw between his gambling and the boxing? Was she right about that?

And finally H came back to the £15,000 he owed Akers. £15,000! Why was it that H was walking along the embankment with absolutely no money to his name? None! Zero! How was it that H, a grown man of thirty-two, could possibly have allowed this to happen? England is the fourth richest nation in the world; was it that H was so dumb, so inadequate, that he couldn't carve himself a slice of that wealth?

All these thoughts and more ran around and round H's head. And the more they ran the more one single thought seemed to dig into him. It was a rising sense of panic that somehow he was becoming invisible. He was walking past people, watching them, and they all seemed to be oblivious to him, to his presence, to his physicality. He was like a ghost, like a shadow, flitting though the streets of London. He wanted to shout, he wanted to jump up and down, wave his arms about: Hey! Look at me! I'm here! I exist! I'm not a shadow, I'm real, I exist!

So deep in thought was H that he missed the turning to Blackie's shebeen and continued on down Wardour Street. As he was passing Meard Street, on the left, he saw a small crowd of people, hanging around outside Gossips nightclub. He stopped. The vague bass line thump of Burning Spear's 'Marcus Garvey' insinuated its way into his head. With its lilting melody a memory floated into H's mind. He and Spiky Conway, a white schoolfriend, had first heard this track in a record shop in Brixton. Something about it immediately appealed to both of them and H had promptly started skanking – the popular dance style of the day – right there in the record shop. As H bent his knees and poked out his small bottom, bobbing it up and down in time to the music, Spiky began to copy him. Neither H nor Spiky could dance particularly and the sight of the two of them – they couldn't have been more than thirteen years old – had the shop assistants in stitches as they bobbed and bounced in time with the music . . .

H's eyes suddenly pricked with tears.

# 21.

**A**s the weak sunlight streamed in through grimy windows, H lay sprawled and sleeping on his mattress. He was still in his lucky suit, still wearing his shoes. Lying next to him on the floor was his talisman and, next to that, his goldfish, swimming in its bowl.

H's eyes opened as he slowly came to. Jesus Christ! His head was killing him. He didn't move a muscle except the small ones that controlled his eyes. He needed these to stare up at the ceiling. His head was pounding, throbbing in waves. For the first time, and it was a surprise to him, he saw what a terrible job somebody had done in painting the bedroom. H wondered why he had never noticed that before.

H tensed his neck and then moved his arms as he propped his body up. He groaned as he looked around. The room was a mess. He swung his feet round, clambered off the mattress and walked stiffly through to the kitchen.

In the cupboard above the small cooker, sitting on top of a tin of pilchards, was a bottle of aspirin. He swallowed two with a glass of water and looked in the fridge. Inside, lurking at the back, was half a carton of milk, a dry, crusty lump of cheese and a mango. H lifted out the carton and put it to his nose. He withdrew it quickly and poured its curdled contents down the sink.

Above the sink was a window that looked out over the back of the flats. Leaning his forehead against the glass, H watched the life of the estate continue, oblivious to his problems. Reggie was outside tinkering with his ancient BMW, which H was sure he had been working on for as long as the two of them had been neighbours. A number of small children played on the nearby swings. Two old ladies, one white, one black, walked slowly arm-in-arm along the grass verges that surrounded the estate. Life went on.

H took off his jacket and threw it over the wooden chair, the only piece of furniture left in the room. He ran the tap in the kitchen sink and dunked his head under it, feeling the revitalising cold of the water. Unable to find a tea-towel, he grabbed his good Lilliard jacket and used it to dry his face. *Plus ça change!*

Feeling refreshed, H stared blankly out of the window again. Slowly he nodded his head, resigning himself to what he would do next.

Dressed in jeans and a clean tee-shirt, H opened the holdall he used for his training kit and stood before his boxing trophies. Carefully, he packed them into the holdall, zipped it up and left the flat.

H knew of a pawn shop in Islington which would take the trophies. He wouldn't get what they were worth, he knew that. But he also knew that for them to go, to justify their passing, that moment, that second, would have to be a new beginning . . .

The rays of the afternoon's weak sunlight had given up their struggle and now hid behind a quickly greying sky. Rain threatened. H looked at the shop on the corner of St John Street and Goswell Road. It was an old Victorian premises and H had been there a number of times in the past as his preoccupation with gambling had increased. On his last visit he'd pawned his Tag Heuer 2000 watch, bought with the winnings of one of his largest purses. It had been a particularly unpleasant occasion since he'd known he was unlikely ever to redeem it. He had sworn then that he would never be back. H navigated St John Street and cautiously entered the shop. The bell tinkled as he crossed the threshold. Fortunately there were no other customers inside; H was in no mood to face the panoply of London's poor and disenfranchised – giving up their baubles, trinkets and the consumer goods that made struggling lives seem less of a struggle.

A middle-aged man, pale and sour-looking, with thinning ginger hair, stepped forward. He eyed H with no particular warmth.

'You again. What can I do for you?'

Grimly, H lifted up his holdall and, one by one, took out his most prized possessions. These were the trophies of a lifetime's endeavour, the tangible symbols of hard-earned excellence; these few possessions gave much of H's life meaning.

# THE LAST CARD

The shopkeeper picked up, turned over, felt the heft of and closely examined each of the statuettes and trophies with meticulous, professional care.

'I'll give you a hundred pounds for the lot.'

\*\*\*

Walking with a heavy tread, H approached the door of his good friend Blue. He needed someone to talk to. Despite being twenty-nine, Blue still lived with his parents in Willesden. The lash of gentrification that had affected other parts of the city had not touched this part of north-west London, but house prices were still rising quickly. It was fortunate that he got on well with his parents as there was little chance for a man like Blue either to buy or rent his own place.

Looking up at the big Victorian house, H thought back to his relationship with his own parents, before they returned to Montserrat. Both had been young teachers when they came to England in the 1950s and had arrived at these shores with the zeal and enthusiasm common to most of that first wave of immigrants. At last! They were feasting in the bosom of the mother country!

Unfortunately, the mother country had other ideas. The depressing weather, the frosty attitude of the people and the lack of career opportunities saw that initial immigrant zeal drift away into memory. Gone! Like the Caribbean sunshine!

Joseph, H's father, eventually settled into work at a paint factory. His mother, Sara, after a number of manual jobs, drifted into secretarial work in an unemployment office.

These facts needn't have blighted H's life, but they had. Again, like most immigrants, H's parents had wanted better for their son. They wanted him to have the kind of career they had been denied: a good, professional job as a doctor, a lawyer, a teacher. When H had first shown prowess as an athlete, his parents had been proud. Particularly his father. Joseph had loved to go to the fights and watch his son dance his way to victory. But as it became clear that Hilary, their youngest son, and the most academic, was gradually allowing the thrill of this game, this hobby, to take precedence over his studies, their pride slowly turned to annoyance. When annoyance turned to anger, H's relationship with his parents became increasingly difficult.

By the time Joseph and Sara returned to Montserrat H was barely in contact with them. He'd moved out some time before and was living in various short-term rooms paid for with part-time work as either a postman or a builder, depending on the season.

With all the career opportunities that England offered, H's parents never understood their son's lifestyle. In the days when H was winning fights and journalists spoke of him as a world championship contender, they found it difficult. But when things began to slide, when, having turned professional, H was mostly losing his fights, they were able to say to him, 'You see? I tol' you dis fightin' is not a t'ing for a man like you! Wid all you education! Why you don' look a proppa job? Proppa!'

Six years ago, both his parents had died in a road accident. That was the worst. And in a way, that was when H had realised that he couldn't stop the boxing. For him to stop a piece of him would have to die. And with the loss of his trophies, a piece of him had.

\*\*\*

H knocked on Blue's door. A moment later it opened and Blue stood before him, in white vest and jeans, tall and dramatic, locks hanging down his back. Blue embraced him in a hug.

'Long time, man, how you doing, H?'

'Not too good, man, not too good.'

'Yeah? Come inside, talk to me, man. Tell me all your troubles. You know I'm gonna make them all go away.' The two entered the house and walked through a hallway leading to the large kitchen at the back. 'I've got a friend here but he's going soon, then we can talk.'

On the way through the hallway they passed the front room, where a photographer was taking pictures, Blue's mother looking on proudly. H poked his head through the doorway and called over to the sprightly Jamaican woman.

'Hello, Mrs G, how are you?'

'Oh, hello, Hilary, I'm all right, t'ank you very much.'

'I see you finally made the cover of *Good Housekeeping* then?' He nodded towards the tall photographer. Mrs Groover laughed appreciatively.

'Oh, no! Dis young man is a journalist. From *The Voice*. 'E's doin' a piece on . . . on, what was it again, young man?'

The journalist stopped taking photos and turned to face H. They shook hands.

'Hi. Kolton. I'm doing a piece for Black History Month on the aesthetics of the West Indian Front Room.'

'Das right, 'is name is "Kolton", not "Carlton".'

'The West Indian Front Room?' H said, puzzled.

'You know, the aesthetics of the flowery wallpaper, the colourful doilies,' he waved a hand airily round the room. 'The plastic that covers the sofa and chairs; where all that stuff comes from, why our parents, the first generation that came over from the Caribbean, designed their front rooms like that.'

'Cool. I'll look out for the article.' H waved again at Mrs G and went to join Blue in the kitchen.

Blue stood at the cooker pouring hot water into two mugs. He handed one to H, and passed the other to another man, who was sitting at a round breakfast table to one side of the room.

'H, meet Wha Gwan, Wha Gwan, this is H.'

As H nodded at Wha Gwan and Wha Gwan nodded back, H looked at him closely. He had half of his hair tightly bound in cane rows, but the other half was loose, a style favoured amongst the brothers in north London. H was sure he'd seen him before but he couldn't remember where.

'Is that fool from *The Voice* still doing his interview with your mum?' The question was squeezed through a scowl that seemed to grip Wha Gwan's entire body.

'Relax, man, my mum likes showing the "nice young man" around. It's not often she gets the chance to show people her doilies and t'ings, you know't I mean!'

'It's a piece for Black History Month, apparently,' said H.

'Black History Month! That's a joke!' snapped Wha Gwan.

'Like that's the only time of the year our history's relevant, you know what I mean!' Blue added.

'You know't I mean,' echoed Wha Gwan, with special emphasis.

'Listen my friend, white people in this country, they don't want people to know our history. They don't even want people to know their history because it's a history of cruelty, barbarity and exploitation. Pure and simple. Hmph! Black History Month!' Wha Gwan dunked a digestive biscuit aggressively into his coffee.

Blue looked across at H.

'Wha Gwan is a Science Fictionist. He's got a theory that white people . . .'

'. . . aren't human like alla we.' Wha Gwan needed no prompting to expound on his own theory. 'They are another species of human altogether and their sole aim is to destroy the planet.' Wha Gwan paused while he bit into the moist digestive. 'They're going to destroy it through the enslavery of other races; the black man, the yellow man, the brown man and the red man. They're also going to destroy the planet's resources; rinse out all the oil in the Middle East, mash up the rain forests, tear out the ozone layer and unleash genetically modified foods on people.' Wha Gwan stared at H as though challenging him to dispute the truth of his statements.

'That's a radical theory,' said H, not quite sure how best to respond.

'These are not theories, my friend, these are facts. Facts! The war between white people in the east and white people in the west has ended. That was the cold war. The war between the Germans and other Europeans has ended. The second European war, which they called the World war. Now that they've finished fighting each other, they're concentrating on taking over everything from everybody. America and Europe. White people.'

H nodded wisely, wondering how, exactly, he was going to ease himself out of this conversation. He'd come round to talk to Blue about his problems with Akers and Beverley, not argue with a Science Fictionist over his theories of Caucasian world domination. Unfortunately, Wha Gwan seemed to be on a roll.

H had met many black people who, when the pressure of being black and a minority in a white man's world became too much, invented all sorts of elaborate reasons for the white man's social, political and cultural dominance. Wha Gwan's Science Fictionist idea was one of the more outlandish, but that seemed merely a testament to Wha Gwan's intelligence and imagination. H's reality however, was bound up in a more physical realm. All the things that you couldn't control, all the petty injustices in life, all of that could be shed in one place: the boxing ring. For H, the ring didn't lie.

'So what's your solution to the plight of the black man?'

'The pen and the sword.' Having reached this point in his train of thought Wha Gwan seemed to calm down. 'You see we need to educate the yout'. Dem man runnin' road, playin' gangster but dey don't know nutten about history and dey don't know nutten about respect. All dey want to do is chat "grime". No, man, we need the pen to educate; to educate is to liberate. And then we need the sword; because, in this society, education is not enough. We need the sword to smite dem! Because you know what? I'm going to get mines! And when I get mines . . .'

H looked down at his coffee. Jesus Christ! Did this guy ever stop talking? He was past caring about Wha Gwan's theory. He looked over at his good friend Blue, who was listening intently. H sighed. It wasn't often that he really needed someone to talk to. He glanced at Wha Gwan, barely hearing the words but still watching the man's jawbone working overtime: up, down, up, down.

'. . . A powerful man is a dangerous thing,' cried Wha Gwan. 'A man that knows himself, knows his worth and the power he has as an individual . . . can accomplish many things!'

# 22.

Nina sat in her BMW Z3 Roadster wearing Jean-Paul Gaultier sunglasses and waiting for H to show up. She was in the car park of a council estate in south London. Battersea. She looked around her. Although it was spring, she was struck by how much of everything looked grey. Even the grass.

Four parking spaces away from her an old dreadlocked black man was leaning into the bonnet of a BMW. It was the oldest, shabbiest and rustiest a vehicle could be and still be called a car. It seemed to have been constructed from at least three different models. The front of the car had no tyres and sat on two rusty wheel ramps. The man was leaning under the bonnet, his dreadlocks – thick and gnarled – reaching down to his waist. They showed flecks of grey. The dirty boiler-suit he wore was a light blue-grey. On the charcoal-grey of the tarmac, next to the dreadlock, was a metallic-grey boom-box. From it poured thick, rhythmic reggae. Nina smiled as the bass line dropped and blasting horns trilled playfully over the top. It was the sole spot of colour in the landscape.

Nina had grown up with reggae and the mechanic's boom-box provided a soundtrack as familiar as the world of grey that currently surrounded her. She liked the music, hated the grey. Opening her car door, Nina stretched her legs out and looked up at the sky. It too was grey; a light, pale shade, then darker and bluer, and finally a wispy, smoky colour hung on the horizon. The sky seemed to sit just above the top of the tower blocks, pressing down, closing her in. While she looked up a small aeroplane droned slowly overhead. It trailed a thin line of vapour. Grey.

Nina sat and pondered the meaning of grey and the reasons that it made her sad. Sitting on H's council estate reminded her of how far she'd come in scrambling away from the poverty of her own child-hood. Like climbing up a sheer rock face without a safety net, she had clung on with the grip of her fingers and toes and will. You gripped that rock face with every bit of your strength because your life depended on it. To fall was to be ripped, broken and bashed on the jagged rocks of poverty.

Nina was jerked from her thoughts by the sight of a man approaching. He walked slowly, shoulders slumped, head down.

'Hilary!'

The man stopped and turned back. The dreadlock also looked over at her. Nina rose from her car, locked it and set the alarm. She walked over to H, suddenly aware of the contrast between herself and her surroundings. It wasn't so much the drama of the French-made, Japanese-designed coat, although it was dramatic, cascading down her shoulders and reaching almost to her ankles. It wasn't the mystery suggested by the ostentation of the large Gaultier sun-glasses, or even the deep red that coloured her lips. It was simpler than all of that. It was the sheen of health and care that emanated from the sheet of dark, straight hair that fell below her shoulders; it was the creamy, smooth glow of her complexion; it was the healthy, upright posture that exuded wellbeing. Nina looked damn good walking over to H, and she knew it.

'What are you doing here?' H was startled by her appearance.

'Yeah, and I'm pleased to see you, too. Where the hell have you been?'

'I've been busy. Why?'

'I was in the area, I thought I'd stop by.' Nina watched as H glanced over at the dreadlock behind her back.

'D'you want to come up?'

Nina smiled sweetly. She'd put him on the spot. He led the way into the tower block.

In the flat H tossed the empty holdall into a corner and disap-peared into an adjoining room, returning with a small cardboard pot. He squatted down by the goldfish bowl and sprinkled in a precise amount of fish food, watching in silence as the fish ate. Nina's eyes lingered on his physique, noting the large thighs and the tightness of his thin, cotton jacket across his shoulders. Yes, H was a solidly built man. A man well capable of doing what she and Gavin needed him to. Nina knew she could toy with him, but the trick was in knowing just how far she could push. From the look on his face today, she judged, not too far.

'How did you find out where I lived?' He seemed distracted and continued to gaze at the bowl, directing his questions at the fish.

'Gavin told me.'

'How did he know?'

'He's a bright man.'

'I don't like people coming here.'

'Why? It's a nice place.' That got his attention. H slowly turned to look at her.

'Don't push me, Nina.' He strode from the room back to wherever he'd gone before. Nina sighed and sauntered slowly after him. He was in the kitchen. She watched as he filled the kettle and put it on the cooker.

'You're in a good mood.'

'I've had a good day.'

'Have you got White Alan's money yet?'

'What's it got to do with you?' He glared at her as he leant against the worktop, arms folded across his chest. Nina removed her sunglasses in a gesture of conciliation.

'Look, let's start again: I knew you wouldn't call me, that's why I came over.' She paused. She was making an effort now and she waited for him to say something. He said nothing. 'We've been through the '90s, women can make the first move now.'

Despite himself, H smiled. Finally.

'That's better! Now whatever your problems are, Hilary, I'm going to make you forget them. Just for this evening.'

H actually snorted through his nose and laughed out loud at that.

'You can drop your hard man act, it doesn't work with me. And just one sugar, please. White.'

H almost smiled again. He turned to the cupboard. When he opened it to take out two mugs Nina could see that he only had two mugs.

The kettle whistled as the water boiled. H made instant coffee, stirring sugar into one of the cups.

'Milk?' Nina asked more in hope than conviction. H shook his head and for a moment the two of them sipped their black coffee in silence. Nina looked at him while H looked out of the window, his thoughts, seemingly, elsewhere.

The afternoon sun must have disappeared behind a cloud because a gloom settled in the small, cramped kitchen. Watching the shadows on H's face, Nina said, 'What would you like to do today?'

\* \* \*

The Roadster flashed down the motorway, heading for Brighton. H sat next to her, his large frame looking cramped in the sports car. When he'd first climbed in, he'd been like a small boy in a toy shop, examining the dashboard in excitement.

'Why do men always do that?'

'Do what?'

'Get huge erections when they see a nice sports car?'

'Why are you driving a car like this, anyway? You don't need a car like this. You're just driving it to pose. You're a poseur.'

She shot him a glance and he grinned.

'The trouble with you women is you don't actually appreciate the technology for its own sake. I'm a man that can do that.'

'Oh, I get it,' Nina smiled. 'A bit of fresh air and you're feeling good now. You're feeling all macho, like . . . you're feeling like you want an argument? You want to prove yourself right?'

'That's what keeps us all breathing, isn't it?'

'No, that's what keeps you breathing. And most men come to think of it.'

'Yeah, well, I'm just glad to be out of London for a while.' The two lapsed into silence. The late afternoon sunshine lit up the country-side around them.

Nina glanced over at the man she and Gavin were ultimately going to manipulate for their own ends. Was he the man for the job?

'Why the sudden urge for fresh air?'

'I've got a headache.'

'Hangover?'

'Yeah. I've had it for about seven years.'

'O . . . kay. Can I at least ask you where we're going?'

'Brighton.'

'I'd gathered that. Whereabouts?'

'Just drive.'

She half-turned to say something, but changed her mind. In the rear-view mirror she saw that the two small, vertical lines had appeared, just above her eyebrows.

H leant forward to switch on the CD player. Quick as a flash Nina slapped his hand away.

'Ow! That hurt! What was that for?'

Nina gave him an evil smirk and H grinned despite himself.

'You think you're so tough, don't you?'

'I am. I wasn't always this beautiful and sophisticated.'

'Is that right?'

As Sussex flashed by, Nina told him a little of her early life, growing up in a council flat in Stoke Newington with her mother and sisters.

'How did you go from the two-bedroom high-rise,' asked H, 'to the mews house in Holland Park with a Z3 Roadster?'

'It's a long story.'

'We've got time.'

'And not one I want to go into right now.'

H shrugged 'Okay.'

'What about you? What's your story?'

He sighed heavily. 'Jesus, you don't want to know.'

'No, I do, really.' Nina glanced round at him encouragingly. She did want to know. She was finding H increasingly intriguing. He was different from the black guys she had grown up around. Here was this big, tough bloke who was a gambler and a boxer who lived in a council flat. That was normal. But aside from this gambling, boxing persona, some things about H weren't normal at all. For starters, he was quiet, he was articulate and he wasn't drooling after her with his tongue hanging out.

'You know what? Let's just get there. I've had a really, really bad day.'

'Okay.' And that was the last word spoken until Nina parked the car in a space just in front of the Old Hilton Hotel, on Brighton seafront.

# 23.

They stumbled over the sliding pebbles, making their way down to the churning water. H led the way, stooping to scoop up a handful of stones. As he neared the water's edge he threw them, one by one, skimming into the waves; watching them bounce once, twice, three times. He was aware that Nina was just behind him and breathing in the heavy, salty air; he wished he was alone. He set off walking, eastwards, towards the pier. He could hear her scrambling to catch up.

The seaside had always been a special place for H. The ocean reminded him of his place in the world, putting his situation, whatever it might be, into a new context. For H the sea represented freedom, abandon and renewal. He could stand before it for hours, just watching.

H neared the pier and slowed down. Looking up at the end of it he could see people on fun-fair rides, people looking out to sea, fishing, smiling, talking; people just enjoying themselves. He didn't want to join them, just wanted to soak up where he was. He knew he would have to return to reality at some point: to London, to Alan Akers, to Beverley, to his empty flat. But for now, he just wanted to be. He stopped walking and sat down on the pebbles, facing the sea.

Nina came up and sat next to him. H glanced round at her. He was grateful that she hadn't bothered him with chatter. She seemed to sense his need for silence, for contemplation, and had given him that space. Despite having driven him all this way at a moment's notice. He was grateful because while he had been walking he had come to two decisions, one more momentous than the other. First, he'd decided to end his gambling holiday. His attempt to win his way out of his financial problems with Akers had been disastrous. He was experienced enough to know that gambling out of necessity was always a disaster. It established an utterly wrong frame of mind from which to operate.

However, the more important decision, the real decision, was to give up the fight game. That was what he had decided when he sold his boxing trophies. That was one of the things he'd wanted to talk through with Blue. He was going to leave boxing. Not even Beverley had dared to suggest it until the end, but now, with everything else in ruins, H could see that it was the only way. She was right. But she'd had to leave for him to realise it.

It was a terrifying thing to contemplate. And not only because it felt like failure to leave the sport without achieving all that he'd dreamed of. On another, more intrinsic level, H defined himself by his boxing. People knew him as the Shuffler for the silky style that had once been his. He was known as a boxer, it was what he did, it was who he was. Beverley was right. If he really was to kick his gambling habit, the boxing had to go. Discovering who else Hilary Chester Zechariah James could be would have to become part of his journey when he left the sport. This was what terrified him.

'When was the last time you were here?' Nina's hair whipped around her face as she asked the question.

H thought before he answered. 'A long time ago.'

'You know what?'

'What?'

'Big deal! I hate looking back! I hate the sea.'

H looked at her, surprised by the aggression in her voice.

'I like people, I like noise, I like traffic, I like bright lights, I like . . .'

Jesus Christ! H wasn't sure where this outburst had come from but he didn't like it. Just as the last of the urban miasma was leaving him, Nina was working hard to replace it! He cut her short.

'Yeah, yeah, yeah, yeah. Always talking tough.' The edge in his voice must have warned her that this was not the time and she lapsed into silence. He quite liked this woman but he wasn't sure what she was doing here. He couldn't work out what her game was, why she was hanging around him. There were some crazy white women out there who couldn't leave black men alone but she didn't look like one of them. And with her money and her looks she could have anybody. So why him?

Nina removed one of her shoes and massaged her bare foot.

'That was a drive I wasn't expecting.' She continued rubbing her toes and gave a sigh of pleasure. H watched her. Under her coat she wore a pale cream skirt that stopped just above her knees. Beneath that, Nina's legs were bare and from where H was sitting they looked in pretty good shape. The thought suddenly hit him with the force of an unexpected shove in the back: he wanted her.

'You know, you could have potential, Hilary.'

'As what?'

'You're . . . kind of . . . good-looking . . .' She laughed girlishly, but H could hear it was fake. She was playing him.

'Is that a compliment?' He said it dry, without interest in the answer.

'Yes.'

'Thanks.'

'That's okay. But you know what you need?'

'What?'

'Money.'

'Is it that obvious?'

Nina removed her other shoe and swung her feet on to H's thigh. 'Please?'

He looked at her. Now she was taking the piss. Having a laugh. And yet her feet were exquisitely shaped: they were delicate, they had perfect proportion, her toenails were painted the same shade of red as her lips; these feet were dying to be massaged. H could feel a stirring in his groin. His penis pushed at the rumpled material around his crotch.

H rested her heels on his lap. He began to knead her right instep. Nina lay back on the pebbles and closed her eyes. Damn, she looked good! With Nina's feet on his lap, her skin soft and smooth, the stirring in H's groin was becoming more and more pronounced.

'I know how you can make lots of it.'

'What?'

'Money.'

'Oh. How?'

'Alan.'

'What about him?'

'Take some of his.'

H laughed bitterly at this. 'I tried that. It cost me fifteen grand, remember?'

'I could tell you how to do it and not get caught.'

'I'm sure you could, Nina, but . . .'

Nina sat up, leaning on her elbows.

'I know when his money comes in, I know when it goes out, I know his movements. I'm talking about two hundred thousand pounds.' Nina looked at him to see how he would react.

He was staring at her as though she was crazy. 'I don't do that kind of thing. I'm a family man.'

'You've got a family?'

'I've got a boy. Cyrus. He's five; big as a house and twice as tough. He's a great little boy.'

'Hard man like you, I didn't take you for the family type.'

'What? A black man can't be a family man?'

'No, I meant . . .'

'I didn't take you for white trash from the slums of Stoke Newington.'

Nina eased her feet from his lap and put them down in front of her. She drew them in close, hugging her knees.

'So where does he live? Your boy?'

'Hanwell. West London. With his mother. And grandmother. His mother and I don't exactly see eye to eye.'

Nina said nothing for a while.

'So. You're not interested in earning some real money?' Nina's tone was hard now, aggressive.

'What's your problem, Nina?' He wasn't angry, he was interested.

'Not even for you and Cyrus?'

'It's not about Cyrus.' H shrugged. 'It's not my style. I'm not that person.'

She gave him the kind of smile that supercilious right-wingers save for young, clean, good-looking homeless people. 'You're a nice guy, Hilary, but – you have to go for it when the chances come your way. People like us don't get many chances.' Nina leant over and kissed him on the cheek. Then she stood and walked back along the beach.

H watched her go. Jesus Christ! What the hell was that all about? He took one last look at the sea and then followed her back to the car. Soon after they were on their way back to London.

# 24.

**. . . IF I WAS FUCKIN' YOU IN YOUR ASS, RIGHT ABOUT NOW,
YOU'D HAVE A DICK STUCK IN YOU . . .**

The following day, in Nick's gym, Mack Daddy was railing obliquely
against the violence of the 'hood. And while Mack railed, boxers from
all over London pounded, banged and skipped their way to physical
fitness, to a state of readiness, to the brink of inflicting yet more
violence.

**. . . IF I WAS FUCKIN' YOU IN YOUR ASS, SHIT!
I BE CAUSING CHAOS . . . !**

While the volume bludgeoned the senses and the lyrics bludgeoned the sensibilities, H lay on his back doing sit-ups. The sweat
rolled off him as he grimaced. H stuck to a routine that he had used
for years. Perhaps he didn't work at it with the vigour of five or six
years before, but the routine remained the same. Three sets of thirty
sit-ups. The third set was always the killer.

'Eighteen . . .' H hissed through clenched teeth, allowing his torso
to drop slowly down, never easing the tension, telling himself that not
boxing was no reason not to keep in shape. 'Nineteen . . .' H hissed
like a knackered steam kettle. Slowly he allowed his torso to descend
back towards the mat. Because he liked the training almost as much
as the boxing. He struggled to hoist himself back up. 'Twenty!'

The hiss now reeked of desperation and H still had ten sit-ups
to go. His abdominal muscles screamed for mercy. He was in better
shape than the vast majority of men his age. He could still pull the
young birds if he put his mind to it. Again H raised his torso, the sweat
dribbling in rivulets down his face into his tee-shirt. 'Twenty-one . . .'
He couldn't maintain the tension and lay down on the mat. He closed
his eyes and panted with the strain of it. There was no way he could

**153**

stop there, he would have to finish, but he needed this breather. He needed this breather. He . . . needed . . . this . . . breather.

H closed his eyes, forced his breathing to be as slow and as deep as he could make it, and relaxed. If there was one thing he'd learnt over the years it was how to recover. H looked up through his closed eyelids. He could see red. A moment later the red became burgundy. He opened his eyes, to see Nick looking down at him.

'How you feeling?' Nick growled at him.

'I didn't know you cared.' H made his answer as terse and sarcastic as the question had been.

'I don't. I've got news for you. You've got a fight coming up. In six weeks.' H showed little interest.

'Yeah? Who is it?'

'Henry Mancini.' There was a long pause. 'De Bugle Boy! Remember him?' Another pause. 'What dya you think?'

'Don't mess me about, Nick. I'm tired.' H wasn't that tired. A shot of adrenaline had squirted through his veins at the mention of the Bugle Boy's name.

'I'm telling you, it's Mancini. He's got a shot at de world title coming up and he wants a warm-up. He was supposed to be foighting a ranker, Mark Hodges, but Hodges got himself shot in some street foight or something. De match was going to be televised and de contracts are all signed. Mancini needs a replacement fast.'

H felt his stomach perform a triple flick-flack. He sat up, resting on his elbows.

'You're serious?'

'Yes, I'm fuckin' serious!'

All thoughts of retirement from the ring were, for the moment, forgotten. H was no longer tired. 'So now I'm fighting . . !'

'I jumped straight in for you. We can sell it as a re-match from your amateur days and wid de TV money involved, we're looking at a pretty decent pay-day.'

'But . . . I haven't had a decent fight in over three years.'

'Who cares?! Your last foight with Mancini was a classic. You've got six weeks.'

'Six weeks! Six weeks! I'll never be ready in . . .'

'Don't worry about it. Mancini's people aren't looking for a fight, dey're looking for a show. I told 'em I'd make sure you could go three, four rounds with deir boy . . .'

'What does that mean?'

'It means you don't need six months to prepare. You just turn up on de day and do de best you can . . .'

'The best I can?' H couldn't quite believe what he was hearing; Nick laughed scornfully.

'Dis isn't a foight, H, you can't win. It's a pay-day to entertain a few million mugs on television. I t'ought you'd be pleased!'

'I'm in there to make Mancini look good and I'm supposed to be pleased?'

Nick's irritation turned to anger. 'What are you fuckin' beefing about, it's an easy fuckin' pay-day!' The gym quietened as some of the other boxers listened in to the latest unfolding drama.

'Come on, Nick, it's Mancini.' H rose to his feet, hands on hips and looked down at the pugnacious Irishman.

Matt had clearly heard the beginning of the argument and stepped forward. 'Dad, why'd you keep . . .'

But Nick ignored his son, turning on H with a passionate, heart-felt scorn. 'You had it all, H. Talent. Dripping out of you.' Nick's piercing eyes shone out of his wizened face as he stared up at H. The hurt in his eyes reminded H of his own father. H looked away, embarrassed.

'What happened to it?' Nick persisted, demanding an answer.

'It went.' H mumbled.

'It went, it went! You let it go!' The gym had fallen into silence. The music had been turned off and the boxers stood around, listening-but-not-listening. 'You fuckin' pissed it all away! Well now dere's twenty t'ousand pound on the fuckin' table for dis fuckin' foight; take it or leave it!'

H shifted his stance, still not looking his coach in the eye. He felt the gaze of the other boxers, his coach and Matt, all looking at him, waiting for an answer.

'I'll take it.'

'Damn roight you'll fuckin' take it! And be glad to take it, too!'

Nick turned and strode away. The gym slowly came back to life, the other boxers gradually returning to their preferred brands of torture. H and Matt were left alone to contemplate this dramatic turn of events.

'I think you should . . .' But H turned his back on Matt, heading for the changing room and the showers. He still had nine more sit-ups to do but, on this occasion, they'd have to wait.

\*\*\*

Back in his street clothes, H wandered slowly down a leafy road in Hanwell, heading towards Alice's house. It was just after six, the sky was darkening and H knew Cyrus would be home from school. H wanted to see him. He wanted to see Beverley. He wanted to see her and tell her about this latest opportunity. H wasn't sure what to do and he missed talking things over with her. But he did not want to see Alice. Thinking about her, H felt his tread slow to a crawl.

H turned into Westcott Crescent and could see Alice's house near the corner. He stopped. The light was on in the living room. Peering in from behind a parked car, H saw Beverley sat on the sofa with her legs tucked to one side. In the armchair across from her he could make out Alice. Cyrus was lying with his head on Beverley's lap, and the flickering light of the television played across their faces. H couldn't make out if his son was also watching or if he was asleep. Across London, across the country, the same scene played out many times: the glowing warmth of security, held within the flickering light of a television. It felt alien to him. He was on the outside.

H backed away and walked back down the street.

# 25.

It was all to do with green-eyed Brenda. The woman was destroying him. Gavin prided himself on being fit, healthy and in top-notch condition. His blond hair might have been a tad thin and his waist not quite as trim as it had been, but Gavin was, he reflected, still a fine figure of a man. He had been an Olympiad, for God's sake! In the 1980 Lake Placid Winter Games – the fourth man in the English bobsleigh team, the man with the most powerful thighs.

But Gavin was worried. Green-eyed Brenda was insatiable. He had come into work today barely able to walk. In the green eyes of Brenda a quickie was something one did when one felt horny. And Gavin was certain nobody could possibly feel more horny than him. The twenty-three-year-old Brenda, he had just this evening decided, must be some kind of freak. She had no concept of foreplay. The idea that two people about to have sex might enjoy the time taken to arouse one another, however one chose to do that, had never entered her beautifully crafted head. No, what green-eyed Brenda wanted, constantly, was a quickie. She would either lie prostrate before him, or occasionally she would thrust her pert little bottom in his direction. She wanted him to do it at a moment's notice. Nothing more, nothing less.

Gavin had tried to sit the poor girl down and explain to her the workings of the male body as opposed to the female body. Men sometimes needed . . . stimulation. And the ability of the male organ to climax repeatedly was something that . . . declined with age. And that was Gavin's big, big mistake. To mention age. Because after a long, detailed and elaborate explanation of the occasional male need for assistance, green-eyed Brenda, with an innocence that would have thrilled a pimp, had asked if this whole conversation was because Gavin was old.

Gavin had stopped dead in his tracks. With one well-aimed question she had felled his love for her, a love that had begun three weeks earlier after a chance meeting in My Old China, a Cantonese restaurant and take-away in the centre of Purley.

Now, Gavin sat at the bar in Roxy's and pondered the many paths of true love, contrasting them with the imponderables of the quickie. Opposite him Nina sat and talked. Something about a trip to Brighton with Hilary James. All he'd gathered of any substance was that things were going according to plan and that she was making moves to encourage him to take on Alan. When she'd begun talking about how they'd driven to the beach and talked about men and women and where she'd grown up and . . . his mind had drifted.

Gavin's legs ached. The previous seven nights with Brenda, plus the quickies he'd encountered during the seven days that went with those seven nights, were wearing him out. That was the truth. He was now walking with a slightly ambling gait that made him resemble an ageing John Wayne. He raised himself from the stool at the bar and looked around him, stretching his aching legs. Nina stopped her chatter in mid-flow, looking up at Gavin with surprise.

'Stretching,' he said, by way of explanation. 'Carry on.' But when Nina resumed talking, Gavin's attention wandered around the club. It was just after nine – still early in the evening. Tonight there would be fewer women punters, more gay men and transvestites. It would be a slightly younger crowd, the atmosphere harder and more conventionally clubby. As Gavin looked around, flexing his knees and legs, he saw H framed in the doorway. He caught his eye and H came over. As Nina rose to greet him, Gavin was surprised to see her blushing.

'Look what the wind blew in.' She said it casually, but Gavin could hear the sudden tension in her voice.

'How are you?' H addressed the question to Nina, but as he said it he swung round to face Gavin. Gavin nodded to him without a word, his expression blank.

It was Nina who responded.

'A lot better for seeing you. So . . .' She leant towards him, taking his arm and half-turning away. As she did so she winked, ever so subtly, at Gavin. Gavin was unable to catch the whispered exchange but when Nina turned to him a moment later, he gathered from the look on her face that she wasn't pleased.

'Gavin,' she said, 'Hilary wants to see Alan.'

\* \* \*

Slightly bow-legged, Gavin stood on the landing outside Alan's office and knocked gently. A muffled 'Come in!' reverberated. Gavin glanced behind him. H was straightening the jacket of his crumpled suit. Gavin opened the door, standing aside to allow him to pass.

'Hilary! The very man!' Gavin noted that Alan seemed to be in a good mood. He was sitting behind his desk, closely examining his teeth in a small mirror. In his free hand he held a plastic flossing fork. His face turned from side to side as he grimaced into his reflection like the head on top of a totem pole. If Gavin played his cards right he thought he might be able to leave work early tonight and perhaps have some kind of conversation with green-eyed Brenda. She was a waitress in the Chinese restaurant and finished work at 2.30 a.m. She was usually home by three. Maybe he could be there before her. Catch her before she jumped on the computer. Which was another thing that was beginning to annoy him about her. She surfed the internet for hours at a time, day or night. He had no idea what she was looking for or what she was –

'You're asking me to throw the fight?' At the far end of the office Gavin was jolted back to the matter in hand by the tone in H's voice.

'I'm happy to waive the matter of the £15,000 you owe me, I'm not greedy. We're all friends here after all.' Gavin held his breath as he waited for H's response. He eased forward on the balls of his feet, ready.

'What? I'm not throwing the fight! I don't care who . . .'

'I'm not asking you, I'm fookin' telling you! You are going to throw that fight an' you're goin' t' throw it in the first fookin' round! I 'ad money riding on Hodges and with 'im out the picture it's now riding on you! A lot of it!'

H was staring at Alan, clearly struggling with his emotions. Gavin sidled closer, letting H know that if he made a move, he would be on him.

'You think you're something special' White Alan continued. 'Well, you're not. You're an ant. I piss on people like you. You're going down in the first round.' H said nothing. But his eyes remained firmly on Alan.

\*\*\*

H had long gone when Gavin left Alan's office. He eased his underpants away from his crotch as he walked slowly to the stairs. So it was true. Alan was definitely looking for a big score. Alan hadn't said so but Gavin thought maybe he was looking for the big pay-day that would see him retire. What about the business? No. Gavin would not allow it to end like this.

At the bottom of the stairs Gavin hobbled along the short corridor and into the club. It was busy now and the bar was crowded. Gavin sat on a stool and turned to the stage, where Nina was singing the final lines of 'I Will Survive'.

She finished her song to enthusiastic applause. She bowed, and when she joined Gavin at the bar he rose and graciously offered her his seat. Gavin could have done with the stool, but he'd made this gesture to Nina for a reason and it certainly wasn't chivalry.

'What are you drinking?' he began.

'Tanqueray and tonic. Thanks.'

Gavin turned to order her drink.

'How's it going with lover-boy?'

'Didn't I tell you how it was going earlier?'

Now that Gavin thought about it, she had. Something about Brighton beach?

'Well, I've got some good news. Hilary has a big fight coming up, as a replacement for one of Alan's boxers, Hodges. The interweaving of life's rich and varied tapestries never ceases to amaze me.'

Nina gave him a blank look. She clearly had no idea what he was talking about.

Gavin elaborated. 'Alan had a large money bet on Hodges on the understanding that Hodges would take a dive against Mancini. Now that Hilary has replaced him, Alan's put an even bigger bet on Mancini and is leaning on Hilary to take the very same dive, but this time in the first round. Trouble is, Hilary doesn't want to.'

# THE LAST CARD

'So? How can he make him?'

'Alan wants you to meet him, accidentally on purpose, and use your charms to make sure that he takes that dive.'

'Great. That's classy.'

'Can you handle it?' There was a pause. And then for the first time in a long time, Gavin saw Nina smile. It was tight, but it was a smile.

'This is what they call irony, isn't it?'

'No, this is what they call serendipity.' Gavin looked smug.

'Alan doesn't know that I've already met Hilary, does he?'

At that moment a short, burly black man pushed himself conspicuously and without ceremony between Gavin and Nina. He signalled a barman. 'Yeah, gimme a rum and black.'

Gavin eyed the man with distaste. He had half of his hair in some kind of tight, plaited style that kept it close to the scalp, while the other half grew loose and wild. He was wearing a full-length quilted coat with 'New Jersey' emblazoned on the front and back.

'Do you mind?'

'Do I mind what?' The man looked back at Gavin with something that made Gavin's pulse quicken. Was it insolence?

'I'm having a conversation here. There's no need to push.'

The black held Gavin's gaze for a moment then turned slowly to look at Nina. As slow as you like he turned back to Gavin, looking him up and down.

'Do I look like I'm stopping your conversation?'

Gavin stood up and squared himself as he now faced him. 'If you have a problem with me perhaps we should take it outside and discuss it.'

'Yeah, man, let's step.' The stranger opened his coat and a small movement with his hand in front of his trousers revealed a bulge. It was a move guaranteed to catch Gavin's attention. Silence.

'Rum and black.' The barman looked at the guy, who was staring at Gavin, who was staring back at him. 'Er . . . that's £3.40.' It was Nina that broke the spell.

'Your drink. It's ready.' One beat. Two beats. The black man turned to Nina, gave her a nod, paid for his drink and then moved away back into the heart of the club.

'What the hell was that?' Gavin said, breathlessly. 'And what the hell is he doing in here?'

'I don't know, but he didn't seem to like the look of you.' Gavin snapped round from looking after the disappearing stranger to looking at Nina.

'What's that supposed to mean?'

'Easy, tiger, he's nothing to do with me!'

'Well, what is to do with you is how to get the other nigger to do what we want.' Gavin saw Nina flinch at the word 'nigger' but he didn't give a damn. 'We now have leverage.'

'What do you mean?' Puzzled.

'If he didn't want to take the dive before, he now has a personal reason to do what we want, doesn't he?'

'I don't need more leverage,' Nina snapped. 'I know exactly what makes Hilary tick. He'd do anything for his little boy, Cyrus.'

'He's got a little boy?'

'Yes.'

'Well, good. I hope you're right. For both our sakes.' Nina turned away and sipped from her drink. Gavin turned back to the body of the club looking for the insolent black who needed teaching a lesson. He couldn't see him. He glanced at Nina's back with a rising contempt. He had a sudden thought; maybe his problem with green-eyed Brenda was that, on some deep, fundamental level . . . he just didn't like women.

# 26.

**D**unstan sat and watched Ade play with his little girl, Tawana. Ade was good with kids generally, but with Tawana in particular. The little girl was almost two years old; she had known Ade for as long as she could remember and she referred to him lovingly as 'Uncle Ade'. Improbably, Tawana was a caring, happy child with a sweet temperament. Ade was very fond of her. But for some reason whenever the little girl called him 'Uncoo Ada' Dunstan found it hilarious. It reminded him of the old black man on boxes of Uncle Ben's rice. Ade had asked Dunstan on a number of occasions what Uncle Ade had to do with Uncle Ben and Dunstan had never been able to come up with an adequate answer. Ade had learnt to ignore him. He considered it beneath him to respond to such childish provocation.

Today, however, Dunstan was serious. In fact he had been in a rather serious mood for at least forty-eight hours. Since the other night when he and Ade had made their drive-by attempt on Paul Akers, things had been very serious. After they had driven off, unsure if they had killed him, the two of them stayed with Dunstan's baby-mother in South Wimbledon. They had been there for two days now and Dunstan was well past stir-crazy.

First, it had been confirmed that Paul Akers was very much alive. That was bad news. You beat an animal badly enough, Dunstan reasoned, it will give up, back away: classic shock and awe tactics. Leave it only slightly wounded, however, it'll keep fighting. In their failure to kill Paul, Dunstan and Ade had shown weakness. Who could tell what Alan's next move might be? Dunstan was driving himself mad thinking about it. And what was the word on the streets of Stokey and Hackney about him and Ade? People would know by now that he and Ade had stepped up to the plate and tried to 'hit' Paul. Most of Dunstan's crew would welcome the hit because they knew that Paul was a liability. However, since he didn't finish the job, how many of his crew would remain loyal in the face of Alan's undoubted response?

Add to all of this the presence of Shirley, Dunstan's babymother, and his troubles were complete. Dunstan loved Tawana and came to see her whenever he could (at least once every two or three months), but Shirley was a different proposition.

Before Dunstan had entered the realms of gangsterism he had been one of a crew of dancers, all black and all from his estate in Stokey. They had called themselves the G-men and been attached to the sound system of the same name. Whenever the sound was on the road, playing in different parts of London, the G-men would go too, performing their routines and doubling as security. One night they were playing an event in Streatham at a community centre called The Castle. As Dunstan and the rest of the boys well knew, going across the river into south London meant dealing with 'pure leggo-beast gial an' savage manhood'. So when, as Dunstan and his dancers were spinning, body-popping, doing the slide and generally going through their paces, a group of girls started to heckle them it was only to be expected, them being leggo-beast. Three of the girls were black, two of them white, and one was wearing a full-length burqa and was therefore of indeterminate race.

Dunstan's attention was drawn to one of the black girls, a redskin who looked to be about fifteen. She was the one with the loudest, most caustic remarks, swearing like a sailor. She had the kind of slackness in her laugh that would make a black man blanch.

'Urrgh! You call dat fuckin' dancin'! My fuckin' grandmuvver could drop moves better dan dat, you know't I mean!'

The next time Dunstan dropped to the rubber mats they danced on, balanced on his head and prepared to spin, his view of the redskin was upside down. Despite the danger of the move he was attempting – it could easily have ended with a broken neck – the redskin continued to heckle.

'Look a' you! You fink you're fuckin' good, don't cha!' She was looking right at Dunstan. 'I seen babies do dem moves, you know't I mean! Dem is old-time moves dat my dad does! Get some new fuckin' moves, man, my dad's got a Chihuahua dat can dance better dan dat, ha, ha, ha, I seen de Chihuahua spinning on its 'ead an' it's got moves dat you ain't even got! Ha, ha, ha!'

That was it. Dunstan dropped his feet back down to the mat, flew over to the redskin and grabbed her by the throat. But not even that could halt the stream of poison issuing forth.

'Go on den, you fuckin' bastard, 'it me, go on, 'it me, I ain't afraida you pussies from up norff you know, you can't fuckin' dance anyhow . . .'

Under the circumstances Dunstan was left with little choice. He let go of her throat and punched her in the face. He knocked her clean off her feet, knocking her front tooth out in the process. At that point DJ Ruffntuff, the sound system stalwart, was flung sideways from behind the deck, the cans were ripped from his ears and someone slammed a chair down on top of the cold cuts that had been keeping the crowd in The Castle bubbling all evening. Suddenly it was a free-for-all, a mass fight that did nothing to dispel the ugly and scurrilous rumour that south Londoners were indeed fine examples of 'savage manhood'.

If Dunstan had been any way unconvinced of the ugliness of the rumour about south London girls, he had it confirmed for him half an hour later round the back of The Castle. It was there that the redskin – he later discovered her name was Shirley – clung to his penis like a woman drowning on storm-tossed seas. She handled his organ with an enthusiasm that Dunstan could only admire.

Two months later she was pregnant with Tawana, was given her own two-bedroomed flat on a nice, leafy estate in south Wimbledon and she and Dunstan were tied together for the foreseeable future. When the stresses and strains of working in the city proved too much, Dunstan would retire to south Wimbledon and impose his will on Shirley to the best of his ability. The problem was that Shirley was a redskin witch; the manner in which she had made herself known to Dunstan – by swearing and heckling him – was a feature of her personality that had remained a fixture. Domesticity for Dunstan could never be bliss with Shirley for a partner.

When Dunstan and Ade had decided to go underground for a while, south Wimbledon had seemed the obvious place. But the reality of sharing the same space with Shirley for anything longer than a few hours was daunting. The forty-eight hours that Dunstan and Ade had been there was fast taking Dunstan to his breaking point. Ade had already stepped in twice to avert a bloodbath: on the last occasion Dunstan had cuffed Shirley when she accidentally spilt some coffee on his lap, and only Ade's quick reactions stopped Dunstan being stabbed in his neck with a sharpened chopstick. In the argument that followed Tawana and then Shirley cried hysterically while Dunstan tried to tear clumps from his own lush afro.

All that had been about three hours ago. Shirley was out for a while to cool off while Ade amused Tawana, and Dunstan sat quietly thinking. And that was when he came up with his plan to get them out of this hell-hole.

'Why don't we just call Alan?'

'What?' Ade looked up from the doll's house that he and Tawana were playing with.

'Why don't we just call Alan up, tell him we want a meeting?'

'And then what?'

'I don't know. We've already knocked out two of his boys. Per'aps we should call it a day, you know't I mean?'

'But what about de globalisation plan?'

'Yeah, but . . .' He glanced round Shirley's flat with an uneasy look on his face. 'Dere's a time and a place, you get me? My man is vex and I man don't know if I'm ready for all-out war, you know't I mean?'

Ade scowled.

'What you looking like that for?'

'I dunno Duns. You sure you wanna ring him now?'

'You gotta better idea?'

'How's it gonna look?'

'It's gonna look like we're doing the right thing; dis is bizniz.' He and Ade maintained eye contact.

'Well . . . it seems to me you started something; let's finish it. Me and you. Maybe there's an opportunity here.' This little speech wasn't much in itself, but in the weeks ahead Dunstan would look back on it as the moment that his and Ade's relationship was to change forever. But that was to come. For now, Dunstan was secure in his connection to Ade.

'No, I don't agree. Later for that.' Dunstan crossed the room and picked up the phone. Ade watched him dial the number.

## THE LAST CARD

'Alan?'
'Dunstan?'
'We need to talk.'

# 27.

**H** stepped out of the tube station at Holland Park and looked around. It was after ten and it was dark. He'd spent the last twenty-four hours in his flat, mostly lying on his back in the dark, hands behind his head, thinking about his next move. What could it be? The money to pay off Akers would soon be his. Great. But now Akers didn't want it. Akers wanted him to take a dive. No. No way. H couldn't bear the thought of that. Making a sham out of something he loved and that the punters believed to be real. No, it wasn't him, he couldn't do it. Akers was forcing him to do something that all of his instincts screamed against. Thoughts went round and round in his head. If he hadn't taken a gambling holiday when he had, he would never have won the big hand with Stammer, which would have meant he would never have intervened when Akers' mobsters had come in to Blackie's demanding money, which meant he would never have come into contact with Akers, which meant he would never have been in the position to tell Akers to fuck right off, which meant Akers would never have . . . and so on and so forth.

In the end, how far back did you have to go when you looked at the events of your life? When you had problems and things weren't working out for you? Since all children are presumably born innocent, H reasoned to himself, surely they should all expect good things to happen in their lives. But since bad things happened to people all the time, H wondered whether that was because they deserved bad things to happen to them? And whether they did or they didn't, the journey from being young and innocent to being older and less innocent meant that a sequence of events had taken place, over the course of a life, from A to Z. Since all events seemed to be interconnected, there had

# THE LAST CARD

to be a point, one single moment in time, when things began to go wrong. You had to be able to pinpoint that moment if you thought about it long enough. H had been thinking about it on and off for the last twenty-four hours, but had yet to pinpoint that moment.

He could remember one of his schoolteachers, Mr Enias, who had posed a similar question one rainy day when H and his mates couldn't go out and play. It was one of those strange but true problems that for some reason had always stayed with H.

The problem was this: a man stands on the platform of a railway station waiting for his train to arrive. Moments later, he looks along the track and sees the train bearing down towards the station. Instead of the train slowing and stopping, however, it keeps its pace up, clearly intent on continuing through to a destination further down the line. In frustration the man rolls up his train ticket and hurls it at the front of the train as it passes him. The rolled-up piece of paper, his ticket, is thrown from right to left and hits the front of the train, which is travelling from left to right. Therefore the train pushes the ticket back the way it came. That means that the ticket has changed direction. And if that is true, there must have been a single moment when the paper was stationary, the exact moment when it changed direction. Physically, that moment of stillness seems an impossibility. But that single moment had to exist. And so it was with H's life. There had to be a single moment when the promise and potential that was his . . . changed directions.

H couldn't remember how Mr Enias had resolved this teaser but it seemed to H that his former teacher had somehow stumbled on a kind of metaphor for H's life.

Outside Holland Park tube station, H was trying to remember the way to Nina's house. He turned right and set off, walking down Holland Park Avenue. He was almost past the second turning when he recognised it and doubled back down Holland Park Terrace, past The Prince of Wales pub, into Pottery Lane. His instincts had been right. The road wasn't cobbled as he'd remembered it, but the lane of small, expensive mews houses was familiar. He found Nina's front door and knocked.

\*\*\*

The living room was bathed in a soft, glowing light. At shoulder height, running along three of its walls, was a long strip about six inches wide, housed in white plastic casing, which looked like a photographer's light box. It was. At one end of this strip the light was a soft white, at the other end the light was violet. In between these two points it went through all the colours of the rainbow. This was the only light source in the room and it gave the space an elegant, mellow, soft glow. H had never seen anything quite like it.

Looking equally elegant was Nina. She wore a faded pair of jeans and a sleeveless, backless top with a '60s print on it, all green and blue swirls. Her feet were bare. The jeans sagged like men's jeans on her narrow hips. H couldn't help but admire the fit. The top revealed more than enough to be a major distraction. Her hair looked clean and well groomed. Overall, Nina radiated casual elegance. Not an elegance that was cold and unapproachable, but the kind of effort-less elegance that was . . . inviting.

Nina and H sat on facing sofas in the middle of the room. In the soft half-light, Nina stared at H. He swirled the glass of whisky he held in his hand, peering in as though the contents of the glass was endlessly fascinating. In his other hand he spun his talisman.

'It's like a nervous tic the way you play with that thing. What kind of lighter is it?'

'It's a Zippo, a replica of the original 1932 model. And it's not a lighter, it's a talisman.'

'Talisman? You? Superstitious?' Nina clearly didn't believe it.

'It's to remind me, to remind me what failure feels like. What it's like to lose. I bought it at a time in my life when things were going badly and now I keep it as a reminder. To make me do better.'

H paused while he chose his next words with care. Earlier in the evening when he knew he needed to speak to somebody, anybody, he'd hit on the idea of calling on Nina for a number of reasons. First, she'd seemed sympathetic to his dilemma with Akers, and secondly, she knew Akers. He wouldn't have to explain anything. But also, and he couldn't tell how important this was, he was finding Nina increasingly attractive. Her tough woman act, with its roots that stretched into the rough parts of north London, and which she maintained despite the wealth that she lived with now, made her an interesting contradiction. H had been out with as many white women as he had black so that wasn't an issue but the fact that he still felt a lot for Beverley – what did he feel? – was confusing him.

'I'm in a jam, Nina.' He said it apologetically, as though real men don't find themselves in jams.

'I know. Gavin told me.'

'Jesus! Does everybody know my business?' He exploded as though he was angry, but actually, H was secretly pleased. He could do 'anger'. 'There's no fucking way on earth that I can throw this fight!'

'That's right.'

'How can I look my little boy in the eye and tell him I'm a fake?'

'You can't.'

'So what the hell am I going to do?'

'Kill White Alan.'

Neither of them laughed and the silence between them was a long one.

'You keep coming out with this . . . stuff.'

'Have you got a better idea?'

'Who do you think I am? A fucking fantasy of yours, a Yardie or something?'

'Please. Do me a favour!'

'Well, I'm not a killer! I don't do murder!'

'What do you do? Apart from gamble?'

'Fuck you!'

'No. I'm serious, what do you do? '

This wasn't a road H wanted to go down. Not now and not with her. 'What is it with you and White Alan, anyway? What's going on with you and him?'

'We were lovers once. But not any more.'

'So leave him! Like any normal woman!'

'I've tried. But with a split of two hundred thousand pounds, I'd find it a lot easier. If you understand what I'm saying. Two hundred thousand pounds.' She stared at H as she repeated the numbers. Just in case he had missed it the first time. 'The only sure way to get the money,' she continued, 'is to get rid of him. Permanently.'

H was finding it all unreal. He couldn't believe he was having this conversation.

'There's no way, Nina . . .'

'I know exactly how . . .'

'I'm not the man for that kind of . . .'

'I've got the combination to the office safe. It's five, five, two . . .'

'No!'

'. . . six, three . . .'

'NO!' H shouted the word at the top of his lungs, spilling his shot of whisky before she would stop.

But even then she didn't stop. Or rather she did stop talking but that wasn't the end of it. She rose, left the room, walked upstairs to her bedroom. H heard her rummaging around in a drawer or closet. She came back into the living room and gently placed something on the sofa next to H. It was a brand-new, fully loaded, snub-nosed Magnum 357.

# 28.

**A**de eased his racing-green Range Rover into the line of traffic at the top of Frith Street. As the car edged its way down the crowded Soho street, past the trendy coffee shops, bars and restaurants, Ade tapped his fingers to the Afro-Cuban beat of the Buena Vista Social Club. Ibrahim Ferrer was crooning an up-tempo number about the passion that he felt for his girlfriend and how every time they made love it felt like the bed was going to catch fire. What! Them was lyrics, boy! Ade couldn't honestly say he was a hardcore fan of Afro-Cuban music, but when this album had first dropped it had reminded him of his father, who'd been a big fan of the hi-life music scene. Ade could remember how his father would drop 'African Woman' on to the record player, take Ade's mother into his arms and swing her round the small living room, mad with the music. Ade's mother was a big woman, and when his father swung her round, bouncing his hip off her large bottom – the two of them would laugh and laugh and laugh. Ade and his sister Maxine would stand by clapping and laughing too.

But Ade hadn't put the album on to remember his father. He'd put it on deliberately because he knew Dunstan didn't like it. Ade wanted to put Dunstan in a certain mood. And he wanted to put Dunstan in a certain mood because he'd been thinking more and more about his ideas about globalisation. Ever since he had phoned White Alan, Dunstan seemed to be backing away from the logic of his own arguments. But if Dunstan didn't want to deal with the real, Ade knew a man who probably would: a soldier from north London, a brer named Wha Gwan that he and Dunstan both knew. Wha Gwan was a brer that didn't ramp. But that was for later. For now, Ade played the Buena

Vista Social Club to irritate and annoy Dunstan, hoping to add some steel to Dunstan's backbone for their meeting with White Alan. He turned the volume up.

> **. . . MARGARITA, QUE ME QUEMO**
> **YO QUIERO SEGUIR GOZANDO . . .**

The Latin rhythms of fire and passion blared inside the car and Dunstan, in truth, had a scowl on his face that would have put fear into a small child. They had just driven past Ronnie Scott's when Ade saw a parking space. Perfect. He nipped out of the line of traffic and slipped in; they were meeting Alan and Paul in Bar Italia just across the road.

> **. . . LA CANDELA ME ESTÁ LLEVANDO**
> **ME GUSTA SEGUIR GUARACHANDO . . .**

Ade snapped the stereo off. He and Dunstan climbed out of the car, locked it and then the two of them high-stepped to the coffee shop. It was the middle of a fresh, April afternoon and Frith Street was busy with gay men and Soho trendies. No wonder Akers wanted the meeting there. As they approached Bar Italia they could see it was crowded. People were sitting round the four tables outside on the street, as well as filling the inside of the coffee shop.

'Dis is no fucking good, is it? De place is cork!' Ade looked around him, aggressively. The sight of so many gays had put him in a bad mood. He bet most of them worked in the media. For the BBC – the Bourgeois Batty Club. Ade noted with a modicum of satisfaction that Dunstan also high-stepped with a look of bad intent on his face. His voluptuous afro was leaning back against the breeze and Ade knew from past experience that he had to watch what he said from this point on. It was allllll good!

'It's all about globalisation.'

'What?'

'Nothing. I was just thinking about what you were saying about globalisation.' They arrived outside the Bar Italia and looked around for a space. There was none.

'Listen, Ade, give it a fuckin' res' about globalisation, will ya? When de time is right I'm gonna be de firs' one to fuckin' move on it, ya get me? Cha! No budder get me vex up now!' As he looked about him for somewhere to sit, the afro comb poked out of the extreme munificence of his hair. It quivered with anticipation.

# THE LAST CARD

'Easy, man, easy. We have to play it cool for dis meeting.'

'Wha'? Who you talkin' to? Listen, dread, when my man finally gets 'ere I ain't playing nuffin cool, ya get me? 'Bou' "fuck all you wogs and niggers"!'

Dunstan was speaking with volume at this point and Ade glanced down at the two men nearest them. They looked to be in their mid-twenties and they drank their coffees from little white coffee cups, both of them frothy with foam. Wrapped in puffa coats against the slight chill in the air, they sipped with an effete diffidence, both now glancing up at Dunstan. No doubt the shouting about 'wogs and niggers' had them worried. Ade saw one of them shake his head warningly and quickly drink down the rest of his coffee. His companion did the same. The first one rose, his friend followed him. Ade waited for them to pick up some bags they had with them and then he and Dunstan bagged the table.

'But we still have to know when to strike,' Dunstan continued. 'Dere's no point in steamin' in dere before we're ready, you know't I mean?' Dunstan kissed his teeth. 'Give me some fuckin' credit, Ade!'

'Hey, relax, Dunstan, you de man, you know dat.' In his heart of hearts Ade already knew that Dunstan was no longer the man but he held up his hand invitingly anyway. Dunstan slapped it and they slid their hands apart, ending the slide with a finger click. 'You know I've got your back.' Ade rose. 'Coffee?'

'What else dey got?'

Ade turned to peer into the coffee shop. On the white board behind the counter was a long list of what they had to offer. Ade pointed to it. 'It's on the board, dere.'

Dunstan peered short-sightedly into the coffee store. He leaned forward and his eyes narrowed as he tried to make out what was on the list. Making sure that Dunstan didn't see, Ade had to smile.

'Dere's a million different types of coffee,' Ade said helpfully, 'but basically it's coffee. Is dat good?'

Suddenly self-conscious, Dunstan leaned back and stopped squinting.

'Dey got chocolate?'

'Judging by the lenffa dat list I would say yes, yes?'

'Good. Get me a chocolate. Large.'

'Moody, Dunstan, moody.' Ade rolled into the coffee shop and eased his way to the counter. Boy, dis place was small! He ordered his drinks and turned to look back out on to the street. As he did, he had to catch his breath. His stomach flipped. He saw the two Akers brothers arrive, Dunstan stand up and the three of them shook hands. Moments later all three looked into the coffee shop. Ade maintained a grim expression as he nodded at them. Alan Akers gave a smile and a theatrical half-bow. It went with the off-white '70s suit he was wearing with the white crew-neck jumper and the white leather boots. The man was a living joke! Paul Akers just nodded at Ade, equally grim, probably still thinking about how Ade had shot at his arse.

Ade picked up his coffee and hot chocolate and carried them outside. Conversation stopped as he placed them on the table. He looked around for a chair. Alan had taken his. Ade saw a free one at another table, picked it up and returned with it. As Ade sat, Alan was looking at him, puzzled.

'What? Don't we get one?' Alan looked between the coffee and Ade, a hurt expression on his face. For a moment Ade looked flustered, then Alan broke out into a broad smile. 'You're all right, I'm only joking!' He looked over at his younger brother. 'Thought I was serious!' Alan chuckled, willing Paul to share the joke. Apparently Paul wasn't in a joking mood because he failed to crack a smile.

'So anyway, Ade, Dunstan and I have had a talk.'

Ade didn't say a word, he just looked between Dunstan, Alan and Paul. 'I know you and Dunstan have been naughty boys. Haven't you?' Both Alan and Paul were looking directly at Ade now, waiting for him to answer. Having been taken by surprise with their comment about the drinks Ade was not going to give them the upper hand now. He was a warrior. He shifted his gaze to his coffee, picked it up, took a careful sip and replaced it on the table. He looked up. White Alan and Paul were both still staring at him.

'Dunstan's already said his piece, Ade, is there anything you'd like to add?' Ade looked at Dunstan, but he kept his eyes on the table and said nothing. Ade looked at Alan, making sure to look him in the eye.

'Like what?' Ade kept his voice even. If they wanted a war, they could have one, whatever Dunstan said. Globalisation, you know't I mean?

'You've been out of order.'

# THE LAST CARD

'Says who?' There it was. The challenge was out in the open, on the table. Alan could pick it up or kick it away, whatever he felt up to. Ade kept his gaze focused on Alan's eyes. Ade didn't blink. He was a warrior. His father taught him that. He was a Nigerian, from the Yoruba tribe. Yoruba were warriors and no fucking dry-up old white man would make him back down.

'I could go on about this,' said Alan. 'But I won't. There's too much money involved.' He now looked at Paul. 'And I know this one has been a right fucking banana. A fool.' He turned back to Ade and Dunstan, looking between them, very serious now. 'It's over.' Paul and Dunstan glanced at each other and quickly glanced away. If body language meant anything it was clear that whatever Alan might say, it wasn't even nearly over.

'Are you two going to kiss and make up, or do I have to bang both your heads together?' Alan looked at both Dunstan and Paul, but he addressed the comment to his brother.

'Come on, Dunstan,' said Paul. 'It's over. No one wins in a war, no one makes any money.' The words stumbled without enthusiasm from Paul's throat. Paul was a man under orders, delivering a script that he clearly did not believe. The look he gave Dunstan did away with any doubt. That was the moment when Ade knew Dunstan's globalisation plan was a winner. For some reason Akers didn't want to take them on! Akers must respect his and Dunstan's power, and if Dunstan wasn't aware of it he, Ade, certainly was.

Dunstan had the vision. He might not have the balls to carry his vision through, but Ade had to give him credit for the breadth of his imagination. If he needed steel in his backbone Ade could provide that, but if that wasn't enough for Dunstan then fuck him. Fuck him! Paul, meanwhile, extended his hand – like a set of defrosted fish fingers – to Dunstan. Dunstan shook it for the briefest moment. White Alan raised his hand to playfully ruffle Dunstan's hair but Dunstan moved his head away just in time. Alan laughed.

'I'm glad you two decided to be smart. I thought I was going to have to kill you right here in the open, you little monkeys!' Alan looked at the pout on Dunstan's face and burst out laughing. Even Paul smiled. Dunstan looked between the two of them saying not a word, the beginnings of a rictus-like grin flirting with the corners of his mouth.

'I'm just kidding,' smirked Alan 'Just kidding!'

Ade looked between the three of them, Paul, Alan and Dunstan. Business might well go on as usual for a while . . . but a day of reckoning was coming. Ade had just seen the future and it didn't include Alan or Paul Akers. In fact, as he looked at the fake grin on his friend's face, he realised it didn't include Dunstan either.

# 29.

H sat in a shadowy part of Blackie's shebeen, in a corner at one of the smaller tables. At the main table in the centre of the room a game of stud poker was in full flow but H wanted no part of it. While Shampa dealt the cards with her usual aplomb, most of the players were unknown to H and even if he had known them he'd still have vowed to give up gambling. And he had . . . kind of. He was playing match kalooki, a card game so boring you could hardly call it gambling – or so H told himself.

Ten o'clock on Sunday night and H found himself sitting opposite Blackie, *mano a mano*. A stack of notes lay in the middle of the table. Grimly, H cast his eyes over it. He still couldn't control the urge to gamble! What was wrong with him? He wanted to scream! H's talisman sat vindictively next to him on the table. Beside that H had a shot glass of JD. While this had hardly been touched, Blackie was uncharacteristically drunk. He drank steadily from the tumbler of Mount Gay which sat next to him.

Blackie and H were nearing the end of a game. Each of them had just one playing card in their hand. H had a nine, Blackie a queen. The deck lay to one side of the money and each of them, in turn, picked from the top. Each was waiting for one card to close out the game. In the joyless, heavy silence between them they picked with the regularity of a metronome.

It was H who picked the winner. A jack. Blackie had a set of three jacks in front of him and H laid his freshly picked jack alongside them. Game over. He scooped up the money in the centre of the table. It was over £300 but the blank manner in which H scooped up and pocketed his winnings would have told Blackie that the win gave

H no pleasure. Blackie looked back at him with the leaden eyes and the slack jowls of a man in serious need of sleep.

'Man, you lucky tonight!' It was Blackie's face that had emitted the words but you could hardly tell; the man was so pickled with rum that the muscles in his face looked as though they'd been pumped with Botox. Blackie collected the cards and shuffled them.

'Really? My life's like a bad plane crash: Beverley wants me to stop gambling, I want to stop gambling, but I can't stop gambling. And I'm "lucky"! Is that right, Blackie?'

'Listen, man, listen. I know dis chap once. He used to come to my old place in Ladbroke Grove, regular! Ibazebo. Nigerian chap. 'E don't come no more since 'is wife ketch 'im wid a nex woman an' brok 'is arm. Now 'e an' 'is wife split up. Anyway, 'e was a sharp Nigerian man, brilliant min'. It was 'im dat did tell me dat 'e t'ought gamblin' was a, was a . . . 'ow did 'e put it?' Blackie's eyes glazed over as his face personified the expression 'the lights were on but nobody was home'. They came back into focus. ''E did say gamblin' was a kind of a comfort; comfort for de . . . "emotionally insecure". Das 'ow de man put it.' Blackie paused as though he'd just revealed the secret of the universe and H should have been be shocked by its simplicity. H was not shocked but he could feel his blood beginning to boil. Blackie carried on talking as he dealt the cards.

'I had to stan' up in de man face and tell 'im 'e tarkin' rrrrrubbish! All de time 'e's gamblin' an' 'e cian see what 'e doin'! Gamblin' . . . is a . . . spiritual t'ing; a t'ing dat can bring us closer . . . closer to Gawd. I mean . . .'

H couldn't contain himself any longer. 'Blackie! You're the one talking rubbish!' He dropped the cards he'd been dealt on to the table and rose.

Blackie looked up at him with uncomprehending eyes. 'I tarking rrrrubbish?'

H bent down to speak directly into Blackie's leaden, black, greasy face. 'Remember Dipak? Did gambling bring him closer to God?'

Blackie's face took on a look of fear. 'Dipak?' Blackie whispered the name.

H turned to leave but turned back. 'You're drunk and you're talking out of your arse!' H jammed his talisman in his pocket and swept out of the shebeen.

# THE LAST CARD

\*\*\*

The night was surprisingly warm as H turned into Wardour Street. The air was still. The street buzzed as H passed through and arrived at Shaftesbury Avenue. He paused. He pulled his talisman out of his pocket, pumping it nervously, turning it over and over and over. Blackie was a good man but when he'd had a few drinks you just couldn't talk to him. H knew he could leave this scene behind for the next ten, fifteen, twenty years, come back and Blackie would be exactly the same. A little more battle-scarred, a few less teeth.

H slipped his talisman back into his pocket and headed towards Chinatown. Out of the endless questions in his life he could hear Nina's low, seductive voice. Providing answers. 'If you wanted to take White Alan out of the game it would be so easy,' the voice said. 'He does the same thing every Sunday night.' H passed Gerrard Street and headed deeper into Chinatown proper, turning left into Lisle Street. He walked a little way until he saw what he was looking for: the brightly lit Chinese restaurant called Yee Tsang's. It was on the corner of Little Newport Street and Newport Place. He could see that the restaurant was busy and the diners, an equal mix of white and Oriental, ate and chatted, enjoying a late Sunday night meal. Life outside the restaurant was equally busy with people, tourists, passing by in both directions, and the shops around the restaurant were all open for business.

H stood across from Yee Tsang's and watched. The voice in his head continued. 'He leaves the club about eleven and goes to Chinatown. He's got a friend there. A Mr Tsang.' H took a step forward, as though in a daze, as though about to approach the restaurant, but then he stepped back. The voice continued.

'He's some kind of business associate. They meet up, they have a drink. They do their business. Alan will stay there for maybe half an hour. He normally has Gavin with him but I'll make sure that he won't be there this time. He'll leave alone.' As the voice in H's head receded, he slipped into a doorway on Lisle Street, disappearing into the shadows.

The street was quiet now and White Alan, looking cool and relaxed, stood at the door to Yee Tsang's finishing a conversation with a short, jovial, stringy-haired Chinese man. Wearing a white short-sleeved linen safari suit, coupled with a silk cravat, Alan looked as though he'd just stepped out of a Laura Ashley fashion shoot. From the recess of the doorway next to Yee Tsang's, H eyed him carefully, asking himself why this man had such an eccentric fascination for white.

Moments later White Alan finished his conversation with the Chinese man, shook hands with him and headed up Newport Place. H remained hidden in the doorway. When Alan was about ten metres away, H stepped out and followed. The voice in his head began again. 'When he approaches Gerrard Street you do it there. It's all small Chinese stores in that area, no one will say a word. It's a tight-knit community, they won't speak to the police.' White Alan was at the top of Newport Place, about to turn into Gerrard Street. H picked up his pace, closing in on White Alan's back. 'Twice. Shoot him twice. Make sure he's dead. Then you go straight back to the office at Roxy's. Before anyone knows he's missing, you clean out the safe. Simple.'

H moved silently and swiftly behind White Alan. He was now close enough to reach out and touch him. Just as White Alan reached the beginning of Gerrard Street, H grabbed his arm and spun him round. For the first time since H had met him, Alan's face betrayed fear.

'What? What do you want?'

'I'm not throwing the fight. I'm not throwing it. You'll get your fifteen grand and then we're quits. It's as simple as that.' White Alan's eyes quickly scanned H for signs of a weapon. Nothing. H looked coolly back at him.

'Is that right?'

'That's more than right. What are you going to do to me, Alan? The bet has been laid.'

Alan stared back at H, an uneasy smile on his face. 'I don't need to do anything to you. The question is: what're you going to do to yourself?'

'What does that mean?'

'It means I know about you, Hilary. You tried to take Mancini as an amateur and he beat the shit outta you. And now you're a gambler stuck on the cards.' H just stared. 'You're one of life's losers, one of the little people, a low-life. You are going to let Mancini win, and not only win, you're going to let him beat the shit out of you. Again. How do I know this?' H still said nothing. Alan leaned in closer so that H could smell the stench of spicy pork on Alan's breath. He whispered in H's ear. 'Because you have no . . . moral integrity.' Alan leaned back and smiled playfully at H. 'But also, if you don't lie down, I'm going to cut you like a fookin' grapefruit.'

White Alan turned his back on H, smoothed out any ruffles that might have disturbed the lines of his linen suit, and continued on his way. H watched him turn the corner into Gerrard Street and go about his business. And only then did he realise that the hand that had spun Alan round was shaking.

# 30.

**W**earing an ankle-length figure-hugging black dress, covered with sparkling black beads, Nina was two-thirds of the way through the last song in her set, Jennifer Holiday's 'I'm not going'. Her shiny black Manolo Blahnik strapless shoes gave her another three inches in height and Nina used them well. She knew she looked damn good and her slowed-down, vamped-up version of the song had the crowd, mostly gay men, cheering their approval.

It was during this cheering that Nina suddenly saw a flurry of activity in the audience. Alan had just entered the club. She saw him barging his way through to the bar to join Gavin. He yanked Gavin's shoulder and the two of them disappeared round the side of the bar and out into the hallway.

Nina was a professional. She took great pride in what she did and she certainly wasn't going to rush the end of the song. But this was one of those moments when she wished she wasn't so professional. At the song's end, instead of ordering her usual Tanqueray and tonic, Nina went round the side of the bar and edged out into the hallway. She couldn't see but she could hear Alan talking with Gavin at the top of the stairs. Alan did not seem too happy.

'He's a fooking liability!'

'I'll watch him, I'll make sure . . .'

'He bloody well told me he's not going to take the fall!'

'Alan, I'll take care of it: I'll see exactly what needs to be done and I'll take care of it. Calm down . . .'

'You fooking calm down! You fooking calm down!' Alan was almost screeching. 'Do you know how much fooking money is riding on this?'

As Nina remembered the conversation she'd had with H she felt the panic rising up in her stomach.

# THE LAST CARD

'Do you want me to pay him a visit? Lean on him?'

'No, I want you to pay him a visit and tell him what great integrity he's got! Of course I want you to fooking lean on him! Break his fooking legs! Do what you have to do but he takes that fooking fall or someone's going to pay! And I'll fooking tell you now it's not going to be me! Do you fooking understand that?'

'Yes, Alan.'

'Yes, Alan. Now fook off and get to work!'

Pause. Nina could feel the thickness of the silence.

'Er . . . Alan, if I physically, if I have, if someone hurts . . . he isn't going to be fit to . . .'

Nina held her breath. She waited for Alan's response to Gavin pointing out the flaw in his plan.

'Has that bitch Nina come up with anything?' Nina flinched at the sound of her own name.

'Has she?'

Before Nina could hear Gavin's reply one of the barmen squeezed past her on his way to the cellar under the stairs. 'Are you going to stand there all day, Nina?'

His mild reproach was loud enough to be heard at the top of the stairs. Nina immediately slipped back into the club. She sat at the bar to think. She wasn't sure what had happened with H that evening but whatever had happened had left Alan in a murderous rage. She was scared. She crossed the dance floor and entered a door, using a security code that she tapped out on the keys. Inside was a small dressing room. This was where Nina had her things: a change of clothes, shoes, her coat, her handbag. Nina opened her handbag and took out her mobile phone. She dialled and listened. After four rings a man's voice answered.

\*\*\*

Nina picked H up outside the Royal Court Theatre by Sloane Square tube station. It was just after three in the morning and he stood alone, in the quiet of the night, smoking a cigarette. He saw her coming and stood next to the kerb as she drove up in her Z3 Roadster. She leant over and opened up the passenger door. He tossed away his cigarette and climbed in.

'I didn't know you smoked.'

'Once in a while.'

'I used to smoke. I gave up on Friday.'

'I'm very happy for you.'

'I give up every Friday.' She looked across at him expecting at least a smile. Nothing.

Nina pulled away from the kerb, drove back around Sloane Square and on to Sloane Street. She knew something serious had happened tonight between H and White Alan and that's why she had called him. That's why she'd called him? Why had she called him? The poor bastard had been through a rough week. She'd take him back to her place which at least looked like somewhere you might want to be and give him a drink. Maybe even a warm bed. Maybe even her bed. She could see the pain in his face and felt like stroking him. She glanced quickly over at him and looked away. He was staring out of the window. Thank God for that! Her face had suddenly flushed! Holy Mary, mother of Jesus!

'You look like shit!'

The look he gave her came slow and hard.

'Is that your idea of conversation?'

Nina kept her eyes fixed on the road. 'I . . . we . . . well, what do you want from me?'

'Nina, you called me.'

'So? Yes, I know I called you. So what of it?' She could feel his eyes boring into the side of her face and she knew why. She was talking gibberish!

'He's on his guard against you now.' What was she saying? Why, why? Where was this going? She turned the car into her road and pulled up outside her house.

'Do you know what happened tonight?'

'Not exactly.'

As she locked the car and the two of them entered the house he told her what had happened. She could feel the two small, vertical lines appear in her forehead, just above her eyebrows. When he'd finished talking she took his arm and, without a word, guided him to one of the sofas in her living room. She sat him down and went to make each of them a drink.

# THE LAST CARD

When she returned she gave him his and sat down next to him. He drank. He looked better.

'Was it bad?' she asked in a soft voice. He didn't say anything, he just looked at her. She reached out a hand and stroked the back of her fingers against his cheek. It felt rough, scratchy. He didn't move, just looked at her. And suddenly she felt the two small, vertical lines in her forehead, just above her eyebrows . . . disappear. They faded away. Nina moved the back of her fingers along H's cheek to his lips, feeling them. She turned her hand over so the tips of her fingers could feel his lips. She suddenly realised she had wanted to do that for almost as long as she had known him.

Slowly, she took her hand away, leant into him and gently kissed him on the mouth. He kissed her back. She sat back, took his drink from his hand, put it down on the floor. She did the same with hers. The two of them simultaneously scooted closer together on the sofa and kissed again, this time deeper, Nina folding her arms around H and feeling him do the same. God, his lips felt good! As soft, as billowy as she had imagined! His arms felt strong and powerful as they wrapped her to him, his hands caressing her back. The front of her body felt alive, tingling, pressed against him. Nina hadn't felt this good about kissing a man in a long, long time.

H moved his hands beneath her jacket, easing her out of it. Once it was off, H's hands danced precariously over the jumper and were soon probing her skin beneath it, moving smoothly up and down her back and sides as though they were slowly searching for something. Each time they moved over her, Nina felt the tingling sensation spread. And the spread was making its way to her groin. Soon, she couldn't stand it. She pulled away from him, flushed, breathless.

'Let's go upstairs.' She rose, took his hand and led him from the room.

The two of them lay down on the bed. H propped himself up on one elbow and Nina rolled into him. They continued where they'd left off on the sofa, H using his free hand to pull Nina's body into his. Again, he played it up and down her spine and, like a cat, Nina arched her body into his with pleasure. Her hands now slipped under the tee-shirt he was wearing and made their way over the smooth contours of his skin. Unbelievably smooth. She moved her hands down his back into the dip of his spine and down below the belt around his trousers. As far as she could go. His buttocks felt hard but smooth. She wanted to go down further. She eased her body away from him, moved her hand round and began to unbuckle the belt around his jeans. His kissing became more urgent, insistent. Nina pulled away from him and used both hands to unbuckle his belt. But before she could finish, he eased back, turned over and sat on the edge of the bed, his back to her.

'I can't.'

Nina dragged herself across the bed and stroked his back.

'What's the matter? We can take our time, there's no rush.'

'It's not that. I've still got Bev in my mind.'

Nina stopped stroking his back. She slipped round to sit next to him. Already the heat of the moment was draining away.

'Girlfriend?'

'Babymother.'

Nina left the bedroom and came back a moment later with two lit cigarettes and an ashtray. She gave one of the cigarettes to H.

'I thought you gave up?'

'I did.'

'Where'd you get these from?'

'They're yours.' They both smiled. He leant over and kissed her on the lips. To Nina, it wasn't a sexy kiss, it was a 'you're actually all right' kiss. She liked it almost as much as the other kind. They sat and smoked.

'I just can't do it.'

'What?'

'Take the fall.'

Nina thought about that for a moment. 'Why not? It would make life a lot easier for all of us.' She laughed without mirth. 'If you were ever going to go for Alan, after what happened tonight, the best time to do it would be straight after the fight. When he's least expecting it.' She looked at him to gauge his reaction to her words. There wasn't one.

'Everything's a mess. The only thing that has any meaning, that isn't shit, is the boxing. It's . . . pure.'

Nina didn't get it. 'So? Who really cares about that, who cares if it's pure?'

'I do!' He swivelled round on the bed to face her. 'Listen. Some days are good, some days are bad, some days are shit; that's life. But when you box, when you box . . . it's different. It's about two athletes, going at each other: all that training, all that energy, against what the other guy can do. It's down to you. There's no place to hide in a boxing ring, there's no one else to blame, it's all down to you. You show people what you're made of.'

As Nina looked searchingly into his eyes he seemed to be willing her to understand.

'Fucking hell, it's about control, Nina! Taking control. If I haven't got control over boxing . . .' He stubbed out his cigarette in the ashtray.

'You're just a romantic . . .' she began.

'I'm a human being, for fuck's sake!' The strength of his feeling surprised her. She took the ashtray from him and stubbed out her own cigarette. She then guided him back down on to the bed, the two of them lying next to each other. And then Nina found herself talking about things that she hadn't spoken about to anyone for a long, long time.

'I used to think I had control. Before Alan. For a woman, being thought of as good-looking is the best possible gift you can have. Men are so stupid they'll do anything for a pretty face. So I was going to be a singer. I didn't know anybody who'd ever done any kind of performing but I just put myself out there and started meeting people. I don't have a fantastic voice, I know that, but it's not bad. And I know I look okay.' H gave a hint of a smile. 'So soon people were asking me to do PA spots in clubs. It wasn't long before owners would take one look at me and bingo! I was in, I was making money. What I didn't know was that Alan Akers was charging protection money from most of the clubs in the area . . .'

'Where's he from? Where's his accent from?'

'Doncaster. Up north. He and his brother Paul came down to London about fifteen years ago. No money and no contacts. Now look at them.' Nina explained to H how they had made London work for them, bent it to their will. 'They're into drug-running, fraud and extorting protection money from clubs. All over north London and the West End. That's how I met him. He took over one of the clubs I used to sing in. The Three Pines, in Stoke Newington. When he opened up Roxy's in Soho he wanted me to be a part of his move. Stupidly, I was flattered.'

'So why isn't it working out for you?'

'Because Alan's losing his grip. He's moved into the West End with Roxy's and he's left Paul in charge of their operations back in north-east London, but he refuses to deal with the fact that Paul is a full-time coke-head. Paul's not up to running things and the whole operation is beginning to unravel. North London now isn't the north London he moved into fifteen years ago. Things are changing there. The young black kids there are growing up and taking over. They're not interested in listening to old-skool crap about 'ways of doing business' from dinosaurs like Alan and Paul Akers. They're listening to all this stuff from America about 'the ghetto' and 'OGs' and 'gangsta rappers' and they want their guns; they're all hip-hop, they want a piece of what's out there and they want it now. I've got a Nigerian girlfriend over in Homerton. Maxine. Her baby brother, Ade, he lives on the Gascoyne Estate, works for a kid called Dunstan. Those kids are still in their nappies; I mean, they are so young, but between them, they're taking over Hackney, Stoke Newington, Dalston, Bethnal Green. Those kids are dangerous. And Alan's feeling the heat.'

'And you won't just leave him because of the money?'

Nina turned to look at him. The scorn in his voice was unambiguous.

'And live like you?' she snapped. She didn't mean it to come out as harshly as it did.

'What do you do for the money?' He asked her straight and her reply was equally straight.

'I sing.' That's what she said but what she thought was 'Fuck you!' Who was he to judge her? What was so great about his life? The next second he leant into her and kissed her deeply. Nina felt more grateful for that kiss than she would have dared admit.

'Whatever we had, it's over. As I'm sure you can tell.'

'I believe you.' The two lay on the bed staring up at the ceiling.

'Maybe . . . maybe you're right,' she almost whispered.

'What?'

'If boxing means that much to you, why don't you take the fight with Mancini . . . and beat him!'

He turned to look at her.

'Win the fight.'

'Me? Beat Mancini!' H's voice was incredulous.

'Hey. Isn't your game all about self-belief and confidence?' Nina now turned towards him. 'Alan's already got me; don't let him get you.' H stared back at her and, as Nina stared back, she felt something stirring but she wasn't sure what. She knew she was playing with fire here. She liked H, there was no doubt about that. She just didn't know how much she liked him.

'I've got six weeks; I'll need to get pretty damn fit if I'm going to beat Mancini.'

'So get fit.' Nina ran her hand through H's dreadlocks. She ran her fingertips lightly over the stubble on his cheeks. She passed a finger over the softness of his lips.

And for the next six weeks, H worked his arse off. He got fit.

# 31.

The gym was busy with boxers, and while Matt watched from the ringside H worked the pads in the ring with Nick. The soundtrack to H's fighter's dance was again the obligatory American rap. The musical mayhem was masterminded by Tim Dogg regaling the gym with 'Low Down Nigga'.

> **YEAH, HA HA! STRAIGHT OUT OF THE MOTHERFUCKIN' BRONX, LETTIN' EVERYBODY KNOW THAT TIM DOGG AIN'T TAKIN' NO MOTHERFUCKIN' SHORTS!**

H threw combination punches at the pads on Nick's hands. The pads were large, black, padded squares. In the centre of each square was a small white circle and it was this that H aimed for when he threw his punches. He danced in front of Nick, bobbing, weaving, moving his feet. Nick took two steps back, one to the side, the pads held up, one by his ear, the other by his chest. H followed him. Bap! Bap! Bap! He threw another combination, a left-right-left, working his body, moving, keeping busy. Nick moved again, one step back, two to the side. He moved his pads to keep H honest, both at the level of his chest this time. Ba-bap! Ba-bap! A left-right, left-right! Different combination, same lethal effect. H was looking good.

Since that night at Nina's H had indeed made the time, and the effort, to ease his body to a level of fitness it hadn't approached for at least five years. The going had been rough but the hard work had paid off. As he one- and two-stepped around the ring, working the pads on Nick's gnarled and battered hands, H could feel a snap and bounce. His knees bent and snapped back with a youthful vigour that felt good. Really good. Every evening H had spent up to two hours stretching. Stretching! Easing his body into unnatural positions, working his joints, lengthening his muscles. Six weeks was not nearly enough time to become really fit but it was enough time to make a difference and that's what H wanted to do. Because he knew that whatever shape his body was in by the time of the fight, his mental condition had to be better. He had to be feeling it and the only way to be feeling it then was to work his body now. H was going to be in the ring, alone, with Henry 'Bugle Boy' Mancini, a man with dynamite in both hands. He was as hard and as rugged a professional as there was. And as H well knew, the ring can be the smallest, loneliest place in the world if you aren't ready for the challenge. Deep down, H was under no illusion that he could beat Mancini over twelve rounds. Not really. But . . . you never know.

\*\*\*

The lives of H and Mancini had taken dramatically different paths since that summer night in 1998 when H had the world at his feet. Why? How had that happened? In the last six weeks, while pounding the roads of Battersea building his stamina, while skipping a series of twelve three-minute rounds, while performing his crunches and his push-ups, his chin-ups, twists, bends, squats . . . H had had time to think. And what he thought was that the person to blame for the different paths taken by himself and Mancini – the only person he could possibly blame – was himself.

It was a painful realisation.

Looking back, H could see that on any objective assessment he had been a vastly more talented boxer than Mancini. He'd had almost everything. He had hand speed, foot speed, he was blessed with an athlete's body, his hand–eye coordination was way above average, he could take a punch and he had a boxer's brain. He could think on his feet, he could change his strategy in the middle of a fight. The one thing he didn't have was a huge, knockout punch, but nobody has everything. And yet despite this formidable arsenal of talent, his career had slipped while Mancini's had gone from strength to strength. Why? All Mancini had going for him was a big punch and a chin like granite.

But, thought H, who was the bravest, who wanted it the most? In a match-up of equal talents, who was going to be the last man standing? H had been thinking about this question a lot recently. He was afraid of the answer. It was one that had been keeping him awake at night.

It was this knowledge – which he had always had! – that was the root of his gambling. He knew that now. And once H had confronted this realisation, he knew this fight with Mancini was going to be his last . . .

\*\*\*

A buzzer sounded for the end of another three-minute round. H stopped throwing punches at the pads and walked round the ring, blowing hard. Nick looked pleased and winked at Matt. He shook the pads off his hands and threw them to his son.

'Can you manage a couple a rounds sparring before you finish, H?'

'Whatever you say, coach.'

Despite the scowl that was an almost permanent fixture on Nick's face, H could tell that he was beaming inside. Over the last weeks of intense training H had thought about what might have been. How things might have been different if the kind of intensity he had brought to his work recently had been the same over the last few years. But he wiped that quickly from his mind. He had to forget what might have been and think about now. Nick's face was as lined as an unmade bed and some of those lines had no doubt been put there by H and his attitude to training over the years. But what was the point of dwelling on what couldn't be changed? H had one chance to redeem himself and he was taking it the best way he knew.

'Roight, you lot! Listen up! I need a couple a loive bodies up here now!' Tim Dogg continued to display a loud and questionable dexterity with words and lyrics. Nick's voice was drowned out and, as usual, he had to bellow and scream to make himself heard. Heads immediately snapped round as the music was turned off. The boxers waited for another of Nick's regular outbursts to blow over.

**. . . HI, MY NAME IS SHEILA FROM HOUSTON.**

**I WAS IN A HOTEL WITH EASY-E, HE GOT A LITTLE ASS DICK . . .**

'Dere's a fuckin' tyranny of rap music in dis fuckin' country and it'll be de fuckin' deatha me and de fuckin' ruination of all roight-moinded people!' Nick glared round the silent room through narrow eyes. 'Why de fuckin' hell can't you listen to de fuckin' bagpoipes or sumten? Sumten wid a fuckin' tune? Jaysus fuckin Chroist!' He continued to glare. 'T'ank fuckin' Chroist for de sound a silence! I need two people up here. Now! You and you!'

He pointed to Blood and one other. The rest of the gym slowly went back to life.

'In you get, Blood. And no punches to the head. You've got t'ree minutes.' Nick climbed out of the ring while Blood, who already had his gloves on his hands and a sheen of perspiration from working the speed bag, climbed in. Nick called over to Matt, 'Got the clock?' Matt reset the clock and nodded to his father.

'Roight,' Nick looked between H and Blood. 'Off you go.'

H and Blood circled each other warily, tossing exploratory jabs. Blood danced, keeping loose, looking good. H stalked. He manoeuvred Blood into a corner and delivered a flurry of combination punches, Blood danced away but no longer looked as casual as he had.

'We've obviously been doing sumten roight,' Nick said to Matt. He turned back to H and Blood. Blood snapped his jabs with more intent, no longer just tossing them. It made no difference to H. He ducked, moved, stepped, tucked; probing, covering up, jabbing. Looking surprisingly smooth, surprisingly fluid. Blood was spurred to greater effort, dancing with more purpose. This wasn't the casual workout he'd expected. He feinted with his left, threw the right, bang! caught H in the face.

Nick screamed at Blood, his face going beetroot red. 'Keep 'em down! Keep 'em down!'

H shook the blow off, came back, aimed at Blood's head, missed! Blood countered and H shuffled, sliding out of range.

'Fuckin' 'ell!' The words burst out of Nick as though chased by a rottweiler. 'Fuckin' 'ell! When's de last toime you saw dat?' It was a question that needed no answer and Matt didn't have one because the last time H had shuffled was too long ago for either Matt or Nick to remember.

Blood and H were now both dancing, using the ring, creating space. H caught Blood flush with a rising right. Bang! Blood hit the canvas. He immediately bounced back and rushed straight at H, his pride dented. Blood and H now stood toe to toe, exchanging furious blows. H then danced away, shuffled, moved, defended. Now Blood was the stalker, the chaser, off-balance, pushing forward. And H was making him taste leather, catching him – bang! Taste that. Bang! Another. Each blow only made Blood come at him faster, losing composure, looking scrappy.

The buzzer sounded to end the round. But Blood pushed on, oblivious to the buzzer. H had played him like a boy and Blood wanted payback.

'Toime!' Nick called it and expected his boys to cool it down. They didn't. 'Toime! Toime!' They still ignored him. The two battled on, H backing up, dancing, jabbing, moving; Blood pushed on, flailing, catching blows, losing it. Other boxers stopped their own work to watch the action. 'Time's up! Blood! H!' But H continued to pepper Blood with jabs, his legs snapping back and forth as he moved; Blood was becoming angrier and looking increasingly amateur. Finally Nick and Matt looked at each other and, simultaneously, jumped into the ring and struggled to separate the two fighters.

With Matt holding Blood and Nick holding H, the two boxers looked at each other, panting heavily. Blood was scowling, still seeing red. But H . . . inside H was smiling. He was beginning to feel it again. What he'd been missing. It felt good. And someone was going to pay for the years of hurt.

# 32.

**G**reen-eyed Brenda had been peremptorily dismissed. The night
before Gavin had returned home to Pampisford Road in Purley
to find green-eyed Brenda at the computer, dressed in the briefest
of shorts, a bra and a ridiculously pink pair of Ugg boots. Which, in
itself, wasn't a problem. The problem was that Brenda was listening,
as she often did, to a strange and particularly tuneless type of music,
very, very loud. Apparently it was called 'grime'. Whatever it was
Gavin didn't like it. He had tried to like it, he had listened while green-
eyed Brenda had tried to 'break it down' for him. But the music
seemed to be a lot of screeching and screaming in a super-fast
manner that allowed you no discernible access to what it was about.
Unintelligible.

After ten minutes, Gavin had asked her to turn the music down.
Unfortunately, five minutes before, he'd refused her request for yet
another quickie and green-eyed Brenda was in no mood to chat. She
had told him to 'mind your own business!' adding, as an afterthought,
'You're too old to understand!'

Gavin had been making his way into the kitchen when he'd asked
the question and, having heard the answer, was now making his way
back out. 'What did you say?'

'You heard!'

In the argument that followed, Gavin decided it was time for
Brenda to move out.

'But I don't have anywhere to . . . I don't have anywhere to go!'

Gavin heard the catch in her voice and knew that she was about to
cry. What could he do? He was a forty-nine-year-old man breaking up
with his beautiful twenty-three-year-old girlfriend, for the sole reason

that she was just . . . young. She was twenty-six years younger than he was.

Gavin steeled his heart, grabbed green-eyed Brenda by the arm and lifted her out of her seat in front of the computer. His seat and his computer.

'Let go of me . . . !'

'Get your stuff and . . . !' Gavin didn't finish his sentence because whilst he had hold of her left arm green-eyed Brenda swung her right fist and punched him in the eye. With a howl, Gavin went down clutching his face.

Twenty-five minutes later and Brenda had most of her few possessions in two army bags and had arranged to move back to the house she had vacated just over two months before. A car waited for her outside. A part of Gavin was sad to see her leave. He would miss her compact body, slim and childlike, and her green eyes which gave her an innocent quality that he liked. Green-eyed Brenda left with a wave and a tear. He watched, unseen, from the upstairs bedroom window as she climbed into the cab and was gone.

As he left the bedroom, Gavin glimpsed his own face in the mirror. He stopped and stepped back to look at his reflection. He ran a hand through his thinning hair and pushed a strand off his forehead. The purple swelling developing round his left eye was a problem that he'd have to explain away at work, but . . . Gavin smiled as he savoured the silence. He was looking forward to his first decent night's sleep in some time. Still smiling, Gavin padded downstairs to make a nice cup of tea.

\*\*\*

It was 8.15 in the morning and Gavin had enjoyed a wonderfully undisturbed night. But his tranquillity had been disturbed by an early morning phone call.

Once again, Gavin had been called on for direct involvement with the kind of unpleasantness Alan seemed to be increasingly reliant upon. Gavin's task today was to wait until the boxer's son, his five-year-old, came into school and then kidnap him. It was what Alan wanted. His final insurance that H would take the dive. This was a major felony for which you could serve major prison time. Gavin thought about the risk he was taking. He thought of the alternatives. Returning to work as a fitness instructor . . . no, he couldn't.

Gavin reconciled himself to his situation by telling himself that it would soon be coming to an end. Akers would soon be going to meet his maker. From what Nina had told him about H, he loved his son with a passion. Gavin wasn't proud of passing on to Alan what Nina had told him about the boxer's son, but the way Alan had been acting, he felt he had no choice. He knew Alan was planning something but Gavin wanted to beat him to it. Get there first. The kidnapping of the young boy was a risky operation but once completed H was sure to be looking for revenge and Nina would do what she had to do to make sure that the desire for revenge would translate into murder. Gavin could then step in and make the kind of money that he deserved to be making while no longer taking the kind of chances he was about to take.

Having thought it through, Gavin sat in his champagne-pink BMW, with its leather seats and its tinted windows, and allowed himself a smile as he watched the stream of mothers enter the school gates with their darling children. Almost all of them said their goodbyes to their cherished ones and left them playing in the school playground. One or two stood chatting. They concerned Gavin slightly, but if he had planned his modus operandi properly there should be no need for violence.

Moments later Gavin saw Cyrus and Beverley get out of their car and make their way towards the school gates. Gavin's smile broadened. Beverley and Cyrus were about twenty metres away when Gavin looked over and saw Emanuel take a .38 from his jacket pocket. His smile vanished.

'What the hell are you doing with that?!'

'Is eensurance pol-ee-cee.' Despite having lived in the country for at least eight years Emanuel spoke with a thick Spanish accent, laced with the sound of garlic and tortilla.

'No, Emanuel, we-don't-need-insurance-policy. That's crazy.' Gavin spoke to Emanuel as though conversing with an imbecile. He tapped the side of his head. 'This-is-my-insurance-policy. English-brain-power. You can put that away.' He pointed to the gun.

Emanuel shook his head vigorously. 'Alan – he say bring gun. In case trouble. Is eensurance pol-ee-cee. Alan say so. If I no want to be driver for ever,' Emanuel sighed heavily, 'I must use if ne-ce-ssary.'

'We don't need-the-gun!' Gavin looked up. Beverley and Cyrus were almost at the school gates. Shit. He would have to go. 'Just do what a driver does and start the engine when you see me come out of those gates. Okay?'

Emanuel nodded. 'Okay. I understand.' He put the .38 back into his jacket pocket, stroking it lovingly, mumbling something under his breath. Gavin shook his head. He was surrounded by Negros, dagos, half-breeds and wogs. What was the country coming to? As Beverley and Cyrus entered the school playground Gavin opened the door. He didn't leave the car just yet, he wanted to see Beverley back out on the street first. The children were allowed into the school building at 8.30 a.m. and it was already 8.19. Beverley was late so she wasn't likely to hang around but that still didn't leave him much time to do what he needed to .

Moments later Beverley walked briskly out of the school gates and back towards her car. Gavin climbed out. Looking back and forth along the road he crossed over quickly and made his way into the school. A night's sleep without Brenda had returned the feeling to his legs and he moved, once again, with what he imagined was the freedom of a cat. As he entered the school gates, Gavin looked around and immediately saw Cyrus. He was playing with a group of six small children. One of them was kicking a tennis ball about while the other five chased after him. The playground attendant, a rather attractive young woman, stood casually by the school door.

To one side of Gavin three mothers stood chatting to each other. Gavin could hear them laughing as they spoke. One of them was olive-skinned, dark-looking. Middle Eastern? In fact, as Gavin looked around the school playground, a lot of the kids looked dark! Of the forty or so children – boys and girls – playing in the playground, over half of them were non-white! Gavin's eyebrows shot to the top of his head. How could that be?

But Gavin did not have time for ruminations on the state of a changing London. He was waiting for an opportunity, a moment of distraction, anything that would allow him to evade the eye of the

# THE LAST CARD

school attendant. Time was running out. He looked at his watch. 8.23. Gavin waited.

And then the moment came. Responding to a call from inside the building, the attendant turned and went in. Just like that! Gavin didn't know how long she would be away from her post but he did know the time was now 8.28. He had two minutes! He steadied himself, took a couple of deep breaths, and then strode quickly over to where Cyrus and his friends were playing.

The tennis ball that the children had been playing with rolled towards him. He stooped and picked it up. There was an immediate wailing of disappointment from the children, the loudest coming from the biggest of them.

'Oi, mister! Can we have our ball back?'

'Of course you can, son. I just want to have a word with little Cyrus.' Gavin looked down at the small children with a beatific smile. He tossed the ball away and the five other children immediately ran after it. Cyrus, however, hesitated, looking up at Gavin.

'Hello, Cyrus. You don't know me but I'm a friend of your father's.'

'You know my dad?' The little boy's eyes lit up.

'I do and he asked me to give you this.' After a quick glance at the door through which the school attendant had disappeared, Gavin moved smoothly into phase two of his plan. Time was short. He squatted down and pulled from his pocket a plastic model of Spiderman.

'Wicked!' Cyrus snatched for the gift. Gavin moved it just out of his reach.

'But you can't have it just yet.' He replaced it in his pocket. He held up his hands as though he were a trainer and his hands were pads. He pretended to shadow box with the small boy. 'Your father tells me you like to watch him boxing?'

The boy's face fell. 'I do but my mum won't let me.'

'Well, today, I have a special treat for you.' He playfully tapped the boy on the cheek, encouraging him to punch his hands. 'Your father asked me to pick you up and take you to see him training.' Gavin backed up a bit while the little boy threw a wild punch at his hand, narrowly missing Gavin's nose. 'He said your mother wouldn't mind because you have been so well-behaved recently and it would be a treat for you. You can play with the Spiderman on the way there.'

But just when it looked as though Gavin could rise and take Cyrus with him, one of the boys playing with the tennis ball called out.

'Come on, Cy! We're losing!'

Cyrus looked round, his attention taken by the children scampering after the tennis ball. Gavin sensed he was losing the boy. He almost panicked, grabbing the boy's hand. He stopped himself, however, pulling out the Spiderman. He waved it in front of him.

'Here. Take it. You can play with it on the way to the gymnasium.' The little boy's hands closed round the toy. Gavin rose up, took Cyrus's hand and, with a last glance at the school door, led him calmly from the playground.

One of the chatting mothers, the Middle Eastern woman, peeled off and waved her goodbyes. She looked over at Gavin and Cyrus and smiled warily at Gavin. Gavin smiled back. The woman looked down at Cyrus.

'Hello, Cyrus, are you being a good boy?'

'Yes, Mrs Slim.' The little boy chanted her name back, his attention focused on the Spiderman toy.

'And where are you off to this morning? You're not going into school today?' By now Gavin was at the gates. All he had to do was pick the boy up, run across the road, jump in the car and he was gone.

'I'm just taking him to meet his father.' The smile vanished from the woman's face and was replaced by a frown. Gavin knew he'd said the wrong thing. He glanced over at Emanuel in the BMW and hoped to Christ he had the engine running. What he saw almost prompted bowel evacuation. Emanuel did not have the engine running. Emanuel was not even in the car. Emanuel stood outside, his right arm tucked not-so-casually into the left side of his jacket. He was looking right at Gavin with a meaningful stare.

'Does Beverley know about this? I don't think she would want Cyrus missing school to see his father.'

'Everything's fine. If you don't believe me ask the school. It's all been arranged with them.' They were now out on the street. Gavin looked both ways and without waiting for the women to reply, he scooted quickly across to the car. He was almost dragging the boy by now. The woman stood on the kerb watching him, clearly suspicious.

# THE LAST CARD

Gavin hissed at Emanuel as he opened the back door and pushed the boy in.

'Get in the car and drive!' He climbed in after the boy. Looking up he saw Emanuel cross the road to meet the woman. What? Gavin looked at him with horror. What the hell was he doing? As he watched, Emanuel slowly withdrew his arm from his jacket. There was something in his hand. The woman looked at it, then up at Emanuel. She began talking rapidly. Gavin climbed out of the car and made his way round to the driver's side. Emanuel had left the keys in the ignition. If the stupid dago was going to shoot this woman right there in the street, Gavin wasn't hanging around.

Just as he was about to start the engine, the woman turned and walked away. Cool as you like. Emanuel strolled back to the car. He met Gavin sitting in the driver's seat.

'What arrre you doing?' He asked the question nonchalantly as Gavin stepped out of the car. Gavin didn't answer, he rounded the back of the car and climbed in next to the boy.

'What were you saying to that woman?' Gavin demanded. Emanuel didn't answer. He started the engine and pulled smoothly away. As they passed the Middle Eastern woman, Emanuel waved at her and smiled. She waved back.

'What did you say to her?' Gavin was almost shouting. He glanced quickly at the boy but Cyrus was playing happily with his new toy.

'You not worry. I ask her the way to Old Kent Road. Then I ask her for telephone number.'

'Her telephone number?'

'Si. Yes.'

'And she gave it to you?' Even Gavin was surprised at the simplicity of the ruse. Emanuel turned back to look at him.

'What you think? You no think Manny is good-looking?' Manny turned back to the road, a broad smile on his face. Gavin could see him in the rear-view mirror. It was a funny thing, Gavin thought, but Emanuel had chauffeured him for almost two years now and Gavin had never really looked at him. He was kind of good-looking.

# 33.

**A**rm-in-arm, H and Nina entered the small Virgin record store in Notting Hill. Bob Marley's 'Jamming' played over the shop's hi-fi system. H was wearing a new Adidas tracksuit, a clean white tee-shirt and old-skool navy-and-white Adidas Gazelles. H looked lean and healthy. He'd also shaved his head. The short dreadlocks that he'd seen as a part of his personality for the last ten years were gone. H's scalp was now as clean as an egg.

H felt good as he browsed the bargain CDs, leaving Nina to search through the Pop/Rock. He was focused in the gym, he hadn't been near a gambling shebeen for weeks, and he and Nina had been seeing more and more of each other.

Nina was not the kind of woman that he would ever expect to see in any kind of a serious way. Yet over the last month she had constantly surprised him with her humour, her knowledge and her drive.

H looked across at her as she stood at the front of the shop waiting to pay. Seeing her head moving in time to the jumping bass line, H had to smile. Always the tough chick was Nina. For some reason, as he looked at her, a lascivious smile playing on his face, she turned and looked right back at him. As though she had read his mind.

They both grinned.

H and Nina left the shop and walked down Holland Park Avenue. It was now only four days before the fight with Mancini and H's rigorous training regime had wound down to almost nothing. Just a light morning run and an hour of gentle sparring.

They approached Nina's house and the chatter between them stopped. As soon as they were in her kitchen H slammed the front door behind them, moved Nina up against the wall and pressed against her body. His lips found their way on to hers while his hands probed inside her jacket, under her shirt and up the side of her stomach and breasts. He gripped her under the armpits. She had her hands under his tee-shirt, down his briefs, digging in her nails, pulling him to her. They stayed like this for a moment, feverish.

They broke apart and ran upstairs to the bedroom. They shed their clothes and with their arms and legs wrapped around each other resumed kissing. Soon Nina had worked her way on top of H and held his face in one hand while she sucked ferociously at his lips. Moments later H had flipped her over and was working his way down her body, kissing, licking, stroking. She lay back, her head raised, looking down at him while his tongue and lips reached her clipped hair. She moaned as she stroked his head.

His turn now, he wriggled higher up the bed. Flushed and glowing, Nina knelt between his legs. She cupped him with one hand, held his girth with the other and made him wish time would stand still.

Some time later they were sprawled across the bed, the bed-clothes a tangled mess on the floor. As H dozed he watched the evening light dying through the bedroom window. Darkness crept through the room and all was still.

The moment was shattered by the shrill ring of H's mobile. H opened his eyes and saw Nina's sleeping face. The ringing continued, jangling, loud and insistent. He sat up and looked around, disorientated. He tried to identify the source of the ringing. His sweatshirt. He leant over Nina to pick it up from the floor. He plucked his mobile from one of the pockets.

'Hel . . .' he coughed, his voice still thick with sleep. 'Hello?' He couldn't hear anything but crying at the other end of the line. 'Hello? Who is this?'

'It's me.'

'What's the matter?' His voice was suddenly full of concern. He scooted his legs round and sat on the edge of the bed.

'It's Cyrus. He's gone missing.'

'He's what?' He was wide awake now. 'He's what did you say?'

'He's gone missing.'

'What do you mean? Where is he?' There was a pause at the other end of the line. Beverley was almost incoherent, but through her sobs she explained what she had been told by the police.

'What?' H's breathing shallowed and he could barely speak. 'Just like that?'

Beverley's response was a sob and a sniff.

'Jesus fucking Christ, so what's happening now?'

Awake now, Nina was sitting up, trying to glean as much as she could from his side of the conversation.

'The police . . .'

H interrupted her. 'Where are you?'

'At my mother's.'

'Stay there! I'm coming over.' He hung up and twisted round on the bed. Nina's eyes were full of concern.

'That was Beverley. Cyrus has gone missing.'

'Missing?'

'Someone took him from his school. This morning.' Grim-faced, H began to dress. Nina sat and watched him. She pulled on some clothes and sat hugging her knees to her chest.

H sat next to her as he laced his trainers. He glanced over at her.

'I think it might be Alan that's got your boy.' She spoke as though in a daze.

H stopped as though he'd been slapped. 'What?'

'I think it might be Alan.'

'Why would you think that?!'

'Earlier today Gavin mentioned something about Cyrus. He said something about telling you that Alan wanted to see you and Cyrus would pass the message.'

H stared at her, dumbfounded.

'Christ, I'm sorry, Hilary, it just . . . we were . . . I had no idea. I think it must be about this.'

'What the fuck is going on, Nina?'

'I know what you want to do, Hilary, but . . .'

'But what?'

'Hilary, you'll get hurt . . .'

'Hurt! I'll fucking hurt somebody! Alan's . . . !'

'Alan's not around!'

'Where is he?'

'Out of town. On business . . .'

'Don't fucking lie to me!'

# THE LAST CARD

'Even if he was here, what good would that do?'

'If he's touched one hair on Cyrus's . . . I'm going to crush his windpipe! I'm going to break his fucking back!'

'Think! Just think about it! If it is Alan that's taken Cyrus – and let's hope that it isn't – but if it is him, he knows you're going to be going crazy! He's taken Cyrus for a reason! He's not going to let you just walk in there and take him back.'

'Call him!'

'Call who?'

'Alan! Call him now. Or Gavin. Find out what the fuck's going on! In fact, give me the number, let me call him.' As Nina left the room, H finished dressing and sat back down on the edge of the bed, thinking. He made himself take slow, deep breaths.

Nina returned and handed him a piece of paper. As she gave it to him she slid an arm over his shoulders. He shook it off and stood up.

'Can I borrow your car?'

'Of course.' She said the words but she knew, they both knew, that their relationship had changed. The honeymoon was over. She knew why he wanted her car and they looked at each other in silence.

'How's Beverley?'

'How do you think?' Nina didn't say anything. H picked up his mobile and tapped in Gavin's number.

\*\*\*

H and Beverley strolled across the grass at the back of her mother's house. It was a large parkland area where the local kids played football, but as the darkness of the evening drew in the place was quiet.

'I'm sorry . . . I just, I just can't . . .'

'It's all right, Bev.' He squeezed her hand. They had been walking along in silence for some time, Beverley crying, allowing the sobs to come unchecked. He recognised that Beverley rarely showed her vulnerability. Despite his own grief, it was H who was being strong, it was H who was taking charge. He put his arm around her and she tried to compose herself.

'How are you, anyway?' she managed to squeeze out. H shrugged, sighing heavily.

'I don't know. Away from all this . . . same shit, different day.'

'I read . . .' she sniffed heavily, '. . . in the paper. You've got this fight coming up soon. Mancini.'

'That's right.'

They walked on in silence for a while.

'One of the last conversations I had with Cyrus was about this fight. We read about it in the papers together. He just looked up at me and said "I want Daddy to win, win, win!"' This set Beverley off crying again and H had to swallow hard. He stopped and turned to face her, drawing her to him. They stood like this for a moment, H feeling the wet of her tears soaking through to his skin.

'Look, Beverley . . . I know I've been an arsehole . . . but I'm serious now. This is going to be my last fight. Ever. And . . . once I do that, I think I can kick the gambling as well. I'm going to get Cyrus back, trust me. Then, is there any chance for us to start again?' He pulled her away from his chest and looked into her red, swollen eyes.

'I think . . . maybe . . . it's too late for us now, H. Best just be friends, eh?'

Again, H had to swallow hard.

\*\*\*

The next day H strode quickly into Roxy's. He'd called Gavin the previous evening and the arrangement had been to come in at 12 o'clock, midday. Gavin had been vague on the telephone but had implied that if H spoke to White Alan today all would be revealed. Without anything more specific H had thought it wise not to mention any of this to Beverley.

That night H had managed very little sleep and today his head felt thick. He'd spent the night disturbed by thoughts of Cyrus, alone and frightened. These were quickly followed by thoughts of what he, Hilary, would do to Akers when he saw him. It was anger that drove him now. As he bowled through the main entrance of the club, H spotted Gavin reading a newspaper at the bar. The club was empty but for three cleaners, two of them working behind the bar, the third gliding round the dance floor with an electric floor-polisher.

Gavin looked up from his paper. 'Hello, Hil . . .'

'Let's cut the shit. Where's Akers?'

# THE LAST CARD

Gavin folded his paper. A lack of pleasantries was fine by him.

'Are you carrying?'

'No.'

'You won't mind if I check then.'

Gavin walked over to him. H raised his arms and Gavin patted him down.

'Right this way.'

They walked through the dark hallway and up the stairs in silence. On the landing H stood behind him as Gavin knocked. Without waiting for an answer Gavin opened the door and leant his head in.

'Hilary James here to see you,' said Gavin. 'He's outside.'

H could just see Akers locking a safe in the wall behind his desk.

'Good. Bring him in.' Akers replaced the mirror that disguised the safe and checked his reflection. Only once he was back in his seat did Gavin usher H into the office. H stood in front of Akers' desk, while Gavin sat in a wooden chair behind him. H could scarcely contain his rage. His words burst out of him.

'Where's my boy? Was it you? Did you do it?'

Alan Akers looked back at H with the inscrutability of a cat. Today he wore a white cashmere jumper and a pair of baggy white woollen slacks.

'You know what I want.' Akers spoke in a soft, confident voice. 'I want insurance that you're going down in the first round. I repeat . . . in the first round.'

H thought his head was going to explode but he made his voice flat, devoid of emotion. 'You've got it. What about Cyrus?'

'He's fine . . .'

'If you've . . .'

'He's fine!' Akers spat out his assurance as though H's concerns were a waste of his valuable time. 'As soon as the fight's over, and you've done what you're supposed to do, he'll be dropped off with the lovely Bever . . .'

That was it. H lunged over the desk for Akers' throat. He grabbed him by his polo-neck, dragged him out of his seat and back over the desk. The next instant Gavin had a choke hold round H's neck and pulled him backwards, across the office. Gagging, H was forced to release his grip on Akers' throat.

Akers rolled off the desk and straightened his clothes. The bruise to his dignity had him so angry he could only bark, 'Out! Get him out of here!'

Gavin shuffled H round so that he was facing the door and then slowly released his hold. He seemed ready to re-apply the pressure if H showed signs of losing it again. But H headed quietly for the door without struggling. Just before he left he stopped and turned back.

'How did you know about Cyrus and Beverley?'

Akers glared back at him. But then he suddenly gave a grim smile. 'Nina, of course. Didn't she tell you?'

H let his face betray no emotion. He dipped into the top pocket of his jacket and pulled out Nina's car keys. He weighed them in his hand for a moment, then tossed them at Akers. 'I guess these belong to you.'

H turned and left. Back out on the street he took some deep breaths of fresh, clean air. He was in shock. Nina had told Akers about Cyrus? He wandered, dazed, up to Oxford Street. He didn't know what to do but he didn't want to go home just yet. He needed time to think.

*** 

H stopped in a Starbucks and ordered a coffee. When it arrived he stirred it, endlessly, thinking, thinking. Did Nina tell White Alan about Cyrus? Deliberately tell him? No, she couldn't have. It must have come out accidentally. But she'd given up badgering him about Akers' money or killing him. Why? H couldn't figure it out. And then other questions crowded their way into his mind: Akers was forcing him to throw the fight. What could he do about that? Akers was forcing him to throw the fight! Akers had Cyrus, H knew he would have to take the dive. But could he live with that?

H laid his head next to his coffee on the counter in front of him. He closed his eyes. He wanted to sleep.

'Are you all right?'

He looked up. The young French waitress was looking down at him with concern.

'Is there anything I can do? Are you feeling ill or something?'

'No, it's all right. I don't think you can help me on this one.'

'You're sure?'

'I'm sure.'

# THE LAST CARD

'You want another cup? This one is cold.'

H looked at his coffee. A thin layer of skin had formed over the top. 'Can I?'

'Of course you can!' She scooped up his mug and returned a moment later with a fresh one. 'Don't tell anyone; it's on the house.' She winked conspiratorially, then gave him a broad smile and walked away. H's eyes followed her as she weaved her way between other customers. Something about this brief, momentary encounter inspired H – this small act of kindness seemed to make the world a better place.

H sat and tried to imagine what he would do if this were a boxing match. What would he do if a 210-pound gorilla was facing him across the ring? How would he deal with it? Would he deal with his opponent head on? Or would he box clever? Dodge, feint, weave? Or would he use his opponent's strength against him?

\*\*\*

At 5.15 p.m., as the late afternoon sunshine faded around him, H found himself on the Gascoyne housing estate in Homerton, Hackney. H didn't know exactly what he was looking for but a chance remark by Nina had given him an idea. It was a crazy, loony idea, but maybe, just maybe, it might work. If H had learnt anything in the ring over the last fifteen years, it was that the most important muscle to flex was the one between his ears. Any 210-pound gorilla could be beaten if you used your boxing brain effectively. Failure to recognise this was why he'd lost to Mancini the first time.

H wandered. Unlike his own small 1960s estate, this one was huge, and ranged from two-storey family homes with neat front gardens to white-painted ten-storey blocks of flats and older red-brick blocks from the 1930s. H estimated that the whole estate must have been spread over almost a square mile.

Gascoyne was one of the new generation of inner-city housing estates. The greying concrete monoliths that had won awards in the 1960s had long since fallen out of fashion and were being replaced. The lessons – of communal walkways, stairs, lifts, places where nobody took responsibility which were therefore permanently vandalised – had apparently sunk in.

H finally headed for a basketball court that bordered Hartlake Road, one of the main arteries running through the estate. He was attracted by a drawling bass-line beat and the urgent clatter of treble.

The basketball court was bordered by an elevated grass verge. Lounging on the court next to a Hackney 'handbag' were a group of kids in their early to late teens. The 'handbag' warbled a track by Tupac so badly distorted that it might have been anybody. The teenagers eyed H warily as he approached.

'Hey, guys, all right?' H ventured.

A skinny white boy – about fifteen, with long, stringy hair that hung in his eyes and dribbled over the collar of a dirty tee-shirt – was sucking hard on the smallest roach H had ever seen, clasped in a pair of metal crocodile clips.

'Wha' 'appen, sah?'

H did a double-take. The skinny white boy spoke in a broad Jamaican patois! Bemused, H watched him pass the crocodile clips to the black boy sitting next to him.

'I'm looking for Joseph Adeyshian. Do you know which flat he lives in?'

'Wha' you say?'

'Do any of you guys know Joseph Adeyshian?'

'Is Babylon you a deal wid?'

This was starting to do H's head in.

'No, I'm not a policeman, I'm a friend of his.' H immediately realised how weak this sounded. The kids must have thought so too – they eyed him suspiciously. The end of the spliff, no bigger than a memory, was passed to one of the white girls. She puckered her lips as she tried to suck the last of the smoke from it.

'Who arrrereuandwyhsssshoieouldhetyelleuianthing?' One of the other black boys was leaning up against the basket now. H looked at him blankly. His puzzled look was clearly expected because the other kids started laughing.

'He said "Who are you and why should he tell you anything?"' That was one of the white girls. She had short blonde hair, wore stone-washed denim head to toe, and small red pimples covered her pasty, pale face. H turned back to the boy.

'I'm just a guy who needs a favour from him.'

# THE LAST CARD

'Yoeulkliookedebbieyst!'

H looked blank and again there was much merriment. He was starting to feel irritable. Whatever happened to respect for one's elders?

'He said you look like the beast!' The white girl again translated and H forced himself to laugh with a mirth he didn't feel.

'I just told you,' H snapped, 'I'm not a policeman! Do you know him? Does he live on this estate?'

There was a pause while the youths decided whether they would answer H's question or not. As they looked him up and down all H could think about was Cyrus and what he might be going through at that exact moment.

'Wydeaouwianthm?' H didn't even bother looking at the boy, he just looked at his improbable translator.

'"Why do you want him?"'

'I'm a friend of Nina McGuire's. I've got a job for Ade and she told me that I could buck up with him and a guy called Dunstan on this estate.'

At the mention of Nina and Dunstan the guy and the girl both seemed to relax. The guy actually smiled.

'OkushioodheaoveminshoondNnaerylr.AdeleeivsuovvaernVyin-Hwos. Nymbatwennynine, sweet.'

'"You should have mentioned Nina earlier. Ade lives over in Vaine House, number twenty-nine."' The young white girl pointed the way.

'Cheers.' H turned to leave.

'Oiymeiytdaouafvegitteotanwyfiaegs?' H turned back to see the black boy with the speech impediment looking at him expectantly. He turned to the girl.

'What?'

'He wants to know if you've got any fags?'

\* \* \*

H rapped loudly on the door of number twenty-nine and took a step back. He could hear the television blaring from the other side so he knew someone was in. Nobody came; he knocked again. He heard what sounded like the unlocking of the national bank: three chains, two bolts and a deadlock.

Standing before H was a lean, sinewy, young black man, twenty-ish, a little bit taller than H. His skin was dark, his head was almost shaved and he stared at H through bright, clear eyes. The young man stood topless, wearing just a pair of huge Evisu jeans, hanging on his hips below a pair of star-spangled Tommy Hilfiger pants. Round his neck he wore a thick, gold rope chain, with a gold 'Lion of Judah' hanging in the middle of his hairless chest.

'Ade?'

'Who wants to know?'

'I'm a friend of Nina McGuire's. Can I come in?'

A woman's voice shouted from inside the flat. 'Who dat, Ade?' The noise from the television suddenly stopped.

'You're a friend of Nina's? How is she?'

'She's good. We've been running around together a little bit.'

'Oh, yeah?' Ade suddenly smiled, showing pearly white teeth. 'What you say your name is?'

'Hilary James. H. Can I come in? I've got something I need to talk to you about.'

'Yeah, man, come in.' Ade stood aside to let him into the flat. H walked through a dark hallway into a bright and airy living room. He had to blink twice to make sure this wasn't some kind of meretricious fantasy. First, the room was hot. The central heating must have been blowing on maximum strength to keep the air as hot as it was, thick and heavy, like a blanket. And the furniture looked as though some-one had spent half a million pounds at a Dalston street market and then installed the purchases in Ade's flat. Ghetto fabulous! The room gloried in the gaudy, the exuberant, the ostentatiously expensive. And at the centre of it, taking pride of place, was a television unit that Steven Spielberg himself would have been proud of. H guessed it must have run to at least five grand. The 52-inch flat-screen model hung from a wall, surrounded by woofers and tweeters and speakers and bouncers and H didn't know what else. The floor was littered with clothes, magazines and other debris and H had to pick his way to an armchair.

Sprawled full-length on the sofa, in her bra and knickers, was the woman who had shouted earlier. She looked to be about the same age as Ade and, apart from her darker skin, had the same long, sinewy look. She reminded H of a young Grace Jones. Hard as nails, but very sexy. H nodded to her. She ignored him and turned back to the television, re-starting the DVD they had been watching. With the speakers now blaring, Ade picked up a half-smoked spliff from an ashtray on the floor and sucked it back to life.

'I hear you and your friend Dunstan,' said H, 'have got problems with a man called Alan Akers. Is that true?' H had to raise his voice to talk over the sound effects of Keanu Reeves fighting about two hundred Agent Smiths. Ade studied H's face with keen eyes.

'I don't have any problems with White Alan.' Ade was guarded, wary, as H had known he would be.

'Listen,' he said, 'I've got problems with him too. I've got big problems with him. I thought maybe we could help each other.'

Ade again thought before he spoke. Despite the wariness H could see that he might like Ade.

'How do I know you're on a level?' The young man turned to the woman lying next to him. 'Turn it down a bit willya, Jan.'

'I'm watching it.'

'I know you are, babe, but turn it down a bit, we're trying to talk, d'you know what I mean.'

'Why don't you go in the other room?' Ade didn't say any more, he just leant across the woman's body, picked up the remote control and switched the television off.

'Oi, Ade!' The woman gave him a murderous look. He returned it with a smile.

'Please, babe. This is business. D'you mind going into the other room? Watching it in there?' Ade leant towards her and kissed her softly on the mouth, completely disarming her. H had to smile. She rose without a whimper and, picking up an empty mug, padded gracefully from the room.

'So how do I know you're on a level?' Ade was harder, more serious now. He took another hit from the spliff and passed it to H. H shook his head. He told the story of his kidnapped son and the fight that he was being forced to fix. He ended by asking Ade a question.

'Not that Nina's chatting your business, but reading between the lines a bit, I reckon the Akers brothers are trying to hang on and control something when maybe . . . their time is over?'

Ade snorted loudly. 'Their time is well over, you get me!'

'So maybe there is a way we can help each other. I'll be completely open with you, I know you're safe. I need Alan . . . out of the way.'

Ade nodded slowly. 'I can see that. But how d'you think me and you could help each other?'

'Well, I can deliver him to you. On a plate. No strings.'

H waited, nervous before this youth, this baby. Ade looked back at him, thinking. When the youth next spoke, H didn't have a clue where he was coming from.

'What do you know about globalisation?'

# 34.

**N**ina had parked her car outside a pub on the Old Kent Road. She was nervous, butterflies fluttering in the pit of her stomach. She hadn't seen H for the last three days, since he'd left that night to see Beverley. She was worried. She hadn't called him, she knew he needed time to deal with what was going on with Cyrus. She gave him the time but that didn't mean she liked doing it. Three days. And he still hadn't called.

And then there was the fact that he'd left her car keys with Alan. Why would he leave her keys with Alan?

Nina liked to be in control. As things stood she didn't know what to think, or what to do. As the days had passed Nina had come to realise something: that H meant more to her than a way of dealing with Alan. She had begun to fantasise about the two of them running away and starting again as Mr and Mrs Nobody. They could go to Birmingham or Manchester or Liverpool. Nina had spent a long time knocking around, singing in pubs, bars and clubs but she had to face facts and the fact was that the longest engagement she had ever had was her stint at Roxy's – because of Alan. Maybe now was the time to move on.

Hilary . . . well, there was something solid about Hilary that she liked. Yes, he was a macho schmuck in his own way and, yes, he had his problems. But he had a streak of decency in him which she admired. All her previous boyfriends, especially White Alan, had treated her like an appendage. H was different. Now that Nina thought about it, maybe she had been treated like that because she hadn't demanded to be treated any other way. But what Nina loved about H was that she didn't need to demand to be treated as anything. And there was another thing. Their sex life wasn't bad either . . .

As Nina locked the car she took one last look at herself, at her reflection in the car window. She wore a full-length black sheepskin coat. Under the coat she wore her favourite Nicole Farhi blouse, grey; some black tailored Comme Des Garçons pants that finished just above her ankles, and a pair of casual black slip-on flat shoes. Prada. To finish off her look she put on a pair of Alain Mikli sunglasses. The overall effect was smart, stylish, bohemian. Not that she was making a special effort or anything.

Nina walked the twenty or so metres past the pub and stepped gracefully into the run-down building next door – the 'Old Kent Road Boys' Club'. As Nina entered the gym, her senses were immediately assailed. Some kind of American rap music pounded out, making her ears throb. The sound mingled with the slap, slap, slapping of the skipping on the wooden floor; the thud, thud, thudding of leather gloves on the heavy leather bags; and the pitter-patter-pitter-patter-pitter-patter-pitter-patter of leather gloves on the speed bag; and all of this combined with the grunts and oomphs and groans of bodies working, pushing, hitting; all in all a cacophony of noise.

The corrosive stench of dried and musty sweat; sweat from bodies that were sweating; sweat from bodies that had been sweating for days but hadn't been washed; sweat from kit that the bodies were wearing that stank with old sweat; sweat from boxing gloves that had been worn by thousands of sweating hands over the years; sweat from old, discarded jock straps that littered the dark corners of the gym; every kind of sweat that you could possibly imagine seemed to exist in this gym and Nina could smell all of it. And this corrosive, acrid sweat smell was lightly flavoured with the stench of battered, worked-over, rubbed-raw leather.

And then the sight of at least twenty young men, most of them in a state of semi-undress, bursting with health and athleticism, glowing with activity. It wasn't quite worth the assault on her nose and ears, but it wasn't far off.

Nina stood at the entrance to the gym and looked around. She was almost certain H would be here today, the day before his big fight, and she wanted to see him. She was desperate to see him. As she looked around, Nina could sense she was causing a stir, but she didn't mind. She knew why she was there.

And then she saw him. H was skipping in a corner of the gym. Two white men, one old, one young, were standing watching him. H wore a sleeveless grey tee-shirt with some shiny black shorts. Nina realised this was the first time she had ever seen him in his boxing kit. He didn't have any pictures of himself boxing in his flat; she was seeing this side of him for the first time. She looked at the sweat flying from his head and running down his face, arms and chest; she watched as his legs, lean and powerful, danced up and down, up and down, up and down. She had to admit it . . . he looked pretty good.

While Nina admired the view, H saw something of the stir she was causing in the mirror in front of him and followed the direction of countless looks. His eyes caught and held hers. She smiled at him, uncertain, sheepish. He looked away. For a while he continued to skip. And then suddenly, to the surprise of the two white men watching him, he threw his rope to the floor and headed for the changing room. He called to one of the white men as he left.

'Remember, Nick, I want the money in cash. Straight after the fight . . .'

'You never moind dat,' the older man shouted after him, 'you just make sure you get some sleep! I'm sending a car over to pick you up at foive tomorra. Sharp!' But H had already left the gym.

Nina stepped outside to wait. The butterflies were still there, more so now. She hovered on the street, near the entrance of the club. She didn't have to wait too long before H sauntered out wearing his navy tracksuit and carrying his kit bag. She walked up to him and kissed him on the cheek. It felt awkward.

'Hi. How are you?' This was ridiculous. Nina felt like a schoolgirl.

'Long time, no see.'

'I was going to say the same thing.'

'I've got a fight coming up. Things on my mind. Like my missing son.'

Right. She had the picture now. And as soon as she had the picture the butterflies began to fly away. To be replaced by anger.

'And I've been trying to find out where Alan's hiding him!' she hissed at him. 'Doesn't that mean something, dick-brain?'

'And?'

Nina was taken aback – H had replied with a blankness that he surely didn't feel. 'No news yet. Alan's keeping everything very tight at the club.' She looked away, jamming her hands into the pockets of her coat and hunching her shoulders. 'What have I done wrong?'

'Nothing. I just told you, I've got things on my mind.'

Oh, please! Why did men do that? She could feel the two small, vertical lines spring to her forehead, just above her eyebrows.

'Kiss me.'

H hesitated, but he bent towards her and tried to give her a quick kiss. That moment's hesitation killed Nina. When H tried to break off she grabbed the back of his head and pulled him towards her. She kissed him with passion, biting his lip, but he jerked away.

'Ow!' He rubbed his bottom lip. There was blood and he glowered at her. She ignored it.

'As soon as this is all over, Hilary, why don't we just go away? As soon as the fight is done, with Cyrus safe and back with his mother, why don't you and me take off somewhere?' She meant what she said but she didn't say it as though she meant it. She knew H wouldn't agree to go away with her. Whatever she had done to him, he had changed. They were on opposite sides of a fence now and that's why she'd bitten him. If she was a man she would have punched him in the face. 'We could just forget about White Alan!'

'You told Akers about Cyrus, didn't you?'

'No! It wasn't me!' And she wasn't lying. Nina knew that the only way White Alan would have known about Cyrus was through Gavin, and it was she who had told Gavin. She felt bad enough about that without admitting this to H. Maybe later. But at least for now she could say with complete confidence that she hadn't told Alan. Despite this, H looked at her with accusing eyes.

'Look at me, Hilary; it wasn't me. You have to believe me.' Silence. 'What are you going to do?'

'I've been to see your man, Ade.'

'Ade?'

'Between us we've cooked up a little "treat" for White Alan. It's all about globalisation, apparently.'

For once, Nina was stumped for words. She took off the sunglasses.

# THE LAST CARD

'What?'

'I need one thing: for you to make sure that Alan is alone on the night after the fight.'

'You're going to do it! You're going to kill White . . . !'

'Shhh!' H grabbed Nina's arm and dragged her away from the entrance to the club. He hissed in her ear. 'What the hell is wrong with you?'

Nina was in shock. Events were moving way too fast for her. H was squeezing her arm, tight now.

'Ow! I can arrange it! I'll arrange with Gavin . . .'

'Are you sure? I don't want that gorilla turning up out of the blue!'

'I'm sure! He's in the same boat as me; he wants Alan . . . got rid of.'

'Gavin! I thought he was White Alan's main man?'

'He was. But people change, don't they?' She glared at H. He let go of her arm. She rubbed it and continued, 'He can see what's going on better than anyone.'

'So what does he get out of it?'

'The top job. Alan's empire.'

'What about the money?'

'Let me deal with that. I can handle him.' H looked at her sternly. 'Are you ready for this?'

'So you're really going to do it?'

'With Ade's help.'

'I don't believe it!'

'Believe it. But can I trust you?'

Nina moved into his arms like a cat curling up by the fire. She kissed him softly and sweetly on the mouth. 'What do you think, Hilary?'

'Just make sure you're waiting for me at your place with a toothbrush and a spare pair of knickers. We fly out that night.'

Nina couldn't believe this. 'Where?'

'Don't worry about it. But . . . about Cyrus . . .'

'I know. I'll keep trying.'

'As soon as you have anything! You'll ring me?'

'Of course.'

H now backed away. 'I've got to go.'

'Hilary! Good luck for tomorrow night!' She smiled encouragingly.

'Don't you want . . .'

'Not this close to the fight!' And he was gone, disappearing back into the gym.

'. . . a ride home?' Nina finished her sentence to herself, the smile lingering on her face like a memory. The butterflies were back again but she knew the lines on her forehead had gone.

Who was it that said women couldn't have it all?

# 35.

A de looked at his co-conspirators Wha Gwan and Dunstan with a thinly veiled scorn. The three of them were sitting round the table in Wha Gwan's ratty kitchen.

'You know what? I think I know the brer.' Wha Gwan.

'Yeah?'

'Where'd you meet him?' Dunstan.

'Frenna mine.'

'Who?' Ade could tell Dunstan didn't like Wha Gwan knowing more than him. Insecure.

'Bwoy, you nose long, eh!'

'How'd you know it's the same brer?'

'You said a boxer, right?'

'Yeah . . .'

'So I met the brer! Six footish, solid, baby dreds.'

'Das alotta brers, you know't I mean.' Wha Gwan cocked his head to one side and squinted at Dunstan.

'Wha Gwan, D? What's your problem?'

'No problem. Just making sure if we're gonna do this we all know what we're getting into.'

'This' was the business of murder.

'You know if we take out a white man there's gonna be hell to pay. Standard.'

'Why? He's a gangster. Just don't touch the civilians.' Ade.

'Listen, star, a white gangster ain't the same as a black gangster, you understand? Five-Oh is not gonna like dat.'

'Dunstan's right.' Wha Gwan. 'We've all heard the term 'black-on-black' violence, but I ain't heard the term 'white-on-white' violence. If we take this guy out there will be repercussions.'

'You know what? You all chatting Kentucky Fried Chicken shit!' Ade glowered at Dunstan and Wha Gwan. 'Alan and Paul are fuckers that need to step! Quicktime! I'm talking black-on-white violence, you get me! Fuck the police! If we're really worried about them we shouldn't be in this fuckin' business!'

'Das de bottom line, G,' said Wha Gwan slowly nodding his head.

'Damn, skippy! I'm the one taking all the risks anyway. Now if we're serious about grabbing a piece of what's ours . . .' Ade was now looking directly at Dunstan, 'we need to step up. Take charge. Let's be some crazy-arsed niggers!'

'How much did you say would be there?' Dunstan. Ade kissed his teeth with irritation.

'Forget de money, Duns! We dus' off de Akers brothers, dere'll be plenty of money. Dis is strictly in and out. Blaps!'

The three lapsed into silence as they thought through the implications of what they were discussing.

'And big blondie, what about him?' enquired Wha Gwan, a sudden casualness entering his tone.

'He's on the down-low. But your job is to keep an eye on him. Make sure he's cool.'

Again Wha Gwan slowly nodded his head. Only this time a hint of a smile crossed his lips.

'If you're gonna dus' Alan, why not take the money anyway?' Dunstan.

'Raartid! Because it's in his safe! He's not just gonna give me de combination!'

'Beat it out of him!'

Both Ade and Wha Gwan stared at Dunstan.

'Dunstan,' said Wha Gwan 'I think what Ade is trying to say is dat time is of de essence: he needs to get in and out; hit it and quit it. He won't have time to torture Alan for the combination to de safe.'

Dunstan looked both disappointed and confused.

'Wassa matta, D, wassup?'

Silence. Ade and Wha Gwan continued to stare at Dunstan.

'I don't know, man. It jus' don't feel right. Akers has connections . . . and . . . it, it feels like dere's too many loose ends.'

From where Ade was sitting it seemed to him that what Dunstan really meant was that there was a power shift happening in his relationship with Ade and he didn't like it.

'Like who?'

'Like what?'

'H for one . . .'

'Dey've got his son! What do you think he's gonna do?'

'And Gavin . . .'

'Fuck Gavin. Don't worry about Gavin.' Wha Gwan.

'He wants de dead man's shoes, he's safe.'

'So why do we need Wha Gwan?'

'No harm in insurance.' Ade could see that he'd said this a little too casually for Dunstan's liking. Dunstan was probably feeling that he was somehow, in some way, being played. And in a way he was. Now was the time for Dunstan to either step up . . . or step away.

'So. Okay y'all?' Ade looked round the table.

'Okay.'

'Okay.'

'So let's do it.'

# 36.

**H** sat in his dressing room. He wore long shiny black shorts. Across the waistband capital letters, in white, read 'HILARY'. He had on black boxing boots. No socks. H knew what he was probably going to have to do and for that he wanted to wear all black. Like Tyson. He was still, but already the adrenaline was coursing through his body.

The dressing room was basic but it was beginning to feel crowded: a long padded table, a metal locker, two wooden chairs, a stool, a full-length mirror. Matt and Nick were also there. H had his clothes hanging in the locker and he couldn't stop himself from glancing at it. His last hope before he went in to face Mancini was a telephone call from Nina telling him that Cyrus was safe. That was it. That was all he needed to know.

He held his hands out in front of him, following the ritual that he had been through a thousand times before but would never go through again. Matt carefully tore off strips of white sticky tape and hung them from the edge of the table. One at a time, Nick carefully, lovingly, wrapped each strip of tape around H's outstretched hands. Nick was turning each fist into a hammer. These quiet moments were the moments that H would miss most. The bond between fighter and trainer. H, Matt and Nick had all completed the preparation but only H was going into the ring. Only H was risking injury to bring triumph and glory to the hundreds of hours of work they had put in together; only H was putting his neck and reputation on the line.

H was acutely aware that this fight was different from any of his previous fights. Even if he didn't throw the fight, he was going into it with little chance of victory. He knew it, Nick knew it, Matt knew it. But H also knew that in the fight game, the boxing ring is not known as 'the killing floor' for no reason. The ring is a dangerous place. Boxing is the only legitimate sport where the object of the exercise is to knock your opponent unconscious. Because of this, and because Nick and Matt both knew that H was approaching the end of the road, the dressing room was especially quiet, especially tense.

Mancini's dressing room was next door. The boom-boom-boom-boom from his ghetto-blaster could be heard, pounding out something insistent, something frantic. The bass line's boom began to seep into H's mind. His thoughts drifted. He thought about the events of the last two months. He thought about Beverley and Nina. Both meant a lot to him. Both had let him down. Did he deserve it? He'd let Beverley down enough times. Gambling, stealing her money, being irresponsible. Had he let Nina down? He didn't think so. Was she just a rebound relationship? Had he been using her? Had she been using him? Akers taking Cyrus must have been her fault. H gave a deep, nervous sigh. Beverley and Nina both meant a lot to him. H sighed again. He had work to do . . .

Yesterday, after he'd left Nina at the gym, H stepped back inside and secretly watched her leave. He'd wanted to go after her but he couldn't. He wasn't certain that he could trust her. If she hadn't told Akers about Cyrus, who had? She must have told Gavin. She must have. And yet . . . and yet he was still attracted by her. He could feel the blood rushing to his groin.

Yesterday, after she'd gone, H had taken a bus to the King's Road. Matt had loaned him a small advance on his fight fee and H needed to do some shopping. He stopped at a men's fashion boutique, Woodhouse, and looked in the window at the tailor's dummies. They looked good and he went in. He was focused now, he had a plan. He pushed thoughts of his son to the back of his mind.

Half an hour later H was back on the street carrying a brand-new leather holdall, a travel holder for a suit and a bag containing a new pair of shoes. Before long he stopped outside another shop, a travel agent. Again he looked in the window. He ran his eye down a list of destinations. Some in Europe, some in North America, some in the Caribbean. His eye stopped over the list of destinations in the Caribbean. He went in.

Another half an hour later H left the travel agency, two airline tickets tucked in his pocket. He made his way home.

\*\*\*

H struggled into his flat. He dumped his new things on the floor of the living room and went over to the stool with his goldfish bowl on it. As he picked up the bowl, his eye snagged on the Caribbean postcard. He held the goldfish bowl up to the light, watching as his fish flashed back and forth in front of him.

He carried the bowl into his small bathroom and sat on the floor, legs on either side of the toilet bowl. He slowly tipped the fish into the toilet. He watched the fish swim round and round and then flushed, watching as it disappeared down the S-bend. One way or another tomorrow's fight meant change. It was the end of the road. But the beginning of a new one.

H rose and went back to look at the postcard. The classic image of the Caribbean: sunset, a beautiful woman in silhouette. Written across the card were the words 'Grab the opportunity – Montserrat is for you!'

\*\*\*

Nick squeezed the last of the tape around H's knuckles.

'Good?'

'Good.' Nick rose on ageing knees from the stool. He put a hand on each of H's trapezium muscles and gently massaged them.

'How you feeling, son?' Nick's voice was almost tender and H half-turned to look at his old trainer in surprise.

'Jesus, Nick, you haven't called me son in years.'

'You haven't fuckin' deserved it, you lazy, fuckin', back-sloidin' bastard!' Matt glanced over as Nick turned away to check the contents of his 'seconds' bag. 'No, I take that back. You've worked bloody hard, I'll say that for you, Hilary.' Matt glanced over again, this time at H. The two smiled at each other.

Nick suddenly turned back and caught the two of them. 'What are you two hyenas grinning at?' Before either could answer H's mobile phone trilled from inside the metal locker.

'Pass it over, Matt!' There was urgency in H's voice.

'Forget it!' Nick growled. 'We've got a job to do!'

'Pass it over!'

# THE LAST CARD

'Hilary!'

H jumped up from his chair, strode over to the locker, pulled it open and answered his telephone. 'Hello?'

'It's me.' Nina.

'Any news?' There was a pause before the news that H least wanted to hear came over the line.

'Sorry, Hila . . .'

He hung up. So this was the way it was going to be. This was how he was going to go out. He tossed the mobile back into the locker and slammed it shut. For a moment he rested his forehead on the locker, eyes closed.

'Gloves!' H suddenly felt as tight as a violin string. He barked the command, mean and low. Matt and Nick looked round at him.

'Are you all right . . . ?' Matt was concerned.

'Put the gloves on, will ya!' H jumped up on the long bench and held his taped hands out.

'Calm down. We're waiting for the referee.'

H had forgotten that. The referee had to come in and inspect the tape job that was done on his hands before the gloves could be put on. H turned and looked at himself in the mirror. He narrowed his eyes, slid off the bench, raised his hands and began to shadow box. Jab, jab, jab. He threw them fast, flicking out his left, snapping it back to his chin. He rose to his toes, dancing, moving, sliding back and forth before the mirror, threw a fierce combination, one-two-three-four, bang-bang-bang-bang! He rolled his shoulders, moved, ducked, weaving his head back and forth, loosening the kinks.

Nick and Matt stood to one side. They watched him work, generating heat, loosening up, dealing with the tension. He knew he looked good, lean, his body was cut. His eyes were clear, focused. He threw another combination – two quick jabs, a big right, a sweeping upper cut, bang! – up on his toes, dancing, dancing. H wasn't using the mirror now, he was working the room turning, sliding, he ducked behind his guard, he looked good, he looked good.

H was in his head now, his eyes closed. This was what the last six weeks had been about: preparing, visualising. But Nina's call was his last chance. He had to go down in the first round. The first round. And make it look convincing. Make it look convincing. That fucker, Akers! As H danced round the dressing room, eyes closed, tossing hand grenades at Mancini – big ones, small ones, ones from under-neath, ones from above – H knew it was over. He had just three minutes in the ring. His last chance to show what he'd taken from the last fifteen years of his life! The poor saps Nick and Matt had no idea what was going on.

H was now whirling round the dressing room, sweat starting to flow.

'Hey, d'you want to slow dat down, now!' The caution came from Nick. 'You want to save some of dat for de ring.'

H ignored him and carried on. The sweat dripped from his nose. It could have been the last round of a twelve-round world title fight the way H attacked the air in front of him.

''Kin 'ell, Hilary, mate! I think you've done enough now! You're warm, you're warm!' But H swept on.

'You're gonna leave it all in here if you don't stop it!' H opened his eyes, he moved to Nick, threw a right, ducked, shuffled out of range, his feet moving in a perpetual glide, stepped back in, tossed a jab, an inch from Nick's face, weaved to the left, weaved to the right, bang! threw another left, bang! an upper cut stopped just under Nick's chin, H danced away, spun round, turned his back, and then Matt grabbed him in a bear hug, pinning his arms to his side.

'What the fuck is wrong with you, Hilary!' The dressing room door opened. Standing in the doorway was the referee, a magic marker in his hand.

'Everything all right in here?'

With Nick and Matt on either side of him, H left the dressing room. They were met by a lone official, a grey-haired man in his fifties, who led them through a long, narrow corridor, lit by a line of harsh striplights from the ceiling. H felt like a man going to the elec-tric chair, to his execution. Dead man walking, dead man walking! Now H was hyperventilating. Both Nick and Matt had a hand on his shoulder, making physical contact with him. H knew they thought he was scared. And he was scared. But not of Mancini! That wasn't it!

They turned a corner and headed towards the entrance to the main arena. They could hear the noise of the crowd now, a low, inhuman roar. Next to the entrance to the arena was a line of four glamorous women, in evening dress, practising their dance steps for the 'before the main bout' dance routine. They laughed and joked as they prac-tised their routine. Fuck them! Fuck them and their dance routine!

# THE LAST CARD

H was petrified. Didn't they know that?

He was still petrified as he listened to the low rumble of the packed twelve-thousand-seater arena. They all seemed to be chanting Mancini's name, again and again, over and over. The noise built to a huge wall of sound. And then Mancini entered from the opposite side of the arena. Mancini! Mancini! Mancini! H was petrified as he entered the arena, ignored by the crowd, and then stepped into the ring. He took off his black robe and bounced around, aggressively. What he wanted to do was go straight back to the dressing-room and curl up into a ball at the foot of the shower stall.

Matt and Nick left the ring and H and Mancini were brought together into the centre. H didn't hear what the referee had to say. Formalities over, H and Mancini banged gloves. H made his way back to his corner for the start of round one. He suddenly felt his bowels loosen.

He turned in his corner and stood facing the ring, waiting for the fight to start. Nick was shouting something in one ear, he could feel Matt's presence on his other side. All H could focus on was Mancini. Mancini had his back to H and was hanging on to the top rope while doing a series of deep knee-bends. Up and down, up and down, up and down. H couldn't hear what Nick was saying, he was completely focused on Mancini's bends. He seemed to be doing them in slow motion.

H glanced down at the judges' table. On it was a pile of ring cards, the figure '1' on the top card. The last card. Next to it was the judges' clock. Its second arm was on the ten. It seemed to crash as it hit the eleven. It stopped for an interminable length of time. It moved again, still in slow motion. It crashed as it hit the twelve. Ding! Round one.

H felt himself kissed on the cheek, first by Nick, then by Matt. He stepped forward into the ring, into silence.

Mancini moved towards him as though he was wading through mud as though he was underwater H seemed to be floating as he stepped towards him Mancini threw a jab H saw it coming from the moment Mancini's brain sent the signal to his arm telling it to move forward H stepped to his right with so much time to spare he had time to notice a glob of Vaseline sticking to Mancini's eyebrow look at it with interest and then punch it with an overhand a stiff jolting right Mancini's head was rocked back and H was aware of a look of surprise flashing across Mancini's face Mancini stood his ground and came straight back at H H took to his toes and danced away from him he dropped his hands to his waist as he backed away moving moving using the ring Mancini followed him still moving as though he was underwater H backed to the ropes and waited for what seemed an eternity for Mancini to catch up with him when Mancini saw him backed up on the ropes he again threw a punch a big right hand this time and again H could see it coming from so early on the merest twitch of Mancini's shoulder muscle seeming to telegraph the intent of the arm that H had time to smack him with a left spin out of his spot on the ropes and smack him again with a right to the side of his head still in slow motion Mancini turned towards him and H caught him with a peach of a combination a left-right-left H danced away Mancini glanced at his corner his trainer and his second H could see both of them screaming something at Mancini he turned back to H with the speed and grace of a tortoise H walked up to him looked into his eyes and saw confusion he saw Mancini loading up to throw another punch H shuffled out of range and slid round the ring Mancini lumbered slowly and painfully after him into H's firing range and H jabbed once twice three times and all of them landed but Mancini still came forward with his back to the ropes H stood his ground and slowly bobbed and wove from the waist even with him moving slowly he still moved faster than the speed at which Mancini threw his punches H looked at the clock and just over a minute had passed he had to go down he had to go down he had no idea how he was going to do it Mancini threw another right-hand H blocked it with his left then threw a one-two combination a right-left the left was an upper-cut that almost took Mancini's head off and for the first time that H could remember he saw Mancini back up in a fight the two steps back that he took allowed H to move from his position on the ropes and take the centre of the ring Mancini was like a wounded drugged bear standing on its hind legs as it came after H H stayed in the centre circle of the ring and now jabbed Mancini at will fending him off digging him moving with him but maintaining his position in the centre of the ring Mancini's face was now looking red puffy and he had a particularly nasty swelling above his right eye H again looked over at the clock and saw that there were about 75 seconds to go before the end of the round he had to do something Cyrus's life was hanging in the balance he saw Mancini making one of his languorous laboured

# THE LAST CARD

lumbering charges once more and this time H slightly dropped his gloves slightly dropped his defence steeled himself and the moment before the blow hit his jaw he closed his eyes . . .

Stars exploded in the darkness, like fireworks on bonfire night, rockets shooting, whistling, up into the black, roman candles flaring their red, white and blue streams, crackers cracking and popping, bursting streams of sparkles dangling, shimmering, hanging, falling, falling, falling . . .

# 37.

The champagne-pink BMW eased along the quiet, dark, residential street. It approached a turning, a road on the left-hand side. The driver leant down, squinting to see the name. Westcott Crescent. He stopped the car and looked at the small child asleep on the back seat.

The driver climbed out and opened the rear passenger door. He gently shook the child awake. He then helped him out of the car and pointed the way to his house. He waited until he was sure the boy knew where he was. He watched him yawn and toddle off, clutching a plastic Spiderman.

# 38.

**C**arrying his brand new holdall, H approached the bar at Roxy's. He walked a little more stiffly than usual. Not because of the new shoes that he wore. And certainly not because of the new black woollen suit, which did not have the extravagance of his lucky suit. The bruising on the left side of his face gave a clue but it wasn't only that. The bruising was the result of the blow H had received from Mancini which had sent him crashing to the canvas. As H fell he'd landed awkwardly on his hip and it was this that hindered him now.

A small crowd of people gathered outside the club and H paused a little distance away. If his plan was to work, the timing was crucial. He pulled out his mobile and looked at the time on the front of it. 10.39 p.m. He tapped the Menu button, went into Personal Numbers and scrolled down the Ds. He came to Dragon. He took two quick deep breaths before dialling the number.

'Hello?'

'Hi, Alice, it's Hilary.' H spoke through jaws that barely opened. 'Is there any . . . ?'

H heard a loud schtups as Beverley's mother kissed her teeth. H winced, holding the telephone inches from his ear. There was a pause.

'Hello?'

'Bev, it's Hilary. Any . . .'

'He's here, he's here, he just turned up, he . . .'

'Is he all right?'

'Oh, Hilary, he's fine, he's fine!' H could hear the happiness, the relief, the excitement in her voice. A lump suddenly sprang to his throat.

'He's a bit shaken up, but he's so good, he's such a good boy! I've put him to bed now and . . .'

'Look, Bev . . .' H was finding it hard to speak. Emotion constricted his throat, bruising constricted his jaws. 'I've got to go now, but I'll . . .'

'But don't you want to . . .'

'I've got to go, bye.' He hung up. He pressed the telephone to his bruised cheek, softly, moving it all about the tender area. They were his family but before he could see them again there was something he had to do.

He removed a slip of paper from his jacket pocket and dialled the number written on it.

'Hello?' The voice at the other end was deep.

'Who dis?'

'H.'

'Yeah, man.'

'Where are you?'

'We're not coming, cowboy . . .'

'You're not coming! What do you mean you're not coming?'

'It's Dunstan, man. He's telling me I'm not a businessman, but when I throw back at 'im 'is own lyrics about globalisation . . .'

'What are you talking about? We had a deal!'

'Easy, star, I'm working on a plan . . .'

'What fucking plan?'

'You need to take some deep breaths . . .'

'Fuck you, arsehole!' H didn't like the advice but he was following it anyway. Nobody said anything over the sound of H's deep, forced breaths.

'Are you still there?'

'Can I talk?' H gave a final deep breath.

'Go on then.'

'Right. Dunstan's out. He's not feeling it. And I need backup, so . . .'

'I'll be your backup.'

'Sorry, blood, I don't know you. I talked to my man but he wants to put things off. He needs time to . . .'

'That's too late. It has to be tonight!'

'Why?'

'It just does. Trust me, I'm your backup, Ade!'

There was another silence.

# THE LAST CARD

'I'm gonna go back and talk to my man. I'll call you.'

Ade hung up. For a long moment H just stared at the useless mobile in his hand. Okay, okay, okay, think, think, think this one through. What to do now? That fuck Ade!

H thought about Beverley. For years he had failed to take responsibility for his actions; she always took responsibility for hers. Always. And suddenly H knew he loved Beverley but he was no longer in love with her. The sudden clarity of the thought took his breath away. He struggled to push the thought from his mind. Later for that. He thought about Nina. Sexy Nina, tough Nina. Whatever else you could say about her there was no way she would ever evade responsibility for her actions. So what was wrong with H? He had to take responsibility. It was as simple as that! He thought of Alan's smiling face. He thought of Mancini's smiling face. He thought of Beverley's smiling face. He thought of Nina's smiling face. He had to take responsibility for himself. Because, because . . . no one else was going to do for him what he had to do for himself.

He switched his mobile off and jammed it into his pocket.

H then put the pain in his hip out of his mind and strode to the entrance of Roxy's. After waiting for some people ahead of him to enter, he paid his money and went in. The atmosphere was busy and there was a party mood in the air. Easing his holdall in front of him as he made his way through the crowd of gay men and transvestites, he approached the bar. He looked up at the Fosters' clock at the back. It was 10.51 p.m.

He beckoned to the barman. 'Where's White Alan tonight?'

The bar man pointed up at the ceiling.

# 39.

Gavin sat at the back of the office, a blank expression on his face disguising his tension as he watched Alan on the telephone. He glanced at his watch. 10.50 p.m. Time was moving on. He had guaranteed Nina that he would have White Alan on his own by 11 p.m. and yet here he was with Ram, the Indian man next to him, quietly sitting in front of Alan like a couple of stale buns at a children's tea party.

Alan hung up, a broad smile on his face. 'Glasses, Ram, glasses. Three.'

The Indian rose and went to the antique drinks cabinet to one side of the office. He carried three champagne glasses to the desk. White Alan lifted a bottle of Dom Perignon out of the bucket at his side and made a big show of opening it. He filled the glasses, inviting Ram and Gavin to join him. He raised his glass for a toast.

'Money in the bin, boys! What a life! The sporting life!' His smile widened, his teeth glistening white.

'The sporting life!' Gavin and Ram choroused politely. The three of them sipped their champagne in silence. To Gavin, the moment felt anti-climactic. White Alan seemed to have no such feelings. 'Now that is what I call a fooking pay-day!' He sat down at his desk and beamed at his two employees.

Gavin looked at his watch. 10.56 p.m. He turned to Ram. 'Go down and get us some Cubans, will you, Ram?'

Ram nodded, no doubt glad of any excuse to remove himself from the oppressive atmosphere of Alan's office.

'Toilet, Alan, back in a minute.' Gavin stepped out of the office, closing the door quietly behind him. He listened to Ram's receding footsteps as he descended the stairs. Gavin looked around in the dim light. And as he looked around a figure melted out of the shadows, carrying a bag. Gavin looked at him, surprised by the sartorial upgrade.

His eyes focused on the holdall. 'Why the bag?'

H held it up apologetically. 'I've come straight from the fight. It's got my kit in it.'

Gavin nodded, satisfied. 'All set?'

'He'll be here soon. Give us fifteen minutes.'

'Ten. You've got ten minutes.' Gavin headed on down the stairs and spotted Ram turning away from the bar, holding a bottle of Dom Perignon and two Cubans. Gavin went over and took them.

'Alan's in a good mood. He says take the rest of the night off.'

Ram's eyes lit up. 'Are you serious?'

'No, delirious. Get lost before I think of something for you to do.'

Ram took no time at all to nod his thanks and disappear. Gavin now turned to one of the barmen, a young man in his mid-twenties who wore his hair in a slick pony-tail. Gavin thought the expression on his face looked vacant and babyish so he made a point of drawing his attention.

'Hey, your name's Graham, isn't it?'

'That's right.'

'I'm the manager. I work directly with Mr Akers. I'd like a tonic water.'

'That's it?'

'Yep. I'm watching my weight.'

Graham returned the smile that Gavin gave him with a weak one of his own. He turned to fetch the drink. Little did Graham know that within, oh, about ten minutes he, Gavin Bishop, would be replacing Mr Akers. He would no longer be the manager, he would be the owner. Gavin made a point of showing his face around and chatting to the bar staff while he waited for his drink because when the shit hit the fan and Alan's death was made known, his alibi would be secure. 'What me, boys? Why, I was down in the bar having a quiet drink with Graham.'

Gavin waited. He kept one eye glued to the entrance to the club, waiting for Ade's appearance.

# 40.

**H** stood in the dim light of the landing and thought about what kind of man he was. He could think of few things more difficult than having had to take the dive against Mancini. It struck at the core of his identity. And yet here he was, about to do something far worse. Yet H knew that at this moment in time, right here, right now, he felt he was doing the right thing. However hard, however questionable.

H dipped his hand into his jacket pocket and took out his talisman. He rubbed its smooth edges with his fingers and pressed it against his bruised cheek. He then slipped it back into his pocket and, without knocking, walked straight into White Alan's office.

Alan was sitting back in his chair examining the recesses of his gaping mouth via his hand-mirror. He looked up at H almost as though he had been expecting him. H was rattled by this and hovered in the middle of the office, awkward, exposed. With Alan's eyes following his every move, he put his bag down on the floor.

'What are you doing here? Our business is over!'

'I thought, I thought . . .' H's voice quavered and he coughed to cover the break in it. 'I thought I'd pay my respects to a true sports fan.'

Alan stared, seemingly unsure how to react. He slowly put the mirror down in front of him. Noting the hesitancy, H drew confidence. He walked forward and picked up one of the empty champagne glasses on Alan's desk. This invasion seemed to be the prompt Alan needed. He sat up in his chair and pulled himself forward, tucking his legs under the desk.

'D'you mind if I have a drink?' H's voice was firm and resolute now.

Alan didn't answer. Instead he raised his hand from under the desk, revealing a handgun pointed at H's chest. A Beretta 9mm.

# THE LAST CARD

H made sure his only visible reaction was to look down, but inside his stomach turned to water.

Alan gestured at the champagne. 'Help yourself.'

Using all his willpower to stop his hand shaking, H picked up the bottle and poured himself a glass.

'I thought your performance tonight was very convincing, Hilary.' Alan seemed confident now, on top of the situation. 'A shame it took little Cyrus to convince you to go through with it.'

H sipped from his glass, trying to contain himself and decide his next move. Since Ade had let him down and told him he wasn't coming tonight H didn't really have a plan. He knew what he had to do but he hadn't thought about how he was going to do it, especially now Alan was pointing a gun at him.

'How much did you make?'

'Do you really want to know?'

'Yeah.'

Alan paused, a smile playing on his lips. 'Put it this way: more money than you're ever likely to see in the whole of your lifetime.' He paused. 'You know what? I admire people like you. Because without people like you, I couldn't exist. You can't have winners without losers and you are a loser. And your son, Cyrus, he's another loser. And his son after him. If I were to kill you right here and now what difference would that make to anybody?'

As H stared at Alan, time seemed to stand still. All H's fear seemed to lift from his body. He sat on the edge of the desk, closer to Alan. He took a good long look at him, the man who had cut his ear with a knife, the man who had slapped his face, the man who had made him throw the fight, the man who now threatened his very life. And suddenly H experienced the clarity of intent that he had experienced in the ring with Mancini.

'Are you a gambling man, Alan? I mean, when the odds aren't fixed?'

'No. It's a fools' game.'

'True. But the feeling you have when you score a tight, heavy bundle of notes . . . it's fantastic.' H laughed, lowering his glass. 'It's brilliant! It may even be as good as it gets, I don't know. But you know what? Somebody once told me that gambling was for the "emotionally insecure".' H paused, waiting for a response from Alan but Alan

241

just stared blankly back at him. 'Attempting to artificially create that buzz through gambling . . . shows a weakness in your personality. Or something. What do you think?'

Alan continued to stare at him with the same blank expression.

'You're not a gambler so I guess you don't have any thoughts on that. But, you see, I think gambling is for the insecure. It really is. And I'm trying hard not to need it because . . .' And that's when H struck. His glass already lowered and poised, he now tossed its contents in Alan's face, blinding him. With a swift jab H knocked the gun aside and, diving across the desk, grabbed Alan by the throat.

The force of H's dive made Alan's chair roll backwards and tip over. H clung to Alan's throat, his thumbs pressing down on his windpipe. Alan thrashed about, trying to smash H's hands away; he bucked, he pounded H's head and face, scratching and clawing at him, he kicked and snapped and snarled, he gurgled and gagged as he gasped for air. But H was used to fielding blows and he squeezed harder, knowing his life depended on it – to let go of Alan's throat was to face failure and almost certain death. H clung on. Alan rose, fell back, scrabbled on the floor, clawing, paddling with his feet. His eyes watered, his voice rasped like a dying cancer patient. He pushed himself up the wall, all the time pushing, pulling, pounding H's arms and hands. And still H clung on pressing, squeezing, choking. As the life slowly began to ebb away from Alan, H felt him thrash about with one last gargantuan effort, pummelling H's face and head. H hunched his shoulders, raising his elbows to shield himself and fend off as much as he could. Still he clung on. The fight began to leave Alan; his blows weakened, his strength left him, his body sagged, his gurgling, bubbling, choking quietened. H saw his eyes roll back in his head as his body slid back down the wall, finally collapsing in a crumpled heap.

H took his hands from Alan's throat and looked down at them, almost unable to believe what they, not he, had done. Where his hands had been were identical, red-raw prints on Alan's flesh, as though to incriminate him directly in an offence for which the maximum sentence was life. H backed away with horror, staring at Alan's body, transfixed by the spectacle of death. But what if he wasn't dead? Slowly he leant down, dropping his ear to Alan's nose and mouth. He tensed, holding his breath, to see if he could hear whether any life still lingered in the carcass. Nothing. He stood back, his flesh crawling. Almost all that could be seen of Alan's eyes were the whites. Gingerly, delicately, H plucked at one of Alan's wrists. He felt for a pulse. Again, nothing. He let go and stepped quickly back, as though death were contagious.

H looked at a clock on the wall. 11.08 p.m. Jesus! He knew he didn't have much time. He darted back round the desk, keeping as far away from Alan's body as possible, and picked up his holdall. Above Alan's body was the mirror that concealed the safe. Leaning with exaggeration over the corpse, his stomach revolting at the thought of touching it, H removed the mirror. He placed it quietly on the floor. Using the code that Nina had given him, H opened the safe. Inside were bundles and bundles of bound fifty-pound notes, and two polythene bags – the size of common house bricks – of what looked like cocaine. Leaving the cocaine where it was, H scooped out all the bundles of cash into his holdall, taking no pleasure in the sight of so much money, still aware of Alan's body lying at his feet.

Fighting a rising nausea, H swiftly picked up a cravat from Alan's desk and wiped down all the surfaces he'd touched. He put the champagne glass with his prints on it into the holdall and left the room.

# 41.

**G**avin looked at the clock behind the bar. 11.13 p.m. Still no sign of the second man. What had happened? Gavin knew that the boxer was still upstairs. He finished his tonic water, took one last look at the club's entrance and headed for the door behind the bar.

He stood silently in the hallway, listening. The low throb of disco pulsated through to him but other than that he couldn't hear anything. He stepped quietly to the stairs, aware that he was walking on tiptoe. As he hit the first step it creaked and, again, he paused. Still nothing. Gavin took the stairs two at a time, acutely aware of every creak and groan underfoot. He silently reached the landing. He stood stock still, his heart pounding.

Gavin peered into the recesses and the shadows that had given up the boxer earlier that night. Nothing. He kept staring, desperate to penetrate the darkness. Finally he moved, taking another step in the direction of Alan's office door. That first step was on a floorboard that must have disliked something about Gavin because its groan was so loud the small, fine hairs at the back of his neck stood to attention. Gavin's heart nearly leapt through his mouth. Again he stopped, frozen. He stood like that for thirty seconds that seemed like thirty minutes. He again moved forward, more carefully this time.

He put his ear to the office door, desperate to divine what was happening behind it. He couldn't hear anything. He looked at the door and knocked. Nothing. He knocked again. Still nothing. He slowly opened the door, poking his head round it.

Everything looked as it should. Gavin stepped into the room. Only now could he see that Alan's chair was tipped over and, and there was Alan! Sitting crumpled on the floor!

# THE LAST CARD

'Alan?' Gavin tentatively called his boss's name. 'Alan? Can you hear me?' Either Alan couldn't hear him or he couldn't answer him. That's when Gavin made his second unpleasant discovery of the night. The mirror above Alan's head was gone and the safe was open.

'Bastard!' He spat the word out through clenched teeth. He looked down at Alan and spat it again. 'Bastard!' He stepped back out of the office and skipped quickly down the stairs.

# 42.

**H** had been hiding behind the door, clutching his now full brand-new holdall to his chest. At last he could breathe again. His breath came quickly, in short bursts. He stepped out of the office. His new suit was suddenly hot and sticky. The pain in his hip was a forgotten memory now as he walked quickly and quietly to the stairs and descended them. He stopped at the bottom and looked along the hallway. He couldn't see Gavin anywhere. He approached the door leading to the side of the bar and opened it a fraction. He peeked into the club, searching through the milling bodies of gays and trans-vestites. Still no sight of the late Alan Akers' main man. He opened the door a fraction more and crouched down to slip through.

As H hovered in the doorway, his eyes scanned the shifting lights and bodies. There he was! He spotted Gavin walking amongst the clubbers, easing, pushing people aside as he looked for him. From his position, crouching by the door, H could see there was something frantic about the way Gavin was moving amongst the Roxy clientele. He was like a shark, leaving in his wake a trail of chaos. People behind Gavin gave him dirty, annoyed looks as he passed.

H waited his moment. It wasn't a large club. He waited until Gavin was at the far end of the dance floor, his back to H. At that moment H rose. He strode quickly through the club. He left by the main entrance.

Outside, H looked around, trying to find a taxi.

# 43.

These fucking poofters! Gavin was becoming increasingly desperate. Where was he? Where was the boxer? How could he have given him the slip? Gavin waded through the gays and the queens; dancing, preening, posing and mincing. How the hell did this happen to London? was the thought going through Gavin's head when he turned on the dance floor to see H's tall silhouette and the back of his head, moving towards the entrance. Fuck! Gavin immediately headed after him, moving with more aggression now, less finesse.

It was a move Gavin was to regret. Dancing next to him, with a carefree charm, was a tall, burly man, built like a construction worker, dressed in a simple red knee-length chiffon dress. He had a blonde wig perched precariously on his head over a dark stubble. In his haste to catch up with the boxer Gavin had planted a hand in the small of the man's back and pushed hard. The man, at that moment twirling to something high in energy, stumbled in his dainty sandals with the kitten heels. He quickly regained his balance, however, and as Gavin moved to go past him the man reached out a muscular, hairy arm and grabbed Gavin by the back of his elegantly coiffured hair, jerking him back.

'Oiy! Wha's your game?'

Gavin spun round and landed a perfect blow high on the man's temple. He let go of Gavin's hair and staggered back, his bulky form knocking aside those merry-makers dancing nearby as he went down. Gavin immediately turned back to the door in hot pursuit of H.

He burst out on to the street, pushing his way past another fucking black man at the door, just in time to see H toss the bag into a black taxi.

'Hey! Come back! Where do you think you're going?' The words were snarled, Gavin angry that the boxer so underestimated him that he thought he could just walk out with the money, right under his nose.

H turned and looked round at Gavin. As Gavin strode towards the boxer he saw him ready himself for combat. And then he saw him look at something to one side. And then Gavin glanced round and saw another man, the one he'd just barged past. And then he recognised him – braided hair on one side, loose hair on the other. And then he saw the Mac 11 pointing at him.

BANG!

And then Gavin . . . forty-nine years old . . . member of the 1984 Olympic bobsleigh team . . . ex-fitness instructor . . . ex-enforcer for Alan Akers . . . murderer of Dipak Chandra . . . was dead.

# 44.

For a moment, out on that busy Soho Street, all was silent. H looked from Gavin, shot through the head and instantly dead, to the black man standing next to him, looking at the body. H knew he'd seen him somewhere before – that hair! Where was it? The man suddenly turned and walked – he didn't run – he walked away through the crowd, into Wardour Street and around the corner. Everybody turned to look. And that was H's cue. He spun round and climbed into the waiting taxi, slamming the door behind him.

'Heathrow Airport.'

'Hang on a minute, mate, don't you think we should wait for . . .'

'Heathrow Airport! I've got a plane to catch!' Something in H's manner must have told the taxi driver that his passenger meant business. Whatever thoughts he might have had about civic duty, he put them to one side and pulled away. Better to not get involved.

H sat in the back of the taxi squinting out the rear window. Jesus Christ! That was close. A large crowd was now beginning to form around Gavin's body.

The taxi drove round Marble Arch, heading into Bayswater Road. The traffic was busy, it was Saturday night after all, and H was on edge. He eyed the big houses and flats as they crawled by, knowing that he wouldn't be seeing anything like this for a while. Not where he was going. He had told the driver to head west, even at this stage still not sure whether to go to Holland Park and Nina, or Hanwell and Beverley. As the taxi brought him ever closer to Holland Park, H's thoughts became more and more confused. Clearly, his feelings about Beverley were wrapped up with Cyrus. If there were no Cyrus, would he be thinking about Beverley? Should he be thinking about Beverley? A part of him still loved her but what had she done for him lately? And what about Nina? Was that love or lust? There were so many things he liked about Nina but he couldn't help thinking . . . could he trust her?

H pulled out a fresh packet of cigarettes. He hadn't had a cigarette in a while and one of the advantages of giving up boxing was that he could now have a cigarette without feeling guilty about it. Or at least that's what he'd told himself when he bought the packet earlier that evening. As he was taking a cigarette out his eye caught the 'No Smoking' sign.

'Excuse me? Driver?' The driver looked round. H waved the cigarette at him with a questioning look. The driver tutted but, no doubt with one eye on the size of his tip, he relented.

'All right then, mate, go on.' He shook his head with disapproval. Fuck you, H thought. If you'd had the evening I'd had you'd want a cigarette as well! He thought back to Akers. He'd killed him with his own bare hands. How did he feel about that? Revulsion? Yes. But . . . but also a sense of . . . power?

H screwed up the plastic and the silver wrapping paper that surrounded the cigarettes. He crushed them into a tight ball, opened the taxi window and tossed them out. The paper ball flew forward, carried by the momentum of the car, hit the windscreen of another oncoming car and bounced back, into the street. H had a sudden flashback to Mr Enias and the teaser he had posed for his class. H thought about the turning point of the paper he'd just thrown and the fact that if it had just changed direction from moving forwards to moving backwards, then at some point, mathematically, it must have been stationary. He thought again about how he'd always perceived his own life in those terms, and he thought about that day, seven years ago, the moment when his own life had become stationary, had changed direction . . .

\*\*\*

**15 JUNE 1998**

'I can't fuckin' hear you!' Nick was shouting at H above the noise in the arena.

'I'm a champ!'

'You're a fuckin' god! Now go out dere and prove it!'

It was the start of the last round. Nick and Matt both took H's head in their hands and kissed him on the cheek before climbing out of the ring. He was their boy. H rose. He looked across at Mancini. Another adrenaline spurt shot through his body. This was his last ever round as an amateur. H shook his arms out, waggling his boxing gloves from side to side, preparing himself for the coming battle. He stared across at Mancini while he eased his gum-shield into a more comfortable place in his mouth. Mancini himself was like a restless horse, prancing, skipping, waiting. Ding! The bell tolled. The referee waved H and Mancini to the centre of the ring. He looked them both in the eye, paying special attention to the bloodied Mancini.

'Are you all right?' The question was shouted above the noise in the arena and delivered sternly. This was a game for men. Keeping his eyes on H, Mancini nodded vigorously. 'You're sure?' Mancini dragged his eyes from H and now glared at the referee. He again nodded his head, but slowly this time. The message was unmistakable. And so the referee waved the two boxers together and stepped quickly back, out of the firing line. H and Mancini dead-stared at each other. They touched boxing gloves in the strange etiquette of the ring. And then it was on, they were ready to bash each other's brains out.

The two boxers circled each other warily. Mancini grimly smiled.

'Are you gonna dance all night, cupcake? Or stand and fight?'

The referee stepped forward. 'No talking!' He stepped back.

And that was when H went to work. He glided forward; he jabbed, bobbed, jabbed again. H was quickly returning to the zone of the last round. He moved, danced on his toes, down, came in, threw a combination, one-two-three, rat-a-tat-tat, back on his toes. He worked the ring, looking good. The crowd loved it and H's support picked up again. Seeing their man doing so well the crowd were turning the event into a carnival.

Mancini ducked, bobbed, bang! caught one in the face, still came in, big right, missed, H was gone, chase, one-two-three, his face is peppered, shit! He still moved forward.

And so it went on, H on his toes, shuffling, the crowd loving it. Coasting his way to victory.

H glanced across at Matt and Nick. Both wore huge smiles, gave him the thumbs up. H turned to Mancini, he advanced to the middle of the ring, planted his feet. H waved Mancini towards him. Come on if you're hard enough! Come and have a go! And, like a wolf, Mancini smiled.

What happened next took just over a minute. H was to suffer the consequences of that minute for the rest of his life. Later, when he replayed the last round in his mind, it was Mancini's smile that he remembered. H had been taking Mancini apart, like a surgeon, skilfully and precisely dismantling him, piece by piece. Yet going into the last round Mancini smiled once when he taunted H, and then again when H waved him on. Mancini must have known something because after that second smile he came at H like a ten-year-old child opening a room full of Christmas presents. H and Mancini now stood toe-to-toe in what was an old-fashioned, macho tear-up. It was a war, vicious and brutal.

Nick and Matt couldn't believe their eyes. They shouted and screamed at H, desperate to be heard above the pandemonium that had broken out in the arena.

'Move!'

'Get out of there!'

'Move away!'

'Dance, H, dance! Shuffle on him!'

'What the hell are you doing?'

'For fuck sake, move!'

# THE LAST CARD

But H didn't move and H didn't dance. He gambled. He gambled himself against the best that Mancini could throw at him; H gambled that he could beat Mancini boxing the way Mancini boxed; H gambled to prove to Mancini that he was as tough as he was. H took that gamble. But as the two of them stood toe to toe, tearing, snarling, pounding each other, H began to tire.

Why didn't the referee step in? Because this was the final round of the final of the ABAs. Nobody wants to see a boxer hurt, but nobody wants to step in too soon and therefore end a fight prematurely; deprive a boxer, a warrior, of the right to snatch first prize. No, the referee wanted to see what these two fine boxers could do.

As H wilted Mancini became stronger, he kept going. H took a big one on the chin, then another. Blood spurted from his eyebrow. Soon there was no power in H's punches. H took another heavy blow and his gum-shield flew out. He stumbled. A final crushing, terrible blow and H went down. His eyes closed. He was out before his head crashed to the canvas.

The pandemonium in the arena turned to silence. Nick and Matt leapt into the ring. Mancini raised his arms in victory but rather than circling the ring in triumph, he went to his own corner and stood with his trainer and seconds, waiting. They could see H was in trouble . . .

H lay on his back. His back on the canvas. A crowd of people around him. A doctor leant over him. The doctor's head was down. The doctor was listening. Listening for signs of life. The doctor snatched at H. Desperate for a pulse. He felt nothing. Now shouting. Cleared people away. Stopped breathing. H was dying. Tilted H's head. Pinched H's nose. Blew into H's mouth . . .

# 45.

**H** took out his talisman to light the cigarette. As he flicked it alight and moved it to the cigarette dangling from his mouth, he paused. He looked at the lighter, his talisman, and thought about what it represented. He lit his cigarette, snapped it shut and buried it deep, back in his jacket pocket. He took a long pull on the cigarette. The sharp intake of nicotine made him feel light-headed for a moment. He looked out the window: they were just passing through Notting Hill. The Virgin record store which he and Nina had shopped in was on his right-hand side. The memory made him smile.

The smile drifted from his face as he again thought about the moment when he'd 'died' in the ring. How that moment had changed the course of his life. And how he'd stood up to Mancini again. It had only been for about two minutes but looking back on those minutes made H break out in goose pimples. He'd gone for it, hadn't he? Just for those brief two minutes, he'd been back in the zone.

But that was over, this was now. And now H was embarking on a new chapter of his life. He had two airline tickets in his pocket and a bag full of money on his lap. Two hundred thousand pounds! What was he going to do? H knew he needed to just go away for a while and think. Think about his life and where he was going with it. He hadn't done that in years. The money would certainly give him the space to do that. But would Nina?

The car was going down Holland Park Avenue now and H could see Nina's turning coming up on the right.

'Turn here, driver. I've got to pick someone up.'

'Right you are, mate.' The taxi slowed as it made the turn into Pottery Lane. A minute later it pulled up some fifty metres from Nina's house. Making sure he left the taxi door open, H stepped out and walked slowly down to Nina's front door. As he approached, his tread slowed even more, stopping outside one of the kitchen windows. The light was on inside and he could see right through into the living room. And there was Nina, waiting for him . . .

# 46.

**N**ina sat on the sofa, legs crossed, reading the magazine section of the *Evening Standard*. She was reading an interview with Julia Roberts but as quickly as she read a sentence, the words and the meaning would float out of her mind. When was Hilary going to arrive? Would he have the money with him?

Nina hated the idea that H might have been hurt. She hadn't seen the fight with Mancini but she had listened to the live report on the radio. She had listened, incredulous, to the commentator's chatter. How he had never seen an unranked fighter begin the opening round of such a big fight in such explosive style; how H was moving with such fluidity and speed that he was picking off the WBA/WBC number-one-ranked super-middleweight with ease; how he was giving Mancini a master-class in the art of boxing.

The superlatives couldn't fly from the lips of the reporter fast enough. Nina listened as the noise of the attendant crowd expanded in the background; the audience had recognised that something amazing was happening. But Nina knew it couldn't last. She knew he was going to take the dive. When it came tears sprang to her eyes.

The commentator's voice leapt from excitement to shock as if someone had thrown a bucket of cold water over him. He couldn't believe what he was seeing! From dancing, moving, controlling the ring, H had suddenly stopped doing everything – and walked into a huge Mancini right-hand. Mancini himself seemed incredulous. The commentator sounded hollow as he described the rest of the round, as Mancini jumped all over the plucky fighter from south London and rained blow after blow on him. H didn't go down immediately and the blows kept coming. Crashing to the canvas, senses probably scrambled, the unranked fighter almost made it to his feet in time, but was counted out.

The reporter concluded that while H had some skill as a boxer he had simply been outclassed by the better fighter, the 'Bugle Boy' from Manchester.

Nina had cried for some time after the fight. She cried for the hurt she knew H would be feeling; she cried for the power that big people like Alan had over little people like herself and H; she cried because she had lied to H about her part in his son's kidnapping, and that had forced him into this humiliation.

After a while she had dried her face. She determined to make it up to H in the best way she could. She had no idea where they were going but she packed a small weekend bag. She dressed simply in black slacks and a black pullover. She pulled her hair back into a bun. Her make-up was light as she sat on the sofa with her travel bag at her feet, passport and purse on top and *ES Magazine* in her hands. Again she read the sentence about Julia Roberts. And she waited.

# 47.

**H** decided that he couldn't trust Nina. Trust was everything. The taxi sailed smoothly out of Pottery Lane, back on to Holland Park Avenue. It arrived at the Holland Park roundabout and waited for a break in the traffic.

'Change of plan, driver. We're going to Hanwell.'

'Hanwell?'

'Yeah, I need to make another stop.'

Irritated at his indecision, the driver glanced at H in the rear-view mirror. H looked away. When the break in the traffic came the taxi pulled on to the roundabout, headed around the green and up the Uxbridge Road.

The taxi pulled up outside Alice's house. It was late now and the house was dark. On his lap H quickly wrapped three stacks of the fifty-pound notes into the pages of a discarded newspaper. He figured the bundle totalled about thirty thousand pounds. Taking a pen from his pocket he wrote a quick note on the front: 'For Beverley and Cyrus – I'm going away for a while but I'll be back. All my love, Hilary.' No, H couldn't stay with Beverley. She'd lost respect for him when he'd needed her most. She had abandoned him. Sure, she'd had her reasons. But, in the end, there will always be reasons, won't there? No, what they'd had was gone. Time would tell if it could ever be rekindled.

With the engine still running, H nipped out of the taxi, walked swiftly to Alice's front door and posted the parcel through the letter-box, squeezing it through.

He climbed back into the taxi.

'Where now, guv'nor?' The taxi driver asked, impassive.

'Heathrow.' The driver nodded and the taxi pulled out.

# THE LAST CARD

'Going away, are you?'

'Yep.'

'Where you off to then, anywhere nice?'

'Montserrat.'

The driver cast H a quizzical look via the rear-view mirror. 'Isn't that where the volcano happened?'

'Yeah . . .'

'Terrible that was. Saw a documentary about that on the telly. How are they coping over there, then?'

'It's tough but . . . life goes on. It's tough over here, isn't it?'

'You're right there, sunshine, you're right there.'

H thought about his brother's house in Virgin Island, in the northern part of Montserrat, far from the exclusion zone around the volcano. The house was set near a cliff face and had broad views of the sea. On a clear day you could see over to St Kitts. Suddenly, H couldn't wait to be there.

He stared out of the window. Suddenly it came to him who Gavin's killer was – Wha Gwan. Blue's friend. H shook his head in amazement, the complexities of the universe far greater than he could possibly fathom. He would sort himself out in Montserrat and then he would come back, a different H. Maybe he would meet up again with Ade. And maybe Wha Gwan – who knew?

H pulled another cigarette from his packet and pulled out his lighter, his talisman. He lit the cigarette and was about to push the Zippo back into his pocket. Only he didn't. He looked at it. This moment was another one of those moments, like the one when he'd almost died in the ring. It was a turning point. Only this time, finally, he was in control. He opened the window and tossed the lighter out. From the speeding taxi, H watched it sail backwards in the dark, hit the asphalt, and bounce forwards.

**THE END**

**Dreda Say Mitchell  RUNNING HOT**     £8.99   ISBN 1 904559 09 3

## WINNER OF THE JOHN CREASEY DAGGER FOR DEBUT CRIME

What's the best thing about Hackney?
The bus outta here!

And that's exactly where Elijah 'Schoolboy'
Campbell needs to be in a week's time,
heading out of London's underworld. He's
taking a great offer to leave it all behind and
start a new life, but the problem is he's got no
spare cash. The possibility of lining his pockets
becomes real when he stumbles across a
mobile phone. But it's marked property, and
the Street won't care that he found it by
accident. The Street won't care that the
phone's his last chance to change his life.
And he can't give it back because the door
to redemption is only open for seven days.

Schoolboy knows that when you're running
hot all it takes is one call, one voicemail, one
text to disconnect you from this life –
permanently. And getting deeper into his old
lifestyle may mean that he never catches that bus . . .

'Lock, stock and a twenty-year-old mobile phone, at last I know my way round
    the North London gun belt!' Nigel Planer, actor, writer & comedian
'An exciting new voice in urban fiction . . . a striking debut' *Guardian*
'Very sharp . . . An impressive first book with a strong sense of place and
    community' *Sunday Telegraph*
'A taut and exhilarating debut . . . The tempo is rapid-fire from the start . . .
    the dialogue is terrific and this is also a very funny novel' *Tribune*
'A fantastic piece of debut writing' Robert Elms, BBC Radio London
'Sharp-eyed, even sharper-tongued chase story . . . distinctly different; well
    worth seeking out' *The Literary Review*
'Fast-moving, colourfully written, touching and informative ' Natasha Cooper, *TLS*
'Swaggeringly cool and incredibly funny' *Stirling Observer*
'Takes urban writing to a whole new level . . . gripping' *The New Nation*

DREDA SAY MITCHELL was born into London's Grenadian community in the 1960s. She
works as an education adviser and lives in London's East End. This is her first novel.

## Danny Rhodes  ASBOVILLE

£8.99   ISBN 1 904559 22 0

'A-S-B-O. You think that makes you special. But it doesn't. It means you were stupid enough to get caught, that's all. I should have one. I should have the biggest ASBO there is. I want a poster with my face on.'

When sixteen-year-old JB is served with an ASBO, he is sent to live with his uncle in a tiny caravan by the sea. Each and every day he must paint one hut on the beach. It's a chance for him to turn his life around, a chance to pay something back for all that happened in the city. As the summer days drag by, JB's feelings of frustration and isolation grow. Only his tentative relationship with Sal offers any chance of rescue. But a storm is coming that threatens to shatter his hopes and destroy the relationship that could redeem him.

'Excellent debut novel, definitely in my top ten of the year' *Bookseller*

'Moving and atmospheric, this coming-of-age tale also has political bite' *Guardian*

'Rhodes asks important questions about social justice, but also tells a compelling human story. An impressive debut' *New Statesman*

DANNY RHODES lives in Canterbury and teaches English in a school by the sea. He has published short stories in the UK and the US. This is his first novel.

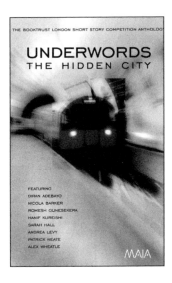

**Merete Morken Andersen OCEANS OF TIME**   £8.99   ISBN 1 904559 11 5
A divorced couple confront a family tragedy in the white night of a Norwegian summer.
International book of the year (*TLS*) and nominated for the IMPAC Award 2006.

**Michael Arditti  A SEA CHANGE**   £8.99   ISBN 1 904559 21 2
A mesmerising journey through history, a tale of dreams, betrayal, courage and romance
told through the memories of a 15-year-old, based on the true story of the Jewish refugees
on the SS *St Louis*, who were forced to criss-cross the ocean in search of asylum in 1939.

**Michael Arditti  GOOD CLEAN FUN**   £8.99   ISBN 1 904559 08 5
A dazzling collection of stories provides a witty, compassionate yet uncompromising look at
love and loss, desire and defiance. 'Witheringly funny, painfully acute' (*Literary Review*)

**Michael Arditti  UNITY**   £8.99   ISBN 1 904559 12 3
A groundbreaking novel on the making of a film about Hitler and Unity Mitford, set against
the background of the Red Army Faction terror campaign in 1970s Germany.

**Marilyn Bowering  WHAT IT TAKES TO BE HUMAN**
£8.99   ISBN 978 1 904559 25 2
Sandy Grey is incarcerated for an apparently unprovoked attack on his father. As World
War II unfolds, the fate of a disparate group of prisoners in a Canadian asylum for the
criminally insane mirrors that of those torn apart by distant conflict.

**Hélène du Coudray  ANOTHER COUNTRY**   £7.99   ISBN 1 904559 04 2
A prize-winning novel, first published in 1928, about a passionate affair between a British
ship's officer and a Russian emigrée governess which promises to end in disaster.

**Lewis DeSoto  A BLADE OF GRASS**   £8.99   ISBN 1 904559 07 7
A lyrical and profound novel set in South Africa during the era of apartheid, in which the
recently widowed Märit struggles to run her farm with the help of her black maid, Tembi.
Longlisted for the Man Booker Prize 2004; shortlisted for the Ondaatje Prize 2005.

**Olivia Fane  THE GLORIOUS FLIGHT OF PERDITA TREE**
£8.99   ISBN 1 904559 13 1
Beautiful, vain Perdita Tree is kidnapped in Albania. Freedom is coming to the country
where flared trousers landed you in prison, but are the Albanians ready for it or, indeed,
Perdita?

**Olivia Fane  GOD'S APOLOGY**   £8.99   ISBN 1 904559 20 7
Patrick German abandons his wife and child, and in his newfound role as a teacher
encounters the mesmerising 10-year-old Joanna. Is she really an angel sent to save him?

**Maggie Hamand, ed. UNCUT DIAMONDS**     £7.99   ISBN 1 904559 03 4
Unusual and challenging, these vibrant, original stories showcase the huge diversity of new writing talent coming out of contemporary London.

**Helen Humphreys WILD DOGS**     £8.99   ISBN 1 904559 15 8
A pack of lost dogs runs wild, and each evening their bereft former owners gather to call them home – a remarkable book about the power of human strength, trust and love.

**Linda Leatherbarrow ESSENTIAL KIT**     £8.99   ISBN 1 904559 10 7
The first collection from a short-story prizewinner – lyrical, uplifting, funny and moving, always pertinent – 'joyously surreal . . . gnomically funny, and touching' (Shena Mackay).

**Sara Maitland ON BECOMING A FAIRY GODMOTHER**
£7.99   ISBN 1 904559 00 X
Fifteen new 'fairy stories' by an acclaimed master of the genre breathe new life into old legends and bring the magic of myth back into modern women's lives.

**Maria Peura AT THE EDGE OF LIGHT**     £8.99   ISBN 978 1 904559 24 5
The story of a girl growing up in the far north of Finland, her first love affair and her desperation to escape from the restricted life of a remote and extraordinary community.

**Anne Redmon IN DENIAL**     £7.99   ISBN 1 904559 01 8
A chilling novel about the relationship between Harriet, a prison visitor, and Gerry, a serial offender, which explores challenging themes with subtlety and intelligence.

**Diane Schoemperlen FORMS OF DEVOTION**     £9.99   ISBN 1 904559 19 0
Eleven stories with a brilliant interplay between words and images – a creative delight, perfectly formed and rich in wit and irony. Illustrated throughout with line engravings.

**Henrietta Seredy LEAVING IMPRINTS**     £7.99   ISBN 1 904559 02 6
Beautifully written and startlingly original, this unusual and memorable novel explores a destructive, passionate relationship between two damaged people.

**Emma Tennant THE FRENCH DANCER'S BASTARD**
£8.99   ISBN 1 904559 23 9
Lonely and homesick, little Adèle finds a new secret world in the attic of the forbidding Mr Rochester, but her curiosity will imperil everyone, including her governess Jane Eyre, shatter their happiness and send her fleeing, frightened and alone, back to Paris.

**Emma Tennant  THE HARP LESSON**     £8.99    ISBN 1 904559 16 6
With the French Revolution looming, little Pamela Sims is taken from England to live at the
French court as the illegitimate daughter of Mme de Genlis. But who is she really?

**Emma Tennant  PEMBERLEY REVISITED**     £8.99    ISBN 1 904559 17 4
Elizabeth wins Darcy, and Jane wins Bingley – but do they 'live happily ever after'? Two
bestselling sequels to Jane Austen's *Pride and Prejudice*, issued together for the first time.

**Norman Thomas  THE THOUSAND-PETALLED DAISY**
£7.99    ISBN 1 904559 05 0
Love, jealousy and violence play a part in this coming-of-age novel set in India, written
with a distinctive, off-beat humour and a delicate but intensely felt spirituality.

**Karel Van Loon  THE INVISIBLE ONES**     £8.99    ISBN 1 904559 18 2
A gripping novel about the life of a refugee in Thailand, in which harrowing accounts of
Burmese political prisoners blend with Buddhist myth and memories of a carefree
childhood.

**Adam Zameenzad  PEPSI AND MARIA**     £8.99    ISBN 1 904559 06 9
A highly original novel about two street children in South America whose zest for life
carries them through the brutal realities of their daily existence.